# How long had it been since she'd touched someone like this?

All that hard flesh Eve had seen on the beach—felt on the bike—pressed back against her fingers as they splayed out across his chest. Across the shadowy eagle that she knew lived there beneath the saturated cotton shirt. Across Marshall's strongly beating heart.

Marshall was right. They weren't going to see each other again. This might be the only chance she had to know what it felt like to have the heat of him pressed against her. To know him. To taste him.

All she had to do was move one finger. Any finger.

She'd never meant to enter some kind of self-imposed physical exile when she'd set off on this odyssey. It had just happened. And before she knew it she'd gone without touching a single person in any way at all for...

She sucked in a tiny breath. All of it. *Eight months*.

Only one way to find out.

Eve trailed her butterfly fingers lightly up to his collarbone. Beyond to the rigid definition of his larynx, which lurched out of touch and then back in again like the scandalous tease it was.

Strong fingers lifted to frame her face—to lift it—and he brought her eyes to his. They simmered, as bottomless as the ocean around them, as he lowered his mouth towards hers.

# How long had it been since she'd touched someone like this?

# HER KNIGHT
# IN THE OUTBACK

BY
NIKKI LOGAN

Published in Great Britain 2015
by Mills & Boon, an imprint of Harlequin (UK) Limited,
Eton House, 18-24 Paradise Road, Richmond, Surrey, TW9 1SR

© 2015 Nikki Logan

ISBN: 978-0-263-25119-7

23-0315

**Nikki Logan** lives on the edge of a string of wetlands in Western Australia, with her partner and a menagerie of animals. She writes captivating nature-based stories full of romance in descriptive natural environments. She believes the danger and richness of wild places perfectly mirror the passion and risk of falling in love.

Nikki loves to hear from readers
via nikkilogan.com.au or through social media.
Find her on Twitter: @ReadNikkiLogan and
Facebook: NikkiLoganAuthor

For Mat

## ACKNOWLEDGEMENTS

With enormous gratitude to Dr Richard O'Regan
for his help with the pharmaceutical aspects of
this story, which were integral to its resolution.
And with deepest respect and compassion for
the families of 'The Missing'.

# CHAPTER ONE

IT WAS MOMENTS like this that Evelyn Read hated. Life-defining moments. Moments when her fears and prejudices reared up before her eyes and confronted her—just like a King Brown snake, surprised while basking on the hot Australian highway.

She squinted at the distant biker limping carefully towards her out of the shimmering heat mirage and curled her fingers more tightly around the steering wheel.

A moment like this one might have taken her brother. Maybe Trav stopped for the wrong stranger; maybe that was where he went when he disappeared all those months ago. Her instincts screamed that she should press down on her accelerator until the man—the danger—was an hour behind her. But a moment like this might have *saved* her brother, too. If a stranger had only been kind enough or brave enough to stop for him. Then maybe Travis would be back with them right now. Safe. Loved.

Instead of alone, scared…or worse.

The fear of never knowing what happened to him tightened her gut the way it always did when she thought too long about this crazy thing she was doing.

The biker limped closer.

Should she listen to her basest instincts and flee, or respond to twenty-four years of social conditioning and help a fellow human being in trouble? There was probably some kind of outback code to be observed, too, but she'd heard too many stories from too many grieving people to be particularly bothered by niceties.

Eve's eyes flicked to the distant motorbike listing on the side of the long, empty road. And then, closer, to the scruffy man now nearing the restored 1956 Bedford bus that was getting her around Australia.

She glanced at her door's lock to make sure it was secure.

The man limped to a halt next to the bus's bifold doors and looked at her expectantly over his full beard. A dagger tattoo poked out from under his dark T-shirt and impenetrable sunglasses hid his eyes—and his intent—from her.

*No.* This was her home. She'd never open her front door to a total stranger. Especially not hours from the nearest other people.

She signalled him around to the driver's window instead.

He didn't look too impressed, but he limped his way around to her side and she slid the antique window open and forced her voice to be light.

*Sociopaths make a decision on whether you're predator or prey in the first few seconds*, she remembered from one of the endless missing-person fact sheets she'd read. She was not about to have 'prey' stamped on her forehead.

'Morning,' she breezed, as if this wasn't potentially a very big deal indeed. 'Looks like you're having a bad day.'

'Emu,' he grunted and she got a glimpse of straight teeth and healthy gums.

Stupidly, that reassured her. As if evil wouldn't floss. She twisted around for evidence of a big damaged bird flailing in the scrub after hitting his motorbike. To validate his claim. 'Was it okay?'

'Yeah, I'm fine, thanks.'

That brought her eyes back to his glasses. 'I can see that. But emus don't always come off the best after a road impact.'

As if she'd know...

'Going that fast, it practically went over the top of me as it ran with its flock. It's probably twenty miles from here now, trying to work out how and when it got black paint on its claws.'

He held up his scratched helmet, which had clearly taken an impact. More evidence. She just nodded, not wanting to give an inch more than necessary. He'd probably already summed her up as a bleeding heart over the emu.

*One for the prey column.*

'Where are you headed?' he asked.

Her radar flashed again at his interest. 'West.'

Duh, since the Bedford was pointing straight at the sun heading for the horizon and there was nothing else out this way *but* west.

'Can I catch a lift to the closest town?'

Was that tetchiness in his voice because she kept foiling him or because hers was the first vehicle to come along in hours and she was stonewalling him on a ride?

She glanced at his crippled bike.

'That'll have to stay until I can get back here with a truck,' he said, following her glance.

There was something in the sag of his shoulders and the way he spared his injured leg that reassured her even as the beard and tattoo and leather did not. He'd clearly come off his bike hard. Maybe he was more injured than she could see?

But the stark reality was that her converted bus only had the one seat up front—hers. 'That's my home back there,' she started.

'So…?'

'So, I don't know you.'

Yep. That was absolutely the insult his hardened lips said it was. But she was not letting a stranger back there. Into her world.

'It's only an hour to the border.' He sighed. 'I'll stand on your steps until Eucla.'

Right next to her. Where he could do anything and she couldn't do a thing to avoid it.

'An hour by motorbike, maybe. We take things a little more easy in this old girl. It'll take at least twice that.'

'Fine. I'll stand for two hours, then.'

Or she could just leave him here and send help back. But the image of Trav, lost and in need of help while someone drove off and left him injured and alone, flitted through her mind.

*If someone had just been brave...*

'I don't know you,' she wavered.

'Look, I get it. A woman travelling alone, big scary biker. You're smart to be cautious but the reality is help might not be able to get to me today so if you leave me here I could be here all night. Freezing my ass off.'

She fumbled for her phone.

His shaggy head shook slightly. 'If we had signal don't you think I'd have used it?'

Sure enough, her phone had diminished to *SOS only.* And as bad as that motorbike looked, it wasn't exactly an emergency.

'Just until we get signal, then?' he pressed, clearly annoyed at having to beg. 'Come on, please?'

How far could that be? They were mostly through the desert now, coming out on the western side of Australia. Where towns and people and telecommunications surely had to exist.

'Have you got some ID?'

He blinked at her and then reached back into his jeans for his wallet.

'No. Not a licence. That could be fake. Got any photos of you?'

He moved slowly, burdened by his incredulity, but pulled his phone out and flicked through a few screens. Then he pressed it up against Eve's window glass.

A serious face looked back at her. Well groomed and in a business shirt. Pretty respectable, really. Almost cute.

*Pffff.* 'That's not you.'

'Yeah, it is.'

She peered at him again. 'No, it's not.'

It might have been a stock photo off the Internet for all

she knew. The sort of search result she used to get when she googled 'corporate guy' for some design job.

'Oh, for pity's sake…'

He flicked through a few more and found another one, this time more bearded. But nothing like the hairy beast in front of her. Her hesitation obviously spoke volumes so he pushed his sunglasses up onto his head, simultaneously revealing grey eyes and slightly taming his rusty blond hair.

Huh. Okay, maybe it was him.

'Licence?'

A breathed bad word clearly tangled in the long hairs of his moustache but he complied—eventually—and slapped that against the window, too.

*Marshall Sullivan.*

She held up her phone and took a photo of him through the glass, with his licence in the shot.

'What's that for?'

'Insurance.'

'I just need a lift. That's it. I have no interest in you beyond that.'

'Easy for you to say.'

Her thumbs got busy texting it to both her closest friend and her father in Melbourne. Just to cover bases. Hard to know if the photo would make them more or less confident in this dusty odyssey she was on, but she had to send it to someone.

The grey eyes she could now see rolled. 'We have no signal.'

'The moment we do it will go.'

She hit Send and let the phone slip back down into its little spot on her dash console.

'You have some pretty serious trust issues, lady, you know that?'

'And this is potentially the oldest con in the book. Broken-down vehicle on remote outback road.' She glanced at his helmet and the marks that could be emu claws. 'I'll admit your story has some pretty convincing details—'

'Because it's the truth.'

'—but I'm travelling alone and I'm not going to take any chances. And I'm not letting you in here with me, sorry.' The cab was just too small and risky. 'You'll have to ride in the back.'

'What about all the biker germs I'm going to get all over your stuff?' he grumbled.

'You want a lift or not?'

Those steady eyes glared out at her. 'Yeah. I do.'

And then, as though he couldn't help himself, he grudgingly rattled off a thankyou.

Okay, so it had to be safer to let him loose in the back than have him squished here in the front with her. Her mind whizzed through all the things he might get up to back there but none of them struck her as bad as what he could do up front if he wasn't really who he said he was.

Or even if he was.

Biker boy and his helmet limped back towards the belongings piled on the side of the road next to his disabled bike. Leather jacket, pair of satchels, a box of mystery equipment.

She ground the gears starting the Bedford back up, but rolled up behind him and, as soon as his arms were otherwise occupied with his own stuff, she unlocked the bus and mouthed through the glass of her window. 'Back doors.'

Sullivan limped to the back of the Bedford, lurched it as he climbed in and then slammed himself in there with all her worldly possessions.

Two hours…

'Come on, old chook,' she murmured to the decades-old bus. 'Let's push it a bit, eh?'

Marshall groped around for a light switch but only found a thick fabric curtain. He pulled it back with a swish and light flooded into the darkened interior of the bus. Something extraordinary unfolded in front of him.

He'd seen converted buses before but they were usually pretty daggy. Kind of worn and soulless and vinyl. But this…

This was rich, warm and natural; nothing at all like the hostile lady up front.

It was like a little cottage in some forest. All timber and plush rugs in dark colours. Small, but fully appointed with kitchenette and living space, flat-screen TV, fridge and a sofa. Even potted palms. Compact and long but all there, like one of those twenty-square-metre, fold-down and pull-out apartments they sold in flat packs. At the far end—the driving end—a closed door that must lead to the only absent feature of the vehicle, the bed.

And suddenly he got a sense of Little Miss Hostile's reluctance to let him back here. It was like inviting a total stranger right into your bedroom. Smack bang in the middle of absolutely nowhere.

The bus lurched as she tortured it back up to speed and Marshall stumbled down onto the sofa built into the left side of the vehicle. Not as comfortable as his big eight-seater in the home theatre of his city apartment, but infinitely better than the hard gravel he'd been polishing with his butt for the couple of hours since the bird strike.

Stupid freaking emu. It could have killed them both.

It wasn't as if a KTM 1190 was a stealth unit but maybe, at the speed the emu had been going, the air rushing past its ears was just as noisy as an approaching motorbike. And then their fates had collided. Literally.

He sagged down against the sofa back and resisted the inclination to examine his left foot. Sometimes boots were the only things that kept fractured bones together after bike accidents so he wasn't keen to take it off unless he was bleeding to death. In fact, particularly if he was bleeding to death because something told him the hostess-with-the-leastest would not be pleased if he bled out all over her timber floor. But he could at least elevate it. That was generally good for what ailed you. He dragged one of his satchels up onto the sofa, turned and stacked a couple of the bouncy, full pillows down the opposite end and then swung his abused limb up onto it, lying out the full length of the sofa.

'Oh, yeah…' Half words, half groan. All good.

He loved his bike. He loved the speed. He loved that direct relationship with the country you had when there was no car between you and it. And he loved the freedom from everything he'd found touring that country.

But he really didn't love how fragile he'd turned out to be when something went wrong at high speed.

As stacks went, it had been pretty controlled. Especially considering the fishtail he'd gone into as the mob of emu shot past and around him. But even a controlled slide hurt—him and the bike—and once the adrenaline wore off and the birds disappeared over the dusty horizon, all he'd been left with was the desert silence and the pain.

And no phone signal.

Normally that wouldn't bother him. There really couldn't be enough alone time in this massive country, as far as he was concerned. If you travelled at the right time of year—and that would be the *wrong* time of year for tourists—you could pretty much have most outback roads to yourself. He was free to do whatever he wanted, wear whatever he wanted, be as hairy as he wanted, shower whenever he wanted. Or not. He'd given up caring what people thought of him right about the time he'd stopped caring about people.

Ancient history.

And life was just simpler that way.

The stoic old Bedford finally shifted into top gear and the rattle of its reconditioned engine evened out to a steady hum, vibrating under his skin as steadily as his bike did. He took the rare opportunity to do what he could never do when at the controls: he closed his eyes and let the hum take him.

Two hours, she'd said. He could be up on his feet with her little home fully restored before she even made it from the front of the bus back to the rear doors. As if no one had ever been there.

Two hours to rest. Recover. And enjoy the roads he loved from a more horizontal perspective.

'Who's been sleeping in my bed?' Eve muttered as she stood looking at the bear of a man fast asleep on her little sofa.

What was this—some kind of reverse Goldilocks thing?

She cleared her throat. Nothing. He didn't even shift in his sleep.

'Mr Sullivan?'

Nada.

For the first time, it occurred to her that maybe this wasn't sleep; maybe this was coma. Maybe he'd been injured more than either of them had realised. She hauled herself up into the back of the bus and crossed straight to his side, all thoughts of dangerous tattooed men cast aside. Her fingertips brushed below the hairy tangle of his jaw.

Steady and strong. And warm.

*Phew.*

'Mr Sullivan,' she said, louder. Those dark blond brows twitched just slightly and something moved briefly behind his eyelids, so she pressed her advantage. 'We're here.'

Her gaze went to his elevated foot and then back up to where his hands lay, folded, across the T-shirt over his midsection. Rather nice hands. Soft and manicured despite the patches of bike grease from his on-road repairs.

The sort of hands you'd see in a magazine.

Which was ridiculous. How many members of motorcycle clubs sidelined in a bit of casual hand modelling?

She forced her focus back up to his face and opened her lips to call his name a little louder, but, where before there was only the barest movement behind his lids, now they were wide open and staring straight at her. This close, with the light streaming in from the open curtains, she saw they weren't grey at all—or not *just* grey, at least. The pewter irises were flecked with rust that neatly matched the tarnished blond of his hair and beard, particularly concentrated around his pupils.

She'd never seen eyes like them. She immediately thought of the burnt umber coastal rocks of the far north, where they slid down to pale, clean ocean. And where she'd started her journey eight months ago.

'We're here,' she said, irritated at her own breathlessness. And at being caught checking him out.

He didn't move, but maybe that was because she was leaning so awkwardly over him from all the pulse-taking.

'Where's here?' he croaked.

She pushed back onto her heels and dragged her hands back from the heat of his body. 'The border. You'll have to get up while they inspect the bus.'

They took border security seriously here on the invisible line between South Australia and Western Australia. Less about gun-running and drug-trafficking and more about fruit flies and honey. Quarantine was king when agriculture was your primary industry.

Sullivan twisted gingerly into an upright position, then carefully pulled himself to his feet and did his best to put the cushions back where they'd started. Not right, but he got points for the effort.

So he hadn't been raised by leather-clad wolves, then.

He bundled up his belongings, tossed them to the ground outside the bus and lowered himself carefully down.

'How is your leg?' Eve asked.

'I'll live.'

Okay. Man of few words. Clearly, he'd spent too much time in his own company.

The inspection team made quick work of hunting over every inch of her converted bus and Sullivan's saddlebags. She'd become proficient at dumping or eating anything that was likely to get picked up at the border and so, this time, the team only found one item to protest—a couple of walnuts not yet consumed.

Into the bin they went.

She lifted her eyes towards Sullivan, deep in discussion with one of the border staff who had him in one ear and their phone on the other. Arranging assistance for his crippled bike, presumably. As soon as they were done, he limped back towards her and hiked his bags up over his shoulder.

'Thanks for the ride,' he said as though the effort half choked him.

'You don't need to go into Eucla?' Just as she'd grown used to him.

'They're sending someone out to grab me and retrieve my bike.'

'Oh. Great that they can do it straight away.'

'Country courtesy.'

*As opposed to her lack of...?* 'Well, good luck with your—'

It was then she realised she had absolutely no idea what he was doing out here, other than hitting random emus. In all her angsting out on the deserted highway, she really hadn't stopped to wonder, let alone ask.

'—with your travels.'

His nod was brisk and businesslike. 'Cheers.'

And then he was gone, back towards the border security office and the little café that catered for people delayed while crossing. Marshall Sullivan didn't seem half so scary here in a bustling border stop, though his beard was no less bushy and the ink dagger under his skin no less menacing. All the what-ifs she'd felt two hours ago on that long empty road hobbled away from her as he did.

And she wondered how she'd possibly missed the first time how well his riding leathers fitted him.

# CHAPTER TWO

IT WAS THE raised voices that first got Marshall's attention. Female, anxious and angry, almost swallowed up by drunk, male and belligerent.

'Stop!'

The fact a gaggle of passers-by had formed a wide, unconscious circle around the spectacle in the middle of town was the only reason he sauntered closer instead of running on his nearly healed leg. If something bad was happening, he had to assume someone in the handful of people assembled would have intervened. Or at least cried out. Him busting in to an unknown situation, half-cocked, was no way to defuse what was clearly an escalating situation.

Instead, he insinuated himself neatly into the heart of the onlookers and nudged his way through to the front until he could get his eyeballs on things. A flutter of paper pieces rained down around them as the biggest of the men tore something up.

'You put another one up, I'm just going to rip it down,' he sneered.

The next thing he saw was the back of a woman's head. Dark, travel-messy ponytail. Dwarfed by the men she was facing but not backing down.

And all too familiar.

*Little Miss Hostile*. Winning friends and influencing people —as usual.

'This is a public noticeboard,' she asserted up at the human mountain, foolishly undeterred by his size.

'For Norseman residents,' he spat. 'Not for blow-ins from the east.'

'Public,' she challenged. 'Do I need to spell it out for you?'

Wow. Someone really needed to give her some basic training in conflict resolution. The guy was clearly a xenophobe and drunk. Calling him stupid in front of a crowd full of locals wasn't the fastest way out of her predicament.

She shoved past him and used a staple gun to pin up another flier.

He'd seen the same poster peppering posts and walls in Madura, Cocklebiddy and Balladonia. Every point along the remote desert highway that could conceivably hold a person. And a sign. Crisp and new against all the bleached, frayed ones from years past.

'Stop!'

Yeah, that guy wasn't going to stop. And now the McTanked Twins were also getting in on the act.

Goddammit.

Marshall pushed out into the centre of the circle. He raised his voice the way he used to in office meetings when they became unruly. Calm but intractable. 'Okay, show's over, people.'

The crowd turned their attention to him, like a bunch of cattle. So did the three drunks. But they weren't so intoxicated they didn't pause at the sight of his beard and tattoos. Just for a moment.

The moment he needed.

'Howzabout we find somewhere else for those?' he suggested straight to Little Miss Hostile, neatly relieving her of the pile of posters with one hand and the staple gun with his other. 'There are probably better locations in town.'

She spun around and glared at him in the heartbeat before she recognised him. 'Give me those.'

He ignored her and spoke to the crowd. 'All done, people. Let's get moving.'

They parted for him as he pushed back through, his hands full of her property. She had little choice but to pursue him.

'Those are mine!'

'Let's have this conversation around the corner,' he gritted back and down towards her.

But just as they'd cleared the crowd, the big guy couldn't help himself.

'Maybe he's gone missing to get away from you!' he called.

A shocked gasp covered the sound of small female feet pivoting on the pavement and she marched straight back towards the jeering threesome.

Marshall shoved the papers under his arm and sprinted after her, catching her just before she re-entered the eye of the storm. All three men had lined up in it, ready. Eager. He curled his arms around her and dragged her back, off her feet, and barked just one word in her ear.

'Don't!'

She twisted and lurched and swore the whole way but he didn't loosen his hold until the crowd and the jeering laughter of the drunks were well behind them.

'Put me down,' she struggled. 'Ass!'

'The only ass around here is the one I just saved.'

'I've dealt with rednecks before.'

'Yeah, you were doing a bang-up job.'

'I have every right to put my posters up.'

'No argument. But you could have just walked away and then come back and done it in ten minutes when the drunks were gone.'

'But there were thirty people there.'

'None of whom were making much of an effort to help you.' In case she hadn't noticed.

'I didn't want their help,' she spat, spinning back to face him. 'I wanted their attention.'

What was this—some kind of performance art thing? 'Come again?'

'Thirty people would have read my poster, remembered it.

The same people that probably would have passed it by without noticing, otherwise.'

'Are you serious?'

She snatched the papers and staple gun back from him and clutched them to her heaving chest. 'Perfectly. You think I'm new to this?'

'I really don't know what to think. You treated me like a pariah because of a bit of leather and ink, but you were quite happy to face off against the Beer Gut Brothers, back there.'

'It got *attention*.'

'So does armed robbery. Are you telling me the bank is on your to-do list in town?'

She glared at him. 'You don't understand.'

And then he was looking at the back of her head again as she turned and marched away from him without so much as a goodbye. Let alone a thankyou.

He cursed under his breath.

'Enlighten me,' he said, catching up with her and ignoring the protest of his aching leg.

'Why should I?'

'Because I just risked my neck entering that fray to help you and that means you owe me one.'

'I rescued you out on the highway. I'd say that makes us even.'

Infuriating woman. He slammed on the brakes. 'Fine. Whatever.'

Her momentum carried her a few metres further but then she spun back. 'Did you look at the poster?'

'I've been looking at them since the border.'

'And?'

'And what?'

'What's on it?'

His brows forked. What the hell *was* on it? 'Guy's face. Bunch of words.' And a particularly big one in red. MISSING. 'It's a missing-person poster.'

'Bingo. And you've been looking at them since the border

but can't tell me what he looked like or what his name was or what it was about.' She took two steps closer. 'That's why getting their attention was so valuable.'

Realisation washed through him and he felt like a schmuck for parachuting in and rescuing her like some damsel in distress. 'Because they'll remember it. You.'

'Him!' But her anger didn't last long. It seemed to desert her like the adrenaline in both their bodies, leaving her flat and exhausted. 'Maybe.'

'What do you do—start a fight in every town you go to?'

'Whatever it takes.'

Cars went by with stereos thumping.

'Listen…' Suddenly, Little Miss Hostile had all new layers. And most of them were laden with sadness. 'I'm sorry if you had that under control. Where I come from you don't walk past a woman crying out in the street.'

Actually, that wasn't strictly true because he came from a pretty rough area and sometimes the best thing to do was keep walking. But while his mother might have raised her kids like that, his grandparents certainly hadn't. And he, at least, had learned from their example even if his brother, Rick, hadn't.

Dark eyes studied him. 'That must get you into a lot of trouble,' she eventually said.

True enough.

'Let me buy you a drink. Give those guys some time to clear out and then I'll help you put the posters up.'

'I don't need your help. Or your protection.'

'Okay, but I'd like to take a proper look at that poster.'

He regarded her steadily as uncertainty flooded her expression. The same that he'd seen out on the highway. 'Or is the leather still bothering you?'

Indecision flooded her face and her eyes flicked from his beard to his eyes, then down to his lips and back again.

'No. You haven't robbed or murdered me yet. I think a few minutes together in a public place will be fine.'

She turned and glanced down the street where a slight *doof-*

*doof* issued from an architecturally classic Aussie hotel. Then her voice filled with warning. 'Just one.'

It was hard not to smile. Her stern little face was like a daisy facing up to a cyclone.

'If I was going to hurt you I've had plenty of opportunity. I don't really need to get you liquored up.'

'Encouraging start to the conversation.'

'You know my name,' he said, moving his feet in a pubward direction. 'I don't know yours.'

She regarded him steadily. Then stuck out the hand with the staple gun clutched in it. 'Evelyn Read. Eve.'

He shook half her hand and half the tool. 'What do you like to drink, Eve?'

'I don't. Not in public. But you go ahead.'

A teetotaller in an outback pub.

*Well, this should be fun.*

Eve trusted Marshall Sullivan with her posters while she used the facilities. When she came back, he'd smoothed out all the crinkles in the top one and was studying it.

'Brother?' he said as she slid into her seat.

'What makes you say that?'

He tapped the surname on the poster where it had *Travis James Read* in big letters.

'He could be my husband.' She shrugged.

His eyes narrowed. 'Same dark hair. Same shape eyes. He looks like you.'

Yeah, he did. Everyone thought so. 'Trav is my little brother.'

'And he's missing?'

God, she hated this bit. The pity. The automatic assumption that something bad had happened. Hard enough not letting herself think it every single day without having the thought planted back in her mind by strangers at every turn.

Virtual strangers.

Though, at least this one did her the courtesy of not referring to Travis in the past tense. Points for that.

'Missing a year next week, actually.'

'Tough anniversary. Is that why you're out here? Is this where he was last seen?'

She lifted her gaze back to his. 'No. In Melbourne.'

'So what brings you out west?'

'I ran out of towns on the east coast.'

Blond brows lowered. 'You've lost me.'

'I'm visiting every town in the country. Looking for him. Putting up notices. Doing the legwork.'

'I assumed you were just on holidays or something.'

'No. This is my job.'

Now. Before that she'd been a pretty decent graphic designer for a pretty decent marketing firm. Until she'd handed in her notice.

'Putting up posters is your job?'

'Finding my brother.' The old defensiveness washed through her. 'Is anything more important?'

His confusion wasn't new. He wasn't the first person not to understand what she was doing. By far. Her own father didn't even get it; he just wanted to grieve Travis's absence as though he were dead. To accept he was gone.

She was light-years and half a country away from being ready to accept such a thing. She and Trav had been so close. If he was dead, wouldn't she feel it?

'So…what, you just drive every highway in the country pinning up notices?'

'Pretty much. Trying to trigger a memory in someone's mind.'

'And it's taken you a year to do the east coast?'

'About eight months. Though I started up north.' And that was where she'd finish.

'What happened before that?'

Guilt hammered low in her gut for those missing couple of months before she'd realised how things really were. How she'd played nice and sat on her hands while the police seemed to achieve less and less. Maybe if she'd started sooner—

'I trusted the system.'

'But the authorities didn't find him?'

'There are tens of thousands of missing people every year. I just figured that the only people who could make Trav priority number one were his family.'

'That many? Really?'

'Teens. Kids. Women. Most are located pretty quickly.'

But ten per cent weren't.

His eyes tracked down to the birthdate on the poster. 'Healthy eighteen-year-old males don't really make it high up the priority list?'

A small fist formed in her throat. 'Not when there's no immediate evidence of foul play.'

And even if they maybe weren't entirely healthy, psychologically. But Travis's depression was hardly unique amongst *The Missing* and his anxiety attacks were longstanding enough that the authorities dismissed them as irrelevant. As if a bathroom cabinet awash with mental health medicines wasn't relevant.

A young woman with bright pink hair badly in need of a recolour brought Marshall's beer and Eve's lime and bitters and sloshed them on the table.

'That explains the bus,' he said. 'It's very…homey.'

'It is my home. Mine went to pay for the trip.'

'You sold your house?'

Her chin kicked up. 'And resigned from my job. I can't afford to be distracted by having to earn an income while I cover the country.'

She waited for the inevitable judgment.

'That's quite a commitment. But it makes sense.'

Such unconditional acceptance threw her. Everyone else she'd told thought she was foolish. Or plain crazy. Implication: like her brother. No one just…nodded.

'That's it? No opinion? No words of wisdom?'

His eyes lifted to hers. 'You're a grown woman. You did what you needed to do. And I assume it was your asset to dispose of.'

She scrutinised him again. The healthy, unmarked skin under the shaggy beard. The bright eyes. The even teeth.

'What's your story?' she asked.

'No story. I'm travelling.'

'You're not a bikie.' Statement, not question.

'Not everyone with a motorbike belongs in an outlaw club,' he pointed out.

'You look like a bikie.'

'I wear leather because it's safest when you get too intimate with asphalt. I have a beard because one of the greatest joys in life is not having to shave, and so I indulge that when I'm travelling alone.'

She glanced down to where the dagger protruded from his T-shirt sleeve. 'And the tattoo?'

His eyes immediately darkened. 'We were all young and impetuous once.'

'Who's Christine?'

'Christine's not relevant to this discussion.'

Bang. Total shutdown. 'Come on, Marshall. I aired my skeleton.'

'Something tells me you air it regularly. To anyone who'll listen.'

Okay, this time the criticism was unmistakable. She pushed more upright in her chair. 'You were asking the questions, if you recall.'

'Don't get all huffy. We barely know each other. Why would I spill my guts to a stranger?'

'I don't know. Why would you rescue a stranger on the street?'

'Not wanting to see you beaten to a pulp and not wanting to share my dirty laundry are very different things.'

'Oh, Christine's dirty laundry?'

His lips thinned even further and he pushed away from the table. 'Thanks for the drink. Good luck with your brother.'

She shot to her feet, too. 'Wait. Marshall?'

He stopped and turned back slowly.

'I'm sorry. I guess I'm out of practice with people,' she said.

'You're not kidding.'

'Where are you staying?'

'In town.'

Nice and non-specific. 'I'm a bit… I get a bit tired of eating in the bus. On my own. Can I interest you in something to eat, later?'

'I don't think so.'

*Walk away, Eve.* That would be the smart thing to do.

'I'll change the subject. Not my brother. Not your…' *Not your Christine?* 'We can talk about places we've been. Favourite sights.' Her voice petered out.

His eyebrows folded down over his eyes briefly and disguised them from her view. But he finally relented. 'There's a café across the street from my motel. End of this road.'

'Sounds good.'

She didn't usually eat out, to save money, but then she didn't usually have the slightest hint of company either. One dinner wouldn't kill her. Alone with a stranger. Across the road from his motel room.

'It's not a date, though,' she hastened to add.

'No.' The moustache twisted up on the left. 'It's not.'

And as he and his leather pants sauntered back out of the bar, she felt like an idiot. An adolescent idiot. *Of course* this was not a date and *of course* he wouldn't have considered it such. Hairy, lone-wolf types who travelled the country on motorbikes probably didn't stand much on ceremony when it came to women. Or bother with dates.

She'd only mentioned a meal at all because she felt bad that she'd pressed an obvious sore point with him after he'd shown her nothing but interest and acceptance about Travis.

*\*facepalm\**

Her brother's favourite saying flittered through her memory and never seemed more appropriate. Hopefully, a few hours and a good shower from now she could be a little more socially appropriate and a lot less hormonal.

Inexplicably so.

Unwashed biker types were definitely not her thing, no matter how nice their smiles. Normally, the *eau de sweaty man* that littered towns in the Australian bush flared her nostrils. But as Marshall Sullivan had hoisted her up against his body out in the street she'd definitely responded to the powerful circle of his hold, the hard heat of his chest and the warmth of his hissed words against her ear.

Even though it came with the tickle of his substantial beard against her skin.

She was *so* not a beard woman.

A man who travelled the country alone was almost certainly doing it for a reason. Running from something or someone. Dropping out of society. Hiding from the authorities. Any number of mysterious and dangerous things.

Or maybe Marshall Sullivan was just as socially challenged as she was.

Maybe that was why she had a sudden and unfathomable desire to sit across a table from the man again.

'See you at seven-thirty, then,' she called after him.


Eve's annoyance at herself for being late—and at caring about that—turned into annoyance at Marshall Sullivan for being even later. What, had he got lost crossing the street?

Her gaze scanned the little café diner as she entered—over the elderly couple with a stumpy candle, past the just-showered Nigel No Friends reading a book and the two men arguing over the sports pages. But as her eyes grazed back around to the service counter, they stumbled over the hands wrapped around *Nigel*'s battered novel. Beautiful hands.

She stepped closer. 'Marshall?'

Rust-flecked eyes glanced up to her. And then he pushed to his feet. To say he was a changed man without the beard would have been an understatement. He was transformed. His hair hadn't been cut but it was slicked back either with product or he truly had just showered. But his face...

Free of the overgrown blondish beard and moustache, his eyes totally stole focus, followed only by his smooth broad forehead. She'd always liked an unsullied forehead. Reliable somehow.

He slid a serviette into the book to mark his place and closed it.

She glanced at the cover. *'Gulliver's Travels?'*

Though what she really wanted to say was…*You shaved?*

'I carry a few favourites around with me in my pack.'

She slid in opposite him, completely unable to take her eyes off his new face. At a loss to reconcile it as the under layer of all that sweat, dust and helmet hair she'd encountered out on the road just a few days ago. 'What makes it a favourite?'

He thought about that for a bit. 'The journeying. It's very human. And Gulliver is a constant reminder that perspective is everything in life.'

Huh. She'd just enjoyed it for all the little people.

They fell to silence.

'You shaved,' she finally blurted.

'I did.'

'For dinner?' Dinner that wasn't a date.

His neatly groomed head shook gently. 'I do that periodically. Take it off and start again. Even symbols of liberty need maintenance.'

'That's what it means to you? Freedom?'

'Isn't that what the Bedford means to you?'

Freedom? No. Sanity, yes. 'The bus is just transport and accommodation conveniently bundled.'

'You forget I've seen inside it. That's not convenience. That's sanctuary.'

Yeah…it was, really. But she didn't know him well enough to open up to that degree.

'I bought the Bedford off this old carpenter after his wife died. He couldn't face travelling any more without her.'

'I wonder if he knows what he's missing.'

'Didn't you just say perspective was everything?'

'True enough.'

A middle-aged waitress came bustling over, puffing, as though six people at once was the most she'd seen in a week. She took their orders from the limited menu and bustled off again.

One blond brow lifted. 'You carb-loading for a marathon?'

'You've seen the stove in the Bedford. I can only cook the basics in her. Every now and again I like to take advantage of a commercial kitchen's deep-fryer.'

Plus, boiling oil would kill anything that might otherwise not get past the health code. There was nothing worse than being stuck in a small town, throwing your guts up. Unless it was being stuck on the side of the road between small towns and kneeling in the roadside gravel.

'So, you know how I'm funding my way around the country,' she said. 'How are you doing it?'

He stared at her steadily. 'Guns and drugs.'

'Ha-ha.'

'That's what you thought when you saw me. Right?'

'I saw a big guy on a lonely road trying really hard to get into my vehicle. What would you have done?'

Those intriguing eyes narrowed just slightly but then flicked away. 'I'm out here working. Like you. Going from district to district.'

'Working for who?'

'Federal Government.'

'Ooh, the Feds. That sounds much more exciting than it probably is. What department?'

He took a long swig of his beer before answering. 'Meteorology.'

She stared. 'You're a *weatherman*?'

'Right. I stand in front of a green screen every night and read maximums and minimums.'

Her smile broadened. 'You're a weatherman.'

He sagged back in his chair and spoke as if he'd heard this one time too many. 'Meteorology is a science.'

'You don't look like a scientist.' Definitely not before and, even clean shaven, Marshall was still too muscular and tattooed.

'Would it help if I was in a lab coat and glasses?'

'Yes.' Because the way he packed out his black T-shirt was the least nerdy thing she'd ever seen. 'So why are my taxes funding your trip around the country, exactly?'

'You're not earning. You don't pay taxes.'

The man had a point. 'Why are you out here, then?'

'I'm auditing the weather stations. I check them, report on their condition.'

Well, that explained the hands. 'I thought you were this free spirit on two wheels. You're an auditor.'

His lips tightened. 'Something tells me that's a step down from weatherman in your eyes.'

She got stuck into her complimentary bread roll, buttering and biting into it. 'How many stations are there?'

'Eight hundred and ninety-two.'

'And they send one man?' Surely they had locals that could check to make sure possums hadn't moved into their million-dollar infrastructure.

'I volunteered to do the whole run. Needed the break.'

*From...?* But she'd promised not to ask. They were supposed to be talking about travel highlights. 'Where was the most remote station?'

'Giles. Seven hundred and fifty clicks west of Alice. Up in the Gibson Desert.'

Alice Springs. Right smack bang in the middle of their massive island continent. 'Where did you start?'

'Start and finish in Perth.'

A day and a half straight drive from here. 'Is Perth home?'

'Sydney.'

She visualised the route he must have taken clockwise around the country from the west. 'So you're nearly done, then?'

His laugh drew the eyes of the other diners. 'Yeah. If two-thirds of the weather stations weren't in the bottom third of the state.'

'Do you get to look around? Or is it all work?'

He shrugged. 'Some places I skip right through. Others I linger. I have some flexibility.'

Eve knew exactly what that was like. Some towns whispered to you like a lover. Others yelled at you to go. She tended to move on quickly from those.

'Favourites so far?'

And he was off… Talking about the places that had captivated him most. The prehistoric, ferny depths of the Claustral Canyon, cave-diving in the crystal-clear ponds on South Australia's limestone coast, the soul-restoring solidity of Katherine Gorge in Australia's north.

'And the run over here goes without saying.'

'The Nullabor?' Pretty striking with its epic treeless stretches of desert but not the most memorable place she could recall.

'The Great Australian Bight,' he clarified.

She just blinked at him.

'You got off the highway on the way over, right? Turned for the coast?'

'My focus is town to town.'

He practically gaped. 'One of the most spectacular natural wonders in the world was just a half-hour drive away.'

'And half an hour back. That was an hour sooner I could have made it to the next town.'

His brows dipped over grey eyes. 'You've got to get out more.'

'I'm on the job.'

'Yeah, me, too, but you have to live as well. What about weekends?'

The criticism rankled. 'Not all of us are on the cushy public servant schedule. An hour—a day—could mean the difference between running across someone who knew Travis and not.'

Or even running into Trav himself.

'What if they came through an hour after you left, and pausing to look at something pretty could have meant your paths crossed?'

Did he think she hadn't tortured herself with those thoughts late at night? The endless what-ifs?

'An hour afterwards and they'll see a poster. An hour before and they'd have no idea their shift buddy is a missing person.' At least that was what she told herself. Sternly.

Marshall blinked at her.

'You don't understand.' How could he?

'Wouldn't it be faster to just email the posters around the country? Ask the post offices to put them up for you.'

'It's not just about the posters. It's about talking to people. Hunting down leads. Making an impression.'

Hoping to God the impression would stick.

'The kind you nearly made this afternoon?'

'Whatever it takes.'

Their meals arrived and the next minute was filled with making space on the table and receiving their drinks.

'Anyway, weren't we supposed to be talking about something else?' Eve said brightly, crunching into a chip. 'Where are you headed next?'

'Up to Kalgoorlie, then Southern Cross.'

North. Complete opposite to her.

'You?' His gaze was neutral enough.

'Esperance. Ravensthorpe. With a side trip out to Israelite Bay.' Jeez—why didn't she just draw him her route on a serviette? 'I'm getting low on posters after the Nullabor run. Need an MP's office.'

His newly groomed head tipped.

'MP's offices are obliged by law to print missing-person posters on request,' she explained. 'And there's one in Esperance.'

'Convenient.'

She glared at her chicken. 'It's the least they could do.'

And pretty much all they did. Though they were usually carefully sympathetic.

'It must be hard,' he murmured between mouthfuls. 'Hitting brick walls everywhere you go.'

'I'd rather hit them out here than stuck back in Melbourne. At least I can be productive here.'

Sitting at home and relying on others to do something to find her brother had nearly killed her.

'Did you leave a big family behind?'

Instantly her mind flashed to her father's grief-stricken face as the only person he had left in the world drove off towards the horizon. 'Just my dad.'

'No mum?'

She sat up straighter in her seat. If Christine-of-the-dagger was off the table for discussion, her drunk mother certainly was. Clearly, the lines in her face were as good as a barometric map. Because Marshall let the subject well and truly drop.

'Well, guess this is our first and last dinner, then,' he said cheerfully, toasting her with a forkful of mashed potato and peas. There was nothing more in that than pure observation. Nothing enough that she felt confident in answering without worrying it would sound like an invitation.

'You never know, we might bump into each other again.'

But, really, how likely was that once they headed off towards opposite points on the compass? The only reason they'd met up this once was because there was only one road in and out of the south half of this vast state and he'd crashed into an emu right in the middle of it.

Thoughtful eyes studied her face, then turned back to his meal.

'So you're not from Sydney, originally?'

Marshall pushed his empty plate away and groaned inwardly. Who knew talking about nothing could be so tiring? This had to be the greatest number of words he'd spoken to anyone in weeks. But it was his fault as much as hers. No dagger tattoo and no missing brother. That was what he'd stipulated. She'd held up her end of the bargain, even though she was clearly itching to know more.

Precisely why he didn't do dinners with women.

Conversation.

He'd much rather get straight to the sex part. Although that was clearly off the table with Eve. So it really made a man wonder why the heck he'd said yes to Eve's 'not a date' invitation. Maybe even *he* got lonely.

And maybe they were now wearing long coats in Hades.

'Brisbane.'

'How old were you when you moved?' she chatted on, oblivious to the rapid congealing of his thoughts. Oblivious to the dangerous territory she'd accidentally stumbled into. Thoughts of his brother, their mother and how tough he'd found Sydney as an adolescent.

'Twelve.'

The word squeezed past his suddenly tight throat. The logical part of him knew it was just polite conversation, but the part of him that was suddenly as taut as a crossbow loaded a whole lot more onto her innocent chatter. Twelve was a crap age to be yanked away from your friends and the school where you were finding your feet and thrust into one of the poorest suburbs of one of the biggest cities in the country. But—for the woman who'd only pumped out a second son for the public benefits—moving states to chase a more generous singleparent allowance was a no-brainer. No matter who it disrupted.

Not that any of that money had ever found its way to him and Rick. They were just a means to an end.

'What was that like?'

Being your mother's meal ticket or watching your older brother forge himself a career as the local drug-mover?

'It was okay.'

Uh-oh…here it came. Verbal shutdown. Probably just as well, given the direction his mind was going.

She watched him steadily, those dark eyes knowing something was up even if she didn't know exactly what. 'Uh-huh...'

Which was code for *Your turn next, Oscar Wilde*. But he couldn't think of a single thing to say, witty or otherwise. So he folded his serviette and gave his chair the slightest of backward pushes.

'Well...'

'What just happened?' Eve asked, watching him with curiosity but not judgment. And not moving an inch.

'It's getting late.'

'It's eight-thirty.'

Seriously? Only an hour? It felt like eternity.

'I'm heading out at sunrise. So I can get to Lake Lefroy before it gets too hot.'

And back to blissful isolation, where he didn't need to explain himself to anyone.

She tipped her head and it caused her dark hair to swing to the right a little. A soft fragrance wafted forwards and teased his receptors. His words stumbled as surely as he did, getting up. 'Thanks for the company.'

She followed suit. 'You're welcome.'

They split the bill in uncomfortable silence, then stepped out into the dark street. Deserted by eight-thirty.

Eve looked to her right, then back at him.

'Listen, I know you're just across the road but could you... would you mind walking me back to the bus?'

Maybe they were both remembering those three jerks from earlier.

'Where do you park at night?' He suddenly realised he had no idea where she'd pulled up. And that his ability to form sentences seemed to have returned with the fresh air.

'I usually find a good spot...'

*Oh, jeez.* She wasn't even sorted for the night.

They walked on in silence and then words just came tumbling out of him.

'My motel booking comes with parking. You could use that if you want. I'll tuck the bike forward.'

'Really?' Gratitude flooded her pretty face. 'That would be great, thank you.'

'Come on.'

He followed her to the right, and walked back through Norseman's quiet main streets. Neither of them spoke. When they reached her bus, she unlocked the side window and reached in to activate the folding front door. He waited while she crossed back around and then stepped up behind her into the cab.

Forbidden territory previously.

But she didn't so much as twitch this time. Which was irrationally pleasing. Clearly he'd passed some kind of test. Maybe it was when the beard came off.

The Bedford rumbled to life and Eve circled the block before heading back to his motel. He directed her into his bay and then jumped out to nudge the KTM forward a little. The back of her bus stuck out of the bay but he was pretty sure there was only one other person in the entire motel and they were already parked up for the night.

'Thanks again for this,' she said, pausing at the back of the bus with one of the two big rear doors open.

Courtesy of the garish motel lights that streamed in her half-closed curtains, he could see the comfortable space he'd fallen asleep in bathed in a yellow glow. And beyond it, behind the door that now stood open at the other end of the bus, Eve's bedroom. The opening was dominated by the foot of a large mattress draped in a burgundy quilt and weighed down with two big cushions.

Nothing like the sterile motel room and single country bed he'd be returning to.

'Caravan parks can be a little isolated this time of year,' she said, a bit tighter, as she caught the direction of his gaze. 'I feel better being close to…people.'

He eased his shoulder against the closed half of the door

and studied her. Had she changed her mind? Was that open door some kind of unconscious overture? And was he really considering taking her up on it if it was? Pretty, uptight girls on crusades didn't really meet his definition of uncomplicated. Yet something deep inside hinted strongly that she might be worth a bit of complication.

He peered down on her in the shadows. 'No problem.'

She shuffled from left foot to right. 'Well…'night, then. See you in the morning. Thanks again.'

A reluctant smile crossed his face at the firm finality of that door slamming shut. And at the zipping across of curtains as he sauntered to the rear of the motel.

Now they were one-for-one in the inappropriate social re-action stakes. He'd gone all strong and silent on her and she'd gone all blushing virgin on him.

Equally awkward.

Equally regrettable.

He dug into his pocket for the worn old key and let himself into his ground floor room. Exactly as soulless and bland as her little bus wasn't.

But exactly as soulless and bland as he preferred.

# CHAPTER THREE

'THIS BUS NEVER stops being versatile, does it?'

Eve's breath caught deep in her throat at the slight twang and comfortable gravel in the voice that came from her left. The few days that had passed since she'd heard his bike rumble out of the motel car park at dawn as she'd rolled the covers more tightly around her and fell back to sleep gave him exactly the right amount of stubble as he let the beard grow back in.

'Marshall?' Her hand clamped down on the pile of fliers that lifted off the table in the brisk Esperance waterfront breeze. 'I thought you'd headed north?'

'I did. But a road train had jack-knifed across the highway just out of Kal and the spill clean-up was going to take twenty-four hours so I adjusted my route. I'll do the south-west anti-clockwise. Like you.'

Was there just the slightest pause before 'like you'? And did that mean anything? Apparently, she took too long wondering because he started up again.

'I assumed I'd have missed you, actually.'

Or hoped? Impossible to know with his eyes hidden behind seriously dark sunglasses. Still, if he'd truly wanted to avoid her he could have just kept walking just now. She was so busy promoting *The Missing* to locals she never would have noticed him.

Eve pushed her shoulders back to improve her posture,

which had slumped as the morning wore on. Convenient co-incidence that it also made the best of her limited assets.

'I had to do Salmon Gums and Gibson on the way,' she said. 'I only arrived last night.'

He took in the two-dozen posters affixed to the tilted up doors of the bus's luggage compartment. It made a great road-side noticeboard to set her fold-out table up in front of.

He strolled up and back, studying every face closely.

'Who are all these people?'

'They're all long-termers.' *The ten per cent.*

'Do you know them all?'

'No,' she murmured. 'But I know most of their families. Online, at least.'

'All missing.' He frowned. 'Doesn't it pull focus from your brother? To do this?'

Yeah. It definitely did.

'I wouldn't be much of a human being if I travelled the entire country only looking after myself. Besides, we kind of have a reciprocal arrangement going. If someone's doing something special—like media or some kind of promotion—they try to include as many others as they can. This is something I can do in the big centres while taking a break from the road.'

Though Esperance was hardly a metropolis and talking to strangers all day wasn't much of a break.

He stopped just in front of her, picked up one of Travis's posters. 'Who's "we"?'

'The network.'

The sunglasses tipped more towards her.

'The missing-persons network,' she explained. 'The families. There are a lot of us.'

'You have a formal network?'

'We have an informal one. We share information. Tips. Successes.'

Failures. Quite a lot of failures.

'Good to have the support, I guess.'

He had no idea. Some days her commitment to a bunch of

people she'd never met face to face was the only thing that got her out of bed.

'When I first started up, I kept my focus on Trav. But these people—' she tipped her head back towards all the faces on her poster display '—are like extended family to me because they're the family of people I'm now close to. How could I not include them amongst *The Missing*?'

A woman stopped to pick up one of her fliers and Eve quickly delivered her spiel, smiling and making a lot of eye contact. Pumping it with energy. Whatever it took…

Marshall waited until the woman had finished perusing the whole display. *'The Missing?'*

She looked behind her. 'Them.'

And her brother had the biggest and most central poster on it.

He nodded to a gap on the top right of the display. 'Looks like one's fallen off.'

'I just took someone down.'

His eyebrows lifted. 'They were found? That's great.'

No, not great. But at least found. That was how it was for the families of long-timers. The Simmons family had the rest of their lives to deal with the mental torture that came with feeling *relief* when their son's remains were found in a gully at the bottom of a popular hiking mountain. Closure. That became the goal somewhere around the ten-month mark.

Emotional euthanasia.

Maybe one day that would be her—loathing herself for being grateful that the question mark that stalked her twenty-four-seven was now gone because her brother was. But there was no way she could explain any of that to someone outside the network. Regular people just didn't get it. It was just so much easier to smile and nod.

'Yes. Great.'

Silence clunked somewhat awkwardly on the table between them.

'Did you get out to Israelite Bay yet?' he finally asked.

'I'll probably do that tomorrow or Wednesday.'

His clear eyes narrowed. 'Listen. I have an idea. You need to travel out to the bay and I need to head out to Cape Arid and Middle Island to survey them for a possible new weather station. Why don't we team up, head out together? Two birds, one stone.'

More together time in which to struggle with conversation and obsess about his tattoos. Was that wise?

'I'll only slow you down. I need to do poster drops at all roadhouses, caravan parks and campsites between here and there.'

'That's okay. As far as the office is concerned, I have a couple of days while the truck mess is cleared up. We can take our time.'

Why did he seem so very reluctant? Almost as if he was speaking against his will. She scrunched her nose as a prelude to an *I don't think so*.

But he beat her to it. 'Middle Island is off-limits to the public. You can't go there without a permit.'

'And you have a permit?'

'I do.'

'Have you forgotten that this isn't a tourist trip for me?'

'You'll get your work done on the way, and then you'll just keep me company for mine.'

'I can get my work done by myself and be back in Esperance by nightfall.'

'Or you can give yourself a few hours off and see a bit of this country that you're totally missing.'

'And why should I be excited by Middle Island?'

'A restricted island could be a great place for someone to hide out if they don't want to be discovered.'

The moment the words left his mouth, colour peaked high on his jaw.

'Sorry—' he winced as she sucked in a breath '—that was... God, I'm sorry. I just thought you might enjoy a bit of downtime. That it might be good for you.'

But his words had had their effect. If you needed a permit and Marshall had one, then she'd be crazy not to tag along. What if she let her natural reticence stop her and Trav was there, camping and lying low?

'I'll let you ride on my bike,' he said, as though that made it better. As if it was some kind of prize.

Instantly her gut curled into a fist. 'Motorbikes kill people.'

'People kill people,' he dismissed. 'Have you ever ridden on one?'

If riding tandem with a woman in the midst of a mid-life crisis counted. 'My mother had a 250cc.'

'Really? Cool.'

Yeah, that was what she and Travis had thought, right up until the day it killed their mother and nearly him.

'But you haven't really *ridden* until you've been on a 1200.'

'No, thanks.'

'Come on… Wouldn't you like to know what it's like to have all that power between your legs?'

'If this is a line, it's spectacularly cheesy.'

He ignored that. 'Or the freedom of tearing along at one hundred clicks with nothing between you and the road?'

'You call that freedom, I call that terror.'

'How will you know until you try it?'

'I'm not interested in trying it.'

He totally failed at masking his disappointment. 'Then you can tail me in the bus. We'll convoy. It'll still be fun.'

Famous last words. Something told her the fun would run out, for him, round about the time she pulled into her third rest stop for the day, to pin up posters.

'There's also a good caravan park out there, according to the travel guides. You can watch a west coast sunset.'

'I've seen plenty of sunsets.'

'Not with me,' he said on a sexy grin.

Something about his intensity really wiggled down under her skin. Tantalising and zingy. 'Why are you so eager for me to do this?'

Grey eyes grew earnest. 'Because you're missing everything. The entire country. The moments of joy that give life its colour.'

'You should really moonlight in greeting-card messages.'

'Come on, Eve. You have to go there, anyway, it's just a few hours of detour.'

'And what if Trav comes through in those few hours?' It sounded ridiculous but it was the fear she lived with every moment of every day.

'Then he'll see one of dozens of posters and know you're looking for him.'

The simple truth of that ached. Every decision she made ached. Each one could bring her closer to her brother or push her further away. It made decision-making pure agony. But this one came with a whole bundle of extra considerations. Marshall-shaped considerations. And the thought of sitting and watching a sunset with him even managed to alleviate some of that ache.

A surprising amount.

She sighed. 'What time?'

'How long are you set up here for?'

'I have permission to be on the waterfront until noon.'

'Five past noon, then?'

So eager. Did he truly think she was that parched for some life experience? It galled her to give him all the points. 'Ten past.'

His smile transformed his face, the way it always did.

'Done.'

'And we're sleeping separately. You know…just for the record.'

'Hey, I'm just buying you a sunset, lady.' His shrug was adorable. And totally disarming.

'Now go, Weatherman—you're scaring off my leads with all that leather.'

Her lips said 'go' but her heart said *stay*. Whispered it, really. But she'd become proficient in drowning out the fancies of her heart. And its fears. Neither were particularly productive in keeping her on track in finding Travis. A nice neutral… nothing…was the best way to proceed.

Emotionally blank, psychologically focused.

Which wasn't to say that Marshall Sullivan couldn't be a useful distraction from all the voices in her head and heart.

And a pleasant one.

And a short one.

They drove the two hundred kilometres east in a weird kind of convoy. Eve chugging along in her ancient bus and him, unable to stand the slow pace, roaring off ahead and pulling over at the turn-off to every conceivable human touch point until she caught up, whacked up a poster and headed out again. Rest stops, roadhouses, campgrounds, lookouts. Whizzing by at one hundred kilometres an hour and only stopping longer for places that had people and rubbish bins and queued-up vehicles.

It was a horrible way to see such a beautiful country.

Eventually, they made it to the campground nestled in the shoulder crook of a pristine bay on the far side of Cape Arid National Park, its land arms reaching left and right in a big, hug-like semicircle. A haven for travellers, fishermen and a whole lot of wildlife.

But not today. Today they had the whole place to themselves.

'So many blues…' Eve commented, stepping down out of the bus and staring at the expansive bay.

And she wasn't wrong. Closer to shore, the water was the pale, almost ice-blue of gentle surf. Then the kind of blue you saw on postcards, until, out near the horizon it graduated to a deep, gorgeous blue before slamming into the endless rich blue of the Australian sky. And, down to their left, a cluster of weathered boulders were freckled by a bunch of sea lions sunning themselves.

God…so good for the soul.

'This is nothing,' he said. Compared to what she'd missed

all along the south coast of Australia. Compared to what she'd driven straight past. 'If you'd just chuck your indicator on from time to time…'

She glanced at him but didn't say anything, busying stringing out her solar blanket to catch the afternoon light. When she opened the back doors of the bus to fill it with fresh sea air, she paused, looking further out to sea. Out to an island.

'Is that where we're going?'

Marshall hauled himself up next to her to follow her gaze. 'Nope. That's one of the closer, smaller islands in the archipelago. Middle Island is further out. One of those big shadows looming on the horizon.'

He leaned half across her to point further out and she followed the line of his arm and finger. It brought them as close together as they'd been since he'd dragged her kicking and cursing away from the thugs back in Norseman. And then he knew how much he'd missed her scent.

It eddied around his nostrils now, in defiance of the strong breeze.

Taunting him.

'How many are there?'

What were they talking about? Right…islands. 'More than a hundred.'

Eve stood, staring, her gaze flicking over every feature in view. Marshall kept his hand hooked around the bus's ceiling, keeping her company up there. Keeping close.

'Trav could be on any of them.'

Not if he also wanted to eat. Or drink. Only two had fresh water.

'Listen, Eve…'

She turned her eyes back up to his and it put their faces much closer than either of them might have intended.

'I really am truly sorry I said that about your brother. It was a cheap shot.' And one that he still didn't fully understand making. He wasn't Eve's keeper. 'The chances of him being out there are—'

'Tiny. I know. But it's in my head now and I'm not going to be able to sleep if I don't chase every possibility.'

'Still, I don't want to cause you pain.'

'That's not hurting, Marshall. That's helping. It's what I'm out here for.'

She said the words extra firmly, as if she was reminding both of them. Didn't make the slightest difference to the tingling in his toes. The tingling said she was here for him.

What did toes ever know?

He held her gaze much longer than was probably polite, their dark depths giving the ocean around them a run for its money.

'Doesn't seem a particularly convenient place to put a weather station,' she said finally, turning back out to the islands.

Subtle subject change. *Not.* But he played along. 'We want remote. To give us better data on southern coastal weather conditions.'

She glanced around them at the whole lot of nothing as far as the eye could see. 'You got it.'

Silent sound cushioned them in layers. The occasional bird cry, far away. The whump of the distant waves hitting the granite face of the south coast. The thrum of the coastal breeze around them. The awkward clearing of her throat as it finally dawned on her that she was shacked up miles from anywhere—and anyone—with a man she barely knew.

'What time are we meeting the boat? And where?'

'First thing in the morning. They'll pull into the bay, then ferry us around. Any closer to Middle Island and we couldn't get in without an off-road vehicle.'

'Right.'

Gravity helped his boots find the dirt and he looked back up at Eve, giving her the space she seemed to need. 'I'm going to go hit the water before the sun gets too low.'

Her eyes said that a swim was exactly what she wanted. But the tightness in her lips said that she wasn't about to go wandering through the sand dunes somewhere this remote with a virtual stranger. Fair enough, they'd only known each other hours. Despite having a couple of life-threatening moments between them. Maybe if she saw him walking away from her, unoffended and unconcerned, she'd feel more comfortable around him. Maybe if he offered no pressure for the two of them to spend time together, she'd relax a bit.

And maybe if he grew a pair he wouldn't care.

'See you later on, then.'

Marshall jogged down to the beach without looking back. When he hit the shore he laid his boots, jeans and T-shirt out on the nearest rock to get nice and toasty for his return and waded into the ice-cold water in his shorts. Normally he'd have gone without, public or not, but that wasn't going to win him any points in the *Is it safe to be here with you?* stakes. The sand beneath his feet had been beaten so fine by the relentless Southern Ocean it was more like squidging into saturated talcum powder than abrasive granules of sand. Soft and welcoming, the kind of thing you could imagine just swallowing you up.

And you wouldn't mind a bit.

His skin instantly thrilled at the kiss of the ice-cold water after the better part of a day smothered in leather and road dust, and he waded the stretch of shallows, then dived through the handful of waves that built up momentum as the rapid rise of land forced them into graceful, white-topped arcs.

This was his first swim since Cactus Beach, a whole state away. The Great Australian Bight was rugged and amazing to look at right the way across the guts of the country but when the rocks down to the sea were fifty metres high and the ocean down there bottomless and deadly, swimming had to take a short sabbatical. But swimming was also one of the things that kept him sane and being barred from it got him all twitchy.

Which made it pretty notable that the first thing he *didn't do* when he pulled up to the beautiful, tranquil and swimmable shores of Esperance earlier today was hit the water.

He went hunting for a dark-haired little obsessive instead.

Oh, he told himself a dozen lies to justify it—that he'd rather swim the private beaches of the capes; that he'd rather swim at sunset; that he'd rather get the Middle Island review out of the way first so he could take a few days to relax—but that was all starting to feel like complete rubbish. Apparently, he was parched for something more than just salt water.

Company.

*Pfff. Right. That was one word for it.*

It had been months since he'd been interested enough in a woman to do something about it, and by 'interested' he meant hungry. Hungry enough to head out and find a woman willing to sleep with a man who had nothing to offer but a hard, one-off lay before blowing town the next day. There seemed to be no shortage of women across the country who were out to salve a broken heart, or pay back a cheating spouse, or numb something broken deep inside them. They were the ones he looked for when he got needy enough because they didn't ask questions and they didn't have expectations.

It took one to know one.

Those encounters scratched the itch when it grew too demanding…and they reminded him how empty and soulless relationships were. All relationships, not just the random strangers in truck stops and bars across the country. Women. Mothers.

Brothers.

At least the women in the bars knew where they stood. No one was getting used. And there was no one to disappoint except himself.

He powered his body harder, arm over arm, and concentrated on how his muscles felt, cutting his limbs through the surf. Burning from within, icy from without. The familiar, heavy ache of lactic acid building up. And when he'd done all the examination it was possible to do on his muscles, he focused on the water: how the last land it had touched was Antarctica, how it was life support for whales and elephant seals and dugongs and colossal squid and mysterious deep-trench blobs eight kilometres below the surface and thousands of odd-shaped sea creatures in between. How humans were a bunch of nimble-fingered, big-brained primates that really only used the millimetre around the edge of the mapped oceans and had absolutely no idea how much of their planet they knew nothing about.

Instant Gulliver.

It reminded him how insignificant he was in the scheme of things. Him and all his human, social problems.

The sun was low on the horizon when he next paid attention, and the south coast of Australia was littered with sharks who liked to feed at dusk and dawn. And while there had certainly been a day he would have happily taken the risk and forgotten the consequences, he'd managed to find a happy place in the *Groundhog Day* blur that was the past six months on the road, and could honestly say—hand on heart—that he'd rather not be shark food now.

He did a final lazy lap parallel with the wide beach back towards his discarded clothes, then stood as soon as the sea floor rose to meet him. His hands squeezed up over his lowered lids and back through his hair, wringing the salt water out of it, then he stood, eyes closed, with his face tipped towards the warmth of the afternoon sun.

Eventually, he opened them and started, just a little, at Eve standing there, her arms full of towel, her mouth hanging open as if he'd interrupted her mid-sentence.

Eve knew she was gaping horribly but she was no more able to close her trap than rip her eyes from Marshall's chest and belly.

His *tattooed* chest and belly.

Air sucked into her lungs in choppy little gasps.

He had some kind of massive bird of prey, wings spread and aloft, across his chest. The lower curve of its majestic wings sat neatly along the ridge of his pectorals and its wing tips followed the line of muscle there up onto his tanned, rounded shoulders. Big enough to accentuate the musculature of his chest, low enough to be invisible when he was wearing a

T-shirt. It should have been trashy but it wasn't; it looked like he'd been born with it.

His arms were still up, squeezing the sea water from his hair, and that gave her a glimpse of a bunch of inked characters—Japanese, maybe Chinese?—on the underside of one full biceps.

Add that to the dagger on the other arm and he had a lot of ink for a weatherman.

'Hey.'

His voice startled her gaze back to his and her tongue into action.

'Wow,' she croaked, then realised that wasn't the most dignified of beginnings. 'You were gone so long…'

Great. Not even capable of a complete sentence.

'I've been missing the ocean. Sorry if I worried you.'

She grasped around in the memories she'd just spent a couple of hours accumulating, studying the map to make sure they hadn't missed a caravan park or town. And she improvised some slightly more intelligent conversation.

'Whoever first explored this area really didn't have the best time doing it.'

Marshall dripped. And frowned. As he lowered his arms to take the towel from her nerveless fingers, the bird of prey's feathers shifted with him, just enough to catch her eye. She struggled to look somewhere other than at him, but it wasn't easy when he filled her field of view so thoroughly. She wanted to step back but then didn't want to give him the satisfaction of knowing she was affected.

'Cape Arid, Mount Ragged, Poison Creek…' she listed with an encouraging lack of wobble in her voice, her clarity restored the moment he pressed the towel to his face and disguised most of that unexpectedly firm and decorated torso.

He stepped over to the rock and hooked up his T-shirt, then swept it on in a smooth, manly shrug. Even with its overstretched neckline, the bird of prey was entirely hidden. The idea of him hanging out in his meteorological workplace in a government-appropriate suit with all of that ink hidden away under it was as secretly pleasing as when she used to wear her best lingerie to section meetings.

Back when stupid things like that had mattered.

'I guess it's not so bad when you have supplies and transport,' he said, totally oblivious to her illicit train of thought, 'but it must have been a pretty treacherous environment for early explorers. Especially if they were thirsty.'

She just blinked at him. What was he saying? What had she asked?

He didn't bother with the rest of his clothes; he just slung the jeans over his shoulder and followed her back up to camp with his boots swinging in his left hand.

'Nice swim?' Yeah. Much easier to think with all that skin and ink covered up.

'I've missed it. The water's so clean down here.'

'Isn't ocean always clean?'

'Not at all. It's so easy to imagine the Southern Ocean being melt straight from Antarctica. Beautiful.'

'Maybe I'll take a dip tomorrow.' When Marshall was otherwise engaged.

They fell to silence as they approached the bus. Suddenly the awkwardness of the situation amplified. One bus. Two people. One of them half-naked and the other fresh from a bout of uncontrollable ogling. As though her-on-the-bed and him-on-the-sofa was the only social nicety to be observed. There was a bathroom and TV space and…air to consider. She was used to having the bus entirely to herself, now she had to share it with a man for twenty-four hours. And not just any man.

A hot man.

A really hot man.

'Um. You take the bus to change, I'll just—' she looked around for inspiration and saw the quirky little public outhouse in the distance '—check out the facilities.'

*Oh, good Lord…*

'Thanks. I'll only be a few minutes.'

Her, too. Most definitely. There was a reason she'd held out until she found a live-in transport with a toilet built into it. Public toilets in remote Australia were not for the faint of heart.

As it turned out, this one was a cut above average. Well maintained and stocked. Some kind of eco-composting number. It was only when she caught herself checking out how the pipework operated that she knew just how badly she was stalling. As if toilets were anywhere near that fascinating.

*Come on, Read, man up.*

Returning revealed Marshall to have been as good as his word. He was changed, loosely groomed and waiting outside the bus already. *Outside.* Almost as though he was trying to minimise his impact on her space.

He held his new bike helmet out to her.

'Come on.' He smiled. 'I promised you a ride. While we still have light.'

It took approximately twenty-five seconds for Eve to get over her concern that Marshall only had one motorbike helmet and he was holding it out to her. After that, she was all about survival of the fittest.

'I don't remember agreeing to this—'

'You'll love it, Eve. I promise.'

She glared up at him. 'Just because you do?'

'Because it's brilliant. And fun.'

No. Not always fun. She'd lost one and nearly two people she loved to a not-so-fun motorbike. Though that could just as easily have been a car, her logical side whispered. Or a bus. Or a 747. Tragedies happened every single day.

Just that day it happened to them.

'Think of it like a theme park ride,' he cajoled. 'A roller coaster.'

'That's not really helping.'

'Come on, Eve. What else are we going to do until it's dark?'

Apart from sit in the bus in awkward silence obsessing on

who was going to sleep where…? She glanced sideways at the big orange bike.

'I'll keep you safe, I promise. We'll only go as fast as you're comfortable with.'

His siren voice chipped away at her resistance. And his vow—*I'll keep you safe*. For so long she'd been all about looking after her father and brother. When was the last time someone offered to look after *her*?

'Just slow?'

Of course there was small print, but it came delightfully packaged in a grin full of promise. 'Until you're ready for more.'

He seemed so incredibly confident that was going to happen. Her bottom lip wiggled its way between her teeth. She *had* always wondered what it would be like to ride something with a bit more power. If by *always* she meant after two hours of watching a leather-clad Marshall dominate the machine under him. And if by *ride* she meant pressing her thighs into his and her front to that broad, strong back, both of them hepped up on adrenaline. It was a seductive picture. The kind of picture that was best reserved for her and a quiet, deluded night in the bus. She hadn't imagined it would ever go from fantasy to opportunity.

He held the helmet out again.

'You'll slow the moment I ask?' she breathed.

'Cross my heart.'

Yeah, not really selling it. Everyone knew what came after that line…

But it was only when she was about to lower her hand away from the helmet that she realised she'd even raised it. What was she going to do, live in fear of motorbikes for the rest of her life? No one was even sure what had caused her mother's accident—even Trav, after he'd come out of the coma, couldn't shed much light. Tragic accident. Could have happened to anyone. That was the final verdict.

'You'll drive safely?'

*Come on, Read, suck it up.*

Sincerity blazed in his solemn grey gaze. 'I'll be a model of conservatism.'

How long had it been since she'd done something outside of the box? Or taken any kind of risk? She used to be edgy, back before life got so very serious and she took responsibility for Travis. And her risks had almost always paid off. That was part of the thrill.

Hadn't she once been known for that?

Here was a gorgeous man offering to wrap her around him for a little bit. And the price—a bit of reckless speed.

It had been years since she'd done something reckless. Maybe it would be good for her.

She took a deep breath and curled her fingers around the helmet's chin strap.

The KTM hit a breath-stealing speed in about the same time it took her to brave opening her eyes. The road whizzed below them in such a blur it was like riding on liquid mercury.

At least that was how it felt.

She immediately remembered the excitement of riding behind her mother, but her mother's bike had never purred like this one. And it had never glued itself to the road like the tyres on this one.

Maybe if it had, all their lives would have been very different now.

She pressed herself more fully into Marshall's hard back and practically punched her fingertips through his leather jacket from clenching it so hard.

'Is this top speed?' she yelled forward to him.

His hair whipped around above her face as he shook his head and shouted back. 'We're only doing seventy kilometres.'

'Don't go any faster,' she called.

She hated the vulnerable note in her voice, but she hated more the thought of hitting the dirt at this kind of speed. In

Travis's case it had been trees but she felt fairly certain that you didn't need trees to be pretty badly injured on a bike.

Marshall turned his face half back to her and smiled beneath his protective sunglasses, nodding once. She'd just have to trust those teeth.

The roads of the national park were long and straight and the bike sat atop them beautifully so, after a few tense minutes, Eve let her death grip on his jacket ease slightly and crept them back to rest on Marshall's hips instead. Still firm, but the blood was able to leach back into her knuckles.

For a death machine he handled it pretty well.

Ahead, the road bent around a monolithic chunk of rock and he eased off the gas to pass it carefully. The bike's lean felt extreme to her and her grasp on his leather jacket completely insufficient, so her fingers found their way under it and hooked onto the eyelets of his jeans.

A few paltry sweatshop stitches were the only thing between her and certain doom.

While the engine was eased, Marshall took the opportunity to call back to her, half turning, 'Doing okay?'

*Eyes front, mister!*

'Stop staring down,' he shouted. 'Look around you.'

She let her eyes flutter upwards as he turned his attention back to the oncoming road. The entire park was bathed in the golden glow of afternoon light, the many different textures changing the way the light reflected and creating the golden equivalent of the ocean. So many different shades.

And—bonus—the speed didn't seem anywhere near as scary as staring down at the asphalt.

It was almost like being in the Bedford. Sans life-saving steel exoskeleton.

She didn't want to look like a complete wuss, and so Eve did her best to ease herself back from where her body had practically fused with his. The problem with that was as soon as he changed up gears, she brushed, breasts first, against his back. And then again.

And again, as he shifted up into fourth.

Okay, now he was just messing with her. She was having a difficult enough reaction to all that leather without adding to the crisis by torturing her own flesh. Leaning into him might be more intimate, but it felt far less gratuitous and so she snuggled forward again, widening her legs to fit more snugly around his. Probably not how a passenger was supposed to ride—the fact her bottom had left the pillion seat in favour of sharing his leathery saddle proved that—but that was how it was going to be for her first ever big boy's motorcycle experience.

And if he didn't like it he could pull over.

Minutes whizzed by and she grew captivated by the long stretches of tufted grass to her left, the parched, salt-crusted trees and coastal heath to her right and the limestone outcrops that practically glowed in the late-afternoon light. So much so that, when Marshall finally pulled them to a halt at a lookout point, she realised she'd forgotten all about the speed. Her pulse was up, her exposed skin was flushed pink and her breath was pleasantly choppy.

But she hadn't died.

And she wasn't ready for it to be over.

'I can see why she—why *you* like this,' she puffed, lifting the visor on her helmet and leaning around him. 'It's a great way to see the country.'

'Are you comfortable?'

His innocuous words immediately reminded her of how close she was pressed against him—wrapped around him, really—and she immediately went to correct that.

'Stay put,' he cautioned. 'We're about to head back.'

She leaned with him as he turned the bike in a big arc on an old salt flat and then bumped back onto the tarmac. As if she'd been doing this forever. And, as he roared back up to speed, she realised how very much in the *now* she'd been. Just her, Marshall, the road, the wind and the national park.

No past. No future. No accidents. No inquests. No Travis.

And how nice that moment of psychological respite was.

The light was totally different heading back. Less golden. More orange. And fading fast. He accessed a fifth gear that he'd spared her on the first leg and even still, when he pulled back in near the bus, the sun was almost gone. She straightened cold-stiffened limbs and pulled off his helmet.

'How was that?' he asked, way more interest in his eyes than a courtesy question. He kicked the stand into position and leaned the bike into the solid embrace of the earth.

'Amazing.'

The word formed a tiny breath cloud in the cool evening air and it was only then she realised how cold she was. The sun's warmth sure departed fast in this part of the country.

He followed her back towards the bus. 'You took a bit to loosen up.'

'Considering how terrified I was, I don't think I did too badly.'

'Not badly at all. I felt the moment when the fear left your body.'

The thought that she'd been pressed closely enough to him to be telegraphing any kind of emotion caused a rush of heat that she was very glad it was too dim for him to see. But he stepped ahead of her and opened the back of the Bedford and caught the last vestiges of her flush.

'How are you feeling now about motorcycles?'

His body blocked the step up into the bus and so she had no choice but to brush past him as she pulled herself up.

'It's still a death trap,' she said, looking back down at him. 'But not entirely without redeeming qualities.'

Not unlike its owner, really.

# CHAPTER FOUR

'I WAS THINKING of steak and salad for dinner,' Eve said, returning from her little bedroom newly clad in a sweater to take the edge off the cool coastal night.

Lord, how domestic. And utterly foreign.

'You don't need to cook for me, Eve. I ate up big at lunchtime in anticipation.'

'I was there, remember? And while it certainly was big you probably burned it all off with that epic swim earlier.'

And Lord knew, between the lusting and the fearing for her life, she'd just burnt all hers off, too.

Preparing food felt natural; she'd been doing it for Travis for so many years. Moreover, it gave her something constructive and normal to do for thirty minutes, but Marshall wasn't so lucky. He hovered, hopelessly. After the comparative intimacy of the bike ride, it seemed ludicrous to be uncomfortable about sharing a simple meal. But he was, a little.

And so was she. A lot.

'Here.' She slid him a bottle opener across the raw timber counter of the Bedford's compact little kitchen. 'Make yourself useful.'

She nodded to a small cabinet above the built-in television and, when he opened it, his eyebrows lifted at the contents. 'I thought you didn't drink?'

That rattled a chuckle from her tight chest.

'Not in bars—' with men she didn't know, and given her

familial history '—but I like to sample the local wines as I move around.'

She brought her solitary wineglass out from under the bench, then added a coffee mug next to it. The best she could do.

'You take the glass,' she offered.

He took both, in fact, poured two generous servings of red and slid the wineglass back her way. 'I guess you don't entertain much?'

'Not really out here for the social life,' she said. But then she relented. 'I did have a second glass once but I have no idea where it's gone. So it's the coffee mug or it's my toothbrush glass.'

And didn't that sound pathetic.

'You're going to need another storage cupboard,' he murmured, bringing the mug back from his lips and licking the final drops off, much to her sudden fascination. 'We're headed for serious wine country.'

'Maybe I just need to drink faster.'

He chuckled and saluted her with the mug. 'Amen to that.'

What was it about a communal glass of vino that instantly broke down the awkwardness barrier? He'd only had one sip and she'd had none, yet, so it wasn't the effects of the alcohol. Just something about popping a cork and swilling a good red around in your glass—or coffee mug—the great equaliser.

Maybe that was how her mother had begun. Social and pleasant. Until one day she woke up and it wasn't social any more. Or pleasant.

'So tell me,' Eve started, continuing with her food prep, 'did you have much competition for half a year in the bush checking on weather stations?'

He smiled and leaned across to relieve her of the chopping knife and vegetables from the fridge. 'I did not.'

It was too easy to respond to that gentle smile. To let her curiosity have wings. To tease. 'Can't imagine why not. Why did you accept it?'

'Travel the country, fully paid. What's not to love?'

'Being away from your friends and family?'

*Being away from your girlfriend.* She concentrated hard to keep her eyes from dropping to the bottom of the biceps dagger that peeked out from under his sleeve.

'Not all families benefit from being in each other's faces,' he said, a little tightly.

She stopped and regarded him. 'Speaking from experience?'

Grey eyes flicked to hers.

'Maybe. Don't tell me,' he nudged. 'You have the perfect parents.'

Oh…so far from the truth it was almost laughable. The steaks chuckled for her as she flipped them. 'Parent singular. Dad.'

He regarded her closely. 'You lost your mum?'

'Final year of school.'

'I'm sorry. New subject?'

'No. It's a long time ago now. It's okay.'

'Want to talk about it?'

Sometimes, desperately. Sometimes when she sat all alone in this little bus that felt so big she just wished she had someone sitting there with her that she could spill it all to. Someone to help her make sense of everything that had happened. Because she still barely understood it.

'Not much to talk about. She was in an accident. Travis was lucky to survive it.'

His fathomless gaze grew deeper. Full of sympathy. 'Car crash?'

Here it came…

'Motorbike, actually.'

His eyes flared and he spun more fully towards her. 'Why didn't you say, Eve?'

'I'm saying now.'

'Before I press-ganged you into taking a ride with me,' he gritted, leaning over the counter.

'I could have said no. At any time. I'm not made of jelly.'

Except when Marshall smiled at her a certain way. Then anyone would be forgiven for thinking so.

'I never would have—'

'It wasn't the bike's fault. It's good for me to remember that.'

He took a long, slow breath and Eve distracted herself poking the steaks.

'A 250cc, you said. Not your usual family wagon.'

'Oh, we had one of those, too. But she got her motorcycle licence not long after having Travis.' Like some kind of statement. 'She rode it whenever she didn't have us with her.'

Which was often in those last five years.

'I think it was her way of fighting suburbia,' she murmured.

Or reality, maybe.

'But she had your brother with her that day?' Then, 'Are you okay to talk about this?'

Surprisingly, she was. Maybe because Marshall was a fellow motorbike fanatic. It somehow felt okay for him to know.

'Yeah—' she sighed '—she did. Trav loved her bike. He couldn't wait to get his bike permit. I think she was going to give him the Kawasaki. He'd started to learn.'

'How old was he when it happened?'

'Fourteen.'

'Five years between you. That's a biggish gap.'

'Thank God for it. Not sure I could have handled any of it if I'd been younger.'

It was hard enough as it was.

It was only when Marshall's voice murmured, soft and low, over her shoulder and he reached past her to turn off the gas to the steaks that she realised how long she'd been standing there mute. Her skin tingled at his closeness.

'New subject?'

'No. I'm happy to talk about my family. I just forget sometimes…'

'Forget what?'

Sorrow washed through her. 'That my family's different now. That it's just me and Dad.'

'You say that like…'

Her eyes lifted. 'That's the reality. If Trav is missing by force, then he's not coming back. And if he's missing by choice…'

*Then he's not coming back.*

Either way, her already truncated family had shrunk by one more.

'You really believe he could be out here somewhere, just… lying low?'

'I have to believe that. That he's hurting. Confused. Off his meds. Maybe he doesn't think he'd be welcome back after leaving like he did. I want him to know we want him back no matter what.'

Marshall's head bobbed slowly. 'No case to answer? For the distress he's caused?'

Her hand fell still on the spatula. For the longest time, the only sound came from the low-burn frying pan. But, eventually, her thoughts collected into something coherent.

'I ask myself is there anything he could do that would make me not want to have him back with us and the answer is no. So giving him grief for what he did, or why he did it, or the manner in which he did it… It has no purpose. I just want him to walk back in that door and scuff the wall with his school bag and start demanding food. The *what*, *why* and *how* is just not relevant.'

Intelligent eyes glanced from her still fingers to her face. 'It's relevant to you.'

'But it's not important. In the scheme of things.'

Besides, she already had a fairly good idea of the *why*. Travis's escalating anxiety and depression seemed blazingly obvious in hindsight, even if she hadn't seen it at the time. Because she hadn't been paying attention. She'd been far too busy shrugging off her substitute mother apron.

Thinking about herself.

She poked at the steak again and delicious juices ran from it and added to the noise in the pan. She lifted her wineglass with her free hand and emptied a bit into the pan. Then she took a generous swig and changed the subject.

'So, who is Christine?'

No-man's-land the last time they spoke, but they weren't spending the night under the same roof then. They barely knew each other then.

*We barely know each other now!* a tiny voice reminded her.

But they did. Maybe not a heap of details, but they knew each other's names and interests and purpose. She'd seen him half naked striding out of the surf, and she'd pressed up against him a grand total of two times now and had a different kind of glimpse at the kind of man he was under all the leather and facial hair. He struck her as…safe.

And sometimes safe was enough.

But right now *safe* didn't look entirely happy at her words. Though he still answered.

'Was,' he clarified. 'Christine was my girlfriend.'

*Clang.* The pan hit the stovetop at his use of the past tense. There was the answer to a question she didn't know she'd been dying to ask. Unexpected butterflies took flight deep in her gut and she busied herself with a second go at moving the frying pan off the heat.

'Recent?'

His strong lips pursed briefly as he considered answering. Or not answering. 'Long time ago.'

Yeah, the ink didn't look new, come to think of it. Unlike the one she'd seen under his biceps.

Which meant he could still be someone else's hairy biker type. That she was having a quiet steak with. Under a gem-filled sky. Miles from anywhere. After a blood-thrilling and skin-tingling motorbike ride…

She shook the thoughts free. 'Childhood sweetheart?'

Tension pumped off him. 'Something like that.'

And suddenly she disliked Christine intensely. 'I'm sorry.'

He shrugged. 'Not your doing.'

She studied the tight lines at the corner of his mouth. The

mouth she'd not been able to stop looking at since he'd shaved and revealed it. Tonight was no different. 'So…there's no Christine now? I mean someone like Christine?'

His eyes found hers. 'You asking if I'm single?'

'Just making conversation. I figured not, since you were on a pilgrimage around the country.'

'It's my job, Eve. Not everyone out here is on some kind of odyssey.'

That stung as much as the sea salt she'd accidentally rubbed in her eye earlier. Because of the judgment those words contained. And the truth. And because they came from him.

But he looked contrite the moment they fell off his lips.

'You don't like talking about her, I take it?' she murmured.

He shook his head but it was no denial.

'Fair enough.' Then she nodded at his arm. 'You might want to get that altered though.'

The tension left his face and a couple of tiny smile lines peeked out the corners of his eyes. 'I couldn't have picked someone with a shorter name, huh? Like Ann. Or Lucy.'

Yep. Christine sure was a long word to tattoo over.

'It's pretty florid, too. A dagger?'

The smile turned into a laugh. 'We were seventeen and in love. And I fancied myself for a bit of a tough guy. What can I say?'

Eve threw some dressing on the salad and gave it a quick toss.

'She got a matching one I hope?'

'Hers just said *Amore*. Multi-purpose.'

'*Pfff.* Non-committal. That should have been your first warning.'

She added a steak to each of their plates.

'With good reason, it turns out.'

'Christine sucked?'

That earned her a chuckle. She loved the rich, warm sound because it came from so deep in his chest. 'No, she didn't. Or I wouldn't have fallen for her.'

'That's very charitable.'

He waved his coffee mug. 'I'm a generous guy.'

'So…I'm confused,' she started. 'You don't want to talk about her, but you don't hold it against her?'

'It's not really about Christine,' he hedged.

'What isn't?' And then, when he didn't respond, 'The awkward silence?'

'How many people end up with their first love, really?'

She wouldn't know. She hadn't had time for love while she was busy raising her family. Or since. More's the pity.

'So where did she end up?'

The look he gave her was enigmatic. But also appraising. And kind of stirring. 'Not important.'

'You're very complicated, Marshall Sullivan.'

His smile crept back. 'Thank you.'

Eve leaned across the counter and lifted the hem of his sleeve with two fingers to have a good look at the design. Her fingertips brushed the smooth strength of his warm biceps and tingled where they travelled.

She cleared her throat. 'Maybe you could change it to *pristine*, like the ocean? That way, you only have to rework the first two letters.'

Three creases formed across his brow as he looked down. 'That could actually work…'

'Or *Sistine*, like the chapel.'

'Or *intestine*, like the pain I get from smelling that steak and not eating it.'

They loaded their plates up with fresh salad and both tucked in.

'This is really good.'

'That surprises you?'

'I didn't pick you as a cook.'

She shrugged. 'I had a rapid apprenticeship after Mum died.'

She munched her way through half her plate before speaking again.

'Can I ask you something personal?'

'Didn't you already do that?'

'About travelling.'

His head tilted. 'Go ahead.'

'Do you…' Lord, how to start this question? 'You travel alone. Do you ever feel like you've forgotten how to be with somebody else? How to behave?'

'What do you mean?'

'I just…I used to be so social. Busy schedule, urban life-style, dinners out most evenings. Meeting new people and chatting to them.' Up until the accident, anyway. 'I feel like I've lost some of my social skills.'

'Honestly?'

She nodded.

'Yeah, you're missing a few of the niceties. But once you get past that, you're all right. We're conversing happily now, aren't we?'

Give or take a few tense undercurrents.

'Maybe you just got good at small talk,' he went on. 'And small talk doesn't take you far in places like this. Situations like this. It's no good at all in silence. It just screams. But we're doing okay, on the whole.'

She rushed to correct him. 'I didn't mean you, specifi-cally—'

'Yeah, you did.'

'What makes you say that?'

'Eve, this feels awkward because it *is* awkward. We don't know each other and yet I was forced into your world unnatu-rally. And now a virtual stranger is sitting ten feet from your bed, drinking your wine and getting personal. Of course it's uncomfortable.'

'I'm not…it's not uncomfortable, exactly. I just feel really rusty. And you don't deserve that. You've been very nice.'

The word *nice* hit him visibly. He actually winced.

'When was the last time you had someone in your bus?' he deviated.

Eve racked her brain… Months. Lots of months. 'Long

enough for that second wineglass to end up right at the back of some cupboard.'

'There you go, then. You're out of shape, socially, that's all.' She stared at him.

'Let's make a pledge. I promise to be my clunky self when you're around if you'll do the same.' He drew a big circle around the two of them and some tiny part of her quite liked being in that circle with him. 'This is a clunk-approved zone.'

'Clunk-approved?'

'Weird moments acknowledged, accepted and forgiven.'

Why was it so easy to smile, with him? 'You're giving me permission to be socially clumsy?'

'I'm saying I'll understand.'

It was so much easier to breathe all of a sudden. 'All right. Sounds good.'

And on that warm and toasty kindred-spirit moment…

'Are you done?' she checked.

He scooped the last of his steak into his mouth and nodded.

'Hop up, I'd like to show you something.'

As soon as he stood up and back, she pinched the tall stool out from under him and clambered onto it. That allowed her to pop the latch on what looked to anyone else like a sunroof. It folded back onto the bus with a thump. She boosted herself up and into the void, wriggling back until her bottom was thoroughly seated and her legs dangled down into the bus.

'Pass the wine up,' she asked.

He did, but not before adding a generous splash to both their vessels. Then he hoisted himself up opposite her—disgustingly effortlessly—and followed her gaze, left, up out into the endless, dark sky over the Southern Ocean.

'Nice view.'

Essentially the same view as when they'd stood up on the Bedford's back step, just a little higher, but somehow it was made all the more spectacular by the location, the wine and the darkness.

And the company.

'I like to do this when the weather's fine.' Though usually alone.

'I can see why.'

The sky was blanketed with light from a gazillion other solar systems. The full you'll-never-see-it-in-the-city cliché. Eve tipped her head back, stared up and sighed.

'Sometimes I feel like I might as well be looking for Trav out there.' She tossed her chin to the trillions of unseen worlds orbiting those million stars. 'It feels just as unachievable.'

He brought his eyes back down from the heavens. Back to hers.

'It was such a simple plan when I set off. Visit every town in Australia and put posters up. Check for myself. But all it's done is reinforce for me how vast this country is and how many ways there are for someone to disappear. Living or dead.'

'It's a good plan, Eve. Don't doubt yourself.'

She shrugged.

'Did you do it because you truly thought you'd find him? Or did you do it because you had to do something?'

Tears suddenly sprang up and she fought them. It took a moment to get the choke out of her words.

'He's so young. Still a kid, even if the law says otherwise. I was going crazy at home. Waiting. Hoping each day would be the day that the police freed up enough time to look into Trav's case a bit. Made some progress. My heart leaping every time the phone rang in case it was news.'

Fighting endlessly with her father, who wanted her to give up. To accept the truth.

His truth.

'So here you are,' he summarised, simply. 'Doing something constructive. Does it feel better?'

'Yeah. When it's not feeling totally futile.'

It was too dark for the colour of his eyes to penetrate, but his focus fairly blazed out from the shadows under his sockets. 'It's only futile when it stops achieving anything. Right now it's keeping you sane.'

How did this total stranger know her better than anyone else—better than she knew herself?

Maybe because it took one to know one.

She saluted him with her wine. 'Well, aren't we a pack of dysfunctional sad sacks.'

'I'm not sad,' Marshall said, pretty proudly.

What was his story? Curiosity burnt, bright and blazing. The intense desire to *know* him.

'Nothing to say about being dysfunctional?'

'Nope. Totally guilty on that charge.'

The wind had changed direction the moment the sun set, and its heat no longer affected the vast pockets of air blanketing the southern hemisphere. They were tickled by its kiss but no longer buffeted, and it brought with it a deep and comfortable silence.

'So,' Marshall started, 'if I want to use the bus's bathroom during the night I'm basically in your bedroom, right? How's that going to work?'

She just about gave herself whiplash glancing up at him.

'Uh…'

The bus's little en suite bathroom was on the other side of the door that separated it from the rest of the bus. And from Marshall.

Groan. Just another practicality she hadn't thought through thoroughly.

*That's because you just about fell over yourself to travel with him for a bit.*

'Or I can use the campsite toilet,' he suggested.

Yes! Thank the Lord for public services.

'It's not too bad, actually.' If you didn't mind rocks on your bare feet at three in the morning and spiders in the dark. 'What time do we need to be up?'

As soon as the words tumbled over her lips she regretted

them. Why was she ending the moment of connection so soon after it had begun?

'The boat's coming at eight.'

And dawn was at six. That was two hours of daylight for the two of them to enjoy sharing the clunk-approved zone together. 'Okay. I'll be ready.'

He passed her his mug, then swung himself down and in and took it and hers and placed them together on the bench below. Eve wiggled to the edge of the hatch and readied her arms to take her weight.

'You all right?'

'Yeah, I do it all the time.' Though she just half tumbled, half swung, usually. Gravity fed. Completely inelegant. 'I don't normally have an audience for this bit.'

His deep voice rumbled, 'Here, let me help…'

Suddenly two strong hands were around her waist, pressed sure and hot against her midriff, and she had no choice but to go with them through the roof and back inside the bus. Marshall eased her down in a far less dramatic manner than she was used to, but not without bunching her sweater up under her breasts and leaving her stomach totally exposed as she slid the length of his body. Fortunately, there were no bare hands on bare skin moments, but it was uncomfortable enough to feel the press of his cold jeans stud against her suddenly scorched tummy.

'Thanks,' she breathed.

He released her and stood back, his lashes lowered. 'No problem.'

Instantly, she wondered what the Japanese symbol for 'awkward' was and whether she'd find that tattooed anywhere on his body.

And instantly she was thinking about hidden parts of his body.

She shook the thought free. 'Well…I guess I'll see you in the morning. I'll try and be quiet if you're not up.'

'I'll be up,' he pledged.

Because he was an early riser or because he wasn't about to let her see him all tousled and vulnerable?

Or because all the touching and sliding was going to keep him awake all night, too.

# CHAPTER FIVE

IT HAD BEEN a long time since Marshall had woken to the sounds of someone tiptoeing around a kitchen. In this particular case, it was extra soft because the kitchen was only two metres from his makeshift bed.

He'd heard Eve wake up, start moving around beyond that door that separated them all night, but then he'd fallen back into a light morning doze to the entirely feminine soundtrack. You had to live with someone to enjoy those moments. And you had to love them to live with them. And trust them to love them.

Unfortunately, trust and he were uneasy companions.

He'd been in one relationship post-Christine—a nice girl with lots of dreams—and that hadn't ended well. Him, of course. Just another reminder why going solo was easier on everyone concerned. Family included.

Thoughts of his brother robbed him of any further shut-eye. He pulled himself upright and forked fingers through his bed hair.

'Morning,' Eve murmured behind him. 'I hope I didn't wake you?'

'No. I was half awake, anyway. What time is it?'

'Just after six.'

Wow. Went to show what fresh air, hours of swimming and a good drop of red could do for a man's insomnia. He sure couldn't attribute it to the comfort of his bed. Every muscle creaked as he sat up, including the ones in his voice box.

'Not comfortable?'

'Better than my swag on the hard outback dirt.' Even though it really wasn't. There was something strangely comfortable about bedding down on the earth. It was very…honest. 'I'll be back in a tick.'

The morning sun was gentle but massively bright and he stumbled most of the way towards the campsite toilet. Even with her not in her room, the thought of wedging all of himself into that compact little en suite bathroom… It was just too personal.

And he didn't do personal.

'I have eggs or I have sausages,' she announced when he walked back in a little later. 'They won't keep much longer so I'm cooking them all up.'

'Nah. I'll be all right.'

'You have to eat something; we're going to be on the water all day.'

'That's exactly why I don't want something.'

She stopped and stared. 'Do you get seasick?'

'Doesn't really fit with the he-man image you have of me, does it?' He slid back onto his stool from the night before and she passed him a coffee. 'Not horribly. But bad enough.'

'How about some toast and jam, then?'

She was determined to play host. 'Yeah, that I could do.'

That wouldn't be too disgusting coming back up in front of an audience.

She added two pieces of frozen bread to the toaster and kept on with her fry-up. If nothing else, the seagulls would love the sausages.

'Is that okay?' she said when she finally slid the buttered toast towards him.

'Just trying to think when was the last time I had toast and jam.' Toast had been about all his mother stretched to when he was a kid. But there was seldom jam.

'Not a breakfast person?'

'In the city I'd grab something from a fast food place near work.'

'I'm sure your blood vessels were grateful.'

Yeah… Not.

'Mostly it was just coffee.' The liquid breakfast of champions.

'What about out here?'

'Depends. Some motels throw a cooked breakfast in with the room. That's not always a nice surprise.'

'Well, this is a full service b & b, so eat up.'

Eating with a woman at six o'clock in the morning should have felt wrong but it didn't. In fact, clunk-approved zone moments aside, he felt pretty relaxed around Eve most of the time. Maybe because she was uptight enough for the both of them.

'Marshall?'

'Sorry. What did you say?'

'I wondered how the boat would know where to come and get us?'

'They'll just putter along the coast until they see us waving.'

'You're kidding.'

'Well, me waving, really. They're not expecting two.'

'That's very casual,' she said. 'What if they don't come?'

'Then I'll call them and they'll come tomorrow.'

Dark eyebrows shot up. 'You're assuming I'd be happy to stay an extra night.'

'If not, we could just head back to Esperance and pick up the boat there,' he admitted. 'That's where it's moored.'

Her jaw gaped. 'Are you serious? Then why are we here?'

'Come on, Eve. Tell me you didn't enjoy the past twenty-four hours. Taking a break. Enjoying the scenery.'

Her pretty eyes narrowed. 'I feel like I've been conned.'

'You have—' he grinned around the crunch of toast smeared with strawberry jam '—by the best.'

She didn't want to laugh—her face struggled with it—but there was no mistaking the twisted smile she tried to hide by turning and plating up her eggs. Twisted and kind of gorgeous. But all she said was…

'So, talk to me about the island.'

The boat came. The *Vista II*'s two-man crew easily spotted the two of them standing on the rocks at the most obvious point of the whole beach. One of them manoeuvred a small inflatable dinghy down onto the stillest part of the early-morning beach to collect them.

The captain reached down for Eve's hands and pulled her up onto the fishing vessel and Marshall gave her a boost from below. Quite a personal boost—both of his hands starting on her waist but sliding onto her bum to do the actual shoving. Then he scrambled up without assistance and so did the old guy who had collected them in the dinghy that he hastily re-tethered to the boat.

'Thanks for that,' she murmured sideways to Marshall before smiling broadly at the captain and thanking him for real.

'Would you have preferred fish-scaly sea-dog hands on your butt?' Marshall murmured back.

Yeah. Maybe. Because she wouldn't have had to endure his heat still soaking into her. She already had enough of a fascination with his hands…

The next ten minutes were all business. Life vests secured, safety lecture given, seating allocated. Hers was an old square cray pot. Marshall perched on a box of safety gear.

'How long is the trip to Middle Island?' she asked the captain as soon as they were underway.

'Twenty minutes. We have to go around the long way to avoid the wrecks.'

'There are shipwrecks out here?' But as she turned and looked back along the one-hundred-strong shadowy islands of the Recherche Archipelago stretching out to the west, the question suddenly felt really foolish.

Of course there were. It was like a visible minefield of islands.

'Two right off Middle Island.'

As long as they didn't add the *Vista II* to that list, she'd be happy. 'So almost no one comes out here?'

'Not onto the islands, but there's plenty of fishing and small boating traffic.'

'And no one's living on Middle Island?'

Marshall's eyes glanced her way.

'Not since the eighteen-thirties, when Black Jack Anderson based himself and his pirating outfit there,' the captain volunteered.

Huh. So it *could* be lived on. Technically.

Eve turned her gaze towards the distant shadow that was becoming more and more defined as the boat ate up the miles and the captain chatted on about the island's resident pirate. Maybe Marshall's theory wasn't so far-fetched. Maybe Trav could be there. Or have been there in the past. Or—

And as she had the thought, she realised.

*Travis.*

She'd been awake two whole hours and not given her brother the slightest thought. Normally he was on her mind when her eyes fluttered open each day and the last thing she thought about at night. It kept her focused and on mission. It kept him alive in her heart.

But last night all she'd been able to think about was the man settling in just metres and a bit of flimsy timber away from her. How complicated he was. How easy he was to be around. How good he smelled.

She'd been pulled off mission by the first handsome, broad-shouldered distraction to come along. Nice. As if she wasn't already excelling at the Bad Sister of the Year award.

Well… No more.

Time to get back in the game.

'Eve?' Marshall's voice drifted to her over the sound of the outboard. 'Are you okay?'

She kept her eyes carefully averted, as though she was focusing on the approaching island, and lied.

'Just thinking about what it would be like to live there...'

They travelled in silence, but Eve could just about feel the moments when Marshall would let his eyes rest on her briefly. Assessing. Wondering. The captain chatted on with his semi-tour talk. About the islands. About the wildlife. About the wallabies and frogs and some special lizard that all lived in harmony on the predator-free island. About the southern rock lobster and abalone that he and his mate fished out of these perilous waters. About how many sharks there were lurking in the depths around them.

The promise of sharks made her pay extra attention as she slid back down the side of the *Vista II* into the inflatable and, before long, her feet were back on dry land. Dry, deserted land.

One glance around them at the remote, untouched, uninhabitable terrain told her Trav wasn't hiding out here.

As if there'd really been a chance.

'Watch where you step. The barking gecko is protected on this island.'

'Of course it is,' she muttered.

Marshall just glanced at her sideways. The fishermen left and promised to return for them in a couple of hours. A nervous anxiety filled her belly. If they didn't return, what would she do? How would she survive here with just a day's supply of water and snacks and no shelter? Just because Black Jack Whatsit got by for a decade didn't mean she'd last more than a day.

'So,' Marshall said after helping to push the inflatable back offshore, 'you want to explore on your own or come with me?'

*Explore on my own*—that was the right answer. But, at the same time, she didn't know anything about this strange little island and she was just as likely to break her ankle on the farthest corner from Marshall and his little first-aid kit.

'Is it safe?' she asked, screening her eyes with her hands and scanning the horizon.

'If you don't count the death adders, yeah.'

She snapped her focus straight back to him. 'Are you kidding?'

'Nope. But if you're watching out for the geckos you'll almost certainly see the snakes before you tread on them.'

Almost certainly.

'I'm coming with you.'

'Good choice. Feel like a climb?' She turned and followed his gaze up to the highest point on the island. 'Flinders Peak is where the weather station would go.'

He assured her it was only one hundred and eighty-five metres above sea level but it felt like Everest when you were also watching every footfall for certain death—yours or a protected gecko's.

Marshall pointed out the highlights to the west, chatted about the nearest islands and their original names. Then he halted his climb and just looked at her.

'What?' she asked, puffing.

'I'm waiting for you to turn around.'

They'd ascended the easiest face of the peak but it had obscured most of the rest of the island from their view. She turned around now.

'Oh, my gosh!'

*Pink.* A crazy, wrong, enormous bubblegum-pink lake lay out on the eastern corner of the island. Somehow everyone had failed to mention a bright pink lake! 'What is it?'

'Lake Hillier.'

'It's so beautiful.' But so unnatural. It just went to show how little she knew about the natural world. 'Why is it pink?'

'Bacteria? The type of salt? Maybe something new to science. Does it matter?'

'I guess not.' It was just curiously beautiful. 'Can we go there?'

'We just got up here.'

'I know, but now I want to go there.'

So much! A bit like riding on his bike, little moments of

pleasure managed to cut through her miserable thoughts about Travis.

He smiled, but it was twisted with curiosity. And something else.

'What?' she queried.

'This is the first time I've seen you get really passionate about anything since I met you.'

'Some things are just worth getting your pulse up about.' And, speaking of which…

He stepped a little closer and her heartbeat responded immediately.

'Lakes and lizards do it for you?'

'*Pink* lakes and geckos that *bark*,' she stressed for the slow of comprehension. Right on cue, a crack of vocalisation issued from a tuft of scrubby foliage to their left. She laughed in delight. But then she caught his expression.

'Seriously, Marshall… *What?*' His focus had grown way too intense. And way too pointed. She struggled against the desire to match it.

'Passion suits you. You should go hiking more often.'

Her chest had grown so tight with the climb, his words worsened her breathlessness. She pushed off again for the final peak. And for the pure distraction of physical distress.

'I get how the birds get here,' she puffed, changing the subject, 'and the crustaceans. But how did the mammals arrive here? And the lizards?'

For a moment, she thought he wasn't going to let it go but he did, gracefully.

'They didn't arrive, they endured. Back from when the whole archipelago were peaks connected to the mainland. There used to be a lot more until explorers came along and virtually wiped them out.'

Eve looked up at a circling sea eagle. 'You can't tell me that the geckos didn't get picked off by hungry birds, before.'

'Yeah, but in balance. They live in *refugia* here, isolation from the world and its threats. Until the first cat overboard, anyway.'

*Isolation from the world and its threats.* She kind of liked the sound of that. Maybe that was what Trav was chasing when he walked out into the darkness a year ago. Emotional *refugia*.

She stumbled on a rock as she realised. Not a year ago…a year ago *tomorrow*. Not only had she failed to think about Travis for entire hours this morning but she'd almost forgotten tomorrow's depressing anniversary.

Her joy at their spectacular view drained away as surely as the water far below them dragged back across the shell-speckled beach where they'd come ashore.

Marshall extended his warm hand and took her suddenly cold one for the final haul up the granite top of Flinders Peak, and the entire south coast of Western Australia—complete with all hundred-plus islands—stretched out before them. The same sense of despair she'd felt when staring up at the stars the night before washed over Eve.

Australia was so incredibly vast and so incredibly empty.

So much freaking country to look in.

She stood, immobile, as he did what they'd come to do. Photographing. Measuring. Recording compass settings and GPS results. Taking copious notes and even some soil and vegetation samples. He threw a concerned glance at her a couple of times, until he finally closed up his pack again.

'Eve…'

'Are you done?'

'Come on, Eve—'

'I'm going to head down to the lake.' But there was no interest in her step, and no breathlessness in her words. Even she could hear the death in her voice.

'Stop.'

She did, and she turned.

'What just happened? What did I do?'

Truth sat like a stone in her gut. 'It wasn't you, Marshall. It was me.'

'What did *you* do?'

More what she didn't do.

'Eve?'

'I shouldn't be here.'

'We have a permit.'

'No, I mean I shouldn't be wasting time like this.'

'You're angry because you let yourself off the hook for a few hours?'

'I'm angry because I only have one thing to do out here. Prioritising Travis. And I didn't do that today.'

Or yesterday, if she was honest. She might have pinned up a bunch of posters, but her memories of yesterday were dominated by Marshall.

'Your life can't only be about your brother, Eve. It's not healthy.'

Health. A bit late now to be paying attention to anyone's health. Her own. Her brother's. Maybe if she'd been more alert a couple of years back...

She took a deep breath. 'Are you done up here?'

A dozen expressions ranged across his face before he answered. But, when he did, his face was carefully neutral. 'We have a couple of hours before the boat gets back. Might as well have a look around with me.'

Fine. He could make her stay...

But he couldn't make her enjoy it.

It took the best part of the remaining ninety minutes on the island but Marshall managed to work the worst of the stiffness from Eve's shoulders. He did it with easy, undemanding conversation and by tapping her natural curiosity, pointing out endless points of interest and intriguing her with imaginary tales of the pirate Anderson and his hidden treasure that had never been recovered.

'Maybe his crew took it when they killed him.' She shrugged, still half-numb.

Cynical, but after the sad silence of the first half-hour he'd take it. 'Seems a reasonable enough motive to kill someone. You know, if you were a bloodthirsty pirate.'

'Or maybe there never was any treasure,' she posed. 'Maybe Anderson only managed to steal and trade enough to keep him and his crew alive, not to accrue a fortune. Maybe they weren't very good pirates!'

'You've seen the island now. Where would you bury it if it did exist?'

She glanced around. 'I wouldn't. It's too open here. Hard to dig up without being seen by the crew.' Her eyes tracked outward and he followed them to the guano-blanketed, rocky outcrop just beyond the shores of Middle Island. 'Maybe over there? Some random little cave or hollow?'

'Want to go look?'

She turned wide eyes on him. 'I'm not about to swim fully clothed across a shark-infested channel to an outcrop covered in bird poo filled with God knows what bacteria to hunt for non-existent treasure.'

'You have no soul, Evelyn Read,' he scoffed.

'I do have one and I'd prefer to keep it firmly tethered to my body, thanks very much.'

He chuckled. 'Fair enough. Come on, let's see if the lake looks as impressive up close.'

It didn't. Of course it didn't. Wasn't there something about rose-coloured glasses? But it wasn't a total disappointment. Still officially pink, even once Eve filled her empty water bottle with it.

'You're not planning on drinking that?' he warned.

'Nope.' She emptied it all back into the lake and tucked the empty bottle into her backpack for later recycling. 'Just trying to catch it out being trickily clear.'

They strolled around the lake the long way, then headed back down to the only decent beach on the island. A tiny but sandy cove formed between two outcrops of rocky reef. The place the boat had left them. Marshall immediately tugged his shoes and socks off and tied them to his own pack, which he

stashed on a nearby rock, then made his way out a half-dozen
metres from where Eve stood discovering that the sand was
actually comprised of teeny-tiny white shells.

'Water's fine…' he hinted. 'Not deep enough for predators.'

She crossed her arms grumpily from the shore. 'What about
a stingray?'

He splashed a little forward in the waves that washed in
from the current surging between the islands. 'Surfing stingrays?'

'Where lakes are pink and lizards bark? Why not?'

'Come on, Eve. Kick your shoes off.'

She glared at him, but eventually she sank onto one hip
and toed her opposite runner and sock off, then she did the
same on the other foot. Though she took her sweet time putting both carefully in her pack and placing the lot next to his
backpack on the hot sand.

'Welcome to heaven,' he murmured as she joined him in
the shallows. Her groan echoed his as her hot and parched feet
drank up the cold water, too. They stood there like that, together, for minutes. Their hearts slowing to synchronise with
the waves washing up and into their little minibay.

Just…being.

'Okay,' Eve breathed, her face turned to the sky. 'This was
a good idea.'

He waded a little further from her. 'My ideas are always
good.'

She didn't even bother looking at him. 'Is that right?'

'Sure is.'

He reached down and brushed his fingers through the crystal-clear water then flicked two of them in her general direction.

She stiffened—in body and in lip—as the droplets hit her.
She turned her head back his way and let her eyes creak open.
'Thanks for that.'

'You had to know that was going to happen.'

'I should have. You with a mental age of twelve and all.'

He grinned. 'One of my many charms.'

She flipped her cap off her head, bent down and filled it with fresh, clean water and then replaced the lot on her head, drenching herself in salty water.

'Well, that killed my fun,' he murmured.

But not his view. The capful of water had the added benefit of making parts of her T-shirt and cargos cling to the curves of her body even more than they already were. And that killed any chance of him cooling down unless he took more serious measures. He lowered himself onto his butt in the shallows and lay back, fully, in the drink.

Pants, shirt and all.

'You know how uncomfortable you're going to be going back?' Her silhouette laughed from high above him, sea water still trickling off her jaw and chin.

He starfished in the two feet of water. 'Small price to pay for being so very comfortable now.'

Even with her eyes mostly shaded by the peak of her cap, he could tell when her glance drifted his way. She was trying not to look—hard—but essentially failing. He experimented by pushing his torso up out of the water and leaning back casually on his hands.

'Easy to say…'

But her words didn't sound easy at all. In fact, they were as tight as her body language all of a sudden.

Well, wasn't *that* interesting.

He pushed to his feet and moved towards her, grinning. Primarily so that he could see her eyes again. Her hands came up, fast, in front of her.

'Don't you dare…'

But he didn't stop until he stood just a centimetre from her upturned hands. And he grinned. 'Don't dare do this, you mean?'

'Come on, Marshall, I don't want to get wet.'

'I'm not the one with a soggy cap dripping down my face.'

'No, you're just soaked entirely through.'

And, with those words, her eyes finally fell where she'd been trying so hard not to look. At his chest, just a finger flex away from her upturned hands.

'I'm beginning to see what Anderson might have liked about this island,' he murmured.

She huffed out a slow breath. 'You imagine he and his crew took the time to roll around in the shallows like seals?'

The thought of rolling around anything with Eve hadn't occurred to him today, but now it was all he could do to squeeze some less charged words past the evocative image. 'Flattering analogy.'

The *pfff* she shot out would have been perfectly at home on a surfacing seal. Her speech was still tinged with a tight breathlessness.

'You know you look good. That was the point of the whole submerge thing, wasn't it? To see how I'd react?'

Actually, getting cool had been the point. Once. But suddenly that original point seemed like a very long time ago. He dropped his voice with his glance. Straight to her lips. 'And how will you react, Eve?'

Her feminine little voice box lurched a few times in her exposed throat. 'I won't. Why would I give you the satisfaction?'

'Of what?'

'Of touching you—'

If she could have bitten her tongue off she would have just then, he was sure. 'Is that what you want to do? I'll step forward. All you have to do is ask.'

Step forward into those still-raised hands that were trembling ever so slightly now.

But she was a tough one. Or stubborn. Or both.

'And why would I do that?'

'Because you really want to. Because we're all alone on a deserted island with time to kill. And because we'll both be going our separate ways after Esperance.'

Though the idea seemed laughable now.

She swallowed, mutely.

He nudged the peak of her cap upwards with his knuckle to better read her expression and murmured, 'And because this might be the only chance we'll have to answer the question.'

Her eyes left his lips and fluttered up to his. 'What question?'

He stared at her. 'No. You have to ask it.'

She didn't, though he'd have bet any body part she wanted to.

'Tell you what, Eve, I'll make it easier for you. You don't have to ask me to do it, you just have to ask me *not* to do it.'

'Not do what?' she croaked.

He looked down at her trembling fingers. So very, very close. 'Not to step forward.'

Beneath the crystal-clear water, his left foot crept forward. Then his right matched it. The whole time he kept his glance down at the place that her palms almost pressed on his wet chest.

'Just one word, Eve. Just tell me to stop.'

But though her lips fell open, nothing but a soft breath came out of them.

'No?' His body sang with elation. 'All righty, then.'

And with the slightest muscle tweak at the backs of his legs, he tipped his torso the tiny distance it needed to make contact with Eve's waiting fingers.

# CHAPTER SIX

*DEAR LORD...*

How long had it been since she'd touched someone like this? More than just a casual brushing glance? All that hard flesh Eve had seen on the beach—*felt* on the bike—pressed back against her fingers as they splayed out across his chest. Across the shadowy eagle that she knew lived there beneath the saturated cotton shirt. Across Marshall's strongly beating heart.

Across the slight rumble of the half-caught groan in his chest.

One he'd not meant to make public, she was sure. Something that told her he wanted this as much as she secretly did.

Or, as her fingers trembled, not so secretly, now.

Marshall was right. They weren't going to see each other again. And this might be the only chance she had to know what it felt like to have the heat of him pressed against her. To know him. To taste him.

All she had to do was move one finger. Any finger.

She'd never meant to enter some kind of self-imposed physical exile when she'd set off on this odyssey. It had just happened. And, before she knew it, she'd gone without touching a single person in any way at all for...

She sucked in a tiny breath. All of it. Eight months.

Puppies and kittens got touch deprivation, but did grown women? Was that what was making her so ridiculously fluttery now? Her father's goodbye hug was the last time she'd had anyone's arms around her and his arms—no matter how strong they'd once been back when she was little—had never felt as sure and rooted in earth as Marshall's had as he'd lowered her from the bus's roof last night. And that had been fairly innocuous.

What kind of damage could they do if they had something other than *help* in mind?

How good—how *bad*—might they feel? Just once. Before he rode off into the sunset and she never got an answer.

Only one way to find out.

Eve inched her thumb down under the ridge of one well-defined pectoral muscle. Nervously jerky. Half expecting to feel the softness of the ink feathers that she could see shadowed through the saturated T-shirt. But there was no softness, only the silken sleeve of white cotton that contained all that hard, hot muscle.

God, he so didn't feel like a weatherman.

Marshall's blazing gaze roasted down on the top of her wet head, but he didn't move. Didn't interrupt. He certainly didn't step back.

Eve trailed her butterfly fingers lightly up along the line of the feathers, up to his collarbone. Beyond it to the rigid definition of his larynx, which lurched out of touch and then back in again like the scandalous tease it was.

Strong fingers lifted to frame her face—to lift it—and he brought her eyes to his. They simmered, as bottomless as the ocean around them as he lowered his mouth towards hers.

'Ahoy!'

Tortured lungs sucked in painfully further as both their gazes snapped out to sea, towards the voice that carried to them on the onshore breeze. Eve stumbled back from all the touching into the buffeting arms of the surf.

'Bugger all decent catch to be had,' the gruff captain shouted as he motored the *Vista II* more fully around the rocks, somehow oblivious to the charged moment he'd just interrupted. 'So we headed back early.'

Irritation mingled with regret in Marshall's storm-grey depths but he masked it quickly and well. It really wasn't the captain's fault that the two of them had chosen the end of a long, warm afternoon to finally decide to do something about the chemistry zinging between them.

'Hold that thought,' he murmured low and earnest as he turned to salute the approaching boat.

Not hard to do while her body screamed in frustration at the interruption, but give her fifteen minutes... Give her the slightest opportunity to think through what she was doing with half her senses and...

Marshall was right to look anxious.

But, despite what she expected, by the time the *Vista II*'s inflatable dinghy transferred them and their gear safely on deck, Eve's awareness hadn't diminished at all. And that was easily fifteen minutes. During the half-hour sea journey back to the campsite beach that followed—past seals sunning themselves and beneath ospreys bobbing on the high currents and over a swarm of small stingrays that passed underneath—still the finely tuned attention her body was paying to Marshall didn't ebb in the slightest.

She forced conversation with the two-man crew, she faked interest in their paltry fishy catch, she smiled and was delightful and totally over-compensated the whole way back.

She did whatever she needed to shake free of the relentless grey eyes that tracked her every move.

After an emotional aeon, her feet were back on mainland sand and the captain lightly tossed their last backpack out of the inflatable and farewelled her before exchanging a few business-related words with Marshall. Moments later, her hand was in the air in a farewell, her smile firmly plastered on and she readied herself for the inevitable.

Marshall turned and locked eyes with her.

'Don't know about you,' he said, 'but I'm famished. Something about boats...'

Really? He was thinking about his stomach while hers was twisted up in sensual knots?

'Have we got any of those sausages from breakfast still in the fridge?'

*Um...*

Not that he was waiting for her answer. Marshall lugged his backpack up over his shoulder and hoisted hers into his free hand and set off towards the track winding from the beach to the campsite. Eve blinked after him. Had she fantasised the entire moment in the cove? Or was he just exceptional at separating moments?

That was then, this was now. Island rules, mainland rules? What gave?

Warm beach sand collapsed under her tread as she followed him up the track, her glare giving his broody stare all the way back from Middle Island a decent run for its money.

They polished off the leftover sausages as soon as they got back to the bus. At least, Marshall ate most of them while she showered and then she nibbled restlessly on the last one while he did, trying very hard not to think about how much naked man was going on just feet from where she was sitting.

Soapy, wet, naked man.

Had the bus always been quite this warm?

'I think I would have been better off washing in the ocean,' he announced when he walked back in not long after, damp and clean and freshly clothed. Well, freshly clothed in the least used of three pairs of clothes he seemed to travel with. 'Lucky I didn't drop the soap because I wouldn't have been able to retrieve it.'

'I think the previous owners were hobbits,' Eve said, determined to match his lightness.

He slumped down next to her on the sofa. 'The hot water was fantastic while it lasted.'

Yeah. The water reservoir was pretty small. Even smaller as it ran through the onboard gas heater. 'Sorry about that. I guess Mr and Mrs Hobbit must have showered at different ends of the day.'

Not usually a problem for a woman travelling alone. The hot water was hers to use or abuse. And that had worked pretty well for her so far.

'So what's the plan for tonight?' Marshall said, glancing at her sideways.

Lord, if she wasn't fighting off visuals of him in the shower, she was hearing smut in every utterance. *Tonight.* It wasn't a very loaded word but somehow, in this tiny space with this über-present man, it took on piles of new meaning.

'Movie and bed—' She practically choked the word off.

But Marshall's full stomach and warm, fresh clothes had clearly put the damper on any lusty intentions. He didn't even blink. 'Sounds good. What have you got?'

Apparently an enormous case of the hormones, if her prickling flesh and fluttery tummy were any indication. But she nodded towards one of the drawers on the opposite side of the bus and left him to pick his way through the DVD choices. The mere act of him increasing the physical distance helped dilute the awareness that swirled around them.

He squatted and rifled through the box, revealing a stretch of brown, even skin at his lower back to taunt her. 'Got a preference?'

'No.'

Yeah. She'd have preferred never to have said yes to this excruciating co-habitation arrangement, to be honest. But done was done. She filled her one wineglass high for Marshall and then poured filtered water into her own mug where he couldn't tell what she was drinking. Maybe if he was sedated, that powerful, pulsing thrum coming off him would ease off a bit.

And maybe if she kept her wits about her she'd have the strength to resist it.

He held up a favourite. 'Speaking of hobbits…'

*Yes!* Something actiony and not at all romantic. He popped the disc at her enthusiastic nod, then settled back and jumped through the opening credits to get straight into the movie. Maybe he was as eager as she was to avoid conversation.

It took about ten minutes for her to remember that Middle Earth was definitely *not* without romance and then the whole movie became about the awkwardness of the longing-filled screen kiss that was swiftly approaching. Which only reminded her of how robbed she'd felt out in that cove to have the press of Marshall's lips snatched away by the approach of the *Vista II*.

Which was a ridiculous thing to be thinking when she should be watching the movie.

Hobbits quested. Wraiths hunted. Dramatic elven horse chase. Into the forests of Rivendell and then—

'Are we in the clunk zone, Eve?' Marshall suddenly queried. She flicked her eyes to her left and encountered his, all rust-flecked and serious and steady.

'What?'

Which was Eve-ish for *Yes…yes, we are.*

'Did I stuff things up this afternoon by kissing you?'

'You didn't kiss me,' she managed to squeeze out through her suddenly dry mouth.

But that gaze didn't waver. 'Not for want of trying.'

A waft of air managed to suck down into her lungs. 'Well, the moment has passed now so I think we're cool.'

'Passed?' he asked without smiling. 'Really?'

Yeah… She was a liar.

'That was hours ago,' she croaked.

'I wouldn't know,' he murmured. 'Time does weird things when you're around.'

Her brain wanted to laugh aloud, but the fluttering creatures inside her twittered girlishly with excitement. And they had the numbers.

'I think you're being adversely affected by the movie,' she said, to be safe.

'I'm definitely affected by something.'

'The wine?'

His smile was as gorgeous as it was slow. 'It is pretty good.'

'The company?'

'Yeah. 'Cos that's been terrific.'

She let her breath out in a long, apologetic hiss. 'I'm being weird.'

'You're weird so often it's starting to feel normal.'

'It's not awkward for you?'

His large hand slid up to brush a strand of hair from across her lips. 'What I'm feeling is not awkwardness.'

There went the whole dry mouth thing again. 'What are you feeling?'

'Anticipation.'

The fantastical world on-screen might as well have been an infomercial for all the attraction it suddenly held. Their already confined surroundings shrank even further.

'Maybe the moment's gone,' she said bravely.

He didn't move. He didn't have to. His body heat reached out and brushed her skin for him. 'Maybe you're in denial.'

'You think I'm that susceptible to low lighting and a romantic movie?'

Sure enough, there was a whole lot of elven-human longing going on on-screen. Longing and whispering against an intimate, beautiful soundtrack. Seriously, why hadn't she insisted on something with guns?

'I think the movie was an admirable attempt.'

'At what?' she whispered.

'At not doing this…'

Marshall twisted himself upright, his fingers finding a safe haven for his nearly empty wineglass. His other hand simultaneously relieved her of her mug and reached past her to place it on the sideboard. It legitimised the sudden, closer press of his body into hers.

'Now,' he breathed, 'what were you about to say?'

Heat and dizziness swilled around her and washed all sense out to sea. 'When?'

'Back in the cove. Was it no?' Grey promise rained down on her. 'Or was it yes?'

Truly? She had to find the courage to do this again? It had been hard enough the first time. Though, somehow, having already confessed her feelings made it easier now to admit the truth. She took the deepest of breaths, just in case it was also her last.

'It wasn't no.'

Those beautiful lips twisted in a confident, utterly masculine smile. 'Good.'

And then they found hers. Hot and hard and yet exquisitely soft. Pressing into her, bonding them together, challenging her to respond. She didn't at first because the sensation of being kissed after so very long with no touch at all threw her mind into a state of befuddlement. And she was drowning pleasantly in the sensation of hard male body pressed against hers. And sinking into the clean, delicious taste of him.

But she'd always been a sure adaptor and it only took moments for her feet to touch bottom and push off again for the bright, glittery surface. Her hands crept up around Marshall's shoulder and nape, fusing them closer. Her chin tilted to better fit the angle of his lips. The humid scorch of his breath teased and tormented and roused her, shamefully.

Revived her.

God, she'd missed hot breath mingling with hers. Someone else's saliva in her mouth, the chemical rush that came with that. Tangling tongues. Sliding teeth. And not just any tongue, breath and teeth but ones that belonged with all that hard flesh and ink and leather.

*Marshall's.*

'You taste of wine, Weatherman,' she breathed.

His eyes fixated on her tongue as she savoured the extra flavour on her lips. 'Maybe it's your own?'

'I had water.'

He lifted back slightly and squinted at her. 'Trying to get me drunk?'

'Trying to fight the inevitable.'

His chuckle rumbled against her chest. 'How's that working out for you?'

Gentle and easy and undemanding and just fine with something as casual as she needed. Wanted. All that she could offer.

And so she gave him access—tempting him with the touch of her tongue—and the very act was a kind of psychological capitulation. Her decision made. Even before she knew she was making it.

She trusted Marshall, even if she didn't know him all that well. He'd been careful and understanding and honest, and her body was *thrumming* its interest in having more access to his. With very little effort she could have his bare, hot skin against hers and her fingertips buried in the sexy curve of all that muscle.

He was gorgeous. He was intriguing. He was male and he was right here in front of her in living, breathing flesh and blood. And he was offering her what she suspected would be a really, really good time.

Did the rest really matter?

One large, hot hand slid up under her T-shirt and curled around her ribcage below her breast as they kissed, monitoring the heart rate that communicated in living braille onto his palm. Letting her get used to him being there. Doing to her exactly what she longed to do to him. Letting her stop him if she wanted. But no matter how many ways he twisted against her, the two of them couldn't get comfortable on the narrow little sofa. No wonder he'd struggled to sleep on it last night. And all the while she had an expansive bed littered with cloud-like pillows just metres away.

Eve levered herself off the sofa, not breaking contact with Marshall's lips or talented hands as he also rose, and she stretched as he straightened to his full height.

'Bed,' she murmured against his teeth.

His escalating kisses seemed to concur. One large foot bumped into hers and nudged it backwards, then another and the first one again. Like some kind of clunky slow dance, they worked their way back through the little kitchen, then through the en suite bathroom and toward unchartered territory. Her darkened bedroom. All the time, Marshall bonded them together either with his lips or his eyes or the hands speared into her hair and curled around her bottom.

There was something delightfully complicit about the way he used his body to steer her backwards into the bedroom while she practically tugged him after her. It said they were equals in this. That they were both accountable and that they both wanted it to happen.

Below her socked feet, the harder external floor of the en suite bathroom gave way to the plush carpet of the bedroom. Marshall's hands slid up to frame her face, holding it steady for the worship of his mouth. His tongue explored the welcome, warm place beyond her teeth just as much as she wanted him to explore this unchartered place beyond the doorway threshold.

A gentle fibrillation set up in the muscles of her legs, begging her to sink backwards onto her bed. The idea of him following her down onto it only weakened them further.

'Eve…' he murmured, but she ignored him, pulling back just slightly to keep the bedward momentum up. It took a moment for the cooler air of the gap she created to register.

Her eyes drifted open. They dropped to his feet, which had stopped, toes on the line between carpet and timber boards.

Hard on the line.

Confusion brought her gaze back up to his.

'I don't expect this,' he whispered, easing the words with a soft brush of his lips. And, when she just blinked at him, his eyes drifted briefly to the bed in case she was too passion-dazzled to comprehend him.

She pulled again.

But those feet didn't shift from the line and so all she achieved was more space between them. Such disappointing, chilly space. At least the hot grasp of his hand still linked them.

'Marshall…?'

'I just wanted to kiss you.'

*Ditto!* 'We can kiss in here. More comfortably.'

But the distance was official now and tugging any more reeked of desperation so she grudgingly let his hand drop.

'If I get on that bed with you we won't just be kissing,' he explained, visibly moderating his breathing.

'And that's a problem because…?'

'This isn't some roadhouse.'

Confusion swelled up around her numb brain. 'What?'

'You don't strike me as the sex-on-the-first-date type.'

Really? There was a type for these things? 'I don't believe in types. Only circumstances.'

'Are you saying you're just up for it because it's convenient?'

*Up for it.* Well, that sucked a little of the romance out of things. Then again, romance was not why she'd put her tongue in his mouth just minutes ago. What she wanted from Marshall was what he'd been unconsciously promising her from the moment they'd met.

No strings.

No rules.

No consequences.

'I'm tired of being alone, Marshall. I'm tired of not feeling anything but sadness. I need to feel something good.' A guarded wariness stole over his flushed face and she realised she needed to give him more than that. 'I have no illusions that it's going to go anywhere; in fact, I need it to be short. I don't want the distraction.'

He still didn't look convinced.

'I haven't so much as touched another human being in months, Marshall.'

'Any port in a storm, then?'

God knew it would be stormy between them. As wild and tempestuous as any sea squall. And just as brief.

'We've covered a lot of ground in our few days together and I trust you. I'm attracted to you. I need *you*, Marshall.'

All kinds of shapes seemed to flicker across the back of his intense gaze.

'But I'm not about to beg. Either you want me or you don't. I'll sleep comfortably tonight either way.' *Such lies!* 'Can you say the same?'

Of course he wanted her. It was written in the heave of his chest and the tightness of his muscles and the very careful way he wasn't making a single unplanned move. He wanted what she was offering, too, but there was something about it that he didn't want. Just…something.

And something was enough.

Eve went to push past him, back to the movie, making the disappointing decision for both of them.

But, as she did, his body blocked her path and his left foot crossed onto carpet. Then his right, backing her towards the bed. And then he closed the door on the sword fights of Middle Earth and plunged them into darkness, leaving only the smells and sounds and tastes of passion between them.

# CHAPTER SEVEN

EVERY MUSCLE IN Eve's body twinged when she tried to move. Not that she could move particularly far with the heavy heat of Marshall's arm weighing her down. But in case she somehow managed to forget how the two of them had passed the long night, her body was there to remind her. In graphic detail.

Languid smugness glugged through her whole system.

She gave up trying to softly wiggle out of captivity and just accepted her fate. After all, there were much worse ways to go. And to wake up. Right now, her brain was still offering spontaneous flashbacks to specific moments of greatness between them last night, and every memory came with a sensation echo.

Beside her, Marshall slept on in all his insensible glory. Buried face first in her pillows, relaxed, untroubled. It was very tempting just to lie here until lunchtime committing Sleeping Beauty to memory.

Although there was her bladder…

Ugh.

She took more decisive action and slid Marshall's arm off her chest, which roused him sufficiently to croak as she sprang to her feet. 'Morning.'

When was the last time she'd *sprung* anywhere? Usually she just hauled herself out of bed and gritted her teeth as she got on with the business of living.

'Morning yourself. Just give me a sec.'

Easing her bladder just a couple of metres and a very thin

en suite bathroom wall away from Marshall was an unexpectedly awkward moment. It seemed ridiculous after everything
they'd shared in the past twelve hours to have to concentrate
her way through a sudden case of bashful bladder. As soon as
she was done and washed, she scampered back into the toasty
warm and semi-occupied bed.

'You're better than an electric blanket,' she sighed, letting
the heat soak into her cold feet.

'Feel free to snuggle in.'

*Don't mind if I do.* She was going to milk this one-night
stand for every moment she could.

Marshall hauled her closer with the same strong arm that
had held her captive earlier, her back to his chest in a pretty
respectable spoon.

His voice rumbled down her spine. 'How are you feeling?'

Wow. Not an easy question to answer, and not one she'd expected him to ask. That was a very *not* one-night stand kind of
question. Thank goodness she wasn't facing him.

'I'm…' What was she? Elated? Reborn? She couldn't say
that aloud. 'I have no regrets. Last night was absolutely what
I expected and needed. And more. It was amazing, Marshall.'

It was only then that she realised how taut the body behind
her had become. Awkwardness saturated his words when they
eventually came.

'Actually, I meant because of today.'

She blinked. 'What's today?'

'One year?'

A bucket of icy Southern Ocean couldn't have been more
effective. The frigid wash chased all the warmth of Marshall's
hold away and left her aching and numb. And barely breathing.

*Travis.* Her poor, lost brother. Twelve months without a boy
she'd loved her whole life and she'd let herself be distracted by
a man she'd known mere moments by comparison.

She struggled for liberty and Marshall let her tumble out
of bed to her feet.

'I'm fine,' she said tightly. 'Just another day.'

He pushed onto his side, giving her a ringside seat for the giant raptor on his chest. She'd so badly wanted to see it last night but the room was too dark. And now she was too gutted to enjoy it.

'Okay…'

Mortification soaked in. What was wrong with her? How much worse to know that, for those first precious moments of consciousness, she hadn't even remembered she *had* a brother. She'd been all about Marshall.

What kind of a sister was she, anyway?

*You wanted to forget*, that little voice inside reminded her cruelly. *Just for one night. Wasn't that the point?*

Yes. But not like this. Not entirely.

She hadn't meant to *erase* Travis.

'It's a number,' she lied, rummaging in a drawer before dragging on panties and then leggings.

'A significant one,' Marshall corrected quietly.

She pulled a comfortable sweater on over the leggings. 'It's not like it took me by surprise. I've been anticipating it.'

Marshall sat up against the bed head and tucked the covers up around his waist ultra-carefully. 'I know.'

'So why are you making it into an issue?'

Ugh… Listen to herself…

Storm-grey eyes regarded her steadily. 'I just wanted to see how you were feeling this morning. Forget I mentioned it. You seem…great.'

The lie was as ridiculous as it was obvious.

'Okay.'

What was wrong with her? It wasn't Marshall's fault that she'd sought to use him for a bit of escapism. He'd fulfilled his purpose well.

Maybe too well.

'So, should we get going right after breakfast?' she asked brightly from the en suite bathroom as she brushed her hair. Hard to know whether all that heat in her cheeks was residual passion from last night, anger at herself for forgetting today or embarrassment at behaving like a neurotic teen.

Or all of the above.

A long pause from the bed followed and she slowed the drag of the bristles through her hair until it stilled in her hand.

'I've got to get back on the road,' she added, for something to fill the silence.

She should never have left it, really. She replaced the brush and then turned to stand in the bathroom doorway. Trying to be grown up about this. 'We both have jobs to do.'

What was going on behind that careful masculine expression? It was impossible to know. He even seemed to blink in slow motion. But his head eventually inclined—just.

'I'll convoy as far as the South Coast Highway,' he started. 'Then I'll head back to Kal. The road should be open by now.'

Right.

Was that disappointment washing through her midsection? Did she imagine that last night would have changed anything? She *wanted* them to go their separate ways. She'd practically shouted at him that this was a one-off thing. Yet bitterness still managed to fight its way through all her self-pity about Travis.

'Yeah. Okay.'

That was probably for the best. Definitely.

'Do you want me to take some posters for the Norseman to Kalgoorlie stretch? That'll save you doubling back down the track.'

It physically hurt that he could still be considerate when she was being a jerk. A twinge bit deep in her chest and she had to push words through it. Her shoulder met the doorframe.

'You're a nice man, Marshall Sullivan.'

His blankness didn't alter. And neither did he move. 'So I've been told.'

Then nothing. For ages. They just stared at each other warily.

Eventually he went to fling back the covers and Eve spun on the spot before having to face the visual temptation of everything she'd explored with her fingers and lips last night, and made the first excuse she could think of.

'I'll get some toast happening.'

*Nice.*

Just what every man wanted to hear from a woman he'd spent the night with. Not 'fantastic' or 'unforgettable'. Not 'awe-inspiring' or 'magnificent'.

*Nice.*

He'd heard that before, from the Sydney kids who had clambered over him in their quest to get closer to Rick and his chemical smorgasbord. From friends and girls and the occasional tragic teacher.

He'd always been the *nicer* brother.

But not the one everyone wanted access to.

Sticks and stones…

Problem was, Eve's lips might have been issuing polite compliments but the rest of her was screaming eviction orders and, though he'd only known her a couple of days, it was long enough for him to recognise the difference. He'd had enough one-off encounters with women to know *get out of my room* when he saw it. Despite all the brave talk last night, she was *not* comfortable with the aftermath of their exhausting night together.

And he was all too familiar with eyes that said something different from words. He'd had them all his life.

He'd been right in assuming Eve wasn't a woman who did this a lot; she was most definitely under-rehearsed in the fine art of the morning-after kiss-off. If he'd realised there'd be no lingering kisses this morning he would have taken greater care to kiss her again last night just before they fell into an exhausted slumber twisted up in each other.

Because Eve had just made it very clear that there would be no more kissing between them.

Ever.

He'd worked his butt off last night giving her the kind of

night she clearly needed from him. Making sure it was memorable. And, if he was honest, giving Eve something to think about. To regret. Maybe that was why it stung even more to see her giving it exactly zero thought this chilly morning.

*Wham-bam, thank you, Marshall.*

Somewhere, the universe chuckled to itself as the cosmic balance evened up. That was what he got for usually hotfooting it out the next morning the way Eve just had.

Only generally to fire up his motorcycle, not the toaster.

What did he expect? Days wrapped up in each other's arms here in this ridiculous little bus while his remaining weeks on the project ticked ever closer to an end and her bank balance slowly drained away? Neither of them had the luxury of indefinite leisure. He wasn't stupid.

Or maybe he was…because Evelyn Read was definitely not a one-off kind of woman and some deep part of him had definitely hoped for more than the single night they'd both agreed on between kisses. Which meant it was probably just as well that was all he was getting. Eve had no room for another man in her single-track life.

And he was done being a means to an end.

He pulled yesterday's T-shirt back on and rather enjoyed the rumples and creases. They were like little trophies. A reminder of how the shirt had been thoroughly trampled underfoot in their haste to get each other naked. A souvenir of the disturbingly good time he'd had with her beyond her bedroom door.

'Don't burn it,' he murmured, passing into the tiny kitchenette intentionally close to her, just to get one more feel of her soft skin. His body brushed the back of hers.

Her feet just about left the floor, she jumped that fast and high. Then a sweet heat coloured along her jawline and her lips parted and he had to curl his fingers to stop himself from taking her by the hand and dragging her back to that big, warm bed and reminding her what lips were made for.

It felt good to torture Eve, just a little bit. It sure felt good to surprise her into showing her hand like that. To shake the ambivalence loose. To watch the unsteadiness of her step. She might call a halt to this thing just getting going between them but he wasn't going to go easily.

He kept on moving past her, ignoring the sweet little catch in her breath, and he stopped at the back doors, flung them open and then stretched his hands high to hook them on the top of the bus, stretching out the kinks of the night, knowing how his back muscles would be flexing. Knowing how the ink there would flash from beneath his T-shirt. Knowing how that ink fascinated her.

If she was going to drive off into the horizon this morning, she sure wasn't going to do it with a steady brake foot.

Yup. He was a jerk.

He leapt down from the bus and turned to his KTM, and murmured to the bitter cold morning.

'*Nice*, my ass.'

The bus's brake lights lit up on the approach to the junction between the Coolgardie and South Coast Highways and Marshall realised he hadn't really thought this through. It was a big intersection but not built for pulling over and undertaking lingering farewells. It was built for turning off in any of the four points of the compass. His road went north, Eve's went further west.

But the uncertain blink of her brake lights meant she, too, was hesitating on the pedal.

She didn't know what to do either.

Marshall gave the KTM some juice and pulled up in the turn lane beside her instead, reassuring himself in the mirror that there was no one on the remote highway behind them. Eve dropped her window as he flipped his helmet visor.

'Good luck with the rest of your trip,' he called over the top of his thrumming engine and her rattling one.

'Thank you.' It was more mouthed than spoken.

God, this was a horrible way of doing this. 'I hope you get some news of your brother soon.'

Eve just nodded.

Then there was nothing much more to say. What could he say? So he just gave her a small salute and went to lower his visor. But, at the last moment, he found inspiration. 'Thank you for coming with me yesterday. I know you would have rather been back on the road.'

Which was code for *Thanks for last night, Eve*. If only he were the slightest bit emotionally mature.

She nodded again. 'I'm glad I did it.'

*Middle Island*, he told himself. Yesterday. That was all.

And then a car appeared on the highway in his mirror, way back in the distance, and he knew they were done.

He saluted again, slid his tinted visor with the obligatory squished bugs down between them and gave the bike some juice. It took only seconds to open up two hundred metres of highway between them and he kept Eve in his mirrors until the Bedford crossed the highway intersection and was gone from view, heading west.

Not the worst morning-after he'd ever participated in, but definitely not the best.

He was easily the flattest he could remember being.

He hadn't left his number. Or asked for hers. Neither of them had volunteered it and that was telling. And, without a contact, they'd never find each other again, even if they wanted to.

Eve Read would just have to be one of those memories he filed away deep inside. He added *The Crusader* to his list of badly handled flings.

Except she didn't feel like a fling. She felt like forever. Or what he imagined forever must feel like. Crazy. He'd known her all of five minutes. So the lingering sense that things weren't done between them was…

Ridiculous.

The shimmering haze of her exhaust as she couldn't speed away from him fast enough told a very different story.

Trees and wire fences and road signs whizzed by the KTM

in a one-hundred-and-ten-kilometre-per-hour blur. Plus a sheep or two.

Would he have stayed if she'd asked? If she'd crawled back into bed this morning and snuggled in instead of running an emotional mile? If he hadn't—like a freaking genius—brought up her most painful memory when she was half-asleep and vulnerable to his words?

Yeah. He would have stayed.

But it was the *why* that had him by the throat.

Eve was pretty but not beautiful, bright but not spectacular, prickly as a cactus and more than a little bit neurotic. She should have just been a charming puzzle. So what was with the whole curl-up-in-bed urge? He really wasn't the curl up type.

*She's your damsel, man.*

The words came burbling up from deep inside him, in his brother's voice. The kind of conversations they used to have way back when. Before they went down opposite off ramps of the values highway. Before Rick's thriving entrepreneurial phase. Certainly before Christine switched teams—and brothers. Back when Rick gave him stick for being a soft touch for girls in need of a knight on a white charger.

Orange charger, in his case.

Relief surfed his veins.

Yeah, this was about Eve's brother. That was all it was, this vague sense that leaving her was wrong. There was nothing more meaningful or complicated going on than that. He hated the helplessness he saw behind Eve's eyes and the flat nothing she carried around with her. It made him feel powerless—his least favourite emotion.

*She's not yours to fix*, Inner Rick nudged.

No, but was there really nothing more he could offer her than platitudes and some help with the posters and one night of sweaty distraction? He was a resourceful guy. He had connections.

And then it hit him…

Exactly why he'd chosen to place a woman he'd just met

and a man he hadn't seen in ten years next to each other at the dinner table of his subconscious.

His brain ticked over as fast as his tyres ate up the highway. If a person was going to go off grid, they might ditch their bank accounts in favour of cash, stop filing tax returns and opt out of claiming against Medicare. But what was Eve the most cut up about—? That Travis was struggling with his panic disorder, alone. And what did people who were being treated for disorders do? They took drugs. And who knew everything there was to know about drugs?

Rick did.

Enough to have driven his kid brother away years before. Enough to have made a thriving business out of supplying half of Sydney with their chemical needs. Enough to have a world of dodgy contacts inside the pharmaceutical industry—legal and otherwise.

Marshall eased off the throttle.

That meant he was just one uncomfortable phone call away from the kind of information that the cops would never think to access. Or be able to. Not ethical, probably not even legal, but since when did Rick let something as insignificant as the law stand between him and his goals?

Of course it would mean speaking to his brother, but maybe a decade was long enough with the silent treatment. Lord knew, Rick owed him.

Marshall down-geared and, as he did, his rapid pulse started to slow along with his bike. The pulse that had kicked up the moment parting from Eve was upon him. Back at the intersection. A kind of anxiety that he hadn't felt in a long, long time—since before he'd stopped letting himself care for people.

The descending thrum of his blood and the guttural throb of his bike colluded to soak him in a kind of certainty about this plan. As if it was somehow cosmically meant to be. As if maybe this was why he'd met Eve in the first place.

Because he could help her.

Because he could save her.

That was all this was. This…unsettling obsession. It was his Galahad tendency. Evelyn Read needed *help*, not *him*. And he was much more comfortable with the helping part.

He hit his indicator and looked for a safe place to pull over. He fished around in the depths of his wallet for a scrap of paper he'd almost forgotten he still carried. Ratty and brown edged, the writing half-faded. Rick's phone number. He punched the number into his phone but stopped short of pressing Dial.

This was Rick. The brother who'd made his teenage years a living hell. Who'd lured his girlfriend away from him just because he could. The brother who'd been the real reason that most of his friends craved his company and half the teachers gave him special treatment. They'd all wanted an in with *The Pharmacist*.

Rick was the reason he couldn't bring himself to trust a single soul, even now. Rick had taken the lessons they'd both learned from their mother about love and loyalty—or absences thereof—and turned the hurt into a thriving new industry where a lack of compassion for others was a corporate asset.

He'd made it work for him, while his little brother struggled in his shadow.

It had taken him years to fortify himself against those early lessons. His mother's. His brother's. And here he was, straddling his bike and contemplating leaping off the edge of his personal fortress of solitude to help someone he barely knew. He'd kicked the door of communication closed between every part of his old life and here he was, poised to take to that door with a crowbar and crack it open again.For a virtual stranger.

No…*for Eve*.

And Eve mattered.

He thumbed the dial button and listened as the number chirped its ominous melody. Took three deep breaths as it rang and rang. Took one more as a gruff voice picked up.

Marshall didn't waste time with niceties.

'You said to call if I ever needed you,' he reminded his brother. 'Did you mean it…?'

*  *  *

Rick had been at first surprised, then wary, when he recognised Marshall's serious tone after so very long. But—typical of the brother he remembered—Rick took the call at face value and accepted the subtext without comment. He listened to the request, grizzled about the dubiousness of what he'd been asked to do, but committed to help. And, despite anything else he'd done in his life, Rick Sullivan was the personification of tenacity. If he said he'd get this done, then, one way or another, some time Marshall's phone would be ringing again.

End of day, that was all that really mattered. Eve needed results more than he needed to maintain the moral high ground.

Rick even managed to go the entire phone call without getting personal.

The leathers of Marshall's jacket creaked as he exhaled. 'Thank you for your help, Rick. I swear it's not for anything too dodgy.'

'This whole thing is dodgy,' his brother muttered. 'But I'll do it because it's you. And because dodgy is where I do my best work. It might take a while, though.'

'No problem.'

Eve had been waiting twelve months. What was one more?

'I might find nothing.'

'Understood.'

'And one day maybe you can tell me what we're doing. And who for.'

He tensed up, mostly at the suggestion that there'd be a 'one day'. As if the door couldn't be closed once jemmied open.

'What makes you think there's a "who"?'

'Because you don't get invested in things, brother. Ever. You're Mr Arm's Length. But I can hear it in your voice. This matters.'

'Just let me know how you go,' he muttered. Eve was not someone he would trust his brother with, even mentally. He wasn't about to share any details.

'So…you want to know whether she's okay?' Rick asked, just before they ended the call.

'Christine?' Speaking of not trusting Rick… A few years ago, he would have felt the residual hurt deep in his gut. But now it just fluttered to earth like a burnt ember. Maybe the history really was history now.

'No, not Christine. I have no idea where she ended up.'

That bit. That Rick hadn't even kept his prize after working so very hard to take it from him.

'I meant Mum,' Rick clarified. 'Remember her?'

Everything locked up tight inside Marshall. He'd closed the door on Laura Sullivan the same day he'd locked Rick out of his life. The two of them were a package deal. The moment she'd realised her enterprising oldest son was going to be a far better provider than the Government, she'd made her allegiance—and her preference—totally clear.

That wasn't something you forgot in a hurry… Your own mother telling you to go.

'No. I'm good.'

There didn't seem much else to say after that.

It took just a moment to wind the call up and slip his phone back into his pocket. He'd get a new number just as soon as Rick gave him the info he needed. But he didn't hit the road again straight away. Instead, he sat there on the highway, bestride his KTM, breathing out the tension.

*You don't get invested in things.*

Well, that pretty much summed him up. Work. Life. He had a good ethic but he never let himself care. Because caring was a sure way of being disappointed. Or hurt. Life in his brother's shadow had taught him that. And as life lessons went, that one had served him well.

Until now.

As Rick had readily pointed out, he was invested now. With Eve—a woman he barely knew. He was more intrigued and conflicted and turned inside out for a woman he'd known just days than the people he'd grown up with. Maybe because she didn't want anything from him that she wasn't prepared to own. She had no agenda. And no ulterior motive.

Eve just…was.

And maybe he'd found a way to help her. Or maybe not. But he sure wasn't going to be able to do it from here.

He'd just sent her off down the highway with absolutely no way of locating her again. No email. No number. No forwarding address. How many Reads might there be in Melbourne? He couldn't shake the screaming thought that this was the only moment he had left. Right now, Eve was rattling down a long, straight road that only went to one place. After that, she could head off in any of five different routes into tourist country and his chances of finding her would evaporate. Tension coiled inside him like a spring…

And that was when he knew.

This wasn't just about helping Eve. If it was, he could just take whatever information his brother dug up straight to the authorities. Let them do the rest. This wasn't just about some cosmic interference to help her find her brother. That unfamiliar, breath-stealing tightness in his chest was panic. And he didn't do panic because that implied caring.

He'd no sooner let himself care for someone than void a ten-year stalemate with his criminal brother to get something that might ease Eve's pain. Eve—a complex, brittle, single-minded angel. The most intriguing woman he'd met in…more than years. The woman who'd barrelled through his defences and wedged herself there between his ribs. Just below his heart.

Oh, crap…

From where he sat, he could see the endless stretch of highway ahead—north to Kalgoorlie, where he could pick up his work trail where he'd left it a few days ago. But, in his mirror, he could see the long straight run behind him, back to the four-way turn-off. Back to a one hundred per cent chance of catching up with the bus before it turned off the western highway.

Back to the possibility he'd been too cowardly to explore.

Back to Eve.

He started his engine, dropped his visor and let his eyes lift to the northern horizon. Towards work and the conclusion of this trip and his safe, comfortable life.

But then they dropped again to the mirror, and the road he'd just travelled.

Sure, she might tell him to get lost. And if she did, he would.

But what if she didn't…?

In the end, his hands made the decision before his head did, and a leathered thumb hit his indicator before pulling the KTM's handlebars right, out across the empty highway and then back onto the opposite shoulder.

Before he could second-guess himself, he gunned the accelerator and roared off towards the south.

Towards the unknown.

# CHAPTER EIGHT

IT COULD BE ANYONE—that speck in the distance behind her.

Car. Bike. Truck. It was too small for one of the massive road trains that liked to thunder past at breakneck speed, but a smaller truck, maybe.

Eve forced her eyes forward and ignored the impulse to check again. Plenty of people drove this road into Western Australia's tourist region. People who had far more legitimate reasons to be heading this way than *he* did.

Marshall was heading north. Back to his weather stations. Back to reality.

Which was exactly what she should be doing. Middle Island had been a nice couple of days of escapism—for both of them—but they both had jobs to be doing.

And Travis was her job.

He always had been.

If the past couple of days had taught her anything, it was that she couldn't take her eyes off the prize—or the map—for a moment. Look how fast she'd been swayed from her purpose. Besides, Marshall couldn't get out of there fast enough this morning. Not once he saw her in full neurotic mode. He was probably congratulating himself right now on a bullet well dodged.

The speck in her rear-vision mirror grew larger. But not large enough to be a truck. A car, then.

Or smaller, her subconscious more than whispered.

No.

Why would Marshall return? He hadn't left anything behind in her bus—she'd checked twice. And their parting had been as unequivocal as it was awkward. And definitely for the best. She was on a mission and didn't need the distraction. No matter how compelling.

And boy, was he ever. He'd been an intriguing curiosity while tattooed and hairy. Clean shorn and well educated, he was entrancing. Naked, he was positively hypnotic. All the better for being a long, long way from her.

She glanced helplessly back at the mirror and her pulse made itself known against the fragile skin of her throat.

Not a car.

Her gaze split its time between looking ahead and looking back, then the forward-looking part became a glance and then a mere flick to keep the bus on a straight and safe line.

Plenty of motorbikes in the sea. Impossible to even know what colour this one was yet.

Her gaze remained locked on her mirror.

If it was orange—if it was *him*—that didn't have to mean anything. Their one night together had probably been so good because it was a one-off. No past, no future. Just the very heated and very comfortable present. Even if Marshall was coming back for a second go at last night, there was nothing that said she had to oblige—no matter what her pulse recommended.

No matter how enticing the promise of a few more hours of mental *weightlessness* he brought.

A dull mass settled between her shoulder blades. She couldn't afford to be weightless. Not until her journey was complete and Travis was home.

Her own thought tripped her up. She'd never thought about this journey being over. What she would do. Would work have her back? She'd resigned with notice, so there were no burnt bridges there, but could she go back to meetings and minutes and deadlines? Would she have the patience? What would she be like after it was all over? Could she be *normal* now that she knew how secretly cruel the world really was?

As for weightless… Would she ever feel that way again?

Or was that just another disloyalty to Travis? To be worrying about any of it?

She'd put herself first once before and look how that had ended. Travis had melted down completely the moment she took her eyes off him.

She glanced up again, just in time to see a flash of black and orange changing into the inside lane and then roaring up beside her.

All the breath squeezed up tight in her suddenly constricted chest.

*He was back.*

Marshall whizzed by on her right, then changed lanes into the vanguard position and weaved in the lane in a kind of high-speed wave. She took several long, steadying breaths to bring the mad thump of her heart back into regular rhythm.

Should she stop? Hear what he had to say?

No. If he wanted her to pull over he'd be braking, slowing her. But he was pacing her, not slowing her. Guiding her onward. Besides, not far now until the turn-off to the Ravensthorpe poster drop. If he had something to say he could say it there.

And she'd listen politely and when it came to the time to part again she'd try and be a bit more erudite than her poor effort this morning.

Two vehicles whizzed by in the opposite direction, marking their entry into tourist country. *Tourism.* That was what she and Marshall were doing, right? Exploring the uncharted country that was each other. Enjoying the novelty. But how many tourists sold up and moved to the places they visited? How many stayed forever? No matter how idyllic.

Right. Because the real world eventually intruded.

And her reality was Travis.

Marshall wiggled his motorbike again and seemed to be

waiting for something. Did he seriously worry that she hadn't recognised him? She gave her headlights a quick flash of acknowledgement and his weaving ceased.

He placed himself squarely in the centre of their lane and let his bike eat up the highway.

And Eve did her best not to fixate on the strong breadth of his back and breathless imaginings about what it would be like to peel all that leather right off him.

The Bedford's front doors were as reluctant to open as Eve was to pass through them. But Marshall had made fast work of slinging the KTM onto its stand and pulling off his helmet. As he sauntered towards her on his thick-soled riding boots, he forked fingers through his thick helmet hair to ruffle it up.

Her first thought—on the clench of her stomach—was that finger-forking his hair was her job.

Her second thought—on the clench of her heart at the sound and smell of his creaking leathers as he stopped in front of her—was that she was completely screwed.

'Forget something?' she managed to squeeze out from the top of the Bedford's steps. More for something to say, really, because if he'd actually come back for his favourite socks she was going to be really crushed. She kept her body language as relaxed as was possible in a body ready to flee.

'Yeah,' he murmured, stepping up onto the bottom step, 'this.'

One gloved hand came up and lifted her chin as if he was holding a crystal flute and his lips brushed against hers. Then the brush got harder, closer. So…*so* much better. He turned his head and deepened the kiss, stroking his tongue into her mouth and against her own. Just when she'd thought no one would ever kiss her like that again.

She wavered there on the top step, the closest thing to a swoon she'd ever experienced.

'I didn't say goodbye properly,' he finally breathed against her astonished mouth. 'Now I don't want to say it at all.'

'You left,' she said between the head spins.

'But I'm back.'

'What about work?'

'What about it? There are plenty of weather stations still on my list. I'll just flex my route.'

*What about* my *work?* was what she really needed to be asking. Because how much of it was she going to get done with him around? If the past couple of days was any indication.

'You just assume I want to carry on where we left off?'

Just because she *did*… He wasn't to know that.

'I'm not assuming anything. If you send me away I've wasted…what…an hour of my time and a couple of bucks in fuel. Those are reasonable stakes.'

She pulled free. 'Charming.'

His grin managed to warm her right through, even as her heart screamed at her not to fall for it.

'Do you want me to go?'

She stared at him. Remembered how it felt to be with him. To be *with* him. And the thought of watching him drive off again was almost unbearable.

'I should,' she breathed.

'That's not a no.'

'No.' She stared at him. 'It's not.'

His puppy-dog grin graduated into a full, brilliant, blazing smile. 'Come on, then. Let's get some posters up. Time's a-wasting.'

He stepped down off the bus and held a hand out to help her. His eyes were screened by sunglasses but she could clearly see the trepidation still in the stiffness of his body. What she did next mattered to him. And that made her feel a whole lot better. She glanced at his outstretched hand. The unexpected chivalry excited and troubled her at the same time. She'd been jumping down off the Bedford's steps all by herself for eight months.

But just because she *could* didn't mean it wasn't a rare treat not to have to.

How would it feel to share this burden, just for a bit?

Would Travis understand?

After an age, she slid her bare fingers into his leathery ones and accepted his help.

But they both knew that taking his hand was saying yes to a whole lot more.

Marshall followed Eve as she chugged the Bedford into the biggest town in the Great Southern region behind the two-dozen cars that constituted peak hour in these parts. When she pulled up in a big open car park, Marshall stood the KTM and then jogged off to find something for them to eat. When he got back with it, she was set up and ready to go. Table and chair in place, bus sides up and covered in posters.

'I need to find the MP's office,' she announced. 'I'm getting low on posters.'

'Didn't you do that before?'

'Nope. Somebody distracted me.'

Yeah. He was probably supposed to feel bad about that. 'Too bad.' He winced.

'You don't look very sympathetic,' she admonished.

He just couldn't stop smiling. What was that about? 'MP's office was a few doors down from where I got lunch. I'll show you.'

Then it was her turn to smile. 'Thank you.'

She weighted down anything on her display that might blow away, grabbed a flash drive from her wallet and hurried alongside him. The door to the MP's office set off an audible alert as they entered.

'Hi there,' a friendly young woman said from behind the reception desk, addressing him. He looked straight at Eve, who slid the flash drive over the counter. 'Welcome to Albany.'

'Can you run off a hundred of these, please?'

The woman frowned and didn't touch the flash drive. 'What is it?'

'A missing-person poster,' Eve elucidated, but it didn't bring any hint of recognition. 'MP's offices are supposed to run off copies for free.'

A little explanation wasn't exactly an Open Sesame.

'Let me just check,' the woman said, stalling.

Eve looked as if she wanted to say more but his hand on her wrist forestalled it. A few moments later the woman came back, smiling, and chirped, 'Won't be long!'

Eve turned to the window and the port view beyond it and curled her arms around her torso.

Every day must have moments like these for her. When simple things like a bit of public bureaucracy suddenly reared up in front of her like a hurdle in her efforts to find her brother. No wonder she was so tired.

That kind of emotional ambush would be exhausting.

'Good morning,' a male voice said and Eve turned from her view.

An overly large, overly suited man with a politician's smile approached, hand outstretched. 'Gerald Harvey, MP.'

'Evelyn Read,' she murmured, sliding her fingers into his.

He followed suit. 'Marshall Sullivan.'

'You have a missing person?' the man asked and barrelled onwards before she could answer. 'I'm very sorry for your loss.'

'My loss?'

The statement seemed to stop Eve cold, and only the new colour in her face gave Gerald Harvey a hint that he might have put his finely shod foot in it. 'Your…uh…circumstances.'

Marshall stepped in closer behind her and placed his hand on Eve's lower back, stroking gently.

'Thank you,' she said to the man, more evenly than he would have expected based on her expression.

Harvey took the first poster that his assistant printed and read it aloud, rolling the name over his tongue like wine. 'Travis James Read.'

Just in case Eve didn't know who she'd been looking for the past year.

'Can't say I've seen him but someone might have. Are you circulating these in town?'

'All over the country.'

The man laughed. 'Not all over it, surely.'

Eve didn't waver. 'All over it. Every town. Every tourist stop.'

He stared as the poster in his hand fell limply over his substantial fist, and Marshall watched the interplay of disbelief and pity play over his ruddy face. Then it coalesced into kind condescension.

'That's a lot of posters.'

Brilliant. Of all the things he could have noted about Eve's extraordinary endeavour...

'Yes.'

'And fuel.'

Okay, enough was enough.

'Eve,' he interjected, 'how about we go back to the bus and I'll come back for the posters in fifteen minutes? You should get started. Don't want to miss anyone.'

Ironic, given her life was all about missing someone.

He thanked the MP and then bustled her out into the street, instantly feeling the absence of the tax payer–funded office heating. She didn't speak. Didn't confront him or rant. She'd turned inwards somewhere in that brief encounter and wasn't coming out any time soon.

He could endure the silence no longer than five minutes.

'Did I ever look at you like that?' he eventually asked as they walked back towards the main street. The mixture of pity and polite concern. As if she might not be all that mentally well herself.

His direct question dragged her focus back to him. Brown eyes reached into his soul like a fist and twisted. 'A little bit.'

Great. No wonder she'd taken a while to warm up to him. Maybe she still was.

'It's not crazy,' he insisted suddenly, stopping and turning her towards him. 'It's not common, sure, but what you're doing is…logical. Under the circumstances. I get it.'

'You do?'

He waved his hand towards her poster display of all *The Missing* as they approached. 'I imagine every one of their families would like to have the courage and commitment to do what you've done. To get out here and look, personally. To do something proactive. To know you've done as much as you possibly can.'

She tossed her head back in the direction of the MP's office. 'That reaction is pretty common.'

'People don't know what to say, I guess.'

She stared up at him. 'You didn't have that problem.'

Something bloomed deep inside on learning that she had forgiven him for whatever first impression he'd left her with. Enough to shrug and joke, 'I'm exceptional.'

The sadness cracked and her mouth tipped up. 'So you say.'

'Go,' he nudged. 'Get started. I'll go back and manage Mr Charm, and then I'll go find us a camping site after I've dropped your new posters to you.'

She seemed to do a full-body sigh. 'Thank you.'

'No problem. Back in a few.'

He turned back for the MP's office but only got a few steps before turning again. He was back beside her in moments.

'Wha—?'

It took no effort at all to pull her into his arms and tuck her safe and warm beneath his chin. To wrap his arms firmly around her so that nothing and no one could get between them.

How had it not occurred to him before now to hug Eve?

This was a woman who needed repeat and regular hugging. On prescription. And he was happy to be her spoonful of sugar. Her slim arms crept around his waist and hooked behind his back, and the rest of her pressed into his chest as she sagged into him. Stroking her hair seemed obvious.

Around them, the sounds of a busy coastal town clattered on. But inside their bubble there was only the two of them.

'That guy was a dick,' he announced against her ear.

'I know,' she muffled into his chest.

'I'm sorry that happened.'

She wriggled in closer. 'You get used to it.'

'You shouldn't have to.'

'Thank you.'

He curled her in closer, resting his chin on her head.

'Um…Marshall?' she eventually mumbled.

'Yeah?'

'Aren't you going to get us a site?'

'Yep. Leaving now.'

Around them traffic did its thing and somewhere a set of traffic lights rattled off their audible alert.

'Marshall?'

His fingers stroked her hair absently. 'Hmm?'

'We're making a scene.'

He opened one eye and, sure enough, a couple of locals walked by, glancing at them with amused smiles on their faces.

He closed the eye again and tucked her in even closer.

'Screw 'em.'

'Gotta say, you have a strange idea of what constitutes a "camping site".'

'I'm funded to stay in motels.' Marshall shrugged. 'You might as well benefit.'

'Are all your *motels* quite this flash?' She leaned on the word purposefully because the waterside complex was more of a resort than anything.

'Well, no. But you put me up the last two nights so I have some budget savings. And there's hardly anyone else here out of season so you can take as much car park room as you need for the bus.'

Because she'd be sleeping in the car park while he spread out in the suite's big bed all alone?

She glanced at him. Maybe she'd misunderstood what his return meant. But she wasn't brave enough to ask aloud. Or maybe that was actually a really good idea. A tempestuous one-night stand was one thing but a second night—that needed some managing.

'Come on. At least check it out since you're here.'

She followed him up to the second storey, where the suite's balcony looked out over a parkland walkway below to the turquoise, pine tree–lined swimming bay that curled left and right of them. The rest of the suite was pretty much made of either sofa or bed. Both enormous. A large flat-screen TV adorned the walls between local art and something tantalising and white peeked out at her, reflected, through the bathroom door.

Her breath sucked in. Was that a…?

'Spa?'

'Yeah, I think so,' he said a little sheepishly. Had it suddenly dawned on him that this was all starting to look a little *boom-chick-a-wah-wah*? 'It came with the room.'

How long had it been since she'd soaked her weary body? And having a spa, or lounging on the sofa, or sitting on the balcony with a glass of wine didn't have to mean she was staying the night here. Her own bed was pretty comfy, thanks very much.

She glanced at the crack in the bathroom door again and wondered how she could ask him for access without it sounding like a come-on. Or an invitation.

As usual, Marshall came to her rescue with the lift of one eloquent eyebrow and the careful and chivalrous choice of words.

'You want first crack?'

It took her about a nanosecond to answer in the positive and about two minutes to sprint back to the bus and get some clean clothes. It was only as she took the stairs back up two by two that she realised what the bundle of comfortable leggings and track top in her arms meant.

They weren't going back out again tonight.

So, that meant room service for dinner. Nice and cosy, just the two of them.

Wow. Her subconscious was really going to make this tough

for her. But the siren song of the bubbles was so strong she didn't care.

*Bubbles.* Heaven.

'It's a fast filler,' Marshall announced as she burst back into the room, more eager than she'd felt in a long time.

Oh, right…filling. Nature's brakes. Eve stood, a bit at a loss, shifting from foot to foot in the room's entryway.

'It has a shower, too,' he volunteered, bright light glinting in the grey of his eyes. 'You could get straight in and then just shower until the water level is high enough.'

She loved her bus, but its shower pressure was as weak as it was brief. The chance for a proper shower was overwhelming. 'Oh, my gosh, really?'

'Your face is priceless.' He grinned. 'You like a spa, I take it.'

'I used to have a jet bath,' Eve admitted to him. And then to herself, 'I miss it.'

Not that she'd given her big four-person bath much thought when she put her house on the market. Because brothers before bubbles, right? But—oh—how she missed the great soak at the end of a long, hard week. And out here where every week was long and hard…

'Go on,' he nudged. 'Get in there.'

Her thanks were practically a squeak as she slipped into the bathroom and closed the door behind her. She waited a moment too long to flip the lock—worrying how Marshall might read the click after such a long, silent pause—but decided to leave it. If he had something nefarious in mind, he'd had plenty of more isolated opportunities to perpetrate his crime. Not to mention the fact they'd already slept together.

Besides, sneaking into a woman's bathroom was beneath a man like Marshall.

*He's a good man.*

It took no time at all to get naked and under the thundering commercial shower as the water slowly rose up over her calves. Hot, hot water pounded down on her shoulders and back, then over her hair as she plunged fully under it.

Warm and reassuring and…home. The water brought with it a full-body rush of tingles.

Unexpected tears rushed to her support.

She'd been doing this so long. Being on the road. Was it okay to admit she was tired? That didn't have to mean she loved Travis any less, did it? The water thundered on and she lifted her face to let the fresh water wash away her guilty tears. Eventually, though, the spa reached a generous level of full-ness and she killed the overhead stream and slid down into the piping-hot pool. Her groan was inevitable and the long sigh that followed the perfect punctuation.

When was the last time she'd felt so…buoyant? When was the last time she'd just closed her eyes and floated? The wa-ter's heat did its job and immediately soaked into muscles she'd forgotten didn't always feel this way, including a few that had only been aching since the marathon of last night.

Was it only twenty-four hours ago that she and Marshall had twisted up in each other's arms? And legs. And tongues. Like some kind of fantasy. Had it even really happened? If it had really happened, wouldn't he be in here with her? Not respectfully waiting on the other side of a closed—but not locked—door.

She lifted one hand to better position it and the cascading tinkle echoed in the silent bathroom.

'Marshall…'

'Yeah?'

Water splashed slightly as she started in the bath at the speed and closeness with which he answered. The door was right next to her head but he sounded close enough to be in here with her. Her eyes went to the mirror reflection of the door instinctively, but she knew before they got there what they'd find.

Marshall wasn't really the Peeping Tom type. If he wanted to look, he'd just knock and enter and stare at her until she was as much a hot puddle as the spa water around her.

*Because he's a good man, and he knows what he wants.*

So what was he doing? Just lurking there? Or did the suite have some kind of weird acoustic thing going on?

She cleared her throat gently. 'Are you busy?'

'Nope. Just unwinding.' Pause. 'Why?'

'I just thought…maybe we could talk.'

'Didn't you want to relax?'

'It's a bit…quiet.'

'I thought you'd be used to that after eight months on the road.'

Yeah. He had a point. Astonishing what two days of company did for a girl.

'Normally I'd have music in my bathroom.' Classical. Mellow.

That deep voice was rich with humour. 'You want me to sing something?'

The very idea added to her hot-water tingles. 'Talking will be fine.'

'Okay.' Another pause. 'What do you want to talk about?'

'I don't know. Where you grew up? Your family? Anything, really.'

The door gave a muffled rattle and Eve wondered if he'd leaned on it. She took the complimentary sponge from its packet and filled it with warm water, then squeezed it down her arms.

*Rinse. Repeat.*

The slow splashes filled the long silence and the steam started working on her pores. And her soul.

'I'm not sure my history will be particularly conducive to relaxation.'

The tightness in his voice paused her sponge mid-swab. 'Really, why?'

'My family's about as functional as yours.'

Dead, drunken mother and AWOL brother was going to be tough to top. But her curiosity was piqued. 'Where are they now?'

'They're still in Sydney.'

'That doesn't sound so very dramatic.'

'Growing up had...its challenges.'

Her sponging resumed. Eve closed her eyes and let herself tune in to the low rumble of his voice. 'Like what?'

Was that a resigned sigh through the door?

'My family weren't all that well off, but we didn't starve. We were okay.'

*Uh-huh...?*

'But it was the nineties. The decade of excess and success, and all that.'

Eve lay her head against the back of the bath and just listened.

'I have a brother, too, Eve,' Marshall went on. 'And poverty wasn't really his thing. So he took matters into his own hands and got quite...creative. Before long, the whole neighbourhood knew he was the go-to for whatever soft-core drug they needed.'

She opened her eyes and stared at the bathroom ceiling. After a moment she murmured, 'Your brother was a dealer?'

'An entrepreneur, according to him.'

*Right.* 'How long did that last?'

'Until very recently I couldn't have answered that at all. But let's just say business is as good as ever for Rick. I don't really see him any more.'

No wonder Marshall could empathise about Travis. He knew exactly what it was like to lose a brother.

'Whose decision was that?'

The only sound in the long, long silence that followed was the dripping of the shower into the spa.

'It's complicated,' he finally said.

Yeah, wasn't it always?

'I struggled growing up with Rick for a brother.'

'Because he was a criminal?'

'Because he was a hero.' He snorted. 'This was the back suburbs, remember. Pretty rough area to grow up. People loved him, they loved what he sold and they scrambled to be part of his inner circle. And sometimes that meant scrambling over me.'

There was something so…suppressed in his voice.

Eve lifted her head. 'Are you talking about girls?'

'Girls. Friends. Even a teacher or two with insalubrious habits.'

Oh, poor teenage Marshall. 'You resented him.'

'No, I loved him.'

'But you hated that,' she guessed.

'It meant I was no different to them. The sycophants. I just wanted to despise him and be done with it.'

So, there were many ways to lose a brother, then.

'Do you miss him?' she whispered.

'I did. For a long while. It felt like he was all I had, growing up. But I just focused my attention on my work and suddenly a decade had passed and I hadn't really thought about him at all. Or my mother. Or Christine. Or what they were all doing together.'

She pushed herself up a little more. 'Christine is with your brother?'

'She was.'

The door rattled slightly again, but not the knob. Down lower. And that was when Eve realised how very close they were sitting to each other. Him sunk down onto the floor of the suite, leaning on the door. Her lying back in warm luxury.

And only a single thin wall between them.

No wonder Marshall was wary of people. And no wonder the tight pain in his voice. 'I'm sorry. I should have asked you about something else.'

'It's okay. I got myself out. It's history now.'

'How do you go from a bad neighbourhood to working for the Federal Government?'

He laughed and she realised how attached she'd become to that sexy little chuckle.

'It will shock you to learn that meteorology is not the sexiest of the sciences.'

Not sexy? Had any of them *seen* Marshall Sullivan?

'But that meant there were scholarships going wasting, and one of them came to me. And it came with on-campus residency.'

'The scholarship was your ticket out?'

'At first, but soon I came to love meteorology. It's predictive. Stats and signs and forecasting. You always know what's coming with weather.'

'No surprises?' she murmured.

'I guess I was just looking for a life where you could spot the truth of something before it found you.'

Yeah. Given he'd been used by his earlier friends, cast off by his mother and then betrayed by his brother, maybe that wasn't surprising.

'It suits you.'

'Being a weatherman?'

'Busting the stereotype.' And how. 'I'm sorry I called you Weatherman.'

'I don't mind it as a nickname. As long as it's coming from you.'

'Why?' She laughed. 'What makes me so special?'

His answer, when it came, was immediate. 'How long have you got?'

The same kind of warmth that was soaking into her from without started to spread out from within. But she wrestled it back down. She couldn't afford to be feeling warm and fuzzy about anyone right now.

She made much of sitting up straighter in the spa bath. The bathroom equivalent of shuffling papers. 'Speaking of specials…what's on the menu tonight?'

*Subtle, Read, real subtle.*

But he let it go after a breath-stealing moment of indecision. 'Give me a second, I'll check.'

*Good man, knows what he wants and compassionate.*

Marshall Sullivan was just getting harder and harder to not like.

# CHAPTER NINE

THIS WASN'T GOING to end well for him...

It had dawned on Marshall, somewhere between sitting at the bathroom door with his head tipped back against the timber and watching Eve tuck so enthusiastically into a bowl of Italian soup, that not everyone was rewarded for goodness. Any more than they were rewarded for doing the right thing.

Hadn't he got that by now?

But done was done. He'd made his choice and he was here. Only time would tell whether it was a crazily fatalistic or brilliantly optimistic decision. But since he was here and since she hadn't driven him off the road, he could use the time practically. He could try and get to know Eve a bit more. Understand her.

Maybe that way he could get a sense of her truth before it hit him like a cyclone.

'Can I ask you what happened with Travis?' he asked, passing his empty plate into the long fingers she reached out and starting at the most obvious point. 'When he disappeared.'

Her bright, just-fed eyes dulled just a little.

'One day he was there—' she shrugged '—the next he was gone.'

'That simple?'

'It wasn't simple.'

'Losing someone never is.'

He fell to silence and waited her out. It had certainly worked well enough on him while she was in the bath. He'd offered up much more than he'd ever shared with anyone else.

'She was drunk,' Eve finally murmured and he didn't need to ask who. 'She'd passed the few hours of Travis's Under-Fifteens hockey at the nearest pub. As far as anyone could tell, she thought she was okay to drive.'

Oh. Crap. Drunk and in charge of the safety of a fourteen-year-old boy.

'Was she an alcoholic?' That certainly explained Eve's moderate approach to liquor.

Her dark head slowly nodded. 'And the whole neighbourhood got to hear about it.'

He let his hands fall between his splayed thighs. Stared at them. 'That's a lot for a girl to handle.'

'It was a lot for all of us to handle,' she defended. 'Travis watched Mum die, Dad endured her reputation being trashed and I...'

'What did you do?'

'I coped. I got on with things. Took over caring for them both.'

'A lot of pressure.'

'Actually, it was okay then.' *Then*... 'It gave me something to focus on. Purpose.

'Dad pulled Trav out of school for the last few months of the year and that might have been a mistake. It took him from his friends, his sport, his structure. He lost his way a bit. He got back into it the next year and got okay grades but he was never cheeky and joyous again. I think we all just got used to the new, flat Travis.' She took a big swallow of water. 'Maybe we got used to a new *us*, too.'

Yeah. Numbness crept up on a person...

'It wasn't easy, those first couple of years. At first it was all about getting him out of the hospital, but then life had to... We had to just get on with it, you know?'

Yep. He certainly did know all about just getting on... Story of his life. But not everyone could do it. There were times *he* really wanted to just opt out. In some ways maybe he had.

'What changed? To make him leave?'

Her beautiful face pinched up slightly. 'Um…'

Whatever it was, it was hurting her.

'There was an inquest the year he went, and there was all this media interest in the accident again.'

'Years later?'

'A legal queue, I guess.' Her slight shoulders shrugged and he'd never wanted to hold someone more in his life. But she looked so fragile he worried she'd shatter. 'So much pressure on all of us again.'

He shifted closer. Leaned into her. 'He couldn't take it?'

Her head came up but she didn't quite meet his eyes. 'I couldn't. I desperately wanted to understand what happened but I couldn't go through it all again. Supporting Dad, mothering Travis. Just as things were getting normal. I just couldn't do it while we relived the accident over and over again.'

Suddenly her blazing need to find her brother began to make more sense.

'What did you do?'

'I went back to my own place. Replaced the dead pot plants with new ones, cleaned the gutters, threw out years of junk mail, started easing back into my own life.'

'And what did Travis do?'

'I didn't abandon them,' she defended hotly. 'I still visited, did sisterly things. But they were both men. They needed to step up, too. They agreed.'

He said nothing, knowing the question was almost certainly in his eyes. *But…?*

'Trav was finding it harder than any of us realised. The inquest brought it all back just as he might have started to become stronger. He turned eighteen, and drifted further and further from us emotionally.' She shook her head. 'And then he just left. Right in the middle of the inquest. We thought he'd just taken off for a few days to avoid the pressure but then it was

a week, and then two. We finally reported him missing when
we hadn't heard anything for a month.'

'You blame yourself.'

Her slim shoulders lifted and then sagged again. 'I wasn't
there for him.'

'Yeah, you were. For years.'

'But I withdrew.'

'You *survived*. Big difference.'

Her tortured eyes lifted. 'Why wouldn't he talk to me? If
he was struggling.'

Yeah—she'd been carrying that around a while; he recognised the signs of soul baggage.

'Eighteen-year-old boys don't talk to anyone about their
feelings, Eve. I've been that kid.'

Old agony changed her face. He pulled her into his arms.
'You aren't responsible for Travis being missing.'

'That's what people say, isn't it,' she said against his chest.
'In this kind of situation. But what if I am?'

Okay, so she'd heard this before and still not believed it. A
rough kind of urgency came over him.

'What if it had nothing to do with you and everything to
do with a young boy who watched his mother die? On top of
the day-to-day trauma of having an alcoholic for a mother.
My own mother was no prize,' he admitted, 'but she was at
least present.'

He'd almost forgotten that she was Eve's mother, too. She
seemed so disconnected from her past. 'What if you had turned
up on his doorstep every single day and he had still done this?'

Tortured eyes glistened over. 'He's my brother.'

'He's a grown man, Eve.'

'Only just. Eighteen is still a kid. And with the anxiety disorder, and depression…'

'Which he was being treated for, right? He was on it.'

'Then why did he leave?'

It was always going to come back to that question, wasn't

it? And Eve was never going to be free of the big, looming question mark. 'Only Travis knows.'

She fell to an anguished kind of silence, picking at the fabric on the sofa beneath her. Marshall stacked up the rest of the dishes and put the lot outside his door on the tray left there by the staff and quietly turned back. He crossed to her and held out a hand.

'Come on.'

She peered up at him with wide, hurt eyes. 'Where are we going?'

'I'm walking you home. I think you need to be in your own place right now, surrounded by familiar things.'

She didn't argue for once. Instead, she slipped her fingers into his and let him pull her up and towards the suite's door.

'It's not really my place,' she murmured as they stepped out into the hall. 'And most of them aren't my things.'

How weird that such sorrowful words could bring him such a lurch of hope. If Eve wasn't all that attached to the Bedford or its contents maybe there was hope for him yet. Maybe he could wedge himself a place in her distracted, driven world.

He kicked off one of his shoes and left it wedged in the doorway so that he didn't lock himself out.

Down in the almost empty car park he opened the bus for her and followed her through to her bedroom. She didn't so much as glance at that presumption, and she didn't look the slightest bit anxious that he might stay. She just accepted it as though they'd been doing it for years.

He pressed his key-card into her hand. 'Breakfast on the balcony at eight?'

'Okay.'

He flipped back her bed covers and waited for her to crawl in, then he folded them back over her and tucked her so firmly in that she resembled something that had just tumbled out of a sarcophagus.

'It's not your fault, Eve.'

He was going to tell her that every day of their lives if he had to.

She nodded, but he wasn't foolish enough to think that she actually believed it. Maybe she just accepted that he didn't think so. Bending brought him dangerously close to her lips, but he veered up at the last moment and pressed his to her hot forehead instead.

'Breakfast. Eight o'clock.'

She didn't agree. She didn't even nod. But her eyes were filled with silent promise and so he killed the lights and backed out of the room and then the bus, giving the big back door a security rattle before leaving her snug and safe inside.

It went against everything in him to leave her in the car park, but Eve had been doing this a long time and she was a grown, competent woman. Just because she'd opened up a little and shown him some of her childhood vulnerability didn't mean he could treat her like the child she'd almost been when her mother killed herself and nearly her brother.

As hard as that was.

He limped along on one shoe and returned to the big, lonely suite.

A gentle kind of rocking roused Marshall out of a deep, comfortable sleep. The suite was as dark as an outback road but he knew, instantly, what was going on.

Except it wasn't eight o'clock. And this wasn't morning.

A warm, soft body slid in next to him, breathing carefully. He shunted over a bit to make room, but she only followed him, keeping their bodies close.

'Eve…?'

As if there was any question.

She snuggled up hard into his side. 'Shh. It's late.'

Or early, he suspected. But he wasn't about to argue with whatever God had sent her back to him, and he wasn't about to ruin a good thing by reading something into this. Instead, he took it—and Eve—at face value and just gathered her into him so that his sleepy heat could soak into her cold limbs.

But he wasn't so strong that he could resist pressing his lips to her hair and leaving them there.

And she wasn't of a mind to move away, apparently.

'I have no expectations,' he murmured against her scalp. 'If you tell me that going our separate ways yesterday felt okay to you then that's cool, I know where I stand. But it felt anything but okay to me and I came back so that we could just—'

'Finish things up more civilly?'

'—*not* finish things up,' he said into the dark. 'Maybe just explore this a little more. See where it goes.'

Her breathing filled his ears. His heart.

'I slept with you because you were riding off into the horizon the next day,' she whispered.

He turned a little more towards her, trying to make her out in the dark. 'And I slept with you knowing that. But then I discovered something about horizons.'

'What?' she mumbled.

'They're an awfully long way away.'

She pushed up onto one elbow, robbing him of her warmth. 'So…you're just going to ride shotgun for the next…what—days? Weeks?'

'Until we know.'

Her voice sounded tantalisingly close to his ear. 'Know what?'

'Whether we have potential.'

'You're in the middle of an epic road trip. It's a terrible time to be looking for potential.'

She was right. He should be aiming for fast, casual and uncomplicated. Like she had.

'That's the thing, Eve. I wasn't looking. It seems to have found me.'

She had nothing to say to that, but her steady breathing told him she was still awake.

Listening.

Thinking.

He bundled her back in close and fell with her—lips to hairline—into a deep slumberous heaven.

# CHAPTER TEN

WAKING THE NEXT morning was like an action replay of the morning before—but without all the action. This time, he didn't catch Eve creeping out of bed. This time, she was not freaking out and sucking all the warmth out of the room. This time, she was not back-pedalling madly from what they'd shared the night before.

Even though what they'd shared overnight was more intimate and meaningful than anything they'd done with each other back at the campsite.

Two bodies, pressed together in sleep. Wrapped around each other. Talking.

No sex.

But infinitely more loaded.

'Morning,' she murmured before her eyes even opened.

'How long have you been awake?'

'Long enough to feel you staring.'

'It's the novelty.' He chuckled.

*Come on. Open them...*

But she just smiled and squirrelled in closer, as if she was getting ready to go back to sleep.

'It's eight o'clock,' he pointed out.

And then her eyes opened—drugged, languorous, and he'd never seen anything quite so beautiful.

'No, it's not.'

'Yeah, it really is.'

And this was a workday for both of them. Technically.

Her eyes fluttered shut and she wiggled deeper into the covers. Okay, so he was going to have to be the brave one.

'So, look at you in my bed…' he hinted.

One eye half opened and he waited for the quip to follow. Something sharp and brilliant and completely protective. But he didn't get one. Her second eye opened and locked on him, clear and steady.

'I just woke up in the middle of the night,' she murmured, 'and knew this is where I wanted to be.'

Right. What could he say to that? This was what he'd come back for, wasn't it? To see what might grow between them. Wasn't that what he'd been murmuring at midnight about? Yet, now that he was faced with it, it suddenly seemed overwhelmingly real.

He cleared his throat. 'Breakfast?'

'In town, maybe? After I get set up.'

Right. Work.

'I have to do my thing today, too.' For the people paying him.

'Where's the weather station?'

He told her and she asked a question or two. More than enough to muddle his mind. He was in bed with a living, breathing, *radiating* woman and they were talking about the weather again. Literally. But somehow it didn't feel like small talk. It felt big.

And then it hit him why.

They were having a *couple* conversation. Comfortable. Easy. And they were having it in bed. Where all conversations should happen. And that was enough to scare him upright.

'I'm going to grab a shower, then I'll get us some food while you set up.'

She pushed up onto her elbows, blinking. 'Sorry if I made things weird.'

He forced a relaxed smile onto his face.

'Not weird. Just—' *dangerously appealing* '—new.'

He padded into the bathroom and put himself under the shower Eve had enjoyed so much the night before. Images filled his head—of Eve standing with the water streaming over her slight body, head tipped back, issuing those sounds he'd heard while he leaned on the doorframe out in the hall. How badly he'd wanted to step inside and join her. Shower with her until the end of time. And now, here he was freaking out that his dreams might be coming true.

In his world, dreams didn't come true.

They shattered.

It was so hard to trust the good feelings.

He nudged the taps and cut out half of the hot water feed and then made sure to keep his shave brief.

When he emerged, Eve was gone.

For half a heartbeat the old doubts lurched to the surface but then he remembered she had no clothes up here, only what she'd crept up the stairs in, and he opened the suite door a crack and peered down through the hallway window. Like a seasoned stalker. Long enough to see Eve heading back across the car park.

*Come on, man. Pull it together. This is what you wanted.*

He'd just learned the hard way not to want. It only led to disappointment.

So Eve had opted for more comfortable accommodation overnight. No biggie. That was hardly a declaration of passion. She'd snuggled in and enjoyed the heat coming off him, and today she was all about Travis again.

Eve was always about Travis.

It was part of what intrigued him about her. That fathomless compassion.

But it was part of what scared him, too. Because how could there be room for him with all that emotion already going on?

He quickly shrugged something decent on and ran a quick comb through his hair so that when she swiped the suite's door he was clothed and everything that needed brushing was brushed.

He threw her a neutral smile. 'Good to go?'

The pause before she answered was full of silent query. 'Yep. Meet you in front of the Town Hall?'

Wherever that was. 'Yup.'

The question mark shifted from her eyes to her soft smile but she simply turned and let him follow her back down to where his bike was parked. She headed for the bus.

'Egg and bacon burger?' he called.

'Sounds great.'

*Great.*

Okay, so it was officially his turn to be off. Most guys would be stoked to wake up to a warm, willing body but, instead of converting the opportunity to a goal, he'd let it get under his skin. Weird him out. Not the best start, true, but Eve didn't look too tragic about it. Her mind was back on her brother already.

As was always the way.

The bumbling MP yesterday was pretty normal, in Eve's experience. In fact, he'd been more tactful than many of the people she'd tried to explain herself to in the past.

Herself... Her choices.

But the only people who'd understood her odyssey the way Marshall had were the other family members in her missing-persons network. Which did, in fact, make him pretty darned exceptional.

Eve smiled and passed a poster to an older lady who stopped to peruse her display. The stranger took her time and looked at every single face before wandering off, which Eve particularly appreciated. Nothing worse than the glancers. Glancing was worse than not looking at all, in some ways. Eve knew it was a big ask to hope that people might remember one face, let alone dozens, but there was no chance of people remembering them from the wall displays in post offices that were half obscured by piles of post packs or pull-down passport photo screens most of the time.

Something inside her had shifted last night when Marshall

told her about his brother. As if he went from adversary to equal in her mind. He'd effectively lost a brother, too—to circumstance—so he knew what it was like to give up on a family member.

Except, in Marshall's case, he was the one who'd walked away.

And didn't that tear her up. Half of her wanted to hug him for the personal strength it must have taken to leave an intolerable family situation so young. The other half wanted to shake him and remind him he had a brother. A living, breathing brother.

And those weren't to be sneezed at.

She never would have picked him for the product of a rough neighbourhood, even with all the tattoos. He was just too *normal*. Beneath the 'keep your distance' leather smokescreen. But to find out that someone so close to him was neck-deep in criminal activity… That just made what he'd done with his life even more remarkable. Finished school, tackled university and then got himself the straightest and smartest of straight, smart jobs.

Meteorology.

A tiny smile crept, unbidden, to her lips. Who knew that she'd ever get quite so hot and bothered by a weatherman?

Yet here she was, very much bothered. And decidedly hot under the covers.

At least she had been last night.

Crawling in with him hadn't been quite the spontaneous exercise she'd confessed. The sprint across the car park had been as sobering as it was chilly and she had plenty of opportunity to think better of it. But she hadn't—because a big part of her had wanted him to roll over, see her and just keep on rolling. Up and over onto her. To make love to her like he had the first time—all breathless and uninhibited.

Another taste of lightness.

Her days were consumed by her brother—couldn't someone

else have her nights? When she'd normally be asleep? Wouldn't
it be okay to let go just for those few short hours? To forget?

But Marshall hadn't taken advantage. He'd just tugged her
close, murmured hot, lovely words in her ear and pulled her
into unconsciousness behind him. And it was only as she'd
fallen asleep that she'd realised how badly she wanted *not to*
do the obvious thing. The easy thing.

Sleeping with Marshall was easy.

Falling for him would be treacherous.

But morning would always come. And it dragged reality
with it.

Eve's reality was that she still had a monumental task ahead
of her. Marshall had chased her up the highway to see what
might form between them if they gave it a chance, but how
could there be any kind of something between them while she
had this dismal marathon to complete?

Good sex was one thing. A *happy families* future was quite
another.

She had no room for anything beyond right now.

And both of them knew that *happy families* was just a myth.
They knew it firsthand.

'Thank you,' she murmured belatedly to the man who took
a poster as though from an unattended pile. She'd been so lost
in thought, that might as well have been true.

Nope, she hadn't promised Marshall anything more than
*right now* and he hadn't asked for it.

Two people could go a long way on *right now*.


The south-western corner of Western Australia was packed
with small, wine-rich country towns, each with unique personality and spaced close enough for tourists to hop from one
to another on their weekend trails.

Papering the two hundred square kilometres ahead with
posters was going to be a much bigger job than the two thousand before it.

But they did a good job together, she and Marshall. When

he wasn't working, or they weren't curled up together in her bus or a motel room, he'd be with her, plastering Trav's face all over the towns they visited. Handing her the pins or the tape or the staple gun. Nothing she couldn't have done for herself but—boy—was it good not to have to.

Somehow, having someone to share all of this with made it more bearable. And she hadn't realised how unbearable it had become. How utterly soul-destroying. Until she felt her soul starting to scab over.

She glanced sideways at Marshall's handsome face. How fast she'd adapted to having him here by her side during her displays of *The Missing*. How willing she'd been to bring him into her journey.

A problem shared…

A man approached from the far end of the street, folded paper in his hands. He looked grim and twitchy.

'Movie tonight?'

Marshall's voice pulled her focus back to him. The two of them hadn't braved a movie since *that* night in her bus. As if the entire art form was now too loaded. The last time they'd settled in to watch a movie together they'd ended up sharing so much more.

'Maybe,' she said breathlessly. A girl couldn't live on spooning alone. And she was fairly sure neither could a man. They were well overdue for a rematch. The way Marshall's eyes locked on hers said maybe he thought so, too.

The stranger still hovered and it was only as he turned away, stuffing the paper in his pocket, that Eve's brain finally comprehended that he wanted to say something.

'I'm sorry,' she called, stretching taller in her seat. 'Can I help you?'

The man slowed. Turned.

'Do you know him?' he said, holding up the crumpled paper as he approached. It was one of her posters.

A tingle tickled between her shoulders and grew outwards

until gooseflesh puckered under her shirt. 'He's my brother. Why? Do you recognise him?'

The man stepped one pace closer. 'Not sure. He looks familiar.'

Eve shot to her feet. 'What do you mean?'

'Just that I feel like I've seen him before. But I don't want to get your hopes up if I'm wrong…'

'I don't need certainty,' she was quick to reassure, 'just leads.'

She felt Marshall's heat as he stood behind her and her heart began to hammer. God, she'd been so wrapped up in the promise in his eyes she'd nearly let this guy walk off. A guy who might know something.

'Where do you think you know him from?' Marshall asked.

The guy switched focus. 'I really can't say. Just…somewhere. And recently.'

'How recent? Two months? Six?' Eve could hear the urgency in her own voice but was incapable of easing it. A big hand fell on her shoulder as if to physically suppress her.

'Where do you live?' Marshall asked, much more casually.

The guy responded to his even tone. 'Here. In Augusta. But I don't think I know him from here.'

God, the idea of that. That Travis might be right here in this little seaside town…

'Somewhere else?'

'I run trucks. Maybe I saw him on one of those. In another—'

'What other town?' Eve pressed, and Marshall squeezed harder.

*Are you freaking kidding me?* The first reasonable lead she'd had in nearly nine months and Marshall wanted her to relax? Every nerve in her body was firing in a soup of adrenaline.

'Where do you do your runs?' Marshall asked calmly.

'Anywhere in the South West,' the man said, visibly uncomfortable at having started the conversation at all. He immediately started retreating from his earlier thoughts. 'Look, I'm probably wrong—'

Deep panic fisted in her gut.

'*No!* Please don't start second-guessing yourself,' Eve rushed on, critically aware that her urgency was pushing him further away. She fought to breathe more evenly. God, how close she'd come to just not calling out to him.

What was happening to her?

'The subconscious is a powerful thing,' she urged. 'It probably knows something your conscious mind can't quite grasp.'

The man's eyes filled with pity and, in that moment, she saw herself as others must. As Marshall must.

Obsessed. Desperate. Pathetic.

And she didn't like his view of her one little bit.

Lines appeared on the man's time-weathered brow. 'I'm just not sure…'

'How about just jotting down the routes you usually take?' Marshall grabbed another poster, flipped it over to the blank side and handed it and a pen to the man. 'We can take it from there.'

More lines formed in his weathered skin. 'I have two-dozen routes. That'll take time…'

They were losing him. And the best lead she'd had in an age…

Eve dashed to the front of the bus and rummaged in the glove box with clammy hands for the maps she carried detailing every region she was in. One was marked up with her own routes—to make sure she never missed a town or junction—but her spare was blank, a clean slate. She thrust the spare into the man's hands.

'On this then, just highlight the routes you take. I can do the rest.'

Possibility flickered over his face. 'Can I take this with me?'

The fist squeezed harder. Not because she risked losing a four-dollar map. But she risked losing a tangible link with Travis. 'Can't you do it here…?'

'Take it,' Marshall interrupted. 'Anything you can give us will be great.'

The stranger's eyes flicked between the two of them 'Hopefully, I can be clearer somewhere…away from here.'

Eve took two steps towards the man as he retreated with the map in his hand. She spun to Marshall. 'I should go with him.'

His strong hand clamped around her wrist. 'No. You should let him go somewhere quiet and do what he has to do. He's not going to be able to concentrate with you hovering over him.'

*Hovering…!* As if they were talking about her chaperoning a teenage date and not possibly finding her brother. 'I just want to—'

'I know exactly what you want, Eve, and how you're feeling right now. But stalking the guy won't get you what you need. Just leave him be. He'll come back.'

'But he's the first person that's seen Travis.'

'*Possibly* seen Travis, and if you push any harder he's going to decide he never actually saw a thing. Leave him to his process, Eve.'

She glanced up the street, hunting for the man's distinctive walk. Two blocks away she spotted him, turning into the local pub. She swung baleful eyes onto Marshall.

'Leave him to his process,' he articulated.

Deep inside she knew he was right, but everything in her screamed for action. Something. Anything.

'Easy for you to say!'

He took a long breath. 'There's nothing easy about watching you suffer, Eve.'

'Try feeling it some time,' she muttered.

She turned away roughly but he caught her. 'I do feel it. In you. Every day—'

'No, I mean try *feeling* it, Marshall. From this side of the fence.'

'It's not about sides—'

'Spoken like someone who's more used to cutting people out of their life than being cut out.'

For a moment she thought he was going to let that go, but he was a man, not a saint. Words blew warmly behind her ear as Marshall murmured in this public place, 'And what's that supposed to mean, exactly?'

'What you imagine it means, I'm sure,' she gritted.

'Eve, I know this is frustrating—'

She spun on him. 'Do you, Marshall? You've been travelling with me all of ten days. Multiply that by twenty-five and then tell me how you think I should be feeling as my only lead walks away from me and into a bar.'

His lips tightened but he took several controlled breaths. 'You need an outlet and I'm convenient.'

*Spare me the psychoanalysis!*

'How did this become about you?' she hissed. 'This is about me and Travis.'

She glanced at the pub again and twisted her hands together.

Warm fingers brought her chin around until her eyes met his. '*Everything* is about Travis with you, Eve. Everything.'

That truly seemed to pain him.

The judgment in his gaze certainly hurt her. 'Forgive me for trying to stay focused on my entire purpose out here.'

The words sounded awful coming off her lips, doubly so because, deep down, she knew he didn't deserve her cruelty. But did he truly not get the importance of this moment? How rare it was. How it felt to go nearly nine months without a single lead and then to finally get one?

A lead she'd almost missed because she was so off mission.

She dropped back into her seat.

All week she'd been going through the motions. Putting up posters, staffing her unhappy little table, answering questions about the faces in her display. But she hadn't actively promoted. She hadn't forced posters on anyone. She hadn't made a single real impression.

All she'd done was sit here looking at Marshall. Or thinking about him when he was gone. Letting herself buy into his hopeless fantasy.

She'd failed Travis. Again.

And she'd nearly missed her only lead.

Marshall sat back and considered her in silence. And when he spoke it was careful but firm.

'I think it might be time to stop, Eve.'

She did stop. All movement, all breath. And just stared.

'Maybe it's time to go home,' he continued. 'This isn't good for you.'

When she finally spoke it was with icy precision.

'How good for me do you imagine it is sitting around the house, wondering whether Travis is alive or dead and whether anyone will give him more than the occasional cursory check twice a year?'

'It's been a year—'

'I know. I've been living it every single day. But I'm nearly done.'

'You're not nearly done. You still have one third of the country to go.'

'But only ten per cent of the population,' she gritted.

'That's assuming that you haven't missed him already.' *And assuming he is still alive.* The words practically trembled on those perfect lips.

She glared. 'What happened to "What you're doing is logical"?'

'I meant that. I completely understand why you're doing it.'

'And so…?'

'I don't like what *it's doing to you*, Eve. This search is hurting you. I hate watching it.'

'Then leave. No one's forcing you to stay.'

'It's not that easy—'

But whatever logical, persuasive thing he was about to say choked as she ran over the top of him. 'Maybe you're just unhappy that I'm putting him ahead of you. Maybe your male ego can't handle taking second place.'

She'd never seen someone's eyes bruise before, but Marshall's did. And it dulled them irreparably.

'Actually, that's the one thing I'm more than used to.'

The fist inside tightened further. How could she do this? How could she choose between two men she cared so much about? Marshall was, at least, stable and healthy and capable of looking after himself. Travis was...

Well, who knew what Travis was? Or where.

But his need was unquestionably greater.

She ripped the emotional plaster off and pushed to her feet. 'I think it's time for us to go our separate ways.'

The bruising intensified. 'Do you?'

'It's been lovely—'

'But you're done now?'

'Come on, Marshall, how long would we have been able to keep this up, anyway? Your circuit's coming to an end.' And her funds were running out.

Her casual dismissal turned the vacuum behind his lids to permafrost. 'Is that right?'

'I don't have room for you, Marshall.'

'No, you really don't, do you.'

'I need to stay focused on Travis.'

'Why?'

'Because he needs me. Who else is going to look for him?' Or look *out* for him. Like she should have all along.

'Face facts, Eve,' he said, face gentle but words brutal. 'He's either gone or he's *choosing* to stay away. You said it yourself.'

Her breaths seemed to have no impact on the oxygen levels in her body. Dark spots began to populate the edges of her vision. 'I can't believe that.'

'People walk away all the time. For all kinds of reasons.'

'Maybe *you* do.'

His voice grew as cold as her fingers. 'Excuse me?'

She started to shake all over. 'I should have thought to seek your perspective before. I have an expert on cutting loose right here with me. You tell me why a perfectly healthy young man would just walk away from his family.'

Marshall's face almost contorted with the control he was trying to exert. 'You think I didn't struggle, leaving them?'

'As far as I can see, you crossed a line through them and walked away and you seem no worse for wear. That's quite a talent.'

'Are you truly that self-absorbed,' he whispered, 'that you can't appreciate what that was like for me?'

'Yet you chose it.'

Where were these words coming from? Just pouring like toxic lava over her lips. Uncontrollable. Unstoppable.

Awful.

'Sometimes, Eve, all your choices are equally bad and you just have to make one.'

'Just go and don't look back?' she gritted. 'Who does that?'

Something flared in his eyes. Realisation. 'You're angry at Travis. For leaving.'

*I'm* furious *at Travis for leaving*, she screamed inside. But outwardly she simply said, 'My brother left against his will.'

How many police counsellors had she had that argument with? Or fights with her father.

'What if he didn't?' Marshall urged. 'What if he left because he couldn't imagine staying?'

*Pfff...* 'Someone's been reading up on the missing-persons websites.'

'Don't mock me, Eve. I wanted to understand you better—'

'Those people were desperate or scared or sick. The Travis I know wouldn't do that.'

'Maybe he wasn't your Travis, have you thought about that? Maybe he's not the kid brother you raised any more.'

The trembles were full-body shudders now.

Marshall stepped closer. Lowered his voice. 'Do you see how much of your life he's consumed, Eve? This obsessive search. It's ruining you.'

'If I don't do it, who will?' she croaked.

'But at what cost?'

'My time. My money. All mine to spend.'

He took her hand. 'And how much of life are you missing while you're out here spending it? I'm right here, Eve. Living. Breathing. But any part of you that might enjoy that is completely occupied by someone who's—'

His teeth cracked shut.

Nausea practically washed over her. 'Go on. Say it.'

'Eve—'

'Say it! You think he's dead.'

'I fear he's a memory, one way or another. And I think that memory is stopping you from living your life just as much as when your mother died.'

'Says the man who hides out behind a face full of hair and leather armour to avoid facing his demons.'

Marshall took a long silent breath.

'This has become an unhealthy obsession for you, Eve. A great idea, practically, but devastating personally. You stripped yourself away from all your support structures. Your colleagues. Your friends. Your family. The people who could have kept you healthy and sane.'

'So we're back to me being crazy?'

'Eve, you're not—'

'You need to go, Marshall,' she urged. 'I can't do what I have to do with you here. That guy nearly walked off because I was off my game. I was busy mooning after you.'

'This is my fault?'

She wrapped her arms around her torso. 'I nearly let my only lead in a year walk off because I was distracted with you.'

'I guess I should at least be happy I'm a distraction.'

Misery soaked through her. 'You are much more than a distraction, but don't you get it? I don't have room for you—for us—in my life. In my heart.'

'You don't have room for happiness? Doesn't that tell you anything?'

'I don't get to be happy, Marshall,' she yelled, heedless of the passers-by. 'Not until Travis is back home where he belongs.'

Those dreadful words echoed out into the seaside air.

'Do you hear yourself, Eve? You're punishing yourself for failing Travis.'

The muscles around her ribs began to squeeze. Hard. 'Thank you for your concern but I'm not your responsibility.'

'So, I just walk away from you, knowing that you're slowly self-destructing?'

'I will be fine.'

'You won't be fine. You'll search the rest of the country and what will you do when you get back to your start point and you've found no sign of him? Start again from the top?'

The thought of walking away from this search without her brother was unimaginable.

'I will always look for him,' she vowed.

And that wasn't fair on someone as vibrant as Marshall. Hadn't he been sidelined enough in his life? She shook her head slowly.

'Find someone else, Marshall. Please.'

Someone who could offer him what he needed. Someone who wouldn't hurt him. Someone who could prioritise him.

'I don't want someone else, Eve,' he breathed. 'I want you.'

Those three simple words stole the oxygen from her cells. The words and the incredibly earnest glitter of Marshall's flecked grey eyes that watched her warily now.

Of all the times. Of all the places. Of all the men.

The seductive rush of just letting all of this go, curling herself into Marshall's arms and letting him look after her. Letting him carry half of all this weight. Of parking the bus for somewhere and building a new life for herself with whatever she had left. With him. Of little grey-eyed kids running amuck in the sand dunes. Learning to fish. Hanging out with their dad.

But the kids of her imagination morphed, as she watched, into Travis when he was little. Scrabbling along the riverbank at the back of their house. Getting muddy. Just being a kid. A kid she loved so completely.

Eve took several long breaths. 'If you care for me as much

as you say you do, then what I need should matter to you. And what I need is my brother. Home. Safe. That's all I've got room for.'

'And then what?'

She lifted her eyes to his.

'After that, Eve. What's the plan then? You going to move in with him to make sure he stays safe? Takes his medication? Stays healthy? How far does this responsibility you feel go?'

The truth…? Just as there was nothing but black after not finding Travis, there was nothing but an opaque, uncertain mist after bringing him home. She'd just never let herself think about either outcome in real terms. She'd just focused on the ten kilometres in front of her at all times.

And the ten kilometres in front of her now needed to be solo.

She twisted her fingers into his. 'You're a fantastic guy, Marshall. Find someone to be happy with.'

'I thought I was working on that.'

It was time for some hard truths. 'You're asking me to choose between a man I've loved my whole life and a man I've—'

She caught herself before the word fell across her lips, but only just.

—*known ten days.*

No matter how long it felt.

Or how like love.

'Would I like to be important to you?' he urged. 'Yes. Would I like, two years from now, to live together in a timber cottage and get to make love to you twice a day in a forest pool beside our timber cabin? Yes. I'm not going to lie. But this is the real world. And in the real world I'm not asking you to choose *me*, Eve. I'm begging you to choose *life*. You cannot keep doing this to yourself.'

She stepped a foot closer to him, close enough to feel his warmth. She slid her unsteady hand up the side of his face and curled her fingers gently around his jaw.

'It's a beautiful image, Marshall,' she said past the ball of hurt in her chest. 'But if I'm going to indulge fantasies, it has to be the one where that guy with the map comes back and it leads me to finding Travis.'

The life drained right out of his face and his eyes dropped, but when they came back up they were filled with something worse than hurt.

Resignation.

This was a man who was used to coming last.

'You deserve to be someone's priority, Marshall,' she whispered. 'I'm so sorry.'

His eyes glittered dangerously with unshed truth and he struggled visibly to master his breathing, and then his larynx.

Finally he spoke.

'I'm scared what will happen to you if I can't be there with you to hold you—to help you—when you find him, or when you don't,' he enunciated. 'Promise me you'll go home to your father and start your life over and pick up where you left off.'

'Marshall—'

'Promise me, Eve. And I'll go. I'll leave you in peace.'

*Peace.* The very idea of that was almost laughable. Not knowing the true nature of the world, as she did now. Blissfully ignorant Eve was long gone.

And so she looked Marshall in the eye.

And she lied.

# CHAPTER ELEVEN

DID EVE HAVE any idea how bad she was at deceit?

Or maybe she just saved her best lies for the ones she told herself. There was no way on earth that this driven, strong woman was going to go back to suburbia after this was all over.

She was too far gone.

And, try as he might, she was not letting him into her life long enough for him to have any kind of influence on what happened from here. His job was to walk away. To respect her decision.

To do what his brain said was right and not what his heart screamed was so very wrong.

*I'm choosing Travis.*

His gut twisted in hard on itself. Wasn't that the story of his life? Had he really expected the very fabric of the universe to have changed overnight? Eve needed to finish this, even if she had no true idea of what that might mean.

He needed her to be whole.

He just hadn't understood he was part of the rending apart.

He rested his hand over Eve's on his cheek, squeezed gently and then tugged hers down and over.

'I hope you find him,' he murmured against the soft skin of her palm.

What a ridiculously lame thing to say.

But it was definitely better than begging her to change her mind. Or condemning her to search, half-crazed, forever.

He stepped back. And then back again. And the cold air between them made it easier to take a very necessary third step. Within a few more, he was turning and crossing the road without a backward glance.

Which was how he generally did things.

*You crossed a line through them and walked away.*

Did she truly believe that he could cauterise entire sections of his life without any ill effect? That he was that cold? His issues arose from caring too much, not too little. But maybe she was also right about it being a life skill, because experience was sure going to help him now.

This was every bit as hard as walking away from his mother and brother.

Eve was not going to be okay. He could feel it in his bones. She had no idea how much she needed him. Someone. Anyone. And if he could feel that protective of her after just a few short weeks, how much must she burn with the need to find and protect the baby brother she'd loved all his life?

He kept walking up the main street through town but then turned down a side street as soon as he was out of her view and doubled back to slide in the side door of a café fronting onto the same road he'd just walked down. From his table he could see Eve, behind her display table, rocking back and forth in the cold air.

If that guy didn't come back soon, he was going to go and drag him out of that pub and frogmarch him back up the street. If Eve wasn't going to walk away from this whole crusade, and she wasn't going to have him by her side, then he was going to do everything he could to make sure that it all came out okay.

So that *she* came out okay.

The waitress delivered his coffee and he cupped his frigid hands around it and watched the woman who'd taken up residence in the heart he'd assumed was empty. The organ he thought had long since atrophied from lack of use.

She sat, hunched, surrounded by *The Missing*, curled for-

wards and eyes downcast. Crying in body if not in tears. Looking for all the world as bereft and miserable as he felt.

She wasn't trying to hurt him. She hadn't turned into a mon-
ster overnight. She was just overwhelmed with the pressure of
this unachievable task she'd set herself.

She just had priorities. And he couldn't be one of them. It
was that simple.

At least she'd been honest.

And if he was going to be, she'd never pretended it was otherwise. She'd never promised him more than right now. No
matter what he'd hoped for.

So maybe he was making progress in life after all. At this
rate he might be ready for a proper relationship by the time he
was in his sixties.

Out on the street, Eve's body language changed. She pushed
to her feet, as alert and rigid as the kangaroos they drove past
regularly, her face turned towards the sea. A moment later,
the guy from the pub shuffled back into view, handed her the
folded map and spoke to her briefly, pointing a couple of times
to places on the map.

Marshall's eyes ignored him, staying fixed on the small
face he'd come to care so much about. Eve nodded, glanced
at the map and said something brief before farewelling him.
Then she sank back down onto her chair and pulled the map
up against her chest, hard.

And then the tears flowed.

Every cell in his body wanted to dump his coffee and jog
back across the road. To be there for her. To hold her. Impossible to know whether the guy had been unable to help, after
all, and the tears were heartbreak. Or maybe they were joy at
finally having a lead. Or maybe they were despair at a map
criss-crossed with dozens of routes which really left her no
further ahead than she'd started.

He'd never know.

And the not ever knowing might just kill him.

His fingers stilled with the coffee cup halfway to his mouth.

At last, he had some small hint of what hell every day was for Eve. Of why she couldn't just walk away from this, no matter how bad it was becoming for her. Of why she had no room for anything—or anyone—else in her heart. Adding to the emotional weight she carried around every day was not going to change the situation. Loving her, no matter how much, was not going to transform her. There was only one thing that would.

Someone needed to dig that brother of hers out from under whatever rock he'd found for himself. For better or worse.

A sudden buzzing in his pocket startled him enough to make him spill hot coffee over the edge of his mug and he scrambled to wipe the spillage with a napkin with one hand while fishing his phone out with the other.

He glanced at the screen and then swiped with suddenly nerveless fingers.

'Rick?'

'Hey,' his brother said. 'I've got something for you.'

Thank God for Rick's shady connections. And for health regulators. And maybe for Big Brother.

And thank God, for Eve's sake, that Travis Read was, apparently, still alive.

Rick had hammered home that the kid's name wouldn't have appeared anywhere on official records, if not for a quietly implemented piece of legislation at the start of the year. Even this was an *unofficial* record.

Accessing it certainly was—his brother had called in a number of very questionable favours getting something useful.

'The trouble with the Y-Gen is that they soon work out how to fly under the digital radar,' Rick had said over the phone. 'But he came undone by refilling his Alprazolam in his real name, even though he did it off the health scheme to stay hidden.

'As of February,' he'd continued, 'it became notifiable in order to reduce the amount of doc-shopping being done by addicts. Your guy wouldn't have known that because the GPs aren't required to advise their patients of its existence; in fact it's actively discouraged. And people call *me* dodgy...'

Marshall had ignored Rick's anti-government mutterings and scribbled the details down on the first thing at hand. The name of the drug. The town it was filled in. Ironic that prioritising his mental health had led to Travis's exposure. An obscure little register inside the Department of Health was pretty much the only official record in the entire country that had recent activity for Travis Read. Lucky for him, his brother knew someone who knew someone who knew some*thing* big about a guy in the Health Department's IT section. Something that guy was happy to have buried in return for a little casual database scrutiny.

Marshall's muttered thanks were beyond awkward. How did you thank someone for breaking innumerable laws on your behalf? Even if they did it every day.

'Whoever you're doing this for, Marsh...' Rick had said before hanging up '...I hope they know what this cost you. I sure do.'

That was the closest he'd come to acknowledging everything that went down between them in the past. He'd added just one more thing before disconnecting.

'Don't leave it so long next time.'

And then his brother was gone. After ten years. And Marshall had a few scribbled words on half a coffee-stained napkin. The pharmacy and town where Travis Read had shown his face a few months earlier.

Northam. A district centre five hours from where he was sitting.

Marshall pulled up his map app and stared at it. If Eve's intelligence was hereditary, then chances were her brother wouldn't be dumb enough to get his medical care in the town in which he was hiding out. So, he desktopped a wobbly fifty-kilometre radius around Northam and ruled out anything in the direction of the capital city. Way too public. It was also ninety-five per cent of the state's population and so that left him with only two-dozen country towns inside his circle.

If it was *him* trying to go underground, he'd find a town that was small enough to be under-resourced with government types, uninteresting enough to be off the tourist trail, but not so small that his arrival and settling in would draw attention. That meant tiny communities were out and so were any of the popular, pretty towns.

Agricultural towns were in because they'd be perfect for a man trying to find cash work off the books.

All of that filtering left him just a couple of strong candidates inside his circle. One was the state's earthquake capital and drew occasional media attention to itself that would be way too uncontrollable for a kid intent on hiding out.

That left only some towns on the southern boundary of his circle.

One was on a main route south—too much passing traffic and risk of exposure. Another too tiny.

The third was Beverley, the unofficial weekend headquarters for a biker gang and must regularly receive police attention.

He was about to cross that one through when he reconsidered. What better place to hide out than in a town filled with people with many more secrets to keep than Travis? People and activity that kept the tourists away and the authorities well and truly occupied. And where better for a newcomer to assimilate seamlessly than a town with a transient male population?

Beverley made it onto his top three. And he made a mental note to wear as much leather as he owned.

One day's drive away and he could spend a day each hunting in all three.

Then at least he would know.

It could be him.

Hard to say under the scrappy attempt at facial hair. The best of all the options he'd seen in the past couple of days, anyway. Marshall settled in at the bar and ordered something that he couldn't remember just five seconds later. Then he pulled out his phone and pretended to check his messages while covertly grabbing an image of the man that might be Eve's brother.

Evidence that Travis was alive and well.

If that even was him. Hard to tell from this far away.

There was an easy kind of camaraderie between the young man and his companions, as if an end-of-day beer was a very common thing amongst them. How nice that Travis got to sit here enjoying a beer with mates while his sister cried herself into an ulcer every night. Well-fed, reasonably groomed, clearly not here under any kind of duress, the kid seemed to have a pretty good gig going here in the small biker town.

Just before six, he pushed back from the table and his mates let him go easily, as if skipping out early was business as usual.

Out on the footpath, Marshall followed at a careful distance. How much better would the photo be if he could give the authorities an address to go with the covertly captured picture?

Authorities.

Not Eve.

This was about giving her back her brother, not getting back into her good books. Something he could do to help. Instead of hurt.

He was no better for Eve than she was for him. He'd finally accepted that.

The guy turned down a quiet street and then turned again almost immediately. Marshall jogged to catch up. The back of these old heritage streets were rabbit warrens of open backyards and skinny laneways. A hundred places for someone to disappear into their house. The guy turned again and Marshall turned his jog into a sprint, but as he took the corner into the quiet laneway he pulled up short.

The guy stood, facing him, dirty steel caps parted, ready to run, arms braced, ready for anything.

In a heartbeat, he recognised how badly he might have blown this for Eve. How easy it would be for Travis to just disappear again, deeper into Australia, where she'd never ever find him. And he realised, on a lurch of his stomach, that this cunning plan was maybe going to come completely unstuck.

And it would have his name all over it.

'Who sent you?' the guy challenged, dark eyes blazing in the dusk light.

Marshall took a single step forward. 'Travis?'

'Who sent you?' he repeated, stepping back. As he moved and the light shifted slightly, the facet of those blazing eyes changed and looked to him more like fear and less like threat.

And he'd know those eyes anywhere…

Marshall lifted both hands, palms outward, to show he came in peace.

'I'm a friend of your sister.'

# CHAPTER TWELVE

'HEY...'

Marshall's voice was startling enough out of the silence without her also being so horribly unprepared for it. Eve's stomach twisted back on itself and washed through with queasiness.

She'd only just resigned herself to him being gone—truly gone—and now he was back? What the hell was he trying to do—snap her last remaining tendrils of emotional strength?

She managed to force some words up her tight throat. 'What are you doing here, Marshall?'

It felt as if she was forever asking him that.

Compassion from him was nearly unbearable, but it rained down on her from those grey eyes she'd thought never to see again.

'Sit down, Eve.'

Instantly her muscles tensed. Muscles that had heard a lot of bad news. 'Why?'

'I need to talk to you.'

'About...?'

'Eve. Will you just sit down?'

*No. No...* He was looking at her like her father had the day Travis was officially declared a missing person.

'I don't think I want to.'

As if what she wanted would, in any way, delay what she feared was to come.

'Okay, we'll do this upright, then.'

His mouth opened to suck in a deep breath but then snapped shut again in surprise. 'I don't know where to start. Despite all the trial runs I've had in my mind on the way back here…'

That threw her. Was he back to make another petition for something between them? She moved to head that off before he could begin. Hurting him once had been bad enough…

'Marshall—'

'I have news.'

*News.* The tightness became a strangle in her throat. Somehow she knew he wouldn't use that word lightly.

'You're freaking me out, Marshall,' she squeezed out.

The words practically blurted themselves onto his lips. 'I've found Travis.'

The rush of blood vacating her face left her suddenly nauseous and her legs started to go.

'He's alive, Eve,' he rushed to add.

That extra piece of information knocked the final support from under her and her buckling legs deposited her onto the bus's sofa.

'Eve…' Marshall dropped down next to her and enveloped her frigid hand between both of his. 'He's okay. He's not hurt. Not sick.'

Eve's lips trembled open but nothing came out and it distantly occurred to her that she might be in shock. He rubbed her frigid fingers and scanned her face, so maybe he thought so, too.

'He's living and working in a small town here in Western Australia. He has a job. A roof over his head. He's okay.'

*Okay.* He kept saying that, but her muddled mind refused to process it. 'If he was okay he'd have been in touch…'

And then his meaning hit her. New job and new house meant new life. They meant *voluntary.* Her heart began to hammer against her ribs. Everything around her took on an other-worldly gleam and it was only then she realised how many tears wobbled right on the edges of her lashes.

'Where is he?' she whispered.

It was then Marshall's anger finally registered and confusion battled through the chaos in her mind. Anger at her? Why? But colour was unquestionably high in his jaw and his eyes were stony.

'I can't tell you, Eve.'

Okay, her brain was seriously losing it. She waited for the actual meaning to sink in but all she was left with was his refusal to tell her where her long-lost brother was.

'But you found him…?'

'He asked me not to say.'

'What? No.' Disbelief stabbed low in her gut. And betrayal. And hurt. 'But I love him.'

'I know. *He* knows,' he hurried to add, though the anger on his face wasn't diminishing. 'He told me that he would disappear again if I exposed him. So that you'd never find him. He made me give him my word.'

Pain sliced across her midsection. 'But you don't even know him. You know me.'

*You* love *me.*

She might as well have said it. They both knew it to be true. Not that it changed anything.

'Eve, he's alive and safe and living a life. He's on his meds and is getting healthy. Every day. He just can't do that at home.'

The thump against her eardrums intensified. 'Okay, he doesn't have to come back to Melbourne. We could move—'

'It's not about Melbourne, Eve. He doesn't want to go *home.*'

Realisation sunk in and she whispered through the devastation, 'He doesn't want to be with his family?'

God, did she look as young and fragile as her disbelief sounded? Maybe, because Marshall looked positively sick to be having this conversation.

'He wants to be healthy, Eve. And he needed to start over for that to happen.'

*Start over…*

'He doesn't have to come back, I can go to him. If he likes where he is—'

'I'm so sorry.' He squeezed both his hands around both of hers and held on. And, after an endless pause, he spoke, leaning forward to hold her stinging eyes with his. 'He doesn't want you to come, Eve. Particularly you.'

*Particularly you.*

Anguish stacked up on top of pain on top of misery. And all of it was wrapped in razor blades.

'But I love him.'

His skin blanched. 'I know. I'm so sorry.'

'I need to see him,' she whispered. 'I've been searching for so long—'

'He wants a fresh start.'

A fissure opened up in her heart and began to tug wider. Her voice, when it came, was low and croaky. 'From me?'

'From everything.'

'Is this…' The fissure stretched painfully. 'Is this about *me*?'

Pity was like a cancer in his gaze. 'He can't be with you any more. Or your dad.'

'Why?' Her cry bounced off the Bedford's timber-lined walls.

Words seemed to fail him. He studied his feet for the barest of moments and then found her gaze again.

'Because of your mother, Eve.'

She stared at him, lost. Confused. But then something surfaced in the muddle of pain and thought. 'The accident?'

His expression confirmed it.

God, she could barely breathe, let alone carry on a conversation. 'But that was years ago.'

'Not for him, Eve. He carries it every day. The trauma. The anxiety. The depression. The guilt.'

*Guilt?* 'But Mum wasn't his fault.'

His fingers tightened around hers again and his gaze remained steady. 'It was, Eve. I'm so sorry.'

She shook the confusion away, annoyed to have to go back

over such old ground. But being angry at him helped. It gave all the pain somewhere to go.

'No. He was with her, but... She was driving drunk.'

But she could read Marshall like a book—even after just a few weeks together—and his book said something else was going on here. Something big. She blinked. Repeatedly.

'Wasn't she?'

'Didn't you say they were both thrown from the bike?'

She was almost too dizzy for words. So she just nodded.

'And the police determined that she was in control?'

'Travis was the only other person there. And he couldn't ride properly then. He was underage.'

Marshall crouched over further and peered right into her face. Lending her his strength. 'No. He couldn't.'

But it was all starting to be horribly, horribly clear.

*Oh, God...*

'Trav was driving?' she choked. Marshall just nodded. 'Because Mum had been drinking?'

No nod this time, just the pitying, horrible creasing of his eyes.

*No... Not little Travis...* 'And he never told anyone?'

'Imagine how terrified he must have been.'

A fourteen-year-old boy driving his drunk mother home to keep her safe and ending up killing her.

'He wouldn't have lied to protect himself.' Her certainty sounded fierce even to her.

'But what if he thought you'd all blame him? Hate him. That's a lot for someone to carry. Young or old. He can't face you.'

She sagged against the sofa back, this new pain having nowhere to go.

'He carried that all alone? All this time?' she whispered. 'Poor Trav. Poor baby...'

'No. Don't you take that on, too. He's getting treatment now. He's got support and he's getting stronger. He's doing pretty bloody well, all things considered.'

So why was Marshall still so very tense?

'But he knows what he wants. And needs. And he isn't going back to your world. And he doesn't want that world coming to him either.' He cursed silently. 'Ever.'

A tiny bit of heat bubbled up beneath her collar and she'd never been so grateful for anger. It cut like a hot knife through the butter of her numb disbelief and reminded her she could still feel something. And not a small something. The feelings she'd been suppressing for twelve months started to simmer and then boil up through the cracks of Marshall's revelation.

*Ever.*

'So…that's it?' she wheezed. 'I gave up a year of my life to find him—I broke my heart searching for him—and all this time he's been living comfortably across the country *starting over*?'

Marshall's lips pressed together. 'He's made his choice.'

'And you've made yours, apparently. You've taken his side pretty darned quick for a man you don't know.'

'Eve, I'm on your side—'

It was as if someone was puffing her with invisible bellows filled with hot air…making this worse and worse.

'Don't! How do I know you're not just making this all up to further your cause?'

'You can't be serious.'

'How would I know? The only evidence I have that any of this is true is your word. You might not have found him at all. You might just want me to think that. You might say anything to get me to stay with you.'

The words poured out uncontrollably.

'What the hell have I done to make you believe that of me?' But he rummaged in his pocket, pulled out his phone and opened his photo app. 'Believe this, then.'

Seeing Travis just about broke her heart.

Her baby brother. Alive. Healthy. Enjoying a beer. Even laughing. *Laughing!* She hadn't seen that in years.

She certainly hadn't done it in as long.

Tears tumbled.

'Eve—'

'What would happen, Marshall?' she asked desperately. 'If you told me where he is. How would he even know?'

She was flying through the stages of grief. At bargaining already.

'I know you, Eve…'

'So you're just going to take the choice away from me? Like some child?'

'You wouldn't be able to stay away. You know it.'

'I'm not about to *stalk him*, Marshall.'

'You already are, Eve! You're scouring the country systematically, hunting him down.'

Her gasp pinged around the little bus. 'Is that how you see it?'

'Why else would you want to know where he is? Unless you were going to keep tabs on him.'

'Because I *love* him. You have no right to keep this from me.'

'I'm not doing this to be a bastard, Eve. I don't want you in any more pain.'

'You think this doesn't hurt? Knowing he's alive and I can't get to him? Can't hold him? Or help him? You think that's kinder than letting me hear from his own lips that he doesn't want to come home?'

Just saying the words was horrible.

He took her chin in his fingers and forced her to look at him and, despite everything, her skin still thrilled at his simple touch. It had been days…

'Hear me, Eve,' he urged. 'If you go there he will disappear again. He knows what to do now, he'll be better at it and he might go off his meds to keep himself hidden. You will never see or hear from your brother again. Is that what you want?'

In all her wildest, worst dreams she'd never imagined she'd be sitting here, across from Marshall—of all people—fighting him for her brother's whereabouts.

But, dear Lord, fight she would.

'How is that any different to what I have now?'

'Because I know where he is and he's agreed to check in with me from time to time.'

The grief and hurt surged up right below her skin, preparing to boil over.

'So…what? You get to be some kind of gatekeeper to my family? Who the hell gave you that authority?'

'He has a legal right to go missing. He wasn't hurt, or forced, or under any kind of duress. He decided to leave.'

'He was sick!'

'And managing his condition.'

He had an answer for every single argument. 'Then he must have been desperate.'

'Maybe, but he's not now. He's doing okay, I swear.' He caught her eyes again and brought everything back to the simple truth. 'You've found him, Eve.'

'No, *you* found him. I have as little as I had before.' Less, really. 'And, whatever he's going through, he clearly needs some kind of psychological help. People don't just walk out on perfectly good families.'

'They do, Eve. For all kinds of reasons. He couldn't stay, not knowing what he'd done. Fearing you'd discover it. Knowing how much you'd sacrificed—'

The inquest. The random timing of his disappearance suddenly came into crystal focus. 'I can help him.'

'You're still protecting him from responsibility? He's an adult, Eve. He doesn't want your help.'

'He needs it.'

'Does he, Eve? Or do you just need to believe that?'

She stiffened where she sat.

'You were his big sister. You looked after him and your father after the accident. That became your role. And for the last twelve months you've been about nothing but him. You chucked in your job. You sold your house. What do you have if you don't have him?'

'I have…plenty, thanks very much. I'll go back to my career, reignite my friendships. Get a new place.'

Oh, such lies. There was no going back. She didn't even know how to be normal now.

'And then what? What are you if you're not all about your brother, Eve? You've been doing this since you were barely out of school.'

Furious heat sped up the back of her neck and she surged to her feet. 'Don't put this on me. You're choosing to protect him instead of me. How about we talk about that for a bit?'

He shot up right behind her and angry fists caught her upper arms. But he didn't shake her. It was more desperate and gentle than that.

'I would *never* protect him, Eve. I hate what he's done to you. I hate that I found him sitting in a pub having a relaxed beer with friends while your soul was haemorrhaging hope *every single day*. I hate that he's got himself a new life when he was gifted with *you* in his old one.'

He said 'you' as if that was something pretty darned special. The stress faults in her heart strained that tiny bit more.

'I hate that he ditched you and your father rather than find the strength to work through it and that he didn't believe in your strength and integrity more.' He sucked in a breath. 'I would never put him ahead of you. I'm choosing *you*. This is all about you.'

'Then tell me where—'

'I can't!' he cried. 'He will disappear, Eve. The first sign of someone else looking for him. The first poster he sees in a neighbouring town. The first time his phone makes a weird noise. The next stranger who looks at him sideways in the street. He's dead serious about this,' he urged. 'Please. Just let it go.'

'How can I possibly do that?' she snarled.

'You once told me that all you wanted was to know he was all right. To have an answer. And nothing else mattered. Well, now you know. He's fine. But you're shifting the goalposts.'

'So, knowing is not enough! Maybe I do want him home, safe, with us. What's wrong with that?'

'Nothing. Except it's not achievable. And you need to accept that. It will be easier.'

'On who?'

'While your head and heart are full of your brother, then no one and nothing else can get through.'

'Are we back to that, Marshall? You and me?'

'No. You've been painfully clear on that front. I just wanted...'

He couldn't finish, so she finished for him. 'To save the day? To be the hero? Guess you weren't expecting to have to come back and be the bad guy, huh?'

'I didn't *have* to be anything.'

'You preferred to have me despise you?'

His eyes flared as if her words hit him like an axe. But he let her go and she stumbled at the sudden loss of his strength.

'You bang on about your great enduring love for your brother,' he grated. 'But you don't recognise it when it's staring you in the face. I chose *you* here today, Eve. Not myself and certainly not Travis. I am critically aware that the end of your suffering means the end of any chance for you and me. Yet here I am. Begging you to come back to the real world. Before it's too late.'

'Reality?' she whispered. 'Life doesn't get much realer than having someone you love ripped from you and held away, just out of reach.'

His eyes bled grey streaks. 'Finally. Something we agree on.'

He pushed away and walked to the bus's back door. But he caught himself there with a clenched fist on each side of the doorframe. His head sagged forward and his back arched.

Everything about his posture screamed pain.

Well, that made two of them.

But he didn't step forward. Instead, he turned back.

'You know what? Yes. Maybe I did want to be the man who

took your pain away. Who ended all your suffering. Maybe I did want to see you look at me with something more heartfelt than curiosity or amusement or plain old lust.'

Haunted eyes bled.

'You're halfway to being missing yourself, emotionally speaking. And if Travis was found, then you'd have no choice but to return to the real, functional, living world. And I wanted to be the man that helped get you there.'

'Why?'

Frustrated hands flew up. 'Why do you think, Eve? Why do any of us do anything, ultimately?'

She blinked her stinging eyes, afraid to answer.

'*Love*, Eve.' So tired. So very weary. Almost a joke on himself. He made the word sound like a terminal condition. 'I love you. And I wanted to *give* you your heart's desire if I couldn't be it.'

'You barely know me,' she breathed.

'You're wrong.' He stepped up closer to her. Towered above her. 'You spend so much time stopping yourself from feeling emotion that you've forgotten to control how much of it you show. You're an open book, Eve.

'I know you're heartbroken about Travis betraying you like this,' he went on, 'and confused about loving him yet hating this thing he's done. I know you're desperate for somewhere to send all that pain, and you don't really want to throw it at me but you can't deal with it all yourself because you've closed down, emotionally, to cope with the past year. Maybe even longer. And it's easier to hate me than him.'

Tears sprang back into her eyes.

'I know it particularly hurts you that it's *me* that's withholding Travis from you because deep down you thought we had a connection even if you didn't have the heart to pursue it. You trusted me, and I've betrayed you. Maybe that's the price I had to pay for trying to rescue you.'

She curled her trembling fingers into a fist.

'I could have told you nothing, Eve. I could have simply kept driving after letting him know that you were all looking for him. Left you thinking well of me. And maybe I could have come back into your life in the future and had a chance. But here I am instead, destroying any chance of us being together by telling you the hard truth about your brother. So you hear it from me rather than from him.'

Her voice was barely more than a croak. 'What do you mean?'

'I've seen your route maps, Eve.' He sighed. 'You would have reached his town before Christmas. And *you* would have found him drinking in that pub, and *you* would have had to stand there, struggling to be strong as he told you how he'd traded up to a better new life rather than the tough old one he'd left, and as he threw everything you've sacrificed and been through back in your face.'

She reached out for something solid to hold on to and found nothing. Because he wasn't there for her any more.

'And you would have knocked on his door the next morning with takeaway coffee, only to find he'd cleared out, with not a single clue. And you would have spent the rest of your life hunting for him.

'And so, even though it hurts like death to do this to you, I would take this pain one hundred times over to spare you from it.'

She stared at him through glistening eyes—wordless—as he stepped up closer.

'I'm not fool enough to think there's a place for me here now, even if you did have some capacity in your heart. I wouldn't expect—or even want—to just slide into the emotional vacancy left by your brother. Or your mother. Or anyone else you've ever loved.

'I deserve my *own* piece of you, Eve. Just mine. I think that's all I've ever really wanted in my sorry excuse for a life. The tiniest patch of your heart to cultivate with beautiful flowering vines and tend and spoil until they can spread up your walls and through your cracks and over your trellises. Until you've forgotten what it was like to *not* have me there. In the garden of your heart.'

He leaned down and kissed her, careless of the puffy, slimy, tear-ravaged parts of her. Long, hard and deep. A farewell. Eve practically clung to the strong heat of his lips.

'But I can't do anything with the rocky, parched earth you'll have left after all this is over. Nothing will ever grow there.'

He tucked a strand of damp hair behind her ears and murmured, 'Go home, Eve. Put him behind you. Put me behind you. Just…heal.'

This time, he didn't pause at the door, he just pushed through, jumped down to the ground and strode off, leaving Eve numb, trembling and destroyed in the little bus that had become her cage.

# CHAPTER THIRTEEN

*Five months later*

MARSHALL SPRINTED UP the valley side to the cottage, sweaty from a morning of post-hole-digging and dusting the rich dirt off his hands as he went. He snatched the phone up just before his voicemail kicked in.

Landline. Not many people called that any more.

'Hello?'

'Marshall?'

A voice familiar yet…not. Courtesy of the long-distance crackle.

'Yeah. Who's this?'

'Travis Read.'

His heart missed a beat. 'Has something happened?'

That was their agreement. Marshall would call twice a year to check in and, apart from that, Travis would only call if something was up. It had only been five months since they'd last spoken. He wasn't yet due.

'No, I'm…uh…I'm in town this afternoon and wondered if I could come and see you.'

Since Travis only had his new Victorian phone number, not his new home address, 'in town' had to mean Melbourne. That was all the area code would have told him. But what could Eve's brother possibly have to say? And why did he sound so tense? Unless it was recriminations. It occurred to him to question why he would have caught a plane anywhere since that would flag him on the Federal Police's radar and risk exposure. Unless he used a fake name. Or drove. Or maybe his family had taken him off the missing-persons register so that scarce resources weren't wasted on a man who wasn't really missing.

He'd given Travis one more go all those months ago for Eve's sake. Pointlessly tried to get him to change his mind, told him the damage it had done to his own life—in the long-term—to walk away from his family, as imperfect as they were. How it hadn't solved any of his problems at all—he'd just learned to function around them.

Or not, as the case may be.

But Travis hadn't budged. He was as stubborn as his sister, it seemed. And now he wanted to meet.

Irritation bubbled just below Marshall's surface. He was already keeping Travis's secret at the expense of his own happiness. Hadn't he done enough?

But then he remembered how important this kid was to the woman he was still struggling to get over and he reluctantly shared his new address and gave Travis a time later in the day before trundling back down the hill to the Zen meditation of punching three-dozen fenceposts into the unsuspecting earth.

About fifteen minutes before Travis was due, Marshall threw some water on his face and washed his filthy hands. The rest… Travis would have to take him as he found him.

About six minutes after their appointed time Marshall heard a knock at his front door and spied a small hire car out of one of the windows as he reached the door.

'Trav—?'

He stopped dead. Not Travis.

Eve.

In the flesh and smiling nervously on his doorstep.

His first urge was to wrap her up in his arms and never, ever let her go again. But he fought that and let himself frown instead. His quick brain ran through the facts and decided that she was obviously here in Travis's place. Which suggested Eve and Travis were in communication.

Which meant—his sinking heart realised—that everything he'd done, everything he'd given up, counted for absolutely nothing.

'How did you find him?'

'Good to see you, too,' she joked. Pretty wanly. But he wasn't in any mood for levity. Not while he was feeling this ambushed.

'I didn't find him,' she finally offered. 'He found me.'

So Travis had finally found the personal courage to pick up the phone. Good for him.

And—yeah—he'd be a hypocrite if not for the fact that he'd since taken his own advice and done the same with Rick. His brother hadn't commented on the new mobile number but Marshall felt certain he'd tried to use the old one. That was why he'd yanked out the SIM and tossed it somewhere along the Bussell Highway the same awful night he'd last seen Eve.

The whole world could just go screw itself. Travis. Eve. Rick.

Everyone.

'I was heading home,' Eve said now. 'Backtracking through Esperance. My phone rang and I thought it might be you, but… it was him.'

The flatness of her tone belied the enormity of what that moment must have meant for Eve.

'Why would you think it was me?' Hadn't they been pretty clear with each other when they'd parted?

She shrugged lightly. 'I'd tried your number several times and it was disconnected, but—you know—hope springs eternal.'

On that cryptic remark, she shuffled from left foot to right on his doorstep.

*Ugh, idiot.* He stepped aside. 'Sorry, come on in.'

There was something about her being here. Here, where he'd had to force himself finally to stop imagining what the cottage would be like with her in it. It felt as if he'd sprinted up the valley side and into an alternate dimension where his dreams had finally turned material.

Inside, she glanced around her and then crossed straight to the full wall window that looked out over the picturesque valley.

'Gorgeous,' she muttered almost to herself.

While she was otherwise occupied with the view, he took the opportunity to look at her. She'd changed, but he couldn't quite put his finger on how. Her hair was shorter and glossier but not that different. Her eyes at the front door had been bright but still essentially held the same wary gaze he remembered. She turned from the window and started to comment further on his view when it hit him. It was the way she carried herself; she seemed…taller. No, not taller—straighter. As if a great burden she'd been carrying around was now gone.

And maybe it was.

But having her here—in his sanctuary—wasn't good for him. It physically hurt to see her in his space, so he cut to the chase and stopped her before she offered some view-related platitude.

'What are you doing here, Eve?'

Maybe she deserved his scepticism. The way they'd left things… Certainly, Eve had known she wouldn't be walking into open arms.

'I'm sorry for the deception,' she began. 'I wasn't sure you'd see me. We didn't really leave things…open…for future contact. Your phone was dead and your infuriating Government privacy procedures meant no one in your department would give me your new one. And you moved, too.'

She caught herself before she revealed even more ways she'd tried to reach out to him. It wasn't as if she'd been short of time.

'Yet here you are.'

'I guilted Travis into hooking this up,' she confessed. 'He

wasn't very happy about betraying you when you've kept his secret in good faith.'

Which explained the tension on the phone earlier. And the long-distance hum. 'To absolutely no purpose, it seems, since you two are now talking.'

'"Talking" is probably an overstatement,' she said. 'We speak. Now and again. Just him and me at this stage but maybe Dad in the future. Trav reached out a few months ago. Said you'd called him again.'

'I did.' Though it had never occurred to him that the contents of that call might some day end up in Eve's ear.

'Talking about everything that happened is pretty hard for him,' she said flatly. 'You were right about that. And you were right that he would have bolted if I'd pushed. He was very close to it.'

'That's partly why I called him again. To make sure he hadn't already done a runner.'

But not the only reason. 'Whatever you talked about, Travis got a lot out of it. It was a real turning point for him.'

Silence fell between them and Eve struggled to know how to continue. His nerves only infected her more.

'So, you went home?' Marshall nudged.

'I was paralysed for a few days,' she admitted. 'Terrified of any forward move in case I accidentally ended up in his town and triggered another disappearance. You could hardly tell me which town not to visit, could you?'

She fought the twist of her lips so that it felt more like a grimace. Great—finally tracked him down and she was grinning like the Joker.

'So I backtracked the way I'd come,' she finished. 'That seemed safe.'

'I wondered if you might still be in Western Australia,' he murmured.

So far away. 'There wasn't anything to stay for.'

Travis in lockdown. Marshall gone. Her journey suspended. She'd never felt so lonely and lost.

'So, here you are.'

'Here I am.' She glanced around. 'And here *you* are.'

All these months he'd been here, within a single day's mountain drive of her family home. God, if only she'd known. She would have come much sooner.

'Do you know where we are?' he asked.

Not exactly warm, but not quite hostile. Just very…restrained.

'The satnav says we're near MacKenzie Falls.' A place they'd both enjoyed so much on their separate trips around the country. 'That's quite a coincidence.'

'Not really. It was somewhere I wanted to come back to.'

Okay. Not giving an inch. She supposed she deserved that.

'You gave up meteorology?'

'No. I consult now. From here, mostly. The wonder of remote technology.'

She glanced out at the carnage in his bottom paddock. 'When you're not building fences?'

'Who knew I'd be so suited to farming.'

'I think you could do pretty much anything you turned your hand to.'

'Thanks for the vote of confidence. Now why are we having this conversation, Eve?'

She sighed and crossed closer to him.

'I wanted to… I *need to* thank you.'

'For what?'

Her fingers were frozen despite the warm day. She rubbed the nerves against her jeans. 'The wake-up call.'

He crossed his arms and leaned on his kitchen island. Okay, he wasn't going to make this any easier.

'When you love a missing person,' she started, 'you can't grieve, you can't move on. You can't plan or make life decisions. So it just becomes easier to…not. It hurts less if you just shut down. And when one system goes down, they all do.

'In my case,' she went on, 'I coped by having a clear, single purpose.'

*Find Travis.*

'And that was all I could deal with. All I could hold in my head and my heart. I developed tunnel vision.'

Marshall studied the tips of his work boots.

'I once told you that if Travis walked in the door, healthy and alive, nothing he'd done would matter.'

He nodded. Just once.

'Me dealing with it so maturely was every bit as much a fantasy as him walking in the door unannounced. Turns out, I'm not so stoic under pressure.' She lifted her eyes. 'It matters, Marshall. It matters a lot. Even as I argued with people who warned me that he might not be alive, I secretly wanted them to be right. Rather than accept he might torture his family like this, deliberately. Leave us wondering forever. And then I hated myself for allowing those thoughts.'

Realisation dawned on his face. 'So when it turned out to be true…'

She shook her head. 'I'm very sorry for the things I said. The way I said them. I thought you were putting Travis ahead of me and that clawed at my heart. I'm sorry to say it took me days to realise that was what I did to you every single day. Put you second. The truth is, you sacrificed yourself—and any chance of us being together—for me. To help spare me pain.'

'So you came to apologise?'

Could a heart swell under pressure? Because hers felt twice its usual size. Heavy and pendulous and thumpy. And it was getting in the way of her breathing.

'You put yourself second.' After a lifetime of coming second. 'For me. Not many men would have done that.'

His voice, when it came, was not quite steady. But still a fortress wall. 'So you came to say thanks?'

She took a breath. Inside her long sleeves she twisted her fingers. Over and over. 'I came to see if I'm too late.'

Marshall didn't move. 'Too late for what?'

'For that vision you had,' she said on a sad, weak laugh.

'The timber cabin in the forest with the clear pools…and me. And you,' she finished on a rush.

And the making love twice a day part. She'd clung to that image for the many lonely nights since he'd left.

Marshall gave nothing away, simply pushed from the island bench and moved to stare out of his window.

'You stuck with me, Eve,' he admitted. 'I finished my audit and returned to Sydney, assuming that a little time was all I needed to get you out of my system. But months passed and you were still there. Under my skin like ink. I couldn't shake you. You were wedged in here.'

He tapped his chest with a closed fist.

'But it doesn't really matter what my heart thinks because my head knows better. And if my life has taught me anything, it's to listen to my head.' He turned back to her. 'I've walked away from much longer relationships than ours when they weren't good for me, Eve. Why would I set myself up to be the second most important person in your life?'

'That's not—'

'So, yes, Eve. I got the cottage in the forest surrounded by pools and, yes, I hope to be happy here. Very happy.' He expelled a long, sad breath. 'But no…there's no *you* in that plan any more.'

A rock of pain lodged in her stomach.

'At all?' she whispered.

'You don't have room for me, Eve. I'd convinced myself that you'd cast me as some kind of substitute for your brother but I no longer think that's true. I just don't think you have any emotional capacity left. And I deserve better than sorry seconds.'

She struggled to steady her breath. But it was touch and go. Every instinct she had told her to go, to flee back home. Except that when she'd come here she'd really hoped that *this* might turn out to be home.

And no home worth having came without risk. It was time to be brave.

'I wasn't out there to find Travis,' she whispered, taking

the chance. 'I think I was out there trying to find a way to let him go.'

She shuddered in a breath. 'But that was terrifying. What if I had nothing but a massive, gaping hole inside where my love and worry and pain for him used to be? What if I could never fill it? Or heal it. Who was I without him? So much of *me* was gone.'

His strong arms wrapped across his chest and all she could think about was wanting them around her.

'And what little was left around the outside was just numb.' She stepped closer to him. 'But then you came in with your ridiculous orange motorbike and your hairy face and your tattoos and you were like…an icebreaker. Shoving your stubborn way through the frost. Inch by inch.'

A tragic kind of light flickered weakly behind his eyes and it sickened her that she'd been the one to extinguish it before. The memory of him standing in her bus, appealing from the heart, in visible, tangible pain. And she'd not been able to feel a thing.

But his body language was giving nothing away now.

'I'm not a plug, Eve. I'm a person. You'll have to find someone else to fill the void.'

'I don't want you to fill it. I want you to bridge it.'

His eyes came up.

Eve picked up a cushion off his sofa and hugged it close. 'When you left, it was horrible. You gone. Travis gone. Mum gone. Dad on the other side of the country. I'd never felt so alone. Which is ridiculous, I realise, given I'd been travelling solo all year.'

His brow twitched with half a frown, so quick she almost missed it. His posture shifted. Straightened. 'What changed?'

'I couldn't stay frozen.' She shrugged. 'I tried to do what I'd done before, just…deal. But all these emotions started bubbling up out of nowhere and I realised that I'd been harbouring the same feelings Travis must have had since Mum died. Despair. Anxiety. I'd been suppressing them, just like he must have.'

'So you developed some empathy for your brother. That's great.'

'I wasn't thinking about him, Marshall,' she rushed to correct. 'God knows, I should have been, and it took me a while to notice, but eventually I thought how strange it was that I should feel such despair about my brother being *alive*. Anger, sure. Resentment, maybe. But despair…?

'Travis has been absent in my life since Mum died. Even back when he was still physically present. I'd learned how to compensate for his absence and not fall apart. But there I was, trundling up the highway, completely unable to manage my feelings about the absence of someone I'd known less than a fortnight.'

His face lifted. His eyes blazed. But he didn't say a word.

'I wasn't thinking about Travis. I wasn't weeping about Travis. I was thinking about you. Missing…you.'

He had nothing to say to that.

'Nothing felt right without you there,' she whispered.

Agony blazed from his tired eyes. 'Do you understand how hard this is to hear? Now?'

It was too late.

Something grasped at her organs and fisted deep in her gut.

She gathered up her handbag. 'I don't want you thinking badly of me, Marshall. I don't want you remembering me as the outback psycho in a bus. I have years' worth of coping mechanisms that I need to unlearn. I barely know where to start. It's going to be a long work in progress.'

She stepped up to him. Determined to get one thing right in their relationship, even if that was goodbye.

'But I'm on my way. Thanks to you. I just didn't want you never knowing how much you helped me. What a difference you made. I'm just sorry I couldn't return the favour. I'm sorry I hurt you.'

She pushed up onto her toes and pressed a kiss to his face, over the corner of his mouth, and then whispered into it, 'Thank you.'

Then she dropped back onto her soles and turned for the door.

'Eve.'

His voice came just as she slid her hand onto the heritage doorknob. But she didn't turn, she only paused.

'What about that bridge?'

The one over the void where her love for Travis used to be?

'I guess I won't be needing it,' she murmured past the ache in her chest. 'It doesn't go anywhere now.'

He stepped up behind her and turned her to face him. 'Where did it go? Before?'

As she spoke, her eyes moistened and threatened to shame her. But she didn't shy away from it. She was done hiding her emotions.

'Someone once told me about a garden,' she breathed, smiling through the gathering tears. 'One which used to be barren rubble. With old stone walls and handmade trellises, and where someone had planted a beautiful, fragrant vine. That's where it went.'

He swallowed hard. 'How will you visit it with no bridge?'

'I won't,' she choked. 'But I'll imagine it. Every day. And it will grow without me—up and over the trellis, through the cracks in the wall. And eventually it will cover up all the rocky and exposed places where nothing could thrive.'

And then she'd be whole again.

Marshall glanced away, visibly composing himself. And then he spoke. 'There's something you need to see.'

He slid his fingers through hers and led her out through the front door and down the paving stones to the rear of the house where a large timber door blocked the path. He moved her in front of him and reached around her to open the door.

It swung inwards.

And Eve burst into tears.

She stepped through into the garden of her imagination. Complete with trellis, flowering vines, stone wall and even a small fishpond. All of it blurred by the tears streaming down her face.

All so much prettier than she could ever have imagined.

'Don't cry, Eve,' Marshall murmured right behind her. Closer than she'd allowed herself even to dream.

Which only escalated the sobs that racked her uncontrollably.

'It's so perfect,' she squeezed out between gasped breaths.

'I made it for you,' he confessed. 'It was the first thing I started when I came here.'

Her body jerked with weeping. 'Why?'

'Because it's yours—' he shrugged, stroking her hair '—it was always yours.'

He turned her into the circle of his arms. Warm. Hard. Sweaty from a day of work. Heartbreakingly close. One arm pulled her tighter, the other curled up behind her head so that he could press his lips there.

'You are not some outback psycho,' he soothed into her hair. 'You're passionate and warm and you feel things intensely.'

Maybe she could now that the ice inside her was starting to thaw.

'I wanted all that love you kept in reserve for your brother,' he breathed. 'I hated that Travis was hoarding it. That he'd just walked away from it as though it wasn't the most precious commodity on earth.'

She pulled back and gave him a watery smile. 'He doesn't want it.'

'Someone else does, Eve. Every single bit of it.' Grey eyes blazed down on her. 'I don't care where it comes from, or where it's been. I just care that it's here, in your garden. With me.'

She curled her hands in his shirt. 'You don't hate me?'

'I never hated you,' he soothed. 'I hated myself. I hated the world and everything in my past that stopped me from being able to just love you. And I was angry at myself for trying to be your champion and fix everything, when all I did was make things worse for you.'

'If you hadn't found Travis, I'd still be driving around the country, heartbroken.'

'If I hadn't found Travis, I'd still be driving around with you,' he avowed. 'I would never have left that easily. I would have just given you some breathing space. I was trying to protect you, not control you.'

'I couldn't face the road without you,' she admitted. 'That's why I went home.'

'I have a confession to make,' he murmured. 'This farm wasn't just about MacKenzie Falls. I picked it so that your father wouldn't have to lose you twice.'

She peered up at him and he tackled her tears with his smudged flannel shirt. 'Lose me where?'

'Lose you to here,' he said, kissing one swollen eyelid and then the other. 'To me.'

Breathless tension coiled in her belly. 'You wanted me to come here?'

'I wanted you with me.'

'Five minutes ago you said it was too late.'

'Eve…if I've learned anything from you it's that surviving is not enough. I survived by leaving my mother and brother behind but it didn't change anything—it didn't change me. I've been on emotional hold since then, just like you. And that can work to a point but it's no good forever. At some point I had to take a risk and start believing in people again. In you.'

'I let you down so badly.'

'I was expecting it. I would have found it no matter what.'

Confused joy tripped and fell over its own feet in her mind. 'You believe in me now?'

'Better, Eve. I believe in myself.'

'And you want me to stay here?'

His lips, hot and heavy, grazed hers, and it wasn't nearly enough contact after so long. She chased his touch with her own.

'I want you to *live* here,' he pledged. And then, in case her addled mind really wasn't keeping up, he added, 'With me.

And the forest. Somewhere we can retreat to when our crazy all-consuming families get too much. Somewhere we can just be us.'

A joyous blooming began somewhere just behind her heart.

'I'll always worry about him,' she warned. She wasn't simply going to be able to excise Travis from her life the way he'd done to her. Once a big sister, always a big sister.

'I know. And I'll always have the family felon to help keep tabs on him.' Then, at her quizzical expression, he added, 'Long story.'

'Everything I said—'

'*Everything* is in the past, Eve. I'm asking you to choose the future. I'm asking you to choose me.'

The last time he'd asked that of her, she'd chosen her brother. And broken Marshall's soul.

She slid her arms around his gorgeous, hard middle and peered up at him from the heart of their fantasy garden.

'No,' she said breathlessly, and then squeezed him reassuringly as he flinched. 'This time *I choose us*.'

\* \* \* \* \*

# Luke hadn't bargained on the new cook.

Sure, Rosa had asked if her niece could take over while she spent some of her vacation time with her daughter, who was expecting a baby soon. Trusting the older woman completely, he'd said sure.

He hadn't thought about Josie being a *woman*.

It had been so long since he'd looked—really looked—at a woman, that when she'd glared at him from her car, blue eyes narrowed, with the pepper spray can in her hand, he'd been shocked to feel the unwelcome rush of attraction. And she was a self-confessed city girl to boot, which was a huge no-no in his book. He'd married a city girl.

He was no longer married.

So to feel something for someone who wore three-inch spiked heels to stomp across a muddy, wet road in the wilds of Montana wasn't a good sign.

But damn, they'd looked good on her, even in the mud and rain.

# FROM CITY GIRL TO RANCHER'S WIFE

BY
AMI WEAVER

Published in Great Britain 2015
by Mills & Boon, an imprint of Harlequin (UK) Limited,
Eton House, 18-24 Paradise Road, Richmond, Surrey, TW9 1SR

© 2015 Ami Weaver

ISBN: 978-0-263-25119-7

23-0315

Harlequin (UK) Limited's policy is to use papers that are natural, renewable and recyclable products and made from wood grown in sustainable forests. The logging and manufacturing processes conform to the legal environmental regulations of the country of origin.

Printed and bound in Spain
by CPI, Barcelona

Two-time Golden Heart Award finalist **Ami Weaver** has been reading romance since she was a teen and writing for even longer, so it was only natural she would put the two together. Now she can be found drinking gallons of iced tea at her local coffee shop while doing one of her very favorite things—convincing two characters they deserve their happy-ever-after. Ami lives in Michigan with her four kids, three cats and her very supportive husband.

To my parents, Jan and Nancy.
Thank you for all you've done and all your support.
It means the world. Love you guys.

## Chapter One

After six hours in a middle-of-nowhere airport, two turbulent flights and a bottom-of-the-barrel rental car, Josie Callahan almost wasn't shocked when she ended up in the ditch on a dark, out-of-the-way Montana road. In what seemed to be a monsoon.

She swallowed what felt dangerously close to hysterical laughter, because at this point, after how awful her day had been, what was the point of getting mad?

Just to check, she dug her phone out of her bag, then almost immediately dropped it back in. No service, of course. It had been hit or miss all day.

Since she had no idea where she was, how far she was from the ranch—this car had no GPS—and her phone wouldn't work, she plopped her head back on the headrest and squeezed her eyes shut. She was hungry, but all she had was a squashed granola bar in her purse and half a bottle of water. No chocolate, unfortunately.

She opened her eyes and gave the rain that was coursing down the windshield a baleful glare.

Where she came from, none of this would be an issue.

Light bounced somewhere down the road. Josie squinted out the rain-streaked window. Lightning? It couldn't possibly be a car out here on this godforsaken road. Could it?

It was getting steadily closer, and she could see the lights were in fact headlights, on what seemed to be a huge truck.

The truck slowed, then stopped on the opposite side of the road, so she wasn't blinded by the lights. Josie scrambled for her pepper spray, her heart pounding. Her hysteria from a few moments ago had turned to a quasi panic. She saw the truck door open, and a tall man stepped out.

She gripped the can tightly. Okay. She was on the road—she hoped—to the Silver River Ranch. Her aunt knew she was on the way. It was possible he was looking for her.

He tapped on her window. She lowered it a few inches and lifted her can of pepper spray so he could see it. The rain splashed in, cold on her skin, but he wore a cowboy hat. The rain ran off the brim. He had sharp blue eyes that caught her attention.

"Are you Josie Callahan?" His voice was deep and a little hoarse, and she blinked.

"I am," she said, holding the can steady. "Who are you?"

"Luke Ryder. Your aunt sent me to check on you." He stooped a little more and lifted a brow. "You don't need the pepper spray, ma'am."

Oh, hell. She lowered the can. No, she didn't need it. Luke Ryder was a well-known retired country star and her aunt's employer. She dropped it in her lap, thankful she hadn't accidentally discharged the can. On herself. The way this day had gone, it wouldn't have surprised her. "Right. Well. Thanks."

"Why don't you get in the truck and I'll grab your bags. You're not that far from the ranch, and Rosa is anxious to see you." There may or may not have been a note of censure in his voice, and she bristled just a bit. Rosa had told her to wait, to come in the daylight, but Josie had had it after everything had gone wrong and had just wanted to *get there*. Guilt swamped her. It seemed as if she was always causing people anxiety. "I couldn't call her. My phone—"

"No service out here for regular cell phones. That's why she sent me." He opened the door as she hit the button to roll the window up. She twisted to grab her coat from the backseat and got her purse and laptop bag. He extended his free hand and, after a second's hesitation, she took it and he pulled her out of the car. She was a little surprised at how tall he was—even though she was in heels he topped her by a head.

Despite the chill in the air, his palm was warm and rough as it slid over hers. The little shiver that ran down her spine had to be from the shock of the cold rain in late August, not his touch.

"Go ahead and get in the truck," he said. "I'll get the rest of your stuff."

"Thank you," she said, and marched across the sodden, uneven road, her boots with their three-inch heels sinking into the dirt. She was afraid she was going to lose one. They, like her, were made for city sidewalks. In retrospect, probably not the best footwear for Montana.

She climbed into the big red dually pickup and sank into the buttery leather seats. This wasn't what she'd expected. She'd thought it'd be threadbare, dirty, more of a working truck for a cowboy. Which she knew from her aunt was what Luke considered himself now. It smelled like—

Luke.

As he opened the back door of the truck and put her bags in, she got another whiff of the fresh air and rain mixed with the scent of laundry soap and something a little spicy. She stopped herself from taking a deep inhale.

She'd been involved with a celebrity once. It had cost her more than she'd ever expected to pay. She wasn't going to fall into that trap again, not for love or money.

"I took everything out of the trunk," he said, turning slightly toward her so she got the whole effect of those eyes. *Oh, my.* "Is there anything else you need?"

"No, that's everything. Thank you." Her tone was a little prim, even to her own ears.

He arched a brow. "Those are two, full, heavy suitcases. How did you get them on the plane?"

She gave him a tight smile. "Paid extra. Of course." She'd packed a few of her favorite pans and utensils. She wasn't going to explain that to him.

"What about the car?" she asked as he climbed in the truck. "Can we just leave it there?"

"We'll have to for tonight. In the morning I'll come back and pull it out. I'd like to be able to see if there's any damage."

She swallowed a sigh. Damage to the rental car. She'd bought the insurance policy that they offered and she hoped it would cover it in this situation. She'd worry about it in the morning. "All right. Thank you."

"You're welcome." He put the truck in gear and made a series of short turns that eventually had the big truck facing the other way on the road. Josie just sat there, her hands in her lap. It was quiet in the truck, except for the rhythmic thumping of the windshield wipers. If she wasn't careful, it could lull her to sleep. Her day was finally catching up to her. She'd gotten up at four that morning to catch her flight. She glanced at the clock on the dash. It was almost nine now.

Los Angeles seemed like a lifetime away. That was probably for the best. She wondered if Aunt Rosa's no-gossip policy extended to her, too. Had she told Luke about Josie's recent troubles?

She sneaked a little look at his profile, which was illuminated by the dash lights. His chin was strong and his hair was cut short under that hat. His shirt was soaked, and did a nice job of outlining strong arms. Aunt Rosa didn't say much about her famous employer, but she had said he was a hard worker. Those arms seemed to be proof of that.

Not that she was looking, of course.

She tore her eyes away and fixed them on the bit

of road she could see in the swath of light from the truck's headlights. The rain ran in rivulets down the sides of the road, and a washout from that was probably what had pulled her off the road and into the ditch.

"Thank you," she said finally, "for your help. I am sorry for making you come out in this weather."

"You're welcome. Did she tell you to wait until morning?"

Now she heard the note of censure in his tone. But all Josie had wanted was to get away from the airports and into a real bed. "She did, yes."

He glanced at her. "You didn't think that maybe she knew what she was talking about?"

Josie threaded her fingers together so tight it hurt. "Of course I did. I just thought—" She trailed off. She'd thought it couldn't be that bad. That *remote* meant a little ways out from town, that roads were paved, that there'd be people around. Somewhere. That she'd just be *out in the country*, not in the middle of nowhere in a monsoon. She combed her hair back from her face. Her neat knot had given up hours ago. "I was stupid. I'm completely aware of that."

"Stupid can get you killed out here," he said mildly, as if he was pointing out the obvious. "Soon enough this won't be rain. It'll be snow. It could take days to find someone who's wandered off."

A little shiver ran over her skin. She'd be gone before the snow set in, thank God. "Point taken. I'll be careful." Not that she'd be driving anywhere. She'd been driving for almost an hour past the last little town when she'd gone in the ditch. There'd be no quick trips out for anything, clearly.

Not like her neighborhood in LA, where she could walk everywhere if she wanted. She massaged her temples with her fingertips.

"Rough day?"

She laughed, because otherwise she'd start crying. And maybe never stop. "You could say that." Her past few months had been a series of *rough days*. She was due for something better. Sometime. Any time. It was why she was up here in Montana instead of back at home in California trying to salvage her career.

Which, of course, was beyond fixing, as was her life as she'd known it. Stupid didn't just kill a person. It could cost them everything.

Luke made a turn onto a tiny road that she didn't even see in the rain and the dark, which meant she'd have missed it if she'd been on her own. They bumped along a rutted road for a quarter mile or so before passing through an open gate under an arch. They wound a little farther, and over a rise the house came into view.

Josie couldn't contain her gasp. Even in the dark, she could see the house was a huge log home. Not a cabin—her aunt had referred to it as a cabin! A cabin was smallish. This place was closer to a mansion. Lights were on in many of the windows, and the front porch was illuminated as well, showing a row of Adirondack chairs. Luke pulled the truck off onto a short gravel drive that opened to a parking area. He stopped next to a low stone wall with soft lights set into it.

"We'll have to make a run for it," he said. "I can't

get any closer than this." He cast a doubtful eye in the direction of her feet. "Don't break an ankle, please."

She snapped out of her awe and grabbed her laptop bag and purse. "Oh, I won't. I can run in these. I'm a city girl, born and raised." This was not a plus out here in the wilds of Montana, but she'd make it work for the next couple of months.

"That's what I was afraid of," he said, low enough she almost didn't catch it, and got out, opened the back door and grabbed a suitcase. She got the other one, and it bumped along behind her as she half walked, half ran to the porch behind Luke, whose long stride made it impossible for her to keep up without trotting.

The heavy front door swung open. Aunt Rosa was framed in the light from the house, anxiety and relief etched on her face. "Josie! Oh, thank God you're okay."

Josie walked into her aunt's embrace, even though it was awkward with all the bags she was juggling and she was soaking wet. "I'm sorry. I'm so sorry."

Aunt Rosa gave her a fierce hug. "Just like your daddy. Stubborn." Her tone was affectionate, not scolding, but Josie still felt bad. "Let me go grab you a towel. Wait right here." She hurried off, and Josie and Luke came all the way in, the suitcases trundling awkwardly over the threshold. Luke came to a stop right behind her, and she felt the heat of his body. It was an odd sort of awareness, one that made her uncomfortable.

"I'll put this in your room," Luke said quietly, and she turned partway around and nodded, making brief eye contact with him.

"All right. Thank you. For all your help."

He tipped his head at her. "You're welcome." He strode off, and Josie pulled her gaze away when it snagged on his broad shoulders and looked around the room instead.

The place was clearly even bigger than it looked, with huge vaulted ceilings and a fire crackling in a massive fireplace with floor-to-ceiling stone on the hearth and up the chimney, all the way to the ceiling. There were two full-size leather sofas and a couple deep chairs covered in what looked like chenille. Magazines were stacked on the end tables. A rug in deep colors anchored the space, in an intricate woven pattern. The walls had been left natural, so the logs seemed to fade away, and she guessed the focus was on an incredible view of the ranch and mountains out the floor-to-ceiling windows that covered the back wall. It was a room that could have been intimidating, but somehow felt homey and lived in, and Josie wanted in that moment to curl up on one of the couches in front of the fire and go to sleep.

Aunt Rosa hurried back down the hall with a towel, which Josie took gratefully.

"Thank you," she said, then gestured at the room. "This is—amazing."

"Yes. Actually, this part is the original house his father built. Luke and his brothers added on to it. Tomorrow you'll be able to see the view. I don't know if Luke told you, but this kind of rain isn't typical for this time of year."

She managed a smile. "So I just got lucky?"

Aunt Rosa smiled and patted her arm. "Something

like that. Now, let's get these bags to your room so you can get into something dry, then I'll feed you."

Josie pulled the handle on her suitcase and looped the other two bags over her shoulders, waving off Aunt Rosa's extended hand. "I've got them. But thank you."

She followed her aunt's trim figure down the hall past that wonderful fireplace and was surprised to meet an older woman coming out of a room right at the beginning of the hall. She moved slower than her age would indicate, with a walker, and a bag of what appeared to be knitting supplies. Her smile was friendly as she saw them. "Well, hello. You must be Josie. I'm Alice Ryder, Luke's mother."

Josie extended her hand. "I am. Nice to meet you, Alice. Thanks for sharing your home with me."

Alice chuckled. "This is Luke's home. I've got my own a little farther down the lane. I'm a temporary guest."

"Alice had her hips replaced," Aunt Rosa explained.

"The boys insisted I stay here so they can keep an eye on me," Alice said cheerfully, and then her smile faded. "I'm glad you got here safe. This place is hard to find in the daylight, much less the rain and dark."

"Yes. I learned that the hard way," Josie admitted. Luke had been clear on her folly, and he'd been right to call her on it. Sheer stubbornness mixed with exhaustion had colored her judgment, and look where that had gotten her. "It's a mistake I won't make again."

Alice smiled at her. "I'm sure you won't. Now you get settled in and relax."

"This is a gorgeous house," Josie said as they continued on.

Rosa nodded "It is lovely. I love it here. But it's time for me to go spend some time with Kelly."

Rosa's first grandchild was due next week. "I know she'll be thrilled to have you around."

Rosa laughed. "Considering how long she waited to have children, she's not surprised that I want to be there." She paused to open a door a few steps down. "This is your room."

Josie followed her in. The bedside lamps were already on, which gave the room a lovely glow. She set her bags down on the floor, next to the one Luke had already dropped off. She thought she could catch a whiff of his scent lingering in the air. *Crazy.*

"You've got a view of the mountains," Rosa said. "In the morning you'll be able to see it."

"It's a lovely room. So—serene," Josie said. And it was. The walls here weren't log. They were painted a very pale lilac gray, a color that felt a little like twilight. The carpet was cream and very thick underfoot. The queen-size bed had a light blue quilt and a white coverlet folded over the end. There were a few framed photos on the wall, shots of what she assumed was the ranch. A small sitting area rounded out the space, with a television.

And a cattle skull over what turned out to be the bathroom.

"Yes," Rosa said, following her gaze with a good-natured sigh, "the senses of humor around here tend

toward warped. I can take it down if you'd rather not
look at it every day."

"Ah, no, it's fine," Josie said, eyeing it warily. She
was in the West after all. "It lends character."

Rosa gave her another hug. "I'm so glad you're
here."

"Me, too." Josie's stomach growled, and they both
laughed. "So there's dinner?"

"Oh, yes," Rosa said and smiled. "Change if you'd
like, then follow your nose to the kitchen." She left,
pulling the door shut behind her.

It took Josie only a few minutes to use the bathroom and put on yoga pants and a long-sleeved
T-shirt. She pulled her hair up in a ponytail and stared
at her reflection with a wince. Pale, with dark circles
under her eyes, she looked as exhausted as she felt.
While she'd jumped at the chance to get out of LA,
she wasn't sure after her adventures today that she
was cut out for this kind of place.

She took a deep breath. She could do it. It was six
weeks in the middle of nowhere, cooking for four
people. She'd spent the past few years cooking for
critics and crowds, her life consumed by her career.
How hard could it be?

## Chapter Two

Josie slept like a rock, and woke up confused when her smartphone alarm went off. She never slept through the night, in fact had prescription sleep medication that she tried not to take but often had to after several restless nights.

Blinking the sleep from her eyes, it took her a few seconds to remember where she was. The Silver River Ranch. She got up and hurried through her morning routine. Rosa had said she was usually in the kitchen by five, and it was nearly that now.

She hurried through the dark house and nearly screamed when a shadow detached itself from the darkness near the fireplace and hurtled itself at her, panting.

She darted behind a chair and whacked her shin on something hard. She bit back a curse and rubbed her aching leg as the shadow—a dark-colored dog— nosed her, tail going a mile a minute.

"You scared me," she said accusingly, and the dog sat, tail still going, apparently unfazed by her tone.

She sighed and gave the dog's head a quick pat, her heart still racing. She wasn't a fan of dogs. Or animals in general, though she'd taken riding lessons as a teen. She'd never had a pet in any of her thirty-two years. Her parents had been too busy, and she'd followed right in their footsteps in terms of throwing herself wholeheartedly into her work. No time for houseplants, much less a pet.

She moved around the dog, who trotted behind her into the kitchen. It already smelled heavenly, and most important, like coffee. Aunt Rosa looked up with a smile. "Good morning. Did you sleep okay? Ah, I see you met Hank."

"Good morning. I did, thanks." She decided not to mention her little run-in in the living room with the furniture. Getting spooked by an animal seemed like a poor start to her job here. "You let the ranch dogs in the house?" Apparently giving up on Josie, Hank trotted over to Rosa, who rubbed his ears.

"Not the working ones. When they get old or can't work for some reason they'll usually get adopted by a family member. Hank is Luke's dog." To the dog, she said, "Go lie down, Hank." He gave Josie another long look, then meandered out of the kitchen.

Rosa nodded toward the stack of white mugs on the counter next to the huge coffeepot. "Help yourself."

"Thanks." She moved around the island and poured a cup, adding a little milk and sugar. She closed her eyes as she took a sip. "Wow. This is really excellent coffee, Aunt Rosa."

"Luke wants only the best," Rosa said cheerfully, and Josie's stomach soured just a little. *Only the best* was a familiar refrain. From her parents, from Russ.

She forced her lips into a smile. "Well, he got it here, for sure." She set the mug down with a solid *clink* on the granite counter, eager to get started. "So...where do I start?"

The next hour passed in a comfortable blur of cooking and preparation. Josie enjoyed the chance to cook with her aunt, and the time passed quickly. She eyed the mountain of food on the platters and Rosa, catching her expression, laughed.

"Yep, only three men and then you and I and Alice. But remember, this isn't just a nice meal out. This has to fuel them for hours and they can't just run in and grab a snack. They'll put a hurting on it."

Almost on cue, Josie heard the low rumble of men's voices and they entered the kitchen. Her gaze landed on Luke first. He just had on worn jeans and a flannel shirt over a T-shirt and the same hat as the night before, but her pulse gave a little skip. He gave her a polite nod. Before she could respond, two big guys stepped between them, and she looked up at them, startled. Her first thought was she'd never seen such good-looking siblings. All of them were tall and lean, with similar blue eyes, but their hair color wasn't all the same. Luke's was darker brown and these two were lighter. Still, they shared the same wide smile, similar to the one Alice had given her last night.

"Good morning," the taller of the two said with a charming grin. "I'm Cade, and this is Jake. You must be Josie."

"I am," she said, shaking first Cade's outstretched hand, then Jake's. No little zings or fizzles of awareness. Which was good, of course, but why had it happened with Luke? Maybe she'd just been tired. "Nice to meet you guys."

Behind them, Luke already had a plate, which he was heaping with food. Cade winked at her and said, "Looking forward to getting to know you better. Rosa's said a lot about you."

Ignoring the flirtatious first part of his comment, a little shiver of worry ran down her spine. Rosa didn't gossip, but what had she said? Josie hadn't talked a lot about her relationship with Russ, or the financial woes that had dogged them, but with his outsize personality and popular cooking show, he often made the gossip pages.

Rosa was beside her then, her hand light on Josie's arm. "I talked up your cooking skills," she said cheerfully. "As you've worked hard for them."

Josie relaxed slightly. "Ah. Well, I'm not sure you guys want the kind of food I've been cooking for the past year or so. More for show than sustenance." There may have been the slightest tinge of bitterness in her tone, so she smiled at both men to soften it. "So I'm looking forward to cooking real meals again."

They exchanged a bit more good-natured chatter as Cade and Jake loaded up their plates and then left for the dining room, where she could hear the clink of silverware and the low rumble of voices.

"I didn't say anything about your personal life," Rosa said quietly as she carried a platter to the sink. "I just said you were between jobs at the moment and could fill in for me temporarily. I don't know all that happened with you, honey, but I know it must have been bad to put those shadows in your eyes and to bring you all the way up here."

The concern in her aunt's voice made Josie want to cry. She blinked away the moisture. "I won't lie. It's been rough. But it'll all work out." She took a deep breath. "What can you tell me about those two?"

There was a slight pause, then apparently her aunt accepted the change in subject. "Cade is a flirt," she said. "Harmless, but a flirt nonetheless. But he won't push you or take it too far. He just loves women of all ages. Luke is the opposite. He won't flirt at all. Jake is in the middle. They're all good boys. Any one of them would be a wonderful catch."

Josie bit back a sigh. While that was good to know, she wasn't looking for any kind of relationship— long-term or temporary. Of all she'd been through personally, the worst had been realizing that *engaged* hadn't meant the same thing to Russ as it did to her. Thank God she'd figured it all out well before the wedding.

She kept her tone noncommittal. "I think it's wonderful that you think so highly of them, but that's not why I'm here." Then she added, "I'm famished. I haven't eaten a breakfast like this in ages." Sad but true. Yogurt and a piece of fruit usually made up her first meal of the day. Eaten in her car on the way to the restaurant. And that was because Russ had made so many comments about her tasting the food. *Be careful. Too many bites will make you fat.* She'd laughed it off at the time, but in retrospect, it made her slightly ill.

Rosa handed her a plate. "Of course, that's not why you're here. But you never know what might develop. If you close yourself off to possibilities, you might miss something special."

Josie didn't fully agree. She wasn't concerned about missing something special. She intended to keep her heart under wraps for the foreseeable future.

Luke hadn't bargained on the new cook.

Sure, Rosa had asked if her niece could take over while she spent some of her vacation time with her daughter, who was expecting a baby soon. Trusting the older woman completely, he'd said sure. He'd listened to Rosa explain with pride that Josie was a trained chef, and had owned her own restaurant in Los Angeles that people flocked to.

He hadn't thought about her being a *woman*.

It had been so long since he'd looked—really looked—at a woman, that when she'd glared at him from her car with her blue eyes narrowed, the pepper spray can in her hand, he'd been shocked to feel the unwelcome rush of attraction. And she was a self-confessed city girl to boot, which was a huge no-no in his book. He'd married a city girl.

He was no longer married.

So to feel something for someone who wore three-inch spike heels to stomp across a muddy, wet road in the wilds of Montana wasn't a good sign.

But damn, they'd looked good on her, even in the mud and rain.

"Don't you think so, Luke?" Cade's question broke into his thoughts.

Luke looked up from the sausage and gravy he'd been demolishing on his plate. "What was that?"

Cade stabbed the egg on his plate. "Josie. She's a looker."

Since she'd just been occupying his thoughts he shook his head, the denial as much for him as his brothers. "I wouldn't know."

Cade looked at Jake incredulously. "He's blind."

"Or stupid," Jake suggested, but there was a glint of humor in his eyes.

"Or both." Cade looked at him hard. "Luke. It's okay to, you know, think a woman is hot."

He shrugged. "She's not my type."

"Maybe she's mine," Cade said thoughtfully, and took a bite of toast.

Luke leveled a glare at him. "Don't even. She's our employee, not a plaything for you."

A slow smile spread across Cade's face and he pointed what was left of the toast in Luke's direction. "You did notice." He turned to Jake, who nodded as he chewed. "He sure as hell did. Well, well. That's a first, isn't it?"

He'd have to be dead not to notice Josie, but he wasn't going to say that to either of his brothers. Ever. Before he could say anything, Jake held up his coffee.

"Leave him alone, Cade. He wants to ignore her, that's his business and his loss. He's hiding, remember?"

Luke bit back a groan. He'd stepped away from performing, from that life to avoid all sorts of entanglements. His brothers might accuse him of hiding, but he'd wanted to just focus on the ranch, to get it into the black and after years of his father running it on the edge of total ruin. To prove he was more than the kid who couldn't wait to bust out of here with big dreams.

He kept his voice steady. "I'm not hiding. I'm retired. Big difference. We've got a lot to do today. I've got to get that car out of the ditch, so I can't go all the way up to the ridge."

The talk changed direction then, and Luke was more than happy to let it go. His brothers meant well, and they'd tease him, but they didn't know just how destructive his marriage had been—and with the benefit of hindsight, how unprepared he'd been, not only for the spotlight but all it entailed.

He'd learned the hard way he was better off on his own, not caught in the bright lights of Nashville's glare.

Finished with his meal, Luke brought his dishes into the kitchen along with his brothers, who then headed out the door. Josie was on the other side of the kitchen, spooning something into a container. Outside, he could see the peaks of the mountains turning pink with the sunrise.

"Josie," he said, and she turned, spoon in hand, polite expression on her face. "I'm going to get your car. Do you have the keys?"

"I do. In my room. Hang on." She set the spoon down and hurried out of the kitchen. His gaze tracked the sway of her hips as she disappeared from sight.

"Thanks for helping her," Rosa said from her perch at the end of the island, and when he snapped his gaze to her, he realized from the bemused expression on her face that not only had he been staring after Josie's slender figure, her aunt had caught him.

Damn.

He cleared his throat. "You're welcome. Least I can do, after all you've done for us."

Rosa waved his words away. "Nonsense. But, Luke? Be careful. She's fragile. Even if she won't admit it."

Before he could either ask what she meant or deny any interest in her niece, Josie came back and handed him the keys. "Thanks for doing this." Her tone was formal and polite, not the easy one she'd used with Cade and Jake. Just as well.

"You're welcome." A tendril of her short blond hair had escaped from her headband, and he curled his fingers around the keys so he didn't tuck it back in. He added, "That car won't do you much good in a few weeks, though. It can snow here as early as October." It wasn't likely, but she needed to understand where she was. He rubbed Hank's ears when the old dog leaned on his leg.

She frowned, whether at his words or the dog, he wasn't sure. "I know that. It was the only one they had."

He gave Hank a last pat. "We'll take it back. You can use one of the ranch trucks. It'll save you money and be safer for you on these roads."

Josie's first instinct was to snap at him and say she was completely capable of making that choice on her own, thank you very much, but then she realized he was right. He knew this area and she, of course, didn't, as she'd proved last night. She most definitely didn't want to get herself in a situation where she needed him to fish her out of the ditch again. Or worse. She sighed. "All right. Thank you."

"You sore or anything from yesterday?"

Surprised at his concern, she lifted her brows. Her shoulder was, in fact, a little sore from the seat belt. She touched the sore spot. "A little. It could have been much worse."

His gaze sharpened as it landed on her hand. "Do you need a doctor? There's a clinic in town, or a hospital in Kalispell."

Josie dropped her hand and shook her head. "Oh, no. It's fine. I took a couple ibuprofen." She'd taken a hot shower last night and that had helped, too. It had been such a low-speed accident, it was a wonder anything had hurt at all.

"If that changes, let us know. I'll let you know when I'm back." He left her standing in the kitchen as he went out, and didn't look back.

Well.

She huffed out an annoyed breath and propped her hands on her hips. She could not read him. At all. She'd apologized for last night. She had to work here and live here with him for the next several weeks. It would be uncomfortable if he didn't like her.

Rosa came back in the kitchen with Alice, who dropped a bagel in the toaster, despite Rosa's fussing that she sit and let Rosa do it. Their cheerful interaction told Josie that this was a regular morning occurrence.

"Every day, we go through this," Alice told her with a laugh. "And every day, same result. Don't we, old friend?"

Rose pulled a jar of preserves out of the fridge. "Yes, we do." To Josie she said, "Don't be put off by Luke's grumpiness. He's a good man."

She gave both women a wry smile. "I'm sure he is. He doesn't seem to like me much, though." Not that they'd gotten off to the best start.

Alice sighed. "Give him time. You might remind him of his ex-wife."

Josie gaped at her. "What? How can you say that?" She pictured Mandy Fairchild, the petite platinum-blonde country singer, with her huge brown eyes and bombshell figure. Josie was tall and thin. No curves. They couldn't be more different. "Um. No."

Rosa laughed. "I don't think she meant physically, honey." She looked at Alice for confirmation.

Alice nodded as she spread the rich red preserves on her bagel. "That's right. I meant your background. From a big city, in a new environment. Mandy lasted about a month out here. He doesn't know you and he probably thinks you'll bolt as soon as things get tough."

Josie raised a brow. "I'm not staying for long," she pointed out.

"No," Alice agreed. "Of course not. But you know how things can trigger the memories even when you're not expecting it. It doesn't have to make sense."

"True," Josie said. But she didn't think there was anything up here that would trigger anything for her. It couldn't be more different from home. She looked out the huge window over the sink. There was no glitz and glam, but the pink-kissed mountains scraped the sky and took her breath away. "Wow. Oh, my gosh. Look at that."

Her aunt came and stood beside her and looked out. "Yes. I see that every morning and it never fails to make me catch my breath. I love it up here."

Alice smiled as she came up beside them. "I've lived my whole life in Montana. And I've never failed to be humbled by the natural beauty up here."

Rosa carried Alice's plate and coffee out of the kitchen. A few minutes later, she was back. "She likes the living room, where she can see the views and watch the news, too. That reminds me. It's satellite TV out here and it can be a little hit-or-miss in bad weather. Now, I'm heading out in a couple of hours. Let's get you up to speed. I'll show you what I do and you can take it from there."

They spent a good hour at the little table in the breakfast room off the kitchen, where Josie could see not only the mountains but the barns and people moving around. It was hard to believe just a couple days ago she'd been in one of the biggest cities in the world. "Feel free to put your own spin on anything. This isn't a sacred document," Rosa said with a chuckle. "It's just things that work well for me and hopefully for you, too. Not haute cuisine, I'm afraid."

Josie ran her hand over the torn and faded cover. "I wouldn't expect that out here. There's no reason for it. It's comfort food, and hearty meals." And she could work with all of it, make little changes and tweaks that wouldn't take away at all from her aunt's meals. "It'll be fun."

She'd work around the awkwardness with Luke and remember it was only for six weeks. She was tough. She could do pretty much anything for six weeks. Even learn how to live in the wilderness of Montana.

# Chapter Three

Josie called the rental company while her aunt went to finish packing for her trip and made sure she could drop the car off earlier than planned. The problem was, she'd need a ride back from Kalispell. Would a taxi come out this far? It didn't seem likely.

Luke came in the kitchen. He tipped his head in her direction as he headed to the sink to wash his hands and then over to the fridge, where he started pulling out the fixings for a sandwich. "Got the car. It's fine. Some grass and dirt stuck up under the front bumper, and it's muddy, but no actual damage."

Josie expelled a long breath and relief slid through her. She wouldn't have to worry about the money, then. "Oh, good. Thank you."

"Did you talk to the car company?"

Josie turned back to the potato casserole she was

preparing for dinner. She'd pop it in the fridge until it was time to put it in the oven. "I did. I can return it anytime."

"Do you want to go tomorrow? May as well get it taken care of." When she hesitated, not wanting to put him out any more than she already had, he added, "I've got to pick up a part for the tractor over there anyway. May as well take care of both things at once."

She nodded. "Okay. As long as you're sure. I can probably make other arrangements."

He chuckled as she covered the pan in tin foil. "No, you couldn't. It'd cost you a fortune."

She sighed. "That's what I was afraid of." And money was at a premium right now. She'd sunk most of it in the restaurant, only to lose it to Russ.

He touched her shoulder as she picked up the heavy casserole pan. She almost fumbled it in surprise. He'd been so cool toward her she'd never expected him to actually touch her. Even if he pulled his hand back awfully fast. "You'll have to get used to it. It's nothing like where you're from."

Before she could say anything, Rosa came in the kitchen, and Luke gave her a hug. They exchanged goodbyes, and before Luke left, he asked Josie, "Is eight okay tomorrow? I'd like to get the part before eleven."

"Eight's fine," she said and tried not to notice Rosa looking between them curiously. Luke left and Josie smiled at her. "Are you ready? You have everything?"

Rosa patted her shoulder bag. "I think so. And the boys gave me a tablet for the trip, so I can watch movies and read. Wasn't that nice of them?"

"It was," she agreed. "I'm sure Kelly can't wait to see you."

Rosa gave her a big hug. "I can't wait to see her and meet my new grandbaby. But I do wish I had more time here with you. Enjoy your time here. Relax."

Josie hugged her back. "I wish we did, too. But Kelly's waiting for you." She didn't touch the "relax" portion of the comment, since it'd been so long since she'd really relaxed that she wasn't sure she knew how to anymore.

"Give Luke time," Rosa said as Josie walked with her through the house. "He'll come around."

Josie laughed. Aunt Rosa was determined to make her point about Luke. "Oh, no. Not going to happen."

Rosa gave her a little smile, then sighed. "I know. I'm sorry, I don't mean to keep bringing it up. I just want to see you happy. Him, too."

Josie stopped in her tracks and looked around for Alice. The last thing she needed was Luke's mother hearing any of this. "Oh, Aunt Rosa. That's nice of you to say, but there's no way I'm staying here. My life is in LA." What was left of it, of course. But she had every intention of salvaging what—if anything—she could and starting over. She didn't need a celebrity chef to give her credibility.

The next morning she had breakfast done and cleaned up in time to leave. She made sure there was sandwich stuff in the fridge from the leftover roast the night before, since she wouldn't be back in time for lunch, but the men had taken box lunches with them when they went out that morning. She heard

Luke asking his mother if she'd be okay while they were gone. Patty, the wife of one of the ranch hands, would be in the house, watching TV with her, but Josie understood his hesitation. He didn't want anything else to happen to her.

She waved him off. "Luke. I'll be fine. We are just going to watch *True Blood* and knit. It's not as if you're leaving me for a week to fend for myself. I'm healing well and this place is crawling with people."

Josie shrugged into her sweatshirt with a smile. Luke might be grumpy toward her, but he clearly had a protective streak a mile wide when it came to his mother.

She stepped out on the porch to wait. It was a lovely morning, but not what she was used to. When was the last time she'd stood outside and appreciated the morning? It wasn't really quiet—the birds were chattering up a storm and she could hear some of the hands down by the barns, their laughter carrying on the still morning air. The grass was damp with dew and the air smelled—fresh. No exhaust, food scents, the general smell of a city in a hot climate. Nothing like what she was used to. It wasn't eighty degrees already—in fact, it was cold—and there was no smog or traffic noise.

It was a little unsettling. As was the fact she'd nearly overslept. Again.

The door opened and closed behind her and she turned to see Luke standing there. "Sorry about that. I just had to make sure Mom was okay."

She smiled at him. "No problem. I understand." She wondered what her own mother was doing right now. Of course, her own mother was much younger than Luke's. She must have had the boys at a much older age.

"Let's go, then. You'll need to follow me. It'll be easier for you."

Josie got in the little rental car and followed the big truck down the lane to the road. He was absolutely right that this kind of car wasn't suited to this area. But the SUV she'd reserved at her aunt's suggestion had been given away when she hadn't made it to the rental place before the cutoff time. This was what they'd had left.

The trip in the daylight was eye-opening. The views were killer and she could see, after they'd gone a half hour before seeing another vehicle as they neared the small town of Powder Keg, just how remote the Silver River was. The roads near the ranch were rough, too. She wondered if that was by design, to help discourage people from tracking Luke down. Or if it was simply that the county had other things to do than maintain roads that were hardly driven.

They drove through the little town with its general store that, from the signs on its front, advertised it sold everything, including animal feed, groceries and clothing. There were two bars, a diner, a bakery, a drug store. A couple churches. One stoplight. The streets were wide and the little town seemed to crouch down in the shadow of the mountains. It was a working town, not a tourist town, but Josie thought it had an Old West appeal all its own.

Having left Powder Keg behind, it was another fifteen minutes before they reached the highway that took them to Kalispell. Josie spotted a couple huge elk grazing off the road and figured a collision with one of them would end badly for all involved. Especially in this car, which probably weighed less than one of those elk.

Kalispell was much busier. A tiny fraction of the size of Los Angeles, but traffic was one thing she knew how to navigate without problems, and there was plenty of it here. The town was charming, something she hadn't appreciated when she'd first arrived, thanks to all the drama she'd endured. Luke pulled in the rental car place at the airport and she parked the car beside him. He opened the door to get out but she shook her head at him. "This will just take a minute."

She ran in and went through the process. The guy came out and gave the car no more than a cursory glance over, even though she'd told them on the phone it had slid in a ditch. When she had her paperwork, she hurried back out to the rumbling truck and hauled herself in rather awkwardly.

"Thanks," she said. "Where to now?"

He put the truck in Reverse. "The equipment dealership."

She hesitated a second, then said, "Would it be all right if we stopped at the grocery store, too? I know you're in a hurry, but it won't take me long. There are a few things I'd like to stock up on while we're here."

"Sure. Actually, why don't I drop you off there. There's a grocery store just down the road from the dealer. I'll just come back and wait in the parking lot."

She agreed, and he left her at the store and she went in, pulling her list out. There were a few things she didn't know if she could get that she might have to order. She'd have to ask how that worked—did the delivery couriers come all the way out to the ranch? She wasn't even sure how mail got there. Maybe she could arrange for delivery in town somewhere and then pick it up. She made a mental note to ask Luke when he came back.

She grabbed a cart and wheeled it down the spice aisle. This store was bright, with wide, well-stocked aisles. They had a surprisingly good collection of spices and fresh items. She loaded up and checked out. When she came out, she spotted the big red truck, Luke at the wheel, his hat tipped back on his head. He pulled forward, stopping in front of her.

"You find what you needed?" he asked as he opened the back door of the truck, and she settled her bags on the floor.

"I did. They've got a lot in there. Just out of curiosity, if I need to order anything, where is it delivered?"

They got in and shut the doors. He put the truck in gear. "Schaffer's—the general store—is where all Silver River deliveries go. Couple times a week someone goes in and gets the mail from the post office and anything that gets delivered. Hungry?"

She hadn't realized it until right that moment, but yes, she was. "Yes."

"There's a good little diner up here. That okay with you or would you rather do a drive-through?"

She laughed. "I can't think of the last time I ate at a drive-through."

He arched a brow in her direction. "Food snob much?"

She shook her head. "Not so much. Just too busy to bother." It was true. It was also true she'd never left the restaurant hungry.

That thought gave her a little twinge.

"Well, this place has great burgers," he said. "And it won't take long. I know you need to get back."

He pulled in the parking lot of a dingy-looking building. The flowers had clearly not been watered in weeks and the blacktop was cracked and weeds grew through them. Luke gave her a full-on grin, and it stole her breath how it transformed his face. Even with the dour expression he usually wore he was handsome. But the smile was something else. "Don't worry. Trust me, okay?"

"Okay," she said, and got out of the truck. The day was starting to heat up. She took her sweatshirt off and tied it around her waist and followed Luke to the door.

Inside it was every bit as small as it looked from the outside. Eight booths and four tables made up the whole place. Three of those were occupied. The floor was cracked vinyl, but clean. The booth the waitress led them to was slightly sticky in the way all diner booths seemed to be, and while it, too, was faded and old, it was clean. The whole place smelled divine. Her mouth watered.

He handed her a small laminated paper. "All you can get here are burgers," he said. "With your choice of fries or onion rings. So there's no real menu, but this is the list of toppings."

Josie took it from him. So this would be an adventure, then. She was game. "All right."

The waitress came back over with tall glasses of water. "What can I get you to drink today?"

Josie chose a diet soda and Luke an iced tea. Then they placed their burger orders. She went with honey mustard, brie and Granny Smith apples on a burger cooked medium. Luke got so many things on his she couldn't keep track.

The waitress left and came back with their drinks.

"So you closed your restaurant?"

His words jarred her. Luke probably thought he was making polite conversation. He had no idea what a minefield that question was. She took a sip of her soda and traced a finger on the laminate tabletop. "It's not quite that easy," she said, settling on a version of the truth. "I had a partner. He has it now."

If he picked up on the bitterness in her tone, he didn't show it. "What made you leave?"

She managed a smile. "It was time to move on. That's why this was perfect timing."

Luke studied her for a second. There was something there she wasn't telling him, but he wasn't going to press. He knew all about keeping things private, and he wasn't going to make her uncomfortable, especially when he didn't know her very well. "Fortunate for us."

Her smile was more real that time and reached her eyes. "I hope so."

She asked some questions about the ranch, and he was more than happy to talk about it, especially since she seemed truly interested in his answers. The waitress delivered two steaming plates of food, and he saw

Josie's eyes widen almost comically. "I guess I forgot to mention it's enough to feed a couple people."

She folded her napkin in her lap with a small laugh. "I guess so."

He took a bite of his fully loaded bacon cheeseburger and chewed reverently. There wasn't another place in the world like this. If there was, he hadn't found it. And he'd looked in all the cities he'd played over the years he'd been touring with his band.

"This is amazing," she said, and her tongue slipped out to catch a dab of ketchup. His gaze snagged on the motion and heat flared inside him, deep and hot. He picked up his tea and took several swallows, hoping the cold liquid would cool him down. He hadn't expected to react to another woman like that—and definitely not another city girl with no plans to stay.

She looked up then, and he was pretty sure she caught him looking at her like something he'd like to eat. She patted her face self-consciously with her napkin. "Did I get ketchup all over?"

"No," he said, and his voice was a little rough in his throat. "No, you're fine."

She gave him a little frown, and he turned his plate and offered her an onion ring to cover the awkward moment. "Want to try one?"

She picked a small one off his plate and took a bite. She closed her eyes as she chewed. "Mmm. Wow. Amazing."

"Not haute cuisine, I guess." It had mattered to Mandy that there was no place, at the time, to get things like sushi in the area. To find a five-star restaurant that wasn't a steak house.

She opened her eyes and frowned at him. "Good food is good food, Luke. It doesn't all have to be fancy and complicated."

He hid a smile. "Sorry. You're right."

She moved her plate out of the way and leaned forward. It was enough to push her breasts up, and he managed to keep his eyes on her face. With great effort. "I'm trained as a chef, but I'm a cook, period. I love to hang out in the kitchen, experiment with recipes and create new ones. Really, the whole idea of haute cuisine doesn't appeal to me. It was part of what led to my split with my partner. Different visions for a lot of things, the very least of which was the menu."

"I understand." He did. She looked at it as an expression of herself, like he had with music. Still did, even if he didn't perform anymore. He wondered if the split had been personal as well as professional, but it wasn't any of his business.

She picked up another fry and nibbled on it. "Do you think I can get a box? I can't take the fries home, but I'd hate to waste the burger."

He'd managed to demolish his. In fact he'd all but licked the plate clean. "I don't know. I'm sure you can. I've never needed one."

She laughed and the sound flowed over him, almost made him smile. "I'm not surprised."

She did get a to-go box and he paid the bill, after she insisted on leaving the tip. They walked through the Montana sunshine to his truck. She made him feel—lighter. She hadn't once referred to his history as a country star. He allowed so few new people into his world it was always a surprise when that happened, because so many over the years had wanted something from him. Or they hadn't wanted him—they'd wanted the country star.

So while it was refreshing to be with someone who didn't have demands or expectations, it was dangerous, too. He didn't want to let down his guard only to learn he'd trusted the wrong person. Again.

## Chapter Four

Two days later, Josie couldn't get the trip they'd made to town out of her mind. Or how easy it had been to be with Luke. When he let down the gruff exterior, he was a charming, funny man. Between the laugh lines around those incredible blue eyes and the small dimple in his cheek—

*Sexy.*

She shook her head to clear the unwelcome thought. She wasn't even going to go there.

"You up for a little walk?"

Josie started and looked up at Alice, who was standing there with a smile. A little thread of embarrassment ran through her. Thank goodness the other woman couldn't read her thoughts.

"Sure. Where to?" She wanted to ask if it was okay for Alice to do that, but she didn't know the other woman well enough to do so.

As if she'd read Josie's mind, Alice smiled a little wider. "It's okay. We're just going to my house, which is the one down the lane a little way. It's a nice, even path. I need a couple of things. If you don't mind."

"I don't mind at all." She followed Alice out the back door, Hank on her heels. She turned to shoo him back in, but Alice shook her head.

"Let him come. He'll be fine, even if he wanders off."

"Okay." Josie held the door for both Alice and the dog, and watched carefully as the older woman navigated the steps. Hank was very courteous as well, waiting for her to be on the ground before trotting after her and looking back at Josie as if to say, *What are you waiting for?* This late in the afternoon it was comfortably warm out, but not hot. She was still trying to adjust to this weather. Cold enough at night for a fire and a quilt, hot enough during the day for short sleeves. The house didn't even have central air.

"Not long now," Alice said cheerfully. "I go back to the doctor next week. Hoping to get the all clear. Then the boys won't argue when I move back into my own house."

Josie rather thought they'd check on her every hour, but she kept it to herself. Hank stopped to examine a bush, then raised his leg.

"I agreed to stay up here because otherwise they'd be checking in with me every ten minutes. Seemed easier to just be where they are. For all of us," she said on a little laugh.

"That makes sense," Josie said, because even after just a few days she could see how devoted these guys were to their mother. It was a refreshing change. Alice hadn't been kidding—her house wasn't far from the main house at all, but around a curve and behind a copse of trees that made it feel farther away than it was. As a bonus, it added to the privacy for all of them.

"Someday Cade and Jake will build their own houses," Alice said. "For now, they all live in the big house since it's a central location. And—well, and Luke remodeled that house thinking he'd have a big family. That didn't happen. But they each have land on this same property."

"That makes sense," Josie said, caught for a moment on the fact Luke had wanted a big family. She wasn't sure, but she thought his marriage had probably been over before the house had even been finished. But she wasn't going to go there, not with his mother. So she asked the safe question. "How big is the ranch?"

"Almost three thousand acres," Alice said. "Some of that is leased from the rancher to the north. He is dialing back his spread but isn't ready to sell."

Josie's eyes bugged. "Three thousand acres?" She couldn't even wrap her mind around that amount of land. True, she'd seen no other people or signs of people on her drive out here, but given the apparent propensity for half-hidden drives, it was likely she'd missed it. Not many, though. Three thousand acres was an awful lot of land.

Alice laughed. "Yes. It's a big place."

"Wow," Josie said. "I had no idea." She lived in a

condo. With lots of other condos and other buildings. Nothing like this.

The wide front porch was one step up. She followed Alice in and was immediately charmed by the little log house. It had a lovely open floor plan, with the kitchen, dining and living area all open to each other. There was another stone fireplace and the fabrics on the couch and chairs were all soft. There were throws all over and another brightly patterned rug, similar to the one in the main house, was on the floor. The end tables were piled high with books. She could see a bed through one of the open doors at the other side of the room, and the bathroom through the other. The back wall of the main room had sliding glass doors, and Josie could see Alice had an incredible view of the mountains. She wasn't sure there was a bad view anywhere on the Silver River.

If she could build a little house here, this was what it'd look like.

"I love this," she said, and Alice smiled.

"Luke had it built for me. He's very generous. Asked what I wanted. He was willing to go big, bless him, but this is all I need, since it's just me now. It suits me to a T. I do miss the main house," she said with a sigh. "But it was just way more than I needed. I really love my own space, though. So will you help me carry a couple things back?"

"Of course." She helped Alice gather a few items and put them in a bag, which Josie carried. She'd been a little worried that Alice might try to push Luke on her, especially since he'd driven her to Kalispell and they'd been alone for a few hours, but she didn't. Her feelings were decidedly mixed when it came to Luke. He put her off balance, which, for someone who had conceded control unwittingly, could develop into a major issue.

She put him out of her mind as she and Alice walked back to the main house. She'd find a way to deal with this. It wasn't for all that long. It was perfectly okay for her to find him attractive. It meant Russ hadn't damaged her beyond repair.

Alice went back to her room and Josie went back into the kitchen. She had dinner almost done, and the men would be back before too long. She put the finishing touches on the meal and got everything set to be served as they came in through the back door. She was getting pretty good on the timing. She didn't know if it was just luck that had them all coming in around the same time or if this was a common occurrence. Each of the four nights she'd been at the Silver River, the men went back out after each meal until dark. Evening chores, they said. It seemed like a hard life, with long, incredible hours and hard work that never ended and a constant battle with the elements. She'd only been here a week and she had an incredible amount of respect for ranchers and those who chose this life, not to mention a newfound respect for Mother Nature.

She looked again out the long window above the kitchen sink. There were no window treatments and she could see why—the view didn't need anything to enhance it. The sharp peaks, the rolling green pastures, the tiny black dots that she knew were cattle all caught her attention. It was both gorgeous and overwhelming.

\* \* \*

"So," Cade said with a smile as he set his dishes on the counter after dinner, "have you been to the barns yet?"

"No," Josie said. She'd actually been kind of avoiding it. She felt comfortable in the house. Outside— well, that was a whole other story. Even her walk with Alice earlier had been a tad unsettling.

Not seeming to catch her reluctance, Cade said, "Can you come down for a tour tomorrow morning? I've got to meet with a potential buyer for one of my horses at eleven, but if you came down about ten, that would give me time to show you around and you'd still have plenty of time to get your things done."

Josie swabbed the counter with the dishrag. She knew she should go and see for herself how this place was run. Not really seeing any way to decline, she smiled at Cade. "That sounds good. Thanks for the offer."

He told her where to meet him and left the kitchen whistling. She finished her cleanup and the prep for the next morning. Already, she was finding a rhythm here. That was good.

So the next morning after breakfast, Josie dutifully left the house at the appointed time and walked down to the barns, Hank the dog trotting after her. She'd asked Alice if it was okay, and she'd said yes. The yard sloped down to the barn area. It was a good walk. She wore jeans and tennis shoes, not real sure of the proper footwear for a barn tour, but reasonably sure her boots with the three-inch spike heels weren't it.

Hank wandered off as she approached the meeting

place. Cade came up while she was looking after the dog, trying to decide if she needed to call him back or not. Alice had told her before to let him go, but she just wasn't sure.

"He'll go back when he's hungry," Cade said, his voice cheerful. "He knows where the food bowl is. Ready?"

She turned her attention to the handsome cowboy in front of her looking at her with a warm smile. She smiled back. "I am."

She followed him into the depths of the huge barn. It was bigger and brighter than she'd thought it would be, and smelled of horses and leather and hay, all things she remembered from her long-ago days of riding. There were a good dozen or so stalls, most with the doors open, unoccupied. It had an indoor arena, with a soaring ceiling and clerestory windows. She stopped.

"Wow. This is amazing." It rivaled the prestigious barn she'd taken lessons at all those years ago, after her mom had gotten a good job and dated the guy who managed the facility. The outside of this barn didn't give a clue to what was inside.

Cade shoved his hat back on his head. "We've put a lot into this. Patty and Jim can train in here all year round. They even hold clinics in here sometimes," he said, nodding toward the small gallery area at one end. "We've all worked hard to build this."

Josie nodded. "I can see that."

Cade was a knowledgeable guide and clearly loved what he did here. They finished in the horse barn and stepped outside, which brought them face-to-face with Luke.

Josie stiffened at his look. His eyes narrowed as he took in her and Cade. But Cade had a smug look on his face he wasn't bothering to hide as he rocked back on his heels.

Cade gave his brother a nod, but Josie saw Luke's face darken a little. Was he unhappy to see her in his space? That seemed unlikely, but he was hard for her to read. Cade looked from her to Luke, and the smug look turned into a smile.

"You want to finish this, big brother? I thought it'd be a good idea to let Josie get acquainted with the ranch while she's here." He looked at his watch. "I've got to get ready for my client anyway." He touched her arm lightly. "Is that okay, Josie? You'll be in good hands with my brother here."

Luke gave her a nod, but his face remained expressionless. "I've got some time."

"Great. See you later." Cade strode off whistling, and Josie stared after him for a minute, wondering if somehow they'd just been played. Cade hadn't seemed very surprised to see Luke.

Well, of course not. They all worked here after all. And now it was just her and Luke. She looked at him and waited for him to say…anything.

"What did Cade show you?" He was ever so polite. No hint of the fun and humor he'd displayed on their trip to town a few days ago. They were back to the stiffness and formality, clearly. She swallowed a sigh.

Josie turned around and indicated with her hand. "Some of the horses, which he explained was his own business on the ranch. I'm not sure where we were going next, actually."

"Okay." Luke walked toward the back of the barn. "Let me show you something."

Curious, she followed him out of the relatively dim barn into the bright light of outside.

Almost immediately her gaze seemed to hone right in on him, rather than the gorgeous scenery around them. He wore worn jeans that looked as if they'd been made just for him, hugging his rear and legs in a way that made her want to reach out and run her hand over the curve of his butt. Appalled, she jerked her gaze back up to his shoulder blades. His broad back was equally as enticing, with the henley shirt he wore stretched nicely across his back. Goodness. She slid her shades off her head and onto her nose. What was wrong with her? She'd never even looked at Russ that way, as if she just wanted to eat him up, and she'd been planning to marry him.

*Maybe that was part of the problem.*

Maybe. But there was no way to follow that to its logical conclusion. Frankly, just because she thought Luke was hot didn't mean anything more than that. She stepped up beside Luke rather than walk behind him and get herself in trouble, and headed toward the large, round, fenced-in paddock where a trim woman was working a horse.

"Hey, Nikki," he said as they approached the fence. "How's he going today?"

The big bay horse tossed his head, but didn't break stride as Nikki slowly rotated to keep up with him as he loped in a circle at the end of a long line. She

was tall and slim, and in her sleeveless top, her arms
were muscular and browned from the sun. Her long
blond hair was caught in a loose ponytail under her
hat, and Josie thought she bore a striking resemblance
to his ex-wife.

But Nikki's smile was wide and open as she
glanced at them next to the fence, with no sign of anything flirty. And why that mattered, Josie didn't want
to even think about. Maybe after so many years of
being on the sidelines and not noticed, being eclipsed
by the guy with her, it was just nice to not have another woman look at her as though she was the enemy.
"Good. Real good, Luke. I think he'll be ready soon.
I already told Cade."

Luke kept his eyes on the horse and Josie sneaked
a look up at him. He was clearly assessing the horse's
movement, and there was a genuine sparkle in his eye.
She nearly peered closer, but that would be rude. So
instead she looked back at the horse, who had slowed
to a trot. She didn't know much about horses, not really, but she did think this one was beautiful.

"Ready for what?" she asked, leaning on the fence.
The smooth wood was cool on her arms. The sun was
getting warm on her back, but it felt good. The pound
of the horse's hooves on the hard ground was steady
background noise.

"Cade trains top-notch cutting horses here," he
said. "Nikki's one of the best around."

Nikki made a motion and the horse stopped, but
his eye was still on her. She walked over, looping
the rope up, and patted his neck as she led him to the
fence. "What Luke didn't tell you is he's just as good

with the horses as his brother is. Modest to a fault."
When Luke shifted beside her she gave him a knowing grin. "You are." To Josie she held out her hand
and said, "Nikki Thurman."

Josie took the other woman's hand, felt the roughness and strength of her palm from all the ropes and
horses she handled. "Josie Callahan. I'm filling in for
my aunt as the cook at the main house."

Nikki nodded. "That's right. So nice to meet you.
How do you like Montana? You're from Cali, right?"

Luke ducked under the fence and took the horse
from Nikki. She stepped back, but he didn't take him
anywhere. Josie watched as he stroked the horse's
legs and ran his hands all over the horse's body. The
horse didn't flinch.

"I am," she said, shifting her attention to Nikki.
"This is—this is different from what I'm used to.
Beautiful, though. Overwhelmingly so."

Nikki nodded. "I understand. I came here from
a small town in the Midwest—nothing like where
you're from—but it wasn't remote like this, nor was
it beautiful in this way. Montana, and this more remote area especially, is rugged and wild in a way few
places are anymore."

"How long have you been here?" Josie was genu-
inely curious. Nikki was young and gorgeous. This
didn't seem like the optimal place for a woman like
her.

Nikki put her hands on her hips and cocked her
head. The breeze blew her ponytail back over her
shoulder. "Six years? Yeah, six years this winter. Yes,
I came out here in the winter," she said on a laugh.

Luke handed the lead back to Nikki. "He's good. Get video of him and get it up on the site in the next week or so."

"Sounds good." To Josie she said, "Nice to meet you. I'm down here every day if you ever want to keep me company."

"Thanks," Josie said, a feeling of warmth in her chest. Nikki could be a friend. She hadn't expected that out here. "I'll do that."

Nikki flashed her another smile before leading the horse away.

"What kind of site?" She'd known Luke did something with horses, but her aunt hadn't really said a whole lot. And Josie didn't know a lot about this type of business anyway.

"For the horses. When they're ready, they go up on the website. People wait for them to go up."

"So you raise and train them?"

"Some," Luke said. "Some are bought at auction. And sometimes Cade will take on someone's horse and train it for them. But that takes a lot of time. Nikki and Jim, who's not here today, are the trainers, and my brothers and I train, too. Cade really runs this end of the operation. No thanks to our father."

"I see," she said carefully.

Luke didn't look at her. Instead, he watched Nikki lead the horse back to the barn. His tone was almost expressionless, but she saw a muscle tick in his jaw. "When I got back here after—after everything ended in Nashville, the ranch was in bad shape financially. My father had made some risky decisions to try to save this place and then he died before he could really make them pan out—if they would have panned out at all. We almost lost the whole thing because of his carelessness. So when Cade wanted to do this it was a far more calculated risk. He's been known for years for his way with horses. We've all worked together to use our strengths to make this place profitable. My dad never would have understood how something like this works. He wasn't any kind of a team player, even when it came to his kids."

*Chapter Five*

There was no real way to respond to that, so Josie just said, "How is it doing?"

"Thankfully, really well. It's been going about seven years now. Cade brought Nikki in as soon as he could and Jim right after. The first year was no profit, but we told Cade to stick with it." He turned from the paddock and started back toward the second barn, the one she hadn't seen yet. "I'm glad he did."

"I'm sure," she agreed.

"Do you ride?"

The question shouldn't have caught her off guard, considering what they were discussing, but it did. "I do. Well, I did. It's been many years since I was on a horse." Like nearly half her life ago, actually, now that she thought about it.

"Do you want to ride out with me tomorrow? I'm going up to the ridge in the northern pasture—" he pointed in the direction "—and it's a pretty easy ride and an amazing view. That way I can show you more of what we do out here."

She snapped her mouth shut before he turned around and saw her standing there with it hanging open in shock. Since he was looking at her expectantly, she said, "Yes. I'd like that."

*What did you just do?*

Not seeming to notice her flustered state, he smiled at her, the full-on smile that made her forget her own name for a heartbeat. That wasn't good. "All right. We'll ride out after breakfast. Say, eight? That give you enough time?"

"Sure," she said weakly. "Eight's fine." What she should have said was "no, thanks." Josie walked next to him, and in this huge space, their arms still managed to bump into each other. It threw her off a little bit, yet neither of them made any move to walk farther apart.

"You'll need boots," he said, glancing at her sneakers. "If you don't have any that are appropriate, Rosa has a few pairs. They are probably in the mudroom. If not, my mom probably has extras for sure."

"I'll find something," she assured him, trying not to laugh at the idea of her boots, which she'd bought on sale but had still cost her more than six hundred dollars, actually on the back of a horse. They were city-girl boots. Not country-girl boots. She'd nearly destroyed them slogging through the mud when she'd gotten here. The death knell for them might just be an actual horse.

He stopped at the barn entrance. "Thanks for coming out here today."

"Thank you for showing me," she said, and meant it. "Cade thought it'd be a good idea for me to see what goes on here. I'm glad I did."

Hank trotted up then, all wagging tail as he sniffed both Josie and Luke. Luke rubbed his ears. "Hey, boy. You come out with Josie?"

Her heart sank as she eyed his coat, which was wet, dirty and matted in places. "He didn't look like that when he came out. Hank! What the heck did you get into?" The dog wagged harder but didn't answer, of course.

Luke laughed, and Josie was momentarily awestruck. God, he was gorgeous when he stopped being grumpy. Apparently being around animals made him happy. "There's a pond down the way. Lots of tall grass around it. He went exploring is my guess." He gave the dog another pat. "You'll need to hose him off and brush him down when you get him back to the house."

This time, Josie didn't even try to stop her jaw from falling open. "Hose him off? How am I supposed to do that?"

He gave her that grin. "There's a doggie shower in the mudroom. Use it and stand back when he shakes it off."

Josie thought of the small handheld shower in the mudroom. So that was what it was. She'd thought it was to clean boots. She looked down at the dog doubtfully, who looked right back up at her, tail still wagging. She would have sworn he was laughing at her. She'd never walked a dog, much less washed one. She sighed. "All right. Let's go, Hank."

\* \* \*

She managed to get the dog mostly clean. She also got herself sopping wet—possibly wetter than Hank himself—and dirty in the process. Alice met her in the kitchen and laughed. "Oh, dear. Did Hank win?"

Josie looked down and plucked her shirt away from her body with a laugh. "Looks that way. That was my first dog bath." And hopefully, her last.

Alice patted her arm. "It's a skill. One that develops over time."

"Mmm." She sighed. "I think he knew I was a novice." They both looked at Hank, who was sprawled on his back in the sun, looking for all the world as if the bath had worn him out. She had to laugh.

"It's a dog's life," Alice said fondly, and Josie couldn't disagree.

Josie hurried down the hall to her room, where she washed up and changed quickly into dry underthings, jeans and a hot pink T-shirt. She hung her wet things in the bathroom, since she didn't have time to do laundry right now. She'd prefer to wait until later, when the place wasn't quite so busy. The last thing she wanted to do was run into Luke with her underwear in her hands. That was way too personal. It seemed as if they danced around some kind of unspoken thing, as though if they didn't acknowledge the thing between them, maybe they could pretend it wasn't there.

She was willing to give it a shot.

That night, Josie lay on her bed, the full moon shining through her window. It bathed the mountains in an unearthly light, a cold glow, even though the night was comfortable enough to have the window open. It had cooled down significantly as the sun had dipped down lower and lower.

But the low fire in her belly jumped every time she thought of Luke.

She had her TV on, and a police drama played that she wasn't paying any attention to. To get her mind off Luke, she called her aunt to see how she was doing in Arizona. She'd gotten an email saying Aunt Rosa had arrived just fine but had wanted to give her a few days to get settled before she checked in.

Her aunt answered on the second ring. "Josie! How is everything up there?"

"Just fine," she assured her aunt. "It's been really easy to settle in here. How was your trip? How's Kelly?"

After asking about Alice, Rosa filled her in on all the details of her daughter's final few days of pregnancy, and Josie was content to let her talk away. When Rosa finished up and asked again about the ranch and how Josie was faring, she cheerfully reassured Rosa all was well and she was managing just fine.

"Are you getting along better with Luke?"

Josie held back a sigh. "Yes. Of course. He's a nice guy. They all are," she added.

"The best," Rosa agreed. Josie was tempted to head her off at the pass, in case her aunt wanted to press the issue. But she feared that could be misconstrued as protesting too much, so she said nothing. "Luke got dealt a raw hand. It'd be wonderful to see him come out of that shell." Before Josie could do much more than open her mouth, shocked, Rosa continued on as if she hadn't said anything of import. "I've been very fortunate to work for them. I'm glad you were able to do this, Josie. Thanks so much."

"It is my pleasure," Josie said. After asking her aunt to call as soon as the baby was born—which should be at any moment—they said goodbye and hung up.

*Dealt a raw hand.* Josie turned off the cordless phone and padded out to the office to return it to the charger base. Was that how Luke looked at it? She had no idea. She hadn't asked. Wouldn't ask, as it was none of her business. He'd been burned. She knew that for sure. But she had no idea if he'd be open to trying with someone new—not that she was volunteering for the position.

Far from it.

There was definitely a little chemistry with her and Luke. But it would be the height of foolishness to get involved in any way when she had to leave—and while she was all for the idea of two consenting adults going into something with eyes wide-open, she wasn't a fling sort of girl.

No, she was a committed kind of girl.

So she'd leave the idea of Luke to fantasy. In her experience, men didn't measure up in real life anyway. Her ex certainly hadn't.

But the memories of Luke's hand on her face and the look in his eyes made her shiver. In a good way. She wasn't sure she'd ever been looked at like that. As if he really saw her. All the way into her.

* * *

The next morning, Luke saddled two horses after breakfast, his usual mount, Kipper, and a paint gelding named Zippy—because he was anything but—for Josie. She'd told him at breakfast she'd be down there today, and while he had no reason to doubt her word, it wouldn't have shocked him if she'd bailed. Mandy would have. She'd been all show—and to be fair, she'd never pretended to be anything but what she had turned out to be. It was his own projections onto her that had gotten them in a mess.

He tightened the cinch on Zippy's girth, then walked him a few steps before tightening it again. This guy was known to hold his breath when being cinched up, and the last thing Luke wanted was for Josie to end up on the ground when the saddle slipped.

Then he looked up and saw her walking toward him. His first thought was, *Holy cow!*

She wore jeans that hugged her curves and her long legs, and disappeared into beat-up old boots she must have found in the mudroom. Her V-neck T-shirt didn't plunge nearly enough, stopping just low enough to give him an enticing peek of what it hugged. She carried a zip-up hoodie. Her hair was in a ponytail, and her face was clear of makeup. This was just Josie, and he was shocked to realize he'd never seen a more beautiful woman.

A small bubble of panic lodged in his throat. He didn't want to see her at all. Maybe he should cancel this ride. Maybe she would have done him a favor by bailing. He still wasn't sure what had made him offer.

She carried box lunches and had a tentative smile.

Well, hell, no wonder. He was no doubt scaring her, staring at her as if he'd lost his mind.

"Hi," he said. "Um, you found boots." Then he just wanted to shut his eyes and bang his head on Zippy's saddle. Awesome. Show him a pretty woman and he turned into a master of the obvious.

But she just smiled as she came to a stop in front of him and looked down at her feet. She turned one of her legs to look at the back of the boot. His eye followed the length of her leg. Lord help him. "I did. Aunt Rosa's. Alice had me pack a little newspaper in the toes so they wouldn't slide around, but otherwise they work just fine."

"Good." He reached for the lunches. "Here, let me take those." Packing them in the saddlebags would give him something to do and give him a minute to redirect his wayward thoughts.

She handed them over and slipped her arms in her sweatshirt. He wasn't sure if he was relieved or not that she'd covered up the view he didn't want to enjoy. He could almost feel her nerves so he started talking.

"This is Kipper. He was born and bred here, and I trained him. One of the first ones. He's a great horse. You get this guy." He finished putting the lunches away and turned to place a hand on Zippy's flank. The horse turned his head and blew out a breath that sounded an awful lot like a resigned sigh. "This is Zippy. Don't worry, his name is a joke. He's not zippy at all. Since I don't know your level of experience or comfort with a horse or trail riding, I thought he'd be a good mount for you." He hadn't wanted to overwhelm her, and despite his laziness, Zippy was calm and dependable. A good trail horse.

Josie walked up and touched Zippy's neck, then stroked her hand down the chestnut's silky coat. "Okay. That sounds good. It's been years, like I said, and I've never been on an actual trail ride."

"Then we'll make this one good. Ready?" Luke took Zippy's head. Not that the gelding was going anywhere. "Go ahead up."

Josie mounted the horse in one fluid motion and settled fairly easily into the saddle. He handed her the reins and Zippy stood still, other than to turn his head and look back at Josie with a small whicker. It made her smile. Luke quickly adjusted her stirrups a bit, then mounted Kipper. He turned to check on her. She looked pretty solid in the saddle, sitting as if she knew what she was doing. That was good. "If you're all set, let's get going." Then a thought occurred to him. "Are you nervous?"

She started to shake her head, then sighed. "Yes. A little. It's been a while and I'm not—" She stopped.

"Not comfortable out here?" It didn't surprise him.

"Not really. Not yet," she admitted.

He appreciated her honesty. "There's nothing out here right now that is going to bother us."

Her brow ached at that. "Right now?"

He gave her a grin, hoping to tease her out of it. "After dark is another story."

She shook her head at him, but there was the glimmer of a smile. She probably didn't know if he was kidding or not. He wasn't, but she didn't need to hear that right now.

They were able to ride side by side through the meadow, and he noted that she had a great seat and light hands. She said it'd been a while, but clearly it was coming back to her. Zippy plodded steadily along, head down. Kipper was steady as well, but alert and ready to go at a moment's notice. He patted the black horse's sleek neck.

"Where are we going today?" she asked. "And what are you doing up there?"

They talked as they went, about nothing in particular. She asked questions about the ranch and daily life there. He was happy to answer because she seemed actually interested in what he had to say. It was more than Mandy had ever done. He wasn't sure what it was about Josie that was bringing out the comparisons. This wasn't anything he'd thought about in ages. Mandy would never have ridden out with him, even on a gentle horse. He'd been unable to get her on a horse, period, even in the confines of the ring, because she was scared, which he could work with, but she hated the animals because they were too big and she thought they were smelly, which he couldn't work with. So he hadn't pressed it, but he had wondered how they'd make a go of life on a ranch if she wasn't willing to make an effort.

With good reason, as it turned out—she'd had no intention of staying.

Neither did Josie. But Josie wasn't Mandy. They weren't involved, much less married, and Josie had planned to leave from the start. She was here temporarily.

He could work with that, too.

Noticing that her expression was looking a little tight and her back was definitely stiffer, and mindful of the fact it had been a long time since she'd ridden, he suggested, "Why don't we walk the last little bit? Give you a chance to stretch out your muscles."

She gave him a grateful look. "That sounds good. Thanks."

They dismounted, and she held up a hand. "Give me a second while I make sure my legs still work."

He couldn't help but laugh as he reached for Zippy's reins. "They do. If you ride enough when you're here, you'll adjust pretty quickly." Would she? Or would this be it?

She walked around in a little circle, then took the horse's reins back. They walked together through the meadow. A little farther and they'd have to leave the horses. The last section was too narrow and rocky for the horses to navigate safely.

"Okay," he said. "Here's where we leave these guys." He nodded toward the trail. "Better if we go on foot."

"Oh. Okay." She frowned at the horses. "We can just leave them here?"

"Yep. They'll be ground tied, and they'll just stay here and graze or doze. They'll be fine."

He took out the lunches and the blanket and they started down the trail. The trees weren't that thick, and the underbrush was pretty scant. She must have been looking at the ground, watching her feet, because when they came out into the clearing it took a moment before he heard her gasp.

"Gorgeous, isn't it?" he said. It was. The mountains were spread in front of them, with the rolling valleys at their feet. They weren't really close, but they still felt majestic and imposing. The ridge they stood on was big enough to be comfortably back from the edge, and he looked at her, with her wide eyes and her ponytail blowing in the wind, and he wanted nothing more than to kiss her right there, under the blue, blue Montana sky.

Instead, he spread out the blanket while she took pictures with her phone. She gave him a wry smile and held it up. "No service, but I can at least use the camera."

"Something to be said for that," he agreed.

"Is any of this yours?" She gestured out at the scene in front of them. "Your mom said you own three thousand acres. I'm having a hard time wrapping my mind around that."

He came up next to her and caught a whiff of her scent, which was mixed with fresh air and sunshine in an almost irresistible combination. He knew he should move away so he didn't keep brushing against her, so he could quell this almost insatiable urge to kiss her, but he couldn't do it. "Yeah. From here you can't really see the fence lines, but that road right there?" He leaned around her to point to a narrow snake of gray in the green landscape. The wind blew a few silky strands of her ponytail against his face. Now he was just torturing himself. That was all there was to it. "That's the division between us and the neighbor to the east. We're not at the right angle to see any of the rest from here."

"Wow," she said, and looked up at him with a

smile, and he couldn't help himself. He brushed a few of the loose hairs that were blowing in her face out of the way with his fingers. Her eyes widened, and then her tongue slipped out to run over her upper lip.

That was all Luke needed. He lowered his head to hers, slowly, giving her time to step away because God knew, he wasn't going to be able to. He heard her breath hitch, and then his mouth was on hers and the world fell away.

## Chapter Six

Josie laid her hands on his chest and leaned into the kiss, which Luke tried to keep light, but she tasted so damn good and was so responsive it all too quickly went from a slow exploration to a hot, urgent claiming. He gripped her hips and pulled her snug against him, and she wound her arms around his neck, giving as good as she got. Her mouth was hot and mobile under his.

Then a bird screeched as it wheeled overhead and the spell snapped. She leaped back, her hands still on his arms, her breath uneven, her cheeks flushed. She looked at him, then away, then backed away.

What had she just done? Holy cow, she'd kissed Luke. And more, she'd nearly climbed up his body to get closer to him. Practically crawled inside him. Nothing civilized about that. It was as if he'd ignited something inside her that had been dormant for years—she'd never felt anything like that before.

Luke's face was impassive. She couldn't read him. A little seed of doubt planted in her mind. Maybe she'd misread him, projected her attraction to him onto him? Imagined that he'd kissed her as if he'd been starving and she was the only thing that could satiate him? The whole idea that it could have been one-sided made her feel a little ill.

He cleared his throat, and before he could do something like apologize, which she really didn't want to hear, she blurted out, "What kind of bird was that?"

He blinked at her for a second, then rubbed his hand over his face and looked up at the sky. All of the ease he'd had with her earlier was gone. She felt its absence keenly. "Ah. A falcon, I think."

She edged away from him and toward the blanket. She tried not to think about other uses for that blanket, and the fact they were in the middle of nowhere, where no one but the falcons would see. Goodness. What was wrong with her?

Deciding to meet this head-on, she asked, "Are we going to be able to be normal?"

He smiled at her, but it didn't reach his eyes. There were tension lines around his eyes and mouth now. "We're adults. We'll manage."

It wasn't the best answer, but she wasn't going to push.

She'd thought kissing him would diffuse the tension building in her, building between them. Instead, she was dismayed to realize it may have done the exact opposite—stoked a fire she'd had no intention of seeing through. Far from being sated, the wanting was coiled even more tightly within her.

*Nuts.*

He pulled out the lunches, and she sat on the opposite corner of the blanket from him. He raised a brow. "Don't trust me?"

Flustered, she shook her head. "Of course not." When he laughed, she blushed even harder. "That's not what I meant." It was herself she didn't trust, not so much him. Something rustled in the bushes, and her pulse jumped as she whipped her head around in the direction of the sound. "What was that?"

He hadn't even moved from his laid-back position on the blanket. She couldn't help but stare for a moment at his prone form, completely relaxed. She wanted to crawl across the blanket and kiss him again. Infuriating man. "Squirrel, most likely."

Right. A squirrel. She took a bite of her sandwich and kept an eye out just in case...what? It tried to charge them? The idea made her feel a little stupid.

"We'd know if it were a bear," Luke said calmly. He didn't look up from his sandwich even when her head jerked up and she stared at him. "They smell bad and would make a fair sight more noise." She made a little strangled sound, trying to decide if he was messing with her or not. She settled for not. He held up the last bite of the sandwich. "Thanks for this, by the way. It was awesome."

She smiled a little, guessing that was his intent. "Thanks."

"When you're ready, we'll go back to the horses.

There's a broken latch on a gate down the way that I'm going to replace. You still okay with that?"

She gathered the leftovers and packed them back up. "Of course." No way was she going to allow a squirrel to spook her. Or a kiss to derail her.

"No attack squirrels. I promise."

She sent him a look and got caught for a minute by the grin on his face. "Ha-ha. The ones at the park near my condo are probably more likely to attack than any you have around here. They get a little pushy."

He smiled and his eyes crinkled at the corners. *Oh, my Lord.* The man needed to stop smiling. "There you go."

She fell in behind him as he started back toward the horses. "We don't have bears, though."

"You have muggers," he pointed out, holding a branch for her. "We don't."

"True," she said thoughtfully, letting her gaze rest on his fantastic rear end as he walked in front of her. Might as well enjoy the view. She'd never been such a fan of jeans as she was today. "But they don't generally eat you."

"Is that what you're afraid of?"

She shrugged even though he couldn't see her. "Kind of. I guess." Might as well be honest.

He stopped at the end of the trail. She could see the horses around him, in the clearing. He settled his hands on her shoulders, and she looked up, startled, into those incredible blue eyes. "I won't let anything happen to you." His tone was dead serious, all teasing gone.

She swallowed and gripped the bag tighter. "Okay.

Thanks." For a heartbeat she thought he might kiss her again, but instead he squeezed her shoulders gently and stepped back. Swallowing her disappointment, she followed him out to the horses.

They spent the rest of the time in a companionable, if not fully comfortable, manner. The little currents flared occasionally, and it seemed to Josie the air hummed if they got too close to each other.

It was a new experience for her, and she wasn't sure if she enjoyed it or not.

She watched him fix the latch, noting the black dots of the cattle way out in the pasture. There weren't any nearby, which was just as well—she was still a little surprised by how big they were up close.

But it was hard to tear her eyes off the play of muscles under his T-shirt. He'd stripped off his long-sleeved shirt, and she was captivated by his back. Zippy shifted underneath her, catching her attention for a second, his head dropped low. She was pretty sure he'd gone to sleep.

Luke strode back toward her, his eyes shaded by his hat, his stride over the uneven ground long and confident. Not unlike his animals, she realized. He belonged here, and moved over this land with a sure-footedness she didn't think she'd ever match. He was completely comfortable in his skin, and that was incredibly sexy.

He smiled at her, but it was a little remote around the edges. While that tugged at her a little bit, she knew it was for the best. He'd had time to process what had happened with them and, like her, had clearly decided to let it go.

"Ready to go back?"

Josie looked out over the huge expanse of land and mountains and felt small. "Yeah."

"How'd it go?" Alice said when she returned to the house. Luke had declined to come back up. She'd helped unsaddle the horses, and the other hands had showed her where things went. Luke had been polite but distant, really no different than he'd been before they'd gone on their ride. She had been able to actually see him withdraw deeper and deeper into himself the closer they got to the barns. No one could probably tell the difference, but she could. It stung a little.

A little shiver ran through her at the memory of Luke's mouth, hot on hers, and his body, hard against her. Heat shot through her.

Oh, goodness.

There was no way she could say any of that to Alice. "It was beautiful," she said instead, because it was true. "A really amazing view."

"Yes. It is gorgeous out here. A little sore?" Alice asked, clearly noting Josie's wince when she sat on a bar stool.

She laughed. "A little." Then she paused, took stock of her aching lower half and amended her answer. "Okay, a lot. But I'll be fine."

"Take a hot bath later," Alice advised her. "That'll help. Or sit in the whirlpool tub tonight. That would work wonders."

Well, since she hadn't brought a bathing suit, the regular tub would have to suffice. In fact, the idea of soaking in hot water was heavenly. "The bath is a good idea. Thanks."

She moved stiffly around the kitchen as she prepared dinner that afternoon, but she wouldn't have traded the soreness for a minute less of the time she'd spent out on the horses today. Nerves built a little as it approached time for Luke to come in for dinner. Would he act as if nothing had happened? Could she keep from letting his family know what had happened with them?

She certainly hoped so. She had a feeling he didn't want them to know he was attracted to her, much less that he'd kissed her.

Luke came in and gave her the same nod he always did, the most restrained of his brothers' greetings. She almost sighed. They'd play this as though nothing had happened, then. Fair enough.

He paused before he went in the dining room, concern on his face. "You doing okay? Mom said you're pretty sore."

"Yes, I am," she told him cheerfully, to hide the awkwardness. "Your mom suggested a bath or the whirlpool tub because hot water can do wonders. But since I have no bathing suit, I'll take the bath when I'm done here."

Was it her imagination or did his eyes get hot? Her fingers curled around the platter she held like a shield. But all he said was, "That'll help."

She nodded and he stood there for another awkward second, then left the kitchen.

She watched him go, unsure if she wanted to laugh or scream. Instead, she lightly banged the platter on her forehead, then set it on the counter. It was too bad they couldn't explore this thing between them. She had friends who had casual relationships all the time. But Josie needed more than a man who blew hot and cold, depending on the day of the week, his mood or what she'd worn that day. She'd been there, done that and wasn't going to repeat the experience, especially for something that would have to be a fling.

She'd never had a fling.

She moved the platter into the sink and considered it. It wasn't because she was against flings—she had friends, both male and female, who had them regularly and moved on when it was over, usually with minimal regrets or drama. But Josie had always been a relationship girl, and even those had been few and far between. She was just too busy. Okay, possibly too picky, as she'd been teased more than once.

But she wasn't starting now. Luke wasn't the guy for her, in any sense, no matter how incredibly he kissed or how he made her toes curl. It was too bad, really. It just wasn't a risk she was comfortable taking.

Luke heard the water running in Josie's room shortly after dinner. He knew that usually she sat in the living room with his mom, watching TV and talking, but tonight she'd gone straight there. She'd admitted she was sore from their ride—she'd been moving pretty stiffly by the time she was cleaning up from dinner. She hadn't complained, though. Her smile had been uncertain when he'd come in. Yeah, he'd sent some weird signals out, and had gotten them back in return.

He needed to back off.

When the water stopped, he wanted to bang his head on the wall. He didn't know how to stop the parade of images that ran through his mind like an X-rated reel. Now she'd be peeling off her clothes and slipping into the water. Her face would be flushed from the steam, and maybe she'd moan a little bit when she sank into the water, like she had in his arms earlier when she'd kissed him. Her full breasts would bob gently in the water, her nipples playing peekaboo if she'd added bubbles...

And hell, he was as hard as a rock and aching for her like he hadn't been with a woman in years. This wasn't a situation that was likely to change.

While she soaked in a hot bath, it'd be a cold shower for him. But, hey. At least they'd be naked at the same time.

As he headed into his bathroom, stripping as he went, he couldn't help but think as far as consolation prizes went, it wasn't much.

After a night spent dreaming about her, Luke couldn't help but notice that Josie did her best to avoid him the next day. If she'd known the role she'd played in his dreams last night, she'd run screaming for the hills. He supposed he should clear the air, and say... what? He wasn't sorry he'd kissed her. He was sorry for the extra stress it was going to cause her. But still, she was perfectly polite, poised and friendly as she had been every morning so far, and he doubted anyone but him noticed the difference.

"What did you do to Josie?" Cade asked as they walked to the barns after breakfast.

Luke winced. So much for that hope. Cade, who was completely clueless about a certain other woman, noticed what was going on with Josie? That was rich. "Nothing."

Cade stopped and glared at him. "Nothing? You took her up to the ridge yesterday. Today, she didn't come near you all morning, and the two of you kept looking at each other when you thought the other wouldn't notice. And let's face it. If I noticed, it must have been pretty damn bad."

Luke rubbed a hand over his face. He could see his breath on the crisp morning air. Fall was on the way. "Nothing happened, Cade. Drop it, okay?" He wasn't going to confess to his brother. He doubted she wanted anyone to know about the kiss, and he sure as hell didn't. He'd never hear the end of it. Not to mention people might get ideas he didn't want them to have.

Cade started walking again. "She's a nice woman. She deserves better than a cowboy who won't leave the ranch unless it's under extreme duress."

"Hey. That's not true," Luke started, but Cade held up a hand.

"Yeah, it is. It is. You'll go to Kalispell, but that's as far as you'll go. And that's only been the past couple of years. For the longest time you wouldn't even do that. For a guy who lived in a bus on the road for weeks at a time—"

"Stop," Luke growled. "Everything changed. You know that." Mandy had left him and he'd been played for a fool in front of millions of people. Many of them happened to live in Montana.

Cade sighed. "Yeah. I do. But that doesn't mean it can't change again." He shook his head and walked away, leaving a completely flummoxed Luke standing there, staring after him. What the hell did that even mean?

Trying to set it all aside, Luke lost himself in the duties of the morning. Ranching took all his time and energy, and he was fine with that. They had a great group of hands who were loyal and hardworking, and he knew he did far more than he needed to, but it kept him busy. And truly, after all these years, he didn't miss Mandy. He knew how badly they'd been suited and how unhappy she'd been here. So he knew better than to act any further on the flash of attraction with him and Josie, no matter how powerful it was.

He also knew he was ten years older and no longer under the influence of hormones and the meteoric rise of his career. Who he'd been then wasn't who he was now. He'd thought he had it all figured out. What he'd actually been was foolish and stupid. Reckless. He wasn't any of those things now.

But he wanted to do more than kiss her. There was no point in denying that fact to himself. To feel her under his hands, under his body. She'd clearly freaked out about it, too, which was actually a good thing. Not that he thought she was after him for his name. She hadn't even asked him anything about his career. No money comments—not that either one of those meant she was a gold digger, of course, but he was primed to look for certain triggers, and those were two for him.

Too many people had looked at him with dollar signs in their eyes and never actually saw *him*.

It made him wary and somewhat cynical about others' motivations. So no, Cade wasn't wrong. He did tend to avoid new people unless he had no choice, allowing his family and friends to do the vetting for him. He'd been gone from the country music scene long enough it was pretty safe for him to venture out. No one in Powder Keg looked at him as anything but Luke Ryder, John Ryder's eldest boy.

He was okay with that.

He wasn't lonely. Alone, yes, but not lonely. There was a difference, and if that was starting to pull at him, well, he just needed to remind himself he had everything he needed here in this small part of Montana.

Didn't he?

He looked up at the sound of running feet and saw Larry, one of the hands, coming toward him, his face tight. "Boss, we've got a problem."

## Chapter Seven

"Uh-oh. I wonder what's going on?" Alice leaned forward and peered out the window. "That's Mike's truck."

Josie looked up from the dough she was kneading for rolls for dinner. The concern in Alice's voice caught her attention. "Who's Mike?"

"The vet." Alice frowned. "He's out here often, of course, but I don't remember any of the guys saying they had anything scheduled. I hope nothing's wrong."

Dinnertime came and went.

Josie packed up the meal and kept the meat warm—rule number one, according to Rosa, was to make sure whatever she made could be kept warm, since you never knew when someone would get held up—and she waited in the living room with Alice and Patty, the wife of the ranch foreman.

Both ladies were knitting and attempting to show Josie how to do it. While they made it look simple, their needles clicking along and the rows unfurling, Josie was having a tough time finishing one single row without swearing.

But they were patient and she was determined. It was a good combination. They'd assured her with practice she'd get better at knitting—she just needed to stick with it. Truthfully, it wasn't anything she thought she'd enjoy. But maybe if she could figure it out, she would.

Alice and Patty were clearly worried. She gathered from them this kind of thing often indicated a serious problem, though they didn't say much, not wanting to borrow trouble.

So when they heard the men come in, all three women looked up sharply, then at each other. Josie caught the look the other two women exchanged, then all three of them rose.

"I guess that's my cue," she murmured, and set her pitiful little knitting aside.

When she went in the kitchen and saw their faces, her heart sank. "What happened?"

"Rough day," Cade said. His face was grim, and he looked tired, but her gaze settled on Luke like a homing beacon. There was a furrow in his brow, and she saw the tension in his body.

"Not over yet," Luke added. "We'll eat quick and go back out. Jake is still there. He'll come in when we get back. We've got some sick cattle. We've already lost four." His voice was flat.

"Oh." Josie lifted her eyes to his, saw the pain there. "I'm sorry." What did you say to that?

Luke managed a small smile, but there was no humor in it. "It's life on a ranch."

She didn't know what to say, so she just hurried and put together plates for each of them. They stood at the counter and basically wolfed it down. They talked to Alice about things that were beyond Josie's scope. Before they left, Alice added, "Send Mike up here for a few minutes if you can spare him. If it's going to be a long night, I'm sure he could use some fuel, too."

After dinner they all trooped back out. Josie didn't say anything, just watched as they each snagged a handful of the cookies she'd left on the end of the counter. These guys were dealing with life or death and all she could offer were cookies. It didn't seem right.

"They'll sleep out there, most likely," said Alice, her tone sad. She sighed and a faraway look crossed her face. "In shifts. Just like their father, looking after the animals as though they are children."

Josie couldn't imagine where there was to sleep in a barn. Even though she'd seen it, and had to admit that as far as barns went, it was clean and neat, she still had no idea where one would crash in it. Seemed as if it'd be loud and dirty, but she kept her thoughts to herself.

She went out and sat with the older women for another hour—they'd DVR'd Alice's favorite show—but both of them seemed a little distracted, and when they packed up for the evening, so did she.

She took her sad little knitting project—it couldn't

yet be called a scarf when it was just a few inches long—and retired to her room. When she stood at the window she could see the moon hanging in the sky and the peaks bathed in its cool light. Somewhere out there Luke was trying to save his cattle. She hoped he would be successful.

They did come in for breakfast, which Alice had told her last night they would. She was ready when they came in, with strong coffee and hot food. They were, to a man, dirty and exhausted looking, but slightly more optimistic than the night before.

"They made it through the night," Luke said before she could ask. "Should be out of the woods now."

"That's good," Josie said quietly. "Just lucky you found them?"

"Jake and Charlie, one of the hands, found them by the creek. We can't check on all of them every day, but we do it regularly. It was just luck we happened on them when we did or we could have lost more." He answered her next question, "The other herds have been checked. This was the only one affected."

"That's good," she said. "What did you do with the rest of them?"

He shrugged as he took a plate and loaded it up. "We moved all the rest of the cows and we'll keep them out of there until we can get rid of all traces of greasewood, which is a plant that can be fatal to cows. We check for it, but apparently we missed this patch. It was just unfortunate it happened when it did. We'll keep an eye on them for a bit longer, but the effects are fast. If any of the rest of them ate it, it'd have shown up by now."

They took a lot of care with the animals and other details. She couldn't help but compare that to her ex and his inability to care about anyone other than himself, much less his employees.

He took a plate loaded with food and followed his brothers into the dining room, and she hurried around putting things away. Alice wasn't up yet. She'd cook a fresh batch of eggs, even though Alice told her not to go to any trouble. Everything else would keep.

She ate her own breakfast and checked her email on the office computer. There was one from her best friend back home, with a link to an article she couldn't open. Allie had promised to send her anything that came up, and from the tone of the email she knew it wasn't a positive article. It was with no small amount of nerves that she fired off a request to cut and paste it into an email.

There was another from a restaurant wondering if she was looking for a new job. Those always gave her pause. She looked at it but just wasn't sure she wanted to work in the same town as Russ again. While LA was huge, the community they'd occupied was relatively small. An awful lot of people had sided with Russ, although part of that could have been that he was simply way more public than she. Still, if she took another job in LA they'd be sure to run into each other. The whole idea made her wary. Just too many memories of things she'd rather put behind her and forget.

Silly, but there it was.

She saved the job offer to an email folder and

was about to close out when a new email pinged in. Allie again.

She opened it, a little curl of dread in her stomach.

Thought you should see this. Do you want me to do anything on my end?

She skimmed the article, which had run in that morning's LA newspaper. The curl of dread turned into a rock, and when she was done, she dropped her head in her hands, tears of anger pressing on her eyelids.

Damn Russ anyway. Was he trying to call her out? Why the hell would he even care?

The article was on the restaurant, on him as the sole owner now. On the changes he'd made, since the previous model hadn't worked well. Due to creative differences, he'd let his partner go and the business was booming.

He didn't mention her by name, of course, but she'd been the partner. She'd been his fiancée. And he hadn't "let her go," he'd ripped the whole thing away from her. It had been her baby. Simple cooking with fresh, local ingredients, lots of which had been grown around the area in inner-city gardens. It had been more of a café than a restaurant, and not the kind of place Russ would have ever started on his own. Which he'd let her know at every turn, even after encouraging her to open it—he'd apparently thought he could control the menu. She'd laughed at him, but he had been the one who laughed last, unfortunately.

"Are you okay?"

Alice's concerned voice broke into her thoughts, and she looked up quickly and sharply, closing out of the email as though it was illicit. "I don't mean to pry," Alice added quietly. "But you didn't hear me come in or greet you."

"Ah." Josie tried to focus on the computer screen she couldn't really see through the sting of angry tears. It would do her no good to cry over it. She'd decided a while ago he wasn't worth it. But this apparent choice to jab at her when she couldn't retaliate—even though she wouldn't—was frustrating. She took a quick breath and tried to get her composure back. "I'm sorry. I'm okay, yes. Just an unwelcome blast from my past, you could say." She'd need to contact her lawyer, see if this was a problem, if it mattered in the pending court case. Russ was arrogant enough to push this as far as he could.

Alice's hand settled on her shoulder and she gave a little squeeze. "I understand. I'll leave you alone. Let me know if I can help."

Josie pushed the office chair back and stood, determined to let it go for now. There was nothing she could do from here anyway. She smiled at Alice. "It'll be fine. Let me fix you breakfast."

Alice laughed and followed Josie back into the kitchen. "I see you and I are continuing the same tradition as your aunt and I. I can make my own breakfast."

Josie smiled as she fetched the jar of berry preserves from the fridge. "I know. I guess you're right." She set it on the counter as Alice fetched a plate and

a butter knife. Hoping to keep the subject off her issues with Russ, she asked, "Did you make this here?"

"The preserves? Yes. Some of the berries grow
wild on the property, some of them I grow in my
garden. It's something I've always enjoyed doing."
Alice spread some on her toasted bagel. "There are a
few jars in the freezer, but they tend not to last long."

"I'm sure," Josie said. "It's delicious." Exactly the
kind of thing she'd have served in her restaurant.

"Well, thank you," Alice said cheerfully. "Now,
did they say anything more about the cattle?"

Josie filled her in on what Luke had told her and
Alice listened with a small frown. She shook her
head. "They take this so hard. They don't like to lose
any of them, and something like this, a poisonous
plant that they check for, is even worse because it
can be prevented." She sighed. "Though really, over
thousands of acres, you can't find every single harm-
ful thing. It's impossible."

"I can see that," Josie said. She could also see that
Luke would do everything he could to keep this from
happening again.

Josie studied the fridge after Alice had left the
room. Clearly, it was time for a trip into Powder Keg
for some supplies. While she could send a list with
someone else who was running into town, she rather
thought she'd like to make this trip. Luke had told her
she could use his truck. She went to the window and
eyed the ranch trucks doubtfully. She'd never driven
anything that big before. Not that she couldn't do it.
But back home her car was more on the sporty side,

not utilitarian. Luke had told her if she needed to drive to take his truck, and showed her where the keys were. She'd listened politely at the time, with no intention of ever taking him up on it.

It almost made her laugh. A month ago, she'd been in LA. Now she was way up north, staring down a huge pickup truck, the likes of which she'd never dealt with. She already knew from riding in this one that she couldn't see over the hood real well.

That could be an issue.

When Luke came in she asked him, "Is it still okay if I borrow your truck?"

He looked at her with surprise for a second. "Sure. You need to go into town?"

"I do. I have some things I need and I'd just like to get them myself." She would also like the opportunity to get a cup of coffee in a café, but didn't say that out loud.

He looked thoughtful. "I was heading that way myself. Want to ride along?"

Part of her wanted to beg off and go another day without him. But the more practical side of her knew it was a waste of gas to go on her own, especially when she was so unfamiliar with the area. Even though it could be a little awkward in the intimate confines of the truck's cab, with the memory of the kiss hanging between them.

"I won't bite," he said, clearly reading her hesitation. She flushed, because it wasn't a bite she was worried about. To cover her embarrassment, she shrugged and smiled.

"That's fine. When are you going?"

He glanced at the clock. "Now. I was just going to check with you and Mom to see if you needed anything."

For a second she was tempted to give him her list and hide here in the kitchen. But there was no real way to back out now. "Okay. Just let me grab my purse." Before he could answer, she hurried from the room. She closed her door and leaned on it, taking a deep breath to settle her nerves. To kill a few more minutes she went into the bathroom and examined her reflection, which was silly, because it really didn't matter what she looked like. She wore skinny jeans and a slim pink T-shirt with a palm tree on the front. Not fancy, and most definitely not very Western. It'd have to do. She smoothed her ponytail, added a touch more lip gloss because she couldn't help herself, then grabbed her purse and went back to the kitchen.

Luke was waiting, a paper in hand.

"Alice need anything?"

He held up the paper. "Yep. And she knows me well enough to write it all down or I'll forget. Ready?"

"Sure." She slipped her feet into flats—also not great footwear, but way better than heels—and followed him out the door.

The atmosphere in the truck was as intimate as it had been the trip home from Kalispell. Luckily this time the trip to town was significantly shorter.

They rode in silence most of the way. Luke had a satellite talk radio channel on, and they were discussing ranching-related business. She didn't understand any of it, talk of grain prices and such, so she tuned it out. She focused instead on the incredible scenery and tried to think of spices in alphabetical order. She also tried with less success not to be tuned in to every move Luke made on the other side of the cab. His long fingers wrapped around the steering wheel, and with every inhale she breathed in his scent. It was making her more than a little crazy, as if she was a teenage girl on a first date with her dream guy.

She wasn't a teenager or on a date, of course. She also knew there were no dream guys.

She was more than a little relieved when they got to Powder Keg. Like before, there were several trucks parked along the main drag, and there were people on the street who waved at Luke as they rolled by. She wondered if they caught sight of her and wondered who she was. She didn't want to start any gossip that might make things uncomfortable for Luke. She'd been so conditioned to fly under the radar, and it was hard to break the habit.

When he parked in front of the store, she got out and went to stand on the sidewalk. An older man winked at her as he walked by. Luke came to join her. She followed him inside and blinked at the way the place was packed from top to bottom.

A woman let out a squeal.

"Well, look who we have here. Long time no see, Luke." There was a definite purr and familiarity in her tone. Because of the layout of the store, Josie was still behind Luke in the entry, and the woman had them both penned in. "Perfect timing. You busy tonight? A group of us are going to the Hole."

Josie could smell the woman's overpowering perfume and coughed.

Luke managed to move forward enough that Josie could step around him. She gave both of them a toothy smile. The woman, a petite bottle-blonde with large breasts that strained at her shirt, frowned.

"If you'll just point me toward where I need to go, I'll get out of your way," she said pleasantly as the other woman looked her over from top to bottom and clearly found her lacking. Josie spotted the grocery section and grabbed a cart from near the door. "Never mind, I see it." She walked away, pushing the cart over the uneven floor, her chin up, her steps deliberate, a sour feeling in her stomach.

"Another city girl, huh, Luke?" Her voice was loud, a little shrill, a little mocking, and it followed Josie as she went down the first aisle she saw. Luke's voice was too low for her to hear his response, and Josie disappeared into the freezer section, her face burning. Her scorn shouldn't matter, since the woman was clearly jealous, and that wasn't Josie's problem. The woman wasn't wrong. Josie already knew she didn't look anything like a local with her designer flats and city clothes. And it shouldn't matter. But she didn't want to cause problems for Luke. Though frankly, if that woman was any indication of the type he preferred, no wonder he'd pushed her away after their kiss.

She stopped to examine a display of snack foods, disturbed by the direction of her thoughts. Why should his type matter? She should be grateful it wasn't her. It'd save her a lot of grief down the line.

## Chapter Eight

Luke found Josie studying two different kinds of frozen corn. He cleared his throat and she turned slightly. Her gaze was cool. Impersonal. Which he deserved. He knew how that had looked, and he'd kissed Josie. It made him look bad.

"I'm sorry about Candy," he said quietly. He wasn't quite sure how to explain his relationship with her—or rather, lack of relationship. He'd had a drunken fling with her years ago after his marriage had imploded, and she'd been on a mission ever since to have a repeat. She had various boyfriends at various times, but she'd made no secret she'd drop them all for him. He suspected that had more to do with his status as a former country star than for him personally. After all, they'd both lived around Powder Keg for their whole lives, and it wasn't until he'd gone to Nashville that she'd shown an interest in him.

"She has some ideas about me that I haven't been able to get her to drop," he explained, even though it was obvious.

Josie set one of the boxes in her cart and met his gaze. "You don't have to explain," she told him. He took his hat off and shoved his hand through his hair, exasperated with himself more than her.

"Yeah, I kinda do. I need you to understand I'm not stringing anyone along, and if I was involved with someone, I'd never have kissed you." This was delivered in a fierce whisper in deference to the fact he never could be sure who was lurking around the next aisle. Everyone meant well, but every one of them talked, or lived with someone who talked. It was the way of a small town, especially one you'd grown up in, where people felt they not only knew you but actually owned part of you. It wasn't something he normally minded—it was part and parcel of a small town and the life he'd chosen. But he didn't want Josie getting tangled up in it all somehow.

She nodded. "I get it. I do. I never thought you were a player, Luke. It was just a weak moment on both our ends."

He wasn't sure if that was a relief or not. He figured either way it was better to move on while he was ahead.

"Did you get everything?" He took in the contents of the cart as she nodded.

"Enough. They've got a lot here. This place is bigger than it looks from the outside."

He smiled. "It is. They use every square inch." Clothes, hardware, tack, even toys as well as groceries filled the space, literally to the ceiling. Outside, there was the feed area, and big things like galvanized water tubs and fencing material. Schaffer's did a brisk and solid business, and had been here as long as Luke could remember. It'd been owned by the same family as well for decades, like a lot of the businesses in town and the surrounding ranches, too. Deep roots. It was amazing how many people stayed or came back.

He left her to gather the things his mom had asked for, then followed Josie to the registers, his mom's items in a basket. Would Josie be willing to put down roots here? Or were hers in Los Angeles? Or did she not have any at all? He wasn't sure what bothered him more, that she might not want to put down roots or that he was even wondering about the damn thing in the first place.

The latter, for sure. He had no business going there. At all.

They each paid for their purchases and loaded everything up into the truck, including the cold items in a battered cooler that Josie looked at askance.

"What do you keep in here?" she asked, eyeing it.

"Food," he said carefully. What else? He opened it up and showed her the inside, which was clean. "It's just beat-up because it slides around in the back of a truck. We use it because typically the trips into town take some time, and that way nothing spoils."

"Okay," she said, and sorted the groceries quickly, pulling out the ones that needed to be kept cold. When she started around to the cab of the truck he asked, "You want to grab a quick bite? Donna's Diner's good and fast. Not on the same level as the burger place," he said with a small smile, "but really good home cooking."

Why had he asked her? She'd say no, for sure, and he'd look stupid. Or, worse, she'd go and just be polite. He opened his mouth to tell her to never mind, but she nodded.

"I'd like that. I like to sample other restaurants."

He didn't point out that this wasn't at the same level as what she'd cooked at. She already knew that, and he knew that she wasn't a food snob. He liked that she was game to give it a try.

They walked in the diner and the place was packed, which wasn't a shock, considering it was lunchtime in the ranching world. They snagged a booth near the entrance. He'd have preferred to be closer to the back, but it couldn't be helped. He didn't know if Josie was aware of the eyes following them, but he sure was. People would look at her because she was young and gorgeous and make assumptions that he couldn't help.

They sat down, and she gave him a weary smile. "Does it bother you?"

"Does what bother me?" he asked, looking up as the waitress popped up to drop off menus and plunk down silverware. After taking drink orders and telling them the specials, she hurried off.

"Being watched like that," she said.

He didn't pretend he didn't know what she was talking about. "It doesn't happen very often here. Besides, it's you they're looking at, not me."

She fussed with her silverware. "Why me?"

He shrugged. "You're new." He didn't add "gorgeous and sexy." That was over-the-top, even if true.

She shrugged. "I imagine that'll wear off soon enough."

He heard what she didn't say—she'd be gone soon enough anyway. Even unsaid, those were the most important words. The ones he needed to focus on when he got the crazy urge to kiss the hell out of her.

Josie was used to the stares, but usually they were directed at the man she was with. This time she was the subject, and it made her uncomfortable. This was a much smaller town, and a whole new world. But these people were looking at the city woman with Luke Ryder, not the woman who was engaged to a high-profile and popular TV chef. With Russ, she'd faded to the background, like she'd preferred.

Like *he'd* preferred, she realized. She was pretty enough to be on his arm, but not so much that she'd overshadow him or distract from him. Anytime the cameras started clicking, he'd started preening, and she'd be relegated to the back. At the time she'd been okay with it. But now, understanding the reasons for it, it made her feel a little ill. How had she been so blind? How could she make sure it didn't happen again?

Luke tapped on her menu. "You okay over there?"

His concern snapped her back to the present, and she realized she'd been staring at the same page for a few minutes. She smiled at him. "Just hungry. Any suggestions?"

"The chicken potpie on special is a popular choice," he said. "And you can't go wrong with the beef stew, either."

She chose the potpie because she was planning to make one herself. He ordered the beef stew. The waitress was friendly and prompt, bringing them coffee and then their meals. Josie had to smile as she looked at the steaming potpie in the huge bowl in front of her. "Everything out here is cowboy-size portions, isn't it?"

He raised a brow at her as he tucked into his stew. "You mean regular size?"

She picked up her fork and thought of the small, perfectly arranged portions they'd served at Aloha's, the restaurant she'd first worked at with Russ. More for art than consumption. Two extremes. "I'm pretty sure this is more than regular."

He grinned and shrugged. "You can get a box to take it home, I'm sure."

Now she had to laugh. "I'm guessing you've never had that problem." She took a bite and closed her eyes. The flavors exploded in her mouth. She tasted tarragon, maybe some lemon and paprika, too. The broth was perfectly done, not too thick, and not runny. The crust was clearly homemade, and no doubt with lard. When she opened her eyes, Luke was looking at her, his fork in the air, his gaze a little intense.

"This is amazing," she said, and he gave her a wry grin as he scooped up more of his stew.

"Is that how you eat everything?" he asked and his voice was a little strangled. "You looked as though you were experiencing it, not just chewing it."

She took a sip of her water. "Not everything, no. But yeah, food should be an experience. Good food should make you stop and savor it. There are differ-

ent levels of flavors as it moves across your palate."
She took another bite, enjoyed it. It'd be a challenge
to top it, even if she wanted to. "The cook here knows
exactly what he or she is doing."

"You can tell her yourself," he said. "Donna is here
every day. These are her own recipes. She's a great
lady. I'm sure you can talk to her. She'd be tickled to
have a real chef in her kitchen."

She rolled her eyes. "She's as much of a chef as I
am, clearly. Maybe more."

They finished eating, and she noticed the stares
had stopped. She hoped it had been more of a new-
person-in-town stare than a who's-with-Luke stare.
When the waitress returned to their table, Josie asked
for a box and Luke added, "Is Donna too busy for a
quick visit?"

The waitress, whose name was Annie, smiled. "I'll
check."

She returned a minute later with her boss in tow.
Donna was a tall woman, with a kind face and a ready
smile. She gave Luke a hug. "Well, Luke Ryder. Wonderful to see you out here." Then she turned to Josie,
her hand extended. "Donna Jones."

Josie shook her hand and introduced herself. Luke
added, "She's filling in for Rosa, Donna."

"Ah," Donna said, and her gaze sharpened. "Rosa
talked a lot about you. You're the chef, correct?"

"I am," Josie confirmed. "And I'm blown away by
your chicken potpie. Was that tarragon and lemon I
tasted in there?"

Donna brightened right up. "Yes. So you know
your stuff."

They spent a few minutes talking shop, and Luke slipped away to talk to another rancher. Henry Parker eyed Luke when he came over. "Who's the woman? You got something you need to tell me? Because I'd say it's about damn time if you do."

Luke shook his head and sat down across from Henry. "Nope. She's my cook. Temporary cook," he corrected himself. "Rosa's niece."

"Quite a looker," Henry observed, but there was nothing inappropriate in his tone, so Luke didn't jump down his throat. Henry's gaze flicked to Luke's. "And a city girl to boot." The last was said quietly, with a concern that Luke understood.

Luke held his gaze. "That she is," he said mildly. "Like I said, temporary cook." Henry wasn't a talker, but he'd tell Brenda, his wife, and she'd set people straight. He liked the Parkers. They were good people.

He steered the conversation toward the ranching question he had, and Henry didn't say anything else about Josie. When Henry looked up with a smile, Luke realized Josie was standing there. He rose and did the introductions. Josie was friendly and open, and he could see that Henry was taken with her quickly. He'd tell Brenda that, too. That was okay. People would be wary of Josie, from the city, after what happened with Mandy. Henry and Brenda vouching for her would go a long way. They were well liked around Powder Keg.

Josie chatted with Henry for a few moments, and Luke could tell the older rancher liked her very much. He didn't blame the guy for being a little dazzled.

As they left the diner, he asked her, "Do you need to go anywhere else?"

"Do we have time to stop in the bakery?" she asked.

"Sure." He led the way and opened the door for her. An old high school friend of his owned it. Katie'd been divorced for going on five years now, and had had quite a time of it getting the place going. She'd stuck with it, and now Sugar was a favorite stop in Powder Keg. She greeted him from behind the counter with a big smile.

"Luke! Good to see you. And who's this?" She came around the counter, her hand outstretched, her smile warm.

"Katie, this is Josie. She's the cook at the ranch." To Josie, as Katie took her hand, he added with pride on her behalf, "Katie has made this place work from scratch."

"Lots of sweat and tears," she said cheerfully as if it hadn't taken her years to get it up and running. "Nice to meet you, Josie."

"You, too," Josie answered, her smile warm. Luke had often wished that he could settle down with some-one like Katie, who was sweet and solid and always had a smile, but the sparks just weren't there. No, in-stead, he just made mistakes.

"So what can I get you today?"

Luke watched as the women walked back to the cases. There were a good amount of cookies and cup-cakes and various other pastries left in the cases. On weekends it was critical to get here early—things sold out fast. Josie chose an assortment of items and paid. She and Katie chatted for a few moments and as Josie turned to go, Katie mouthed, "I like her" and gave him a thumbs-up. He gave her a small smile and shook his head, then followed Josie out the door. He didn't want Katie to get the wrong impression. Or anyone to get the wrong idea. Least of all himself.

In the truck, she opened the bakery bag, took out a big frosted sugar cookie, then held the bag out to him. "Want one?"

"What if I wanted that one?" he teased as she took a bite. She shook her head at him.

"This one was mine. I figured you weren't the pink frosted type." She arched a brow. "Perhaps I was wrong?"

"Busted. You'd be right." He selected a white frosted one. It had sprinkles, but he couldn't win them all. He took a big bite and looked over at Josie. She had a smudge of frosting on her cheek, and a couple random crumbs. He couldn't stop himself. He reached over and brushed the crumbs off. Her eyes got wide when his gaze snagged on her full, sexy mouth. Her breath whispered out and he nearly leaned in, over the console, over the bakery bag, and kissed her.

She must have read his intent, because alarm filled her eyes. She shook her head. "Luke." That one word managed to convey both a plea and regret. He sat back and took a frustrated bite of the cookie instead and looked up to see Mrs. Mitty, one of the town's biggest talkers, smiling broadly at him from the sidewalk in front of the truck.

Fact was, he'd nearly kissed Josie right in the middle of town. And they'd been caught.

He heard a strangled little sound from Josie and knew she'd read Mrs. Mitty's expression, as well. The bright smile on her face gave it away, pride in the fact that she'd been the one to catch the moment.

A moment that shouldn't have happened at all.

He put the truck in gear and backed out of the spot.

There was no mistaking the fact it had been building all day, in the little bumps and touches and glances. He knew what was happening here, and it seemed to be happening despite their best efforts to avoid it. They rode the rest of the way, small talk filling the space between them, and she finally asked the question he'd been wondering if he'd hear.

"Do you miss it? Performing?"

There was the standard answer he gave everyone, and then there was the truth. Josie had been nothing but open with him. So she deserved the truth. "I do. I miss it a lot. I miss connecting with people through music. I don't miss the grind of touring, that's for sure." He gave a half laugh. "It was a rush at the beginning. But after a while, you forget where you are. You stop all these places, but you can't ever really see them. It's tough to just run out and grab a burger, or go for a run, or catch a movie. All of a sudden, you belong to all these people and you've traded your privacy for their loyalty." He stopped, realizing he'd said more than he'd meant to. Somehow he'd bottled it all up and convinced himself it didn't matter. Yet once he'd started talking about it, it had fizzed out of him like soda out of a shaken bottle.

He glanced at her and cleared his throat. Her face was soft, pensive. "So, yeah. I miss it."

She reached over and touched his leg. He felt the heat of it through his jeans. "Have you ever thought about going back?"

That was an easy one. "No."

"No?" He heard the skepticism in her tone and shook his head. He understood, after what he'd just said—it sounded as though he wanted nothing more than to get back to that life.

"No. I haven't. I don't want to get back under the fishbowl of that life. Be scrutinized like that. Or put my family back in it, either." Right there was a huge issue—they'd been caught in the glare of his life, even all the way out here.

She nodded. "I can understand that. Do you still write songs?"

He hesitated. "Not really, no. I haven't picked up my guitar in ages." That wasn't entirely true. He'd written snatches of songs over the years, but couldn't bring himself to play the guitar. Not because he hadn't wanted to. He did. He missed it. But he'd come to view it as part of his past life and bringing it out, reminding people—his family—he'd left, then come back too late, didn't feel right. Even if there was a hole that the songwriting had filled for him. He'd never done it for the fame. He'd done it for the love of the music. The fame had surprised him completely.

"That's too bad," she said quietly after a moment. There was no judgment in her tone, and he was absurdly grateful for it. "I can't imagine not cooking anymore. It's not the same, of course, in terms of the fame and the performing you did—but it's still a huge creative outlet, and I need it to keep me grounded."

He couldn't swallow around the weird lump in his throat. That was it exactly, and he'd cut himself off from it.

## Chapter Nine

Josie left her window open for a while in the evenings, even though the night air was cool. It wasn't real quiet here, and she found she didn't miss the noises of the city anymore. She'd gotten accustomed to the sounds of nature instead.

A chorus of otherworldly howls rose on the night and came in through her window. Josie froze, goose bumps rising on her skin as the sound rose and fell, followed by a high-pitched yipping. Slightly freaked out, she left her room and went out in the living room, where Luke stood. He turned when she got close, and gave her a half smile.

"What is that?" The sound rose again, fell. The hairs rose on her arms. She rubbed them, the chill she felt much more primal than the coolness of the air.

"Coyotes. Look at Hank."

Hank was as still as a statue, his body tight and his hackles up. A low growl rumbled in his throat. Josie wrapped her arms around her torso.

"Cold?"

She looked down at herself, in her yoga pants and long-sleeved T-shirt. "Not really. Just— I've never heard them before. Or seen Hank like that." Suddenly, LA seemed really far away. It was at night that this place seemed most wild. There was a complete, velvety darkness that she'd never experienced in Southern California. And in it, things howled and prowled that didn't live in the city.

The room was dark but for one small lamp in the corner that gave off more of a glow than any real light. The moon was full, though, and thin clouds scuttled in front of it. It was enough light that she could see Luke standing by the sliding door, which was open. His pose was deceptively relaxed. He was on alert, too, she realized.

She came and stood beside him, breathing in the scent of his aftershave and the scent that was just— him. A slight breeze blew in.

"Will we see them?" Even her hushed tones seemed loud in this darkness.

"Probably not." Luke's gaze was trained outside, much like Hank's. She peered, too, but didn't see anything. There was more yipping and howling, and then Hank dropped to his haunches and let out a howl of his own. Startled, Josie stepped back quickly. Luke grabbed her elbow and she was pressed against his chest. He hadn't moved when she'd jumped. She could feel his heat and the beat of his heart through the thin undershirt he wore. For a moment, it was all she could concentrate on.

The side of his face brushed her hair as she turned her head slightly. "Um. Thanks. Sorry, I still get a little spooked out here."

He let go of her elbow and she felt the loss of contact keenly, but he didn't move away from her. "I know. It's not for everyone. You don't have coyotes in Los Angeles?" His tone was hushed.

She moved away just slightly. "I don't know. I don't think so. I've never heard them. But we don't have this—quietness that you do out here. There are different sounds here."

"Bugs, frogs, big and small night creatures," he filled in.

"Exactly." She wanted him to understand. "Where I live, I can hear the sound of the 405 freeway. It's not real close, but it's a constant background noise. I hear dogs barking, people talking, doors slamming, whatever. I look out my living room doors, like these, and I see an absolute sea of lights. It's never fully dark, the way it is here, and never fully quiet the way it is here." She'd been disconnected from nature, she could see now. Maybe it was inevitable with the life she led. She never would have noticed or missed it, but being here had opened her eyes.

"Here you look out and can see the stars," he said softly. "All of them. You can see far more than you could ever see down there. The light washes them out."

"Yes." She'd noticed that right away, the first clear night she'd been here. Tonight, as well. So many stars, the night sky looked like a glittery celestial pincushion. "It's amazing. I never knew what was out there."

"It's not all bad here, is it?" His voice was joking, but there was something under it, some tone that she couldn't quite understand or define. She wondered at it.

"No. Of course not. Just a lot different than what I'm used to." She couldn't say she'd be sorry to get back to the city, but this place had grown on her. It pulled at her in a way that surprised her. She'd never expected to feel a connection out here, to nature and the people who lived here. To feel, oddly, as if she belonged here. They were quiet for a few moments and the sounds were farther away, then gone. The silence between them wasn't awkward, but it was a little heavy. Josie was very aware of the man next to her.

"They've moved on for now," Luke said finally, his voice loud in the quiet room. Hank still sat at attention, but he was more alert than tense and his hackles were down. That had to be a good sign. She figured he knew what was going on.

She rubbed her arms and moved away from the door. "That's good, right?"

He shrugged. "They are out of earshot, but they're out there somewhere. Unlike wolves, they are pretty adaptable. Which is why I wondered if you'd ever heard them down there."

She shook her head. "Nope." Aware of the sudden change in the air between them, she murmured, "Well, I guess I'll go back to bed."

She looked up at him and caught her breath at her thoughtless comment. His gaze was intense on her.

Suddenly she was very aware of the fact she was braless under her shirt. It was loose enough it didn't cling, but she crossed her arms over her chest, hoping to hide the evidence of her sudden reaction. From the chill of the air through the doors or his suddenly hot gaze, she didn't know.

From the heat pooling between her thighs, she could guess.

He moved a little closer, and she didn't move. Not only because the dog was behind her, but because she didn't want to. She wanted, more than anything, to feel his mouth on hers again and feel his arms around her. When he moved in and slid his hands up her arms, she didn't resist, caught in the spell, and tipped her head back. He lowered his mouth to hers slowly.

"Tell me this is a bad idea," he murmured, his breath whispering over her mouth. She couldn't, for the life of her, say the words. Not with her body humming and her toes curling in anticipation.

In reply, she lifted on her toes and pressed her mouth to his.

He opened to her right away with a groan, and wrapped his arms around her and pulled her in close. She felt the hardness of his chest, the pound of his heart that matched her own, the heat of his skin that seeped through the thin fabric of her own shirt. The pressure of his chest on her breasts was exquisite. When his hands came up, slid under her shirt and cupped her breasts, she moaned and arched into his hands. He brushed her nipples with his thumbs and she nipped his lower lip with her teeth. He gave a startled laugh, then a growl. "That how you want to play?"

He walked her back against the wall, away from the door, kissing her the whole way, then lifted her shirt and took one nipple in his mouth. He tugged and played with it, his free hand doing the same to the other breast, and she buried her hands in his hair. The pleasure shot straight to her core, and the flash of heat was intense, more than anything she'd ever felt.

"Luke," she gasped, her head rolling back and forth on the wall. She wanted—more. So much more. For this fire to consume her, consume them both.

But he stood back up and tugged her shirt down, taking her mouth in a crushing kiss instead that had her head spinning even more than it had before. She felt his hardness on her belly and she ached for him. When they came up for air, he rested his forehead on hers and she laid her hands on his chest, feeling the unevenness of breath that matched her own. Josie fought for some semblance of control over her feelings. There were so many, too many, and she'd had no idea pleasure was such a razor's edge. She wasn't a virgin, and her earlier experiences had been pleasant enough, but nothing like this. Like this fire that roared through her and threatened to burn from the inside out. She wondered what he'd be like in bed. Wondered if she'd be able to find out. The heat that already was searing her body kicked up another notch.

Then she wondered why the hell she was wanting things she couldn't have.

She pushed him away gently so she could duck away, where she could breathe air that didn't smell like him and her hormones had a chance to settle back down. She couldn't think when she was basking in his body heat and all she wanted to do was curl into him and hold on.

What was happening to her? She was so good at being in control. What was it about Luke that made all that evaporate?

He let her go and turned slowly to face her. "Did I scare you?"

His voice was low and rough and sent exciting little chills down her spine. She turned and took quick small steps back to him. Shook her head as she laid her hand on his face. His cheek was deliciously rough under her palm. "No. Oh, no. You couldn't do that."

Not in the way he meant anyway.

"That's good. I'm not real sure what to think about this." He shoved his hands into his pockets and rocked back a little on his heels. She dropped her hand and moved away again. Hank had given up on staring outside at some point when they were—um, busy— and had wandered off.

That made two of them. "Me, either."

She stood there for another moment, staring at him. Then she said, "I guess I'll go to bed." Even from her vantage point she saw his eyes flare. "Alone," she amended weakly. She wasn't sure if she said it to re- mind him, or herself.

He came toward her and she didn't move, just tilted her head back when he stopped in front of her. He lowered his head and kissed her again, a softer, searching kiss this time, slow and deep. She gripped his strong arms to keep from melting into a puddle right at his feet.

When he released her mouth, he ran his thumb lightly over her lips. She knew if she sucked it into her mouth the way she wanted to, they'd end up in her bed. And she wasn't ready for that. He whispered, "Good night. Sweet dreams."

"You, too," she murmured, and fled to her room.

There was no point in pretending there wasn't something going on with her and Luke. And no point in pretending the whole ranch didn't know it. It was a close-knit community and word traveled fast—even though far less had happened than many of them thought, no doubt. The connection between them was almost a living thing. She thought of it as a shiny band she couldn't seem to slip...and wasn't sure she wanted to.

Josie recognized a losing battle when she saw one. So though she had told Nikki, whom she had come to consider a friend, that no, she hadn't slept with Luke, she kept her mouth shut with everyone else. The idea of his family wondering about their relationship was mortifying. She wondered if she needed to say something, then realized Luke would have to deal with that end of it. Thankfully, none of them ever said a word to her.

But that didn't stop the knowing looks and the teasing grins. And in some cases, suspicion. This was from the older employees, the ones who remembered his marriage and divorce to a woman who'd been an avowed city girl. Like Raphael, the hand who helped her with Zippy's tack that morning. She was going riding with Nikki, who was taking her current charge out for some experience on the trail.

Raphael had been polite and helpful, but distant and cool, too. She might have written it off as simply his personality, except she got the same treatment from a few others, as well. Never disrespectful or rude, just wary, no doubt of her and her motives. Looking out for their boss, to whom many of them were devoted.

She understood and respected it.

All she could do was make a point of being friendly and warm. Why it mattered to her if they accepted her or not was a mystery. She wasn't staying. She supposed she didn't want to be lumped in with Luke's ex-wife any more than she already was.

There'd be no broken hearts when she left.

She led Zippy to the corral after thanking Raphael and waited for Nikki. She wasn't far behind. "All set?" she asked as she walked up with Firefly.

"All set," Josie replied. They mounted the horses and started out. They'd planned an easy ride. Nikki figured it'd be about two and a half hours, which was plenty of time for Josie to get back to the house to start making dinner. They'd become friends over their shared love of shoes and food. Nikki was a horse-woman all the way through, but she'd grown up in her family's Greek restaurant. She had some family recipes she'd offered to share with Josie, and Josie was looking forward to giving them a try—after a trip to Kalispell to get the ingredients she needed.

Josie had, in fact, noticed some tension with Nikki and Cade. She hadn't asked about it, mindful of her own issue with a Ryder brother, but Nikki had known she'd seen. There had been sparks and definite heat, but Nikki said there was nothing going on with them.

Later, she'd admitted that she'd shared a hot night with Cade a year or so ago, and ever since then, it had been awkward. He wouldn't commit, but he wouldn't just sleep with her, either. It was frustrating, and if it wasn't for the fact she loved this job and they took such good care of her as an employee, she'd leave.

Josie understood, but she also thought it was a long time to be caught in that kind of limbo. She was ready to combust and she had only been around Luke barely two weeks. Nikki had explained they were pretty good at avoiding each other. But still. They lived a stone's throw away from each other on an isolated ranch. It couldn't be easy.

Today, though it didn't take long for the conversation to turn to Luke.

"Was Raphael rude to you?"

Surprised, Josie shook her head. They rode side by side through the field. "No. Why?"

She sighed. "They are worried for him because you're leaving."

Josie shut her eyes for just a moment, felt Zippy underneath her. "I know. I understand. But I've never been anything but open about it. I don't think I should be punished for that."

Nikki nodded. "I agree. But I guess it was really bad here after she left. You'll need to ask him the details, if it gets that far, but they were really worried about him."

Josie thought of all she knew about Luke's marriage. It really wasn't much. She'd been sympathetic at the time, but only in a fleeting way as she'd seen it on the tabloid front pages, in the way you were as a fellow human, but not someone you actually knew. She also understood, having been in a few tabloids herself, that what was printed wasn't necessarily true, or in some cases, even based in truth. "I don't know everything that happened. But I understand people being protective of him. I think that's a good thing."

"Yeah," Nikki said. "You don't think you'll stay?"

Josie looked around at the gorgeous scenery and thought of how different from home it was. "No. But it's not because I can't hack it out here. It's because my life is elsewhere and I have to get back to it." Of course, her life outside the Silver River Ranch was in ruins, but there was no point in bringing that up.

Nikki gave her a grin. "You've done well, city girl." Then she sobered. "Not that you had to prove anything to anybody."

Josie shook her head. "I did. This was way different than I thought it'd be. Even talking to Aunt Rosa over the years, I didn't really grasp what it's like out here."

Nikki nodded. "It took me a while to adjust, too. Plus being female creates some issues. I'm outnumbered quite a lot. I had to earn the respect of each of them, more than if I'd been another guy with the same skills. That took time. If it helps, Luke would be a hell of a catch."

Josie shook her head. "You know it doesn't."

Nikki's smile was wry. "I know. I just thought I'd point it out."

* * *

A while later, Nikki frowned at the sky. Clouds were gathering and they were dark. But they were still an hour from the ranch. Josie looked up and asked, "Is that rain only?"

"I'm not sure," Nikki said. Flashes of light answered that question—lightning. She swore and immediately wheeled Firefly around, and Josie followed suit with Zippy. "Let's go. We'll get as far as we can before the storm hits. I knew this was coming, but it wasn't supposed to be here until after our ride."

Josie didn't answer as Nikki urged her horse into a canter and she followed suit. She dropped low in the saddle as they went across the field. Soon enough, there was a bit of a rocky point in the trail that would mean they needed to slow down. The wind rushed past her ears and she felt the change in the wind—it got a little cooler, and as they slowed the horses to a walk for the rocky part of the trail, Josie didn't dare look up at the sky. Nikki's worried face when she turned in her saddle was enough.

"You okay?" she shouted, and Josie nodded, giving her a thumbs-up. Tree branches swayed and thrashed around them, but by the thunder and lightning count that even Josie knew, the storm was still a few miles off, even though the rain was starting to pelt them. Zippy tossed his head, but stayed steady under her, and Josie pretty much just gave him his head. He knew where he was going better than she did.

By the time they came out the other side, the rain was a downpour and Josie had lost her sunglasses somewhere. She'd put them on the top of her head and they'd fallen off either from the wind or the rain. They'd been expensive but she didn't even care. Right now she wanted to be sure she got Zippy back where it was safe.

Now the thunder rolled and shook the ground and both horses were clearly spooked. Nikki's mount was dancing a bit under her steady hand, but kept her head pretty well. The count was much closer—the storm would be on them in a matter of moments.

It was then she realized that they weren't going to make it.

## Chapter Ten

"Luke." Raphael's face was tight with tension and worry. "Nikki and Josie aren't back yet."

Luke rounded on the man. "Back? From where?"

"They went for a ride. Took Firefly and Zippy. But the storm—"

Luke ran to the barn entrance and stared out at the rain and the thunder that shook the barn. He swore and shoved his hat back on his head. "Where did they go, Raphael?"

The man told him. "Nikki knows to stick to the plan. She knew the storm was coming, but we thought they had an extra couple hours. They would have been an hour out." There was agony in the other man's tone. There were various shelters out there. It was anyone's guess if they'd made it to one in time, or which one Nikki had chosen.

Cade and Jake came in the barn. "Everything okay?"

Luke was blunt. "Nikki and Josie are out in this." Even in his own worry and fear he saw the same expression cross both of his brothers' faces.

"Where?" Jake asked.

Luke told him what Raphael knew. "We can each take a truck and find them." Even as he said it he knew it was impractical. Some of those places weren't accessible by any type of vehicle larger than a four-wheeler. Some were on foot or horseback. So even if they drove out, there wasn't any way, in this storm, to get to them.

Jake spoke, his voice calm. "Nikki knows her stuff. She knows this ranch as well as we do. She'll have found shelter for them and the horses."

While Luke knew his brother was right, he still thought he might crawl up the walls waiting.

Cade blew out a breath. "That's true. She does." He looked at Luke. "Hey, man. Jake is right. And as soon as it's clear, we'll take four-wheelers and go looking. Though I'm going to guess that as soon as it's safe, Nikki will move out. Again, she knows what she's doing."

"I know." He didn't doubt her, or Cade's words. But he couldn't suppress the panicky feeling that pressed on his chest and made it tough to take a full breath. He scanned the sheet of rain, so heavy that visibility was nearly zero. He couldn't see the house, much less fifty feet out.

Josie was out there, and Josie didn't know what the hell she was doing. She wasn't the strongest rider and she was still somewhat fearful, though brave, about the outdoors. Some of those shelters weren't more than shacks with leaky roofs and no doubt rodents or some other animal in residence.

He stood in the door of the barn, sheltered from the rain, with his brothers, who were equally tense and quiet for different reasons, and watched it pour down, and the lightning put on quite a show for what felt like forever. When they deemed it far enough away to start the ride out, the three men went and got the four-wheelers out and each took a slightly different route, not too far off the original one Nikki had planned. There were four possible shelters in the area, depending on which way they'd decided to go, but one of them was a cave, and they agreed that she'd most likely avoid that one unless absolutely necessary as there was no place for the horses.

Luke split off at his designated spot, pushing the four-wheeler as fast as it would comfortably go on this terrain—which wasn't nearly fast enough. The wind rushed past his helmet and the noise of the engine made it hard to think about anything but where he was going. He wasn't going to examine his fear for Josie. He tried to tell himself that it was equaled by his concern for Nikki, but that just wasn't true. He was worried about them both, yes. But he was half-insane over Josie.

The shack in front of him was empty. He could tell as soon as he came over the small ridge. There were no hoofprints in the mud, no sign they'd been anywhere near here. His heart sank and he ground out a curse that he couldn't hear over the roar of the ATV.

His radio crackled right before he'd reached the shack and Jake's voice came over it. "Found them. They're fine." The relief he felt was more than he could have imagined. More than he wanted to feel.

He turned around and went back.

It wasn't until he saw her, wet and muddy and with Cade's arms around her, that he could take a full breath. And then with the next one he wanted to punch the hell out of his brother. But she turned from Cade and looked at him and gave him, improbably, a small smile.

He wanted to run and pull her in his arms, then carry her inside and check every inch of her to make sure she was okay. He forced himself to walk, albeit quickly, over to where she stood. He could see Raphael and another groom disappearing into the barn with the horses.

"Are you okay?" Some of the intensity of what he was feeling must have shown on his face, because Josie took a small step back.

"Yes." It was one word, just one word, but it eased something coiled inside him.

"She's a tough one," Nikki said, and gave her friend a weary smile. Josie returned it. "Let her tell you about it on the way to the house. I'm sure she wants out of her wet clothes as much as I do." She gave Josie a hug. "You did good."

"Thanks. You don't have to come with me," she said quietly when Luke turned and started toward the house with her. "I'm fine."

He still wasn't convinced of that. She was awfully pale. "That's good. What happened?"

She took a deep breath, then started the story. In the house, they toed off their boots and he caught her arm before they left the mudroom. "Can I come with you?" He wondered exactly what he was asking. Wondered exactly what he was going to answer. But she lifted solemn eyes to his and nodded.

So he went in her room and she closed the door. Before he even really knew what he was doing he kissed her, hot and hard and deep and with all of the urgency and all of the fear he'd had inside him while she'd been out there. She leaned into him and kissed him right back. He stepped back and lifted her shirt at the hem, then looked into her eyes. She took the hem from him and lifted the shirt over her head. Her nipples beaded against the black lace of her bra, which was low cut over the tops of her breasts. He groaned and freed both nipples for his mouth and hands, getting some of the lace in his mouth as he laved her nipple and she arched against him.

"Luke," she whispered, and it was a plea, a demand. He lifted his head, and she reached around and unhooked the bra. She let it slide down her arms, and he filled his hands with her before it even hit the ground. Her breasts were round and soft, and he wanted to bury himself in them for days. Her skin was cold, a reminder of what she'd just been through.

"Josie. God." He kissed her, his hands on her breasts still when she slid her hand between them and cupped him. He groaned and pressed against her hand.

It only took a few more minutes—her jeans were wet

and took a little extra effort to get off—but they were naked soon enough, and she was pressed against him, her nipples brushing his chest, his hard length firm against her belly. As they sort of fell onto the bed, he shifted to avoid landing on her. His fingers brushed her thigh and she thought she'd combust if he didn't touch her, if he didn't move his hand over just a little bit…

Then he did, and his fingers sank inside her. She bucked and reached for his length, but he pinned her with a kiss. "If you touch me, I'll lose it." He pulled away, his hand stilled and she whimpered. "Condoms. I don't—"

"I'm protected," she told him. "And I was careful, always." With Russ, they'd always used a condom, which in retrospect was a good idea.

"I was, too," he said, and positioned himself over her, and she was touched that he trusted her. She opened her thighs wider and he sank in, inch by inch, the tight set of his jaw telling her just how hard he was holding on to control.

"Josie," he groaned, and she lifted up to meet him.

The rhythm was hard and fast, and she thought she'd fly apart all too soon. The pressure built and when she couldn't hold it back, at his urging, "Let it go, Josie, so I can go with you," she did, and even as she shattered she knew from his hoarse cry that he'd gone over the edge with her.

Whoa.

Josie lay there, under Luke, feeling the pounding of his heart and the unsteadiness of his breathing, both of which matched her own. He shifted slightly and rested next to her. It was then that she realized they'd barely made it to the bed and were sideways across it. She was still wearing her wet socks. As a bonus, she was no longer cold.

"Wow," he said after a moment. "Josie." He turned his head to look at her, and she saw warmth in his blue, blue eyes and something else, something that looked a lot like regret. But he leaned in and kissed her, a soft kiss. "Let me start a shower for you."

What she wanted to do was curl up in his warmth and soak it in. But that wasn't an option. Instead, she got up and gathered clean, dry clothes from her dresser and peeled out of her socks as she picked up her wet and scattered things from the floor. Luke came out of the bathroom and steered her toward it gently, where he'd started the shower on hot. The room was full of steam. When he kissed her again, she pulled him toward it with her. "Shower with me?"

He hesitated, then shook his head. "I don't think that's a good idea."

Josie's face flamed. Just like that, all the warm feelings she'd been enjoying crashed to the floor. Not wanting him to see it, she simply said, "Okay," and walked into the bathroom. And shut the door in his face.

She wouldn't cry. Goodness, it wasn't worth that. But she was more than a little embarrassed to have been so bold only to be shut down.

Obviously, making love hadn't meant the same thing to him as it did to her.

Lesson learned.

Josie knew she should have walked away. She'd allowed herself to be swayed by a look, by what she'd wanted to be true and real and bright. But then Alice had bustled in, all concern, and she'd found herself trying to hide her feelings while telling her the story.

She and Nikki had taken shelter in a building that was little more than a shack. It had three sides and was deep enough they could stand back from the worst of the splashing as the rain ran off the roof. However, the roof had leaked almost as much as it had kept out and the rain had driven in through the gaping cracks in the sides of it, but it had kept them and the horses out of the worst of the weather. It had quickly smelled of wet horse and leather, as well as the scent of the rain itself. She'd been waiting for it to come down on their heads, with the way it had creaked in the wind.

Nikki had explained that there were a couple small cabins on the property that were weather tight and had things like blankets and canned goods, and were checked fairly regularly to make sure there were no animals living in them, but none of them were more than an hour's ride of the main buildings.

The worst of the storm had gone through pretty quickly, and as soon as Nikki had deemed it safe, they'd headed back out.

The whine of the four-wheeler had reached them about ten minutes in, and Josie had been very glad to see Jake.

"Ladies," he'd greeted them, his smile not masking the concern in his eyes as he'd looked them over, and the horses, too. "Everything okay?"

"We're fine," Nikki had assured him. "We stayed

at the lean-to back over the hill. Damp and chilly, but out of the weather."

"All right. Good." The relief in his voice had been clear. He'd radioed Luke and Cade and let them know they were safe. "Been pretty worried about you."

"It came up fast," Nikki had admitted. "I thought we should have had more time."

"It happens to all of us." He'd gone on back and they'd followed.

Cade had been there right away, and he'd given her a hug. Luke had shown up only a couple minutes later.

The intense way he'd looked at her had heated her from the inside out. Of course, she'd left the part about what had happened after out of the version she'd told Alice.

Which brought her right back to the fact he'd bolted from her room as if his hair was on fire. After she'd asked him to stay. Her face burned, and she was grateful Alice had left the room.

Josie took one of the trucks into town that afternoon—not Luke's. It was her first solo trip, because there was a rumor she could get real, actual cell phone service if she parked behind the Laundromat.

Plus, she could avoid Luke. That was a bonus right about now.

So here she was, on a few errands, but the most important one was to call Allie.

"Josie! How are you, up there in the wilds of Montana?"

It was so good to hear her voice. A wave of homesickness washed over Josie. "I'm making the best of it. You know me."

"Yeah." Allie's voice softened. "Did you call your lawyer?"

"Yes." She sighed, even though right now it all seemed very far away. "I'm not there to defend myself, and he's trying to make himself the victim. Annoying, but not a surprise."

"And he has the new girlfriend," Allie said quietly.

Josie shook her head even though Allie couldn't see her. "Not new. She was one of the ones on the side. His favorite one." A few weeks ago that would have burned Josie, made her angry and sad and sick. Now? She was disgusted with him, but detached. It was a wonderful step.

Allie huffed out a half laugh. "God. Well, he'll get what's coming to him, Jo. Men like him always do."

Maybe. But it wouldn't be from Bree, the current honey. As far as she could tell, neither of them cared enough about the other to be able to cause any real or lasting damage. That had been her mistake—actually caring for Russ and thinking he cared for her.

Luke flashed in her mind. He had more integrity in his left eyebrow than Russ had in his whole body. Even if he confused her.

"I hope so," she said finally.

"So what's it like working for Luke Ryder? Can you tell me anything about him without violating his privacy?"

Josie nearly choked. Allie had no idea what a loaded question that was. She settled for a half answer and hoped Allie wouldn't pick up on it. She didn't want to go into how he'd kissed her and had made love to her that morning. Allie would never let her hear the end of it. "He's just a normal guy. Nice. They all are. It's different working in a private kitchen, but they're open to anything as long as it's hearty."

"So a nice change from the pressure cooker of your old job and good fit for you, then," Allie said. "Even though it's temporary."

"Yes," Josie agreed, ignoring the little pang the word *temporary* gave her. Though after what had happened earlier, it was just as well. "Even though."

They chatted a bit longer, and Josie assured her friend she missed plenty about California and she had no plans to stay in Montana. When she disconnected, she knew she hadn't been fully honest. She wasn't sure she would be returning to Cali for good. But she did know she wouldn't be staying in Powder Keg, Montana, on the Silver River Ranch, either.

## *Chapter Eleven*

Luke felt like an ass. No. He was an ass. Damn it. Not only had he broken his promise to himself, he'd made Josie feel bad. He couldn't get the hurt look in her eyes out of his mind. She hadn't deserved him running away.

*Thwack!* He buried the ax right in the middle of the log and split it cleanly in two. There was a growing pile nearby, but he hadn't succeeded in wiping out the image of her pained expression.

She deserved a hell of a lot more than he could offer her. But that was already a given.

Cade strolled up, brow cocked. "Is it working?"

Luke didn't even pretend. He was too tired. "Does it look like it's working?"

Cade shoved his hands in his pockets. "No. Have you tried just talking to her?"

Luke stared at him like he was mad. "Why would I do that?" What could he say? "Sorry" wasn't exactly right. He was sorry for hurting her, but not for the time spent with her, and he knew himself well enough to know he'd blow it if he tried to make the distinction.

"Oh, I don't know. Maybe because you're both adults? And I don't want her to leave because you've screwed something up."

"She's not going to leave," Luke mumbled as he lined the next log up. He hoped she wouldn't anyway. *Thwack!*

"Right. Fix it, damn it. She's as grumpy as you are. Whatever you did, you did it wrong."

Luke's head came up and his hand tightened on the ax handle. "What are you saying, Cade?"

Cade met his gaze squarely. "I'm saying you messed up and you need to fix it. That's all." His footsteps crunched on the gravel as he walked away.

Luke let out a breath. He'd heard a criticism that wasn't there. Cade had only been talking about the here and now, about how he'd hurt Josie. He tossed the wood into the pile and spent the next hour transporting it to the rest of the pile, where it'd wait until winter. He also tried to work out exactly what he'd say to make sure he didn't diminish what they'd shared.

It had been more than he'd expected. She was more than he'd expected. Way more. And it was wrong to make her feel bad just because he had some issues.

He snagged his shirt off the ground. Cade was right, as much as he hated to admit it. He'd go apologize for being an ass. Hopefully, she'd accept it.

* * *

He came in the kitchen and realized, when Josie looked at him with a little frown between her brows, that he was maybe not dressed for groveling. He was sweaty and dirty and probably smelled bad. But it was now or never. He doffed his hat and wished he hadn't put that cautious look in her beautiful eyes. Or earned that blank look on her face.

"I'm sorry," he blurted, and winced as soon as the words were out and her expression went cool. "I'm an ass," he added. When she simply stared at him, he wondered how he could write song lyrics that affected millions, but when it came to an apology to a woman who mattered he couldn't manage to keep his foot out of his mouth. He took a deep breath and started over, since she didn't seem inclined to say anything. "I'm not remotely sorry for what happened between us. I am sorry I freaked out and left you like that. I'm an ass," he repeated, and waited. For whatever she wanted to throw at him. He'd take it because he'd earned it.

Because she mattered and she deserved more than he'd given her.

Josie came around the island and approached him slowly. He was filthy, sweaty and dirty. "What have you been doing?" He didn't normally look as if he'd been through the wringer when he came in.

"Chopping wood." His gaze was cautious and level.

"You made me feel crappy." She managed to keep the hurt out of her tone, but she felt he should hear the truth.

His gaze softened with regret, and he shifted in place, his fingers kneading the brim of his hat. "I know. It wasn't my intention."

His clear discomfort, as much as his words, softened her. "I can't say the way you handled it was okay. It is fine that you didn't want—to stay. It was—it was pretty intense." She'd been ridiculously hurt. Shunted aside, not good enough. So it meant a lot that he would make sure she knew—clumsily, at that—that it hadn't been her.

"I wanted to stay." He reached out one hand, then stopped before he touched her. "More than you know. I just— I panicked, I guess."

She understood that. For two people who hadn't been looking for anything, they'd sure fallen into something. "I know."

"Am I forgiven? I don't want you to leave. Or be uncomfortable around me."

He sounded so earnest, if he hadn't been such a mess she'd have gone up and kissed him. "Yes. Of course."

Now they were at a crossroads. There was so much she wanted that she wasn't going to get. But still, she took a deep breath and looked him in the eye. In for a penny...

"What do you want, Luke? Where do you want to go with this?" She gestured between them. Might as well get this out in the open, where no one could hear them. It needed to be dealt with, one way or another.

He stepped closer and she saw his eyes go hot. "What do I want?" he repeated. "I want the chance to show you that I'm not going to leave you like that."

His voice got a little rough. "I want a chance to do it right."

Josie's mind went blank. *Do it right?* Her whole body hummed to life at his words. When she recovered enough she managed to say, "I do, too. But— it'd be good to set the lines now, so we don't—make any mistakes."

His eyes flared. "You think we'd be a mistake?"

She shook her head. A mistake implied there was something wrong with them together. She didn't think that, not at all. "Oh, no. No, I don't." Her voice was nearly a whisper.

He moved closer and set his hat aside so he could lay his hands on her shoulders. "Josie." Her name, full of wonderment and confusion. He was as torn up as she was. Which way to go? Did she dare to take the risk that might ultimately cost her her heart?

She cleared her throat. "I have to leave. There is a very set end here. I'm not sure I'm the fling type, Luke." She needed to lay that down before this went any further.

His gaze was intense on hers. "I'm not asking you for a fling."

"What do you want from me? Are you willing to see where it goes? To just keep things casual?" Her boldness took her by surprise. If he turned her down, it'd be awkward. *More* awkward, rather. At least she'd know where she stood. There was power in that, too.

He was quiet for a moment, and her heart pounded and her face started to heat. When she opened her mouth to tell him to forget it, he spoke. There was heat in his eyes and a wariness, too, that she wished he would let her help him erase. There wasn't time for that, of course.

"Are you sure, Josie?"

She had no intention of falling in love. None whatsoever. She liked Luke, and enjoyed the fact they were so attracted to each other. He made her burn in ways she never had, made her want in a way she never had. It was a little scary, but she was pretty sure her heart was safe. If it wasn't, she'd find a way to heal and move on. Luke had been nothing but clear on his intent to stay single and live on this ranch. That wasn't going to work for her long-term. She had a life in another state, another city, hundreds of miles away. There was no real way to meet in the middle. Which was too bad, since she thought they'd be good together. But could she let this chance, possibly her only chance at something like this, slip away because it might hurt her?

She swallowed hard and lifted her gaze to meet his serious ice-blue one. "I'm sure." Her voice was low, but steady. And with those two words, she changed everything.

A pleasant week passed, with Josie feeling a little like a college girl in the throes of her first real romance. Sadly enough, it sort of was. Her previous relationship hadn't had any romance to speak of. Luke was sweetly romantic.

It was killing her, in a good way.

"You free tomorrow morning?" Luke's question was posed as he set his dinner dishes on the counter. She looked up, momentarily distracted by his nearness. She gave a quick mental run-through of her menu for the next day.

"Yes, I can spare a couple hours," she said. "I need to be back by three, if that'll work."

"That's not a problem." He leaned one hip on the counter and crossed his arms. "If we leave right after breakfast, we'll be back in time."

Josie made some mental adjustments to breakfast. "All right. Where are we going?"

"Kalispell. That's all you need to know right now." He gave her a lazy smile and her heart turned over.

"Mmm. A surprise, huh?" She'd never been big on surprises. They'd often ended up being more about the giver than her, and many of them had been flat-out unpleasant.

Luke must have heard the doubtful tone in her voice because he tipped her chin up with one finger. "Hey. Do you trust me?"

He wasn't joking now. His expression was completely serious, and she realized he was asking about more than just a trip into town. So her answer was about more than that, too.

"Yes, Luke. I trust you."

A smile quirked the corners of his mouth. "Good. Then we'll head out as soon as you're ready in the morning." He settled a light kiss on her mouth, just a promise of what could be later, when Cade walked in the room.

"Whoa. I didn't see anything," he said loudly as he crossed the room. Josie's first instinct was to jump away from Luke, but he settled a light hand on her shoulder and squeezed.

"There's a woman out there who would let you kiss her. After she kicked your ass for being—well, for being an ass," Luke said, and Cade's face darkened.

"That's not the same," Cade mumbled. "You know that."

Luke shook his head but didn't say anything else. Cade gave them both a cocky smile, but now Josie could see the pain underneath it. He hid it well, but the better she got to know him, the more she realized there was far more to him than the carefree-cowboy front he so carefully nurtured.

"You kids have a good night," he said, and waggled his eyebrows at them. "Don't do anything I wouldn't do."

"That doesn't narrow it down very much," Luke said, and Cade just laughed as he left the room.

Josie looked at Luke. "Nikki?"

He nodded. "Yeah. They've been dancing around this for a long time. I don't see either of them changing. Too damn stubborn."

She thought of the story Nikki had told her. She wasn't going to share her friend's confidence, but she did think it was too bad they couldn't see their way to each other. But all she said was "I think stubbornness runs in the Ryder family." Then she gave him a big smile.

Luke grunted what could have been assent, then took his leave, as well. She finished up in the kitchen and prepared the coffeepot for the morning—she set the timer to start it ten minutes before her alarm went off, so when she came into the kitchen, the wonderful aroma was already filling the room. It was a little trick she'd used at home, too.

She hurried up to her room. They'd developed a system over the past week, she and Luke. He'd come to her in a bit, and stay with her—they'd make love, then he'd leave before they could fall asleep.

He never spent the night.

On the one hand, she understood. There were other family members in this house, although she didn't think any of them were fooled by what was going on under their noses. And other than Cade tonight, no one said anything.

On the other hand, she didn't think it had anything to do with family. She suspected it was deeper than that. That it was a way for him to hold back from her, to keep himself separate from the deeper intimacy of sleeping together. If he stayed all night, it would signal a level of commitment neither one of them was comfortable with.

She didn't let it bother her. Well, she tried not to let it bother her. It wasn't worth it, wanting more, asking for more, when she already knew she was leaving in two weeks. There was no point in getting emotionally involved—more so than they already were. It would make her leaving a messy thing, and she was all about avoiding an emotional mess.

But she was kind of worried there already would be one. On her end, at least.

She darted into the bathroom to brush her teeth. Just as she was dropping the toothbrush back in the holder, the knock came. Soft, but she'd been waiting for it, her whole body vibrating like a tuning fork.

She opened her door and stepped back to let him in. "Hi," she said, trying to hide the giddiness, as if she hadn't just seen him fifteen minutes ago.

He gave her a slow grin. "Hi yourself."

She closed the door and locked it, then turned into his arms and gave herself over to the feelings.

Luke lay awake, Josie's breathing steady and deep beside him. She was so beautiful. The moonlight streamed in the room, just enough that he could see her. The sheet was still bunched around her waist, but dipped low enough he could see the shadow of hair between her legs. Her breasts were plumped against the mattress, the rosy nipples calling his name. Her hair fanned on the pillow, and he touched it lightly. He laid a hand on the curve of her waist, then pulled the sheet and blankets up over her as he carefully got out of bed. The mattress dipped as he did so, and he held his breath as she stirred slightly, but didn't wake up.

He pulled his pants on and just stood for another minute, wanting to stay, wanting to curl up behind her, to wake with her in the morning. But he couldn't. He needed some kind of distance, and this was it. It was understood between them, even if they didn't ever mention it.

Regretful it couldn't be more, he slipped out and pulled her door shut, only to see his mother standing there. Shock, then disapproval crossed her face.

Hell. He had no shirt on, but thank God he'd put his pants on. "Mom."

She tilted her head. "Luke Jackson Ryder, what do you think you're doing?"

There were a lot of answers to that question, but none of them were probably what she wanted to hear. "I don't think I need to explain, Mom. We know what we're doing." Then he attempted to change the subject. "Are you okay? Why are you up?"

She poked him in the chest, hard. "I'm fine. Went in the kitchen for a drink. We are not talking about me. You can't even stay the night with her?" She gave her head a firm shake.

He shut his eyes. "Mom. It's just best I don't." So that Josie didn't think there was more here than there actually was? So *he* didn't think there was more than there actually was? He wasn't sure.

"Don't break her heart," she said sharply. "Because you and I both know if you didn't care about her—a lot—you wouldn't be in her bed."

Luke scrubbed his hand over his face. "Mom. We're not going to talk about this." Of course he cared about her. He wasn't a total heel.

His mother harrumphed and walked off into her room and shut the door. He was left in the hallway, feeling chastised—rightly or not, he wasn't sure—and embarrassed. Then he shook his head and returned to his room.

Yes, he and Josie made love. No, he couldn't wait to get naked with her. But it was more than that. They talked, they watched TV, they laughed. They had a relationship—a friendship—and it was based on more than mutual attraction. No, they weren't in love. But that had never been on the table anyway. He thought she was gorgeous and sexy. He liked her a lot. Liked her company a lot. Liked that she didn't push him, that she just accepted him for—well, for him. For who he really was, not as the country star.

Which was good, because it'd been a long damn time since he'd been a star. He'd been out of the business far longer than he'd been in it. But lately he was getting the itch to write songs again. So he'd started jotting some lines down, listening to the music in his head. He hadn't tried to get the guitar out and do any actual composing, because that made it too real. He still hadn't gone down to the recording studio in the basement. He wasn't ready to visit that part of his past yet.

He did not miss performing and touring. Well, maybe a little bit. He missed singing and the energy of the crowd and the music and the band. When it all merged together properly, it was an almost holy experience.

Okay, yeah, he missed it. And he wasn't sure why it was surfacing now.

He could already tell sleep was going to be hard for him. So he got out his notebook and worked on the song.

## Chapter Twelve

Josie was ready the next morning, dressed in jeans and a light sweater—it was going to be a cool day, but sunny. Luke gave her a smile and a kiss on the temple, but he seemed tired and distracted.

"You okay?"

He nodded. "Just tired. Nothing new there. Bring a pair of regular socks, too."

She went and grabbed a pair of argyle knee socks and shoved them in her purse, then joined him in the kitchen. Alice had told her not to worry about dinner; if they were a little late, she'd start things for Josie. Josie had thanked her, but hoped she'd be back in time.

She started the dishwasher and followed Luke out the door. He opened the passenger door of the red truck for her and she hopped in smoothly.

She felt a little bloom of pride. It was true—she'd gotten much better at entering and exiting the truck over the weeks she'd been here. In fact, she'd garnered lots of new skills she'd never thought she'd need. Like dog washing and caring for horses.

Luke got in and started the truck. Even though he'd said he was fine, his jaw was a little tight. She'd thought things had seemed a little strained with him and Alice this morning, but she wasn't completely sure. Nor would she ask. It wasn't her business.

"Can you tell me now what we're going for? Why do I need socks?" She did trust he wouldn't pull any kind of crap with her but she was still a little leery. She'd had plenty of surprises foisted on her over her life. *What do you mean you want an open relationship, Russ?* Yeah, that had been one of the nastier ones.

He gave her a grin. "No. You'll see. You trust me, remember?" When she nodded, he added, "It's nothing bad or unpleasant. Just something I want to do for you, as a thank-you for all you've done for us. Okay?"

She exhaled. Put that way… "Okay. Fair enough. Even though you don't owe me anything," she added.

He reached over and laced his fingers in hers. "More than you know."

They talked on the trip, and she was surprised again at how comfortable she was with him, and how much he'd opened up to her. It was such a change from the beginning. A little thread of regret snaked through her. To think they'd found this kind of ease with each other, and she had to leave.

But she knew that bringing up the future would

only ruin the moment, when they'd been very clear on the fact there was no future. It just wouldn't work. And maybe the ease was only there because there was a time limit on this and it was fast approaching the end. Maybe it allowed him to relax, when he knew she wouldn't be around much longer.

She hoped that wasn't it. She didn't think that was the truth. But it was hard to tell and she couldn't imagine asking. What if it ended things earlier than expected? She wanted every moment they could get.

In Kalispell, he found a parking spot just off the main drag and rubbed his hands together. "Ready?"

She smiled at him. She couldn't help it. He was excited—almost giddy—about whatever this was. Like a kid. "I'm ready."

"Good." He leaned toward her and she met him halfway, and he kissed her quick and hard and thoroughly. She lost her breath for a moment and he touched her face. There was a tenderness in his touch that spoke to something deep inside her. "Let's go."

She grabbed her purse and met him on the sidewalk. He didn't take her hand, but they did walk close enough their arms brushed, and he rested his hand on the small of her back as they navigated the pedestrian traffic on the main drag. She stopped in front of a boutique Western store with an incredible display of gorgeous Western boots that made her stop for a second. These, with their intricate scrollwork and details, were far from the beat-up old boots of Aunt Rosa's she'd been wearing. These were works of art.

"Oh, wow," she said, awed.

Luke bent close, and his breath feathered over her ear. "Lucky for you, this is where we're going."

She twisted to look up at him, delight blooming in her chest. "Really?"

He dropped a quick kiss on her forehead and reached past her for the door handle. "Really."

The bell jangled over the door and a gorgeous woman, probably in her late twenties, looked up with a smile that quickly grew more genuine when she saw Luke. Josie heaved an internal sigh. Not much of a shock here.

She came around the end of the counter, her long black hair in a thick braid down her back. "Luke. So good to see you. And you must be Josie."

She held out her hand and her friendliness didn't dim at all. This wasn't a woman who was out for Luke. Josie relaxed a little.

Not because it really mattered—Josie was leaving, and if Luke could have a woman nearby, that'd be better anyway. Right? Her stomach immediately clenched. Okay, so she had a little work to do on convincing herself.

She took her hand. "I am."

"Nice to meet you. I'm Skye Howard. This is my shop. Luke said you're in the market for new boots?"

"Ah." She glanced at Luke, who looked a little bit as if he was up to something. "I don't own any."

Luke stepped in. "Skye makes them herself. She's a master craftswoman. And this is my treat. Like I told you in the truck, I just wanted to thank you for all the work you've done for us."

"Oh." Josie was touched, and she caught Skye's

avid expression. No doubt she could see there was...
something between her and Luke. "Wow. Are you
sure?" Because she was willing to bet Skye's handi-
work didn't come cheap. Even for a friend.

He brushed his hand down her arm, lightly, then
nudged her forward toward Skye. "I am." He told
her he had another errand to run and left them to it.

Skye smiled at her. "Are you ready?"

"Oh, yes." Josie followed her over to a chair where
Skye indicated she should sit and slipped off her
shoes, understanding now why Luke had told her to
bring regular socks. She pulled them on. "Are all
these your work?" she asked, looking around the
shop.

"No." Skye fitted her foot in to the measuring de-
vice and made a note on a pad. "I do this mostly on
commission. The ones in the window are mine, and
I have a few pairs in here, but mostly I carry other
brands. Not everyone wants or can afford custom-
made boots. I do a pretty solid online business, as
well."

Josie examined the top of Skye's head as she
crouched at her feet. Her hair was jet black and long.
The braid came nearly to her waist. Her skin was a
golden brown and her eyes were a sparkling brown.
She was small and slender, but her quick fingers were
long and nimble. Skye took a tablet and set it up on
the table between them. "Here are some samples of
my work. See what works for you, if there's anything
you like or don't like. Some are more everyday, some
are more special occasion, but I make them all to
withstand real use, not just for show."

There was pride in her voice, and Josie could quickly see that it was well deserved. As she swiped through the album, she was more and more impressed. Some of the detail work, with flowers and vines, was truly amazing. "Skye. Wow. You do all this yourself?"

"Right now I do. If the business keeps growing, I'll need to bring in others to help, but I'll keep a close eye on it and stick with the designing. That's what I love, and what makes each pair individual, even if someone chooses the same design as someone else. They'll never be identical."

Josie decided to go simple. She chose black leather with a rambling rose in deep pink and green vines. It would twine up the side of the boot on the outside and over the toes. Skye drew it freehand out for her quickly so she could see, and then made a copy of it for Josie.

"I know you're leaving soon, so I'll put a rush on this. If you have to leave before I get them done, I'll mail them to you, but I'd really like to have your feet in the store if possible, to make sure that they fit you properly."

Josie smiled. "Thanks, Skye. I can come back, just let me know when."

Skye hesitated, then said, "This is none of my business and I know it, but are you and Luke an item? He looks at you— Well, he looks at you. I've gotten to know him and his family over the past couple of years and I've never seen him look at someone like he does at you."

Josie hesitated. She didn't know Skye, not really.

She liked her, but wasn't sure how much to say. So she just smiled at her. "It's fine. I like him a lot, but I'm leaving." She gave a little shrug that was not nearly as carefree as she'd have liked it to be. "So no, there's not really anything there."

Skye studied her for a second. "Fair enough." Then her gaze drifted behind Josie. "Hey, Luke. You're just in time."

Luke was polite to her, but when they left the store, Josie wondered if he'd overheard and misconstrued her shot at being nonchalant about them. Because in reality, it wasn't nearly as casual as she'd made it sound. She was trying to pretend it was, but deep down she knew better. To test the waters, she said, "Thanks for doing that for me. They're going to be beautiful. And Skye is awesome."

He nodded, his jaw still seeming a little tense. "She is. She's been a great addition to the city. Her work is in high demand. And you're welcome."

Luke didn't know why her comment had bothered him so much. They'd been pretty much operating on the assumption that it was going to be over soon, but to hear her classify it as "not really anything" had hit him oddly hard. It didn't do him any good to want it to be more. Or her either, for that matter.

But she mattered to him. He wanted to think he mattered to her. That *they* mattered.

He had no idea how to even say that, so he kept it to himself. Better to keep it that way than run the risk of making things awkward and weird for both of them.

"I can't wait to see them," Josie was saying. Her smile was wide and a little worried, so he smiled back and made himself relax. It was okay. They were okay. He wasn't going to push her.

"She'll get them done as soon as she can. She knows you're on a tight schedule."

"Yes," Josie agreed. "I just hope she's not putting a lot of other things to the side to accommodate me."

Skye had assured him it would be no problem to make the boots for Josie. She'd been excited to do it. "I think she would have said if she couldn't get them done in time. She's a good businesswoman on top of being a design genius. She's not going to do anything to risk her reputation." And Luke already knew her reputation had been built with care. She didn't say much about her past, of course, but he'd heard that she came from a rough family. More power to her if she was able to rise above that and make her own way.

"That's good," she said with a sigh. "I don't want to put her out."

Again, he was struck by the difference between her and Mandy—it wouldn't have occurred to his ex-wife that Skye might be inconvenienced by what she wanted. Mandy wouldn't have been mean about it, it just simply never would have crossed her mind to ask. She'd spent so much time being told how it was all about her that she'd wholeheartedly believed it. It had made things difficult when Luke had finally realized she wasn't ever going to change. She'd wanted him more as a satellite than as a partner, which was not his view of marriage.

They stopped for a quick lunch—not the burger

place or the diner this time, not enough time—and headed back to the ranch.

He did pull over, down a remote road, and leaned over for a hot kiss. It nearly led to more, right there in the truck, but she eased back and smiled at him. "Something to look forward to?"

He half laughed, half groaned. "Yeah. Okay." Not for the first time he wished there would be no one in his house so he could have his way with her as soon as they walked in the door.

She laughed at him as she eased back into her seat. "You'll be fine. Let's just get there, shall we?"

"Did you have a good time in Kalispell?" Alice asked her a little later. Josie smiled at her.

"I did. It was so sweet of Luke to think of that for me. I can't wait until they're done."

Alice smiled back. "He's a good man. A very good one. And you make him smile."

This was the most direct Alice had been about her and Luke yet, though she'd been dropping hints for days. Josie decided to respond in kind. "It's mutual, Alice. You raised good boys."

Her smile turned a little sad around the edges. "Yes. No thanks to their mother."

Confused, Josie set the knife on the counter. "What? Aren't you their mother?"

Alice eased herself on a chair at the island. She folded her hands on the counter and lifted her somber gaze to Josie's. "I'm going to tell you something that I'm not even sure his ex-wife knew. Luke never talks about it—I don't know if any of them do. But their mother left when they were young. Really young. Luke was four, so he has some hazy memories of her. The other two don't remember her at all."

Josie sucked in a breath. "Oh. Oh, Alice." Her heart broke a little for the small boys who'd lost their mom—who'd left them behind.

Alice ran her hands over the cool stone of the counter, her pensive gaze on her hands. "She wasn't ready to be a mother, much less ready to be a wife. John loved her madly but she didn't feel the same. She tried, but she was just too selfish to make it work." There was no trace of bitterness in her voice. Just sadness and maybe a bit of bewilderment.

Josie wondered at "loved her madly." Why had he remarried if he was so in love with the woman who'd left him? Maybe the question was written on her face, because Alice gave her a sad smile. "He married me a few months later. He wanted a mother for his boys, whom he loved but was in way over his head with, and I—" She stopped, then took a deep breath. "I wanted what my sister had, what she threw away like it was no more than trash. A family."

"Your sister," Josie said slowly, and then it dawned on her. "You're their biological aunt." It explained the family resemblance. She never would have guessed Alice wasn't their mom. They all shared the same smile.

Alice nodded. "I am. But I'm also their mother in every way that counts." There was a bit of fierceness in her tone.

Josie didn't doubt that. "What happened to—to your sister?"

Alice sighed. "She was an addict, as well. She died five years after she left. In New York City, of all places. And I only found that out by accident."

Sympathy flooded her. "Oh, Alice." Saying she was sorry didn't seem like enough, but her heart ached for Luke, Cade and Jake, who would never get the chance to make amends with their mother.

"I know. It— I know it left a hole. But it has to be said, John and I had a good marriage. He was a loving husband, a good father. He and Luke butted heads a lot, but that was because they were very similar in a lot of ways. At the time you couldn't convince Luke of that." There was a faint smile on her lips now. "We make a good family. I'm so grateful I got to be their mom."

Josie realized, after Alice had left, that the older woman had another point. The women in Luke's life left him. His mother, his wife. She was going to leave him, too, but of course she wasn't a part of his life the way they had been, or should have been. But it probably only validated what he felt—that he was somehow unworthy. This broke her heart a little. She wasn't leaving because she wanted to. Not now. She was leaving because she'd never pretended any different. Nothing had changed in that respect. She hadn't come in here with any intentions other than to cook for the family. But she was going to be leaving a lot behind. Friends, to be sure, and possibly her heart, as well.

She wasn't going to dwell on that last point. There was no reason to. Nothing was going to change, no matter how much she wished it.

## Chapter Thirteen

"Help me move back to my house, please?"

Luke frowned as he surveyed the packed bags lined up neatly on the bed behind his mother. "Are you sure you're ready? Maybe you should give it another week." What if she fell?

She reached up and patted his cheek. "Of course I'm ready. I would have been just fine weeks ago. I only stayed up here because I knew if I didn't, the three of you would be trekking your way down to check on me at all hours of the day and night. But you need your own space back. And I think it's time for Cade and Jake to look into building their own places."

Startled, Luke looked at her. "What? Why?" They'd lived like this for years. There was no reason for him to be in that big house all by himself. Was it really okay for her to leave?

Alice sighed and turned to lift the smaller of the duffels off the bed and set it on the floor. "Luke. At some point you're going to want the place to yourself. You and Josie—"

He held up a hand. "There is no me and Josie—"

She gave him a look and kept on talking. "You and Josie together got me to thinking. You're not going to be single your whole life. None of you are. None of you should be."

Numbly, he repeated, "There is no me and Josie." Even though, yes, there was a relationship there. It wasn't going anywhere.

The other two bags joined the first on the floor. Alice started to strip the sheets off the bed, and he jumped in to help.

"Well, there should be. There's something between you, more than just the physical, it's crystal clear to everyone here. It'd be a damn shame to let her go, don't you think?" Before he could answer, she kept right on talking. "But if you do, you might find another woman to marry. Such a shame to keep letting Mandy win."

Luke stood there, completely poleaxed, the sheets balled up in his hands, not sure where to start to respond. Or if he even should try. She'd said an awful lot in just a few words.

She lifted the duffel, and Luke immediately dropped the sheets and took it from her. "I'll carry this and I'll take care of the rest of the room later."

His mind reeling, he followed his mother over to her house. He noted her pace was slow but her steps were steady. No limping or sign of pain. He wondered if she'd told Cade and Jake they should think about moving out. They each had their own lots on the ranch. Neither had opted to build on them yet because they were all single, so it made more sense to just bunk in the same house, where they shared a cook. But if they wanted to do their own thing, obviously there wasn't anything he could do about it.

What had she meant about letting Mandy win?

He followed his mother into her little house and set the bags on the bed where she directed him to. She pulled him in for a hug. "Thanks for the help. I love you. I just want you to be happy, but you seem to think that's not in the cards for you. That you had only one shot at it with a woman you weren't a good match with to begin with. Don't write it off. Don't just let Josie go because Rosa is coming back. Please."

Those weren't promises he could make, because he knew most of them couldn't be kept. So all he said was, "I love you, too, Mom."

After she assured him she was fine and would let them know if she had any issues, he left her little cabin. Down the lane another half mile or so was the lot Cade owned. It wouldn't be within eyeshot, but close enough. They'd all been given parcels that would allow them privacy, but yet be close enough that working on the ranch wouldn't be an issue. It had been his mother's idea, he suspected. And he knew she was right. If Cade and Jake were ready to build, he wasn't going to stop them. Sure, he'd rattle around that big house all by himself, but when his brothers married there'd be wives and kids and plenty of people. Or maybe he'd offer the house to them, and take one of the parcels and build himself a little cabin, like his mother's.

\* \* \*

Josie frowned at the ball of sheets in the hall in front of Alice's room. She wasn't anywhere to be found. So when Luke came in the back door, she met him in the mudroom. "What's going on with your mom? Is she okay?"

"She's fine." Luke toed off his boots. "She moved out."

"Alice moved back out?" Shocked, Josie could only stare at Luke. Alice hadn't said anything to her. "Why? Oh, gosh. Should I take her a plate? Will she come up here for meals?"

Luke settled his hands on her shoulders and squeezed gently. "Josie. Relax. I said that wrong. She didn't move out, she went back home. She'll cook for herself, but come up here often for meals."

"Oh. Why?"

Luke shrugged, but there was something in his posture that made her think there was more to the situation than he was telling her. "Luke. What happened?"

He sighed and rubbed his hand over his face. "She thinks I need space. My own space," he clarified. "I ran into her the other night after I left your room. Apparently that was enough to make her decide to go home. She insists she was ready anyway."

Josie's face burned. "She saw you leave?" This was new, as Alice hadn't given her any indication she was aware of an actual relationship with Josie and Luke. But— Oh, my. How to face her now? *Yes, Alice, I'm having excellent sex with your son.* Oh, God. No.

"Yeah. She didn't say much—we're both adults

after all, and it's no one's business but ours, but yeah. It wasn't my favorite mother-son moment."

Josie cringed. "Oh, God." Adults or not, there was something mortifying about being caught like that, and him leaving made it seem as if he wasn't willing to spend the night with her, as if he was hiding something. Hiding her.

He pulled her in and kissed her, hard. She held on and kissed him right back. He pulled away lightly and nuzzled her cheek. "Are you going to tell me not to come to your bed anymore?" His breath feathered on her cheek.

She sighed and leaned on him, her cheek now on his chest. "Sadly, no."

A chuckle rumbled through him and she had to smile. She wasn't willing to give him up. These next two weeks would be priceless for her. She'd already accepted that she'd be leaving and he'd be staying— no shock there. But she was determined to get everything out of this experience since it was unlikely she'd connect with another man the same way. It just didn't seem possible. If she'd been wondering if she'd been in love with Russ before, she had her answer now— no. She didn't know exactly what she felt for Luke, didn't want to dig too hard into it, but she knew it was far more than she'd ever felt for Russ. And that alone was a win in her book.

Luke gave her another kiss and went back outside, and Josie returned to her work.

When he walked into the kitchen the first thing he saw—the first thing he always saw lately—was Josie.

She gave him a quick smile as she looked over her shoulder from the stove, where she was stirring something that smelled wonderful. He washed his hands and came up behind her, wrapping his arms around her lightly and kissing her neck. She went perfectly still, spoon in hand.

"What was that for?" she asked, her tone light, but her eyes were serious. Luke knew he'd just advanced them another step, past the point they'd been toeing for a while now, that they seemed to have tacitly agreed they wouldn't cross. But his mother's words had shaken something loose in him.

"No reason other than you looked like you needed it," he said lightly, and she smiled at him, then returned to her pan. "What is that?"

"Gravy. My bugaboo." She gave a little laugh and pushed her hair back with her free hand. "If I blink too many times it gets lumpy. Or thick. Or doesn't come together."

"You're a professional and it still happens?"

She shrugged and sent him a little look. "Oh, all the time. In fact, it was one of the things—" She stopped and hunched her shoulders a little bit. As if she'd gone too far.

"One of the things what?" he prompted, curious since this was the most she'd referenced her past. He'd figured there was a good reason she wasn't at her restaurant anymore, but since she hadn't said anything he hadn't wanted to push.

She gave her head a quick shake. "Nothing."

But he wasn't in the mood to be brushed off. Not today. "Josie. Please don't shut me out."

She took the pan off the stove and turned to face him. She took a deep breath. "It was one of the things my relationship broke up over. I didn't do it his way."

Luke went very, very still. *His way.* So there was a guy mixed up in all this. "Over gravy?" He couldn't help his incredulous tone.

She gave a little laugh and a half shrug. "Yes. And no. It was more that I didn't do things the way he considered the right way. His way, which as it turned out was the only way."

Luke's hands fisted. He forced them to relax. "And who is that?"

Josie went to the sink to fiddle with the dirty pans she'd put there. If she was going to tell this story, she needed to keep busy. "It's a long story. But I met Russ Crosby at a party hosted by mutual friends. I know you're not a big TV watcher, but he's big on the Cook's Network and often appears on talk shows and things. So really well-known. He took me under his wing, you could say, even though I was not interested in a career in television. He also owns three restaurants—two in LA and one in New York City. I worked for him for a while in LA and things kind of—kind of developed." She'd been flattered he'd taken the time to notice her, to compliment her and eventually to ask her out. "We dated for nearly three years. He did a lot of travel and I started my own place, which he eventually took over. Only it was by little increments. I didn't even really realize what was happening until one day, when I thought we were going to get married, I found out he'd been unfaithful. Very unfaithful."

Luke made a sound that could have been a growl. She looked over her shoulder, then grabbed the dish towel and turned to face him, wiping her hands on the towel. "Oh, yes. All the way along. And he'd inserted himself neatly in my restaurant so that when I left him, I had to leave that behind, too. He'd loaned me the money and it was all set up so that if I left, he'd get it." She shut her eyes. This was the part that made her the most angry. She'd been so stupid. So blind. "I missed it, Luke. I didn't know—I knew I had to pay him back, but he'd been undermining me the whole time."

Luke got up and came around the counter, wrapping his arms around her when he got there. She didn't cry—she had no tears for Russ—but she did lean on Luke and let him just hold her. "So that's why you came here?"

She nodded her head against his chest, enjoying the solid feel of him. "Yes. It'd been about three months since it all went down and I needed to get away." She also needed the money from a paycheck, since their very public breakup had been engineered by Russ to look as if he was the injured party, just helping his struggling fiancée out, and look how she repaid him by leaving him, blah, blah, blah. "I also—I also couldn't get a job at that same level. No one in the city or nearby wanted to hire me. Not because I wasn't any good, but because Russ is so very much larger-than-life that no one wants to mess with him." There was bitterness in her words and she knew it. Could taste it. Luke's arms tightened around her. "There were signs all the way along. Like I said, little things like how I made gravy. Or plated an entrée. Or what-ever. He'd come in and correct me or tease me—now I can see how very controlling he was, but he was so subtle about it, at the time I just couldn't.''

She hadn't listened to those who had tried to warn her. She hadn't wanted to believe it, or believe that she could be such a fool. And in the end, she'd been a far bigger fool than she'd ever imagined.

"So what happened with your restaurant? How did he get it?"

Josie explained the loan he'd given her had had a clause written in by his lawyer—and she'd trusted him enough not to hire her own, a mistake she'd not make again—that the whole thing reverted to him if business struggled according to the stringent terms he'd set. It had struggled in the beginning, as new places were likely to do, but he hadn't given her all his support like he'd promised. And if she'd realized how it was all set up, she would have done things a little differently. She hadn't needed him to make her a success, and that had completely burned him. But it was too late now.

"Wow. What a bastard."

Josie rose up on her tiptoes and kissed his cheek. He made her feel better, as weird as it sounded. Hav-ing someone completely on her side, with no knowl-edge of Russ, was wonderful. "Thank you. Yes, he is."

"So you can't go back?"

She shrugged. "To work at my place? No. I can't. I have a lawsuit against him, but it won't give me the restaurant back. People's memories are short, you know?" Still, she didn't know how short, or if she wanted to risk it. And the more she thought about it, the more she thought that maybe it was time for a change. "I spent ten years there. That's a long time. I have a condo. I have friends there. I have other options that I'm considering." She'd had a life, such as it was, but it was run by her career. Another mistake she wasn't going to make.

He ran his hand down her hair. "It's not easy."

She supposed he'd know, having been through something similar. Though hers wasn't nearly as high-profile as his breakup. She'd been a nobody all the way along. "No. It's not. But I'm looking at options. I love to cook. It's what I want to do. Now I just have to figure out where I'm going to do it."

It was time she put some of those irons in the fire. Russ had knocked her down, but she wasn't out of the game. Not yet. Not unless and until she wanted to be.

Josie felt better for telling Luke her story. She hadn't really told anyone all the details, other than Allie, because she'd been embarrassed to have been so thoroughly duped. Luke hadn't judged her. He hadn't laughed at her or asked her how she hadn't seen it coming. He'd just listened.

She valued that beyond measure.

She'd spent a lot of time beating herself up over this. How had she not seen it, how could she have trusted Russ, etc. But she'd come to realize that though the signs were all there, in the context of their relationship they simply hadn't been warning signs. She hadn't liked being treated in the kitchen the way he'd treated her, and she'd told him so. He'd apologized, improved and eventually they'd fall back into the same pattern. She hadn't been a doormat, and that was important.

But still.

So Luke's unquestioning support felt good. She'd never really had anyone who sat solidly in her corner before. Not her parents, who had insinuated that she'd screwed this up on her own, and not her coworkers, who'd known where their bread was buttered— by Russ's hand. He was petty enough that he would have used their support against her, or worse, as reason to fire someone and make it hard for them to find a new job. She wasn't going to hold any of that against them. They'd done what they could and they all needed the work.

Taking out her phone, Josie pulled up her list of potential places. She called her former mentor, who had a few suggestions for her, as well. She'd never really considered being a personal chef, for example. She'd gotten used to being in the pressure-cooker atmosphere of a commercial kitchen in a popular, world-renowned restaurant. Her experience here at the Silver River, though, was reminding her how much she loved food. How much she just loved to cook. So maybe it was an option after all.

Her mentor promised to put out feelers and let her know if anything came up. It was exciting to realize there were a lot of prospects out there for her that were beyond Russ's reach.

She was ready to find them.

## *Chapter Fourteen*

Josie heard it as soon as she stepped in the house, returning from a trip to town the next afternoon. The notes of a guitar, muffled slightly by what probably was a closed door, but there was no mistaking the music.

Luke was playing.

She shut the door behind her softly, not that he'd hear it. But she didn't want to risk him sensing her arrival and stopping. The song was melancholy, and he kept stopping and starting, as though he was trying to work out the exact notes. She set the groceries and the mail on the counter and listened. The guitar was an extension of his soul. To hear it now, when he'd said himself that he'd given it up for years, was a gift.

Far too soon, the music stopped and she heard the door open. She held her breath, feeling as if she'd intruded when all she'd done was return from town early. He came in the kitchen and stopped. Discomfort crossed his face. She preempted him from making any excuses by smiling at him, keeping her tone casual. The last thing he'd want was her to make a big deal of it. "That was lovely, Luke. New song?"

He shoved his hand through his hair. "I— Yeah. Listen, Josie—"

She held up a hand. "I won't say anything. But I have to ask—why do you want to hide it?"

He shook his head. "It's just not a good idea. That's all."

"Oh, Luke." But there was no more for her to say, nothing that would matter. She didn't know how to help him heal the wound left too long ago. Maybe, by playing today, he'd started down that road himself.

He shrugged. "Water under the bridge now," he said as he left the kitchen. She heard him in the mudroom, and then the back door opened and closed.

She watched him walk down the path toward the barns, her heart aching. Music and the guitar were part of him. A part of him he'd cut off. It had to have felt like he'd given up something vital and critical to his well-being. There was a recording studio in the basement. She'd found it one of the first days she'd been here, when she was down there to visit the root cellar. The door had a window in it, and she'd glanced in. It looked as if it hadn't been touched in years. At the time she hadn't thought too much about it. But now, knowing what she did, she wondered if it ever had been used—his marriage had been short and he'd left the industry right after that. From what Alice had told her, the house hadn't been all the way completed at that time. So she figured it was a good bet the recording studio had always been empty.

She turned from the window and started taking items from the bags on the counter. Whatever Luke was punishing himself for, it seemed as though it went a lot deeper than a marriage that had been ill-fated from the start.

Luke mentally cursed himself for getting the guitar out. He'd come in the house to take care of some paperwork in the office and had realized that the house was empty. He'd been unable to stop himself from going upstairs and taking the instrument out of his closet.

Lately it had been calling to him. Every time he opened the doors, it had been the first thing he'd looked at. As if it was done being ignored. It was all coming back, the songwriting, the need to play—he'd locked it all away for so long that to have it come back now was disconcerting at best.

The beat-up old Gibson felt like coming home in his hands. He could tell the story behind almost every ding and scratch. He could still feel the guitar in his hands. All he'd had to do was close his eyes and his fingers…and the music…took over. He'd plucked out a few bars of the melody he'd envisioned to go with the song he'd written, played with it, and felt the rush he'd been missing.

He stared at the hay bales in front of him, barely seeing them. Then he'd come in the kitchen and realized he'd been caught. By Josie, who looked at him with soft eyes and a knowing smile. He'd panicked, as though he'd accidentally let her in deeper than he'd intended. Which was silly. But he had the feeling that she had seen and understood what it had meant for him to play again. He wasn't sure how he felt about that.

Movement caught his eye, and he turned to smile at Nikki as she approached him, the phone clutched in her hand. The he noticed her face was set in tense lines. His smile faded. "Nikki. What's going on?"

"I need to go home. My mom just called. My father had a stroke. It's not— They don't know—" Her voice trailed off as she took a gulping breath and Luke caught her arm.

"I'm so sorry, Nikki. We'll get you right out of here. Did you make flight reservations yet?"

Cade strode over and his gaze zeroed right in on Nikki. "Nik. Are you okay? What happened?" To Luke he repeated, "What the hell happened?"

Nikki spoke before Luke could. "I'm going home. I've got a flight out of Kalispell at six."

"I'll drive you," Luke said. "You packed?" He checked the time. "We'll need to leave in about fifteen minutes to make it."

She looked at him gratefully, and Cade's mouth tightened. "I'll be ready. Thanks, Luke."

As she hurried off, Cade turned to him. "I'll drive her."

Luke wasn't going to get in the middle of whatever was between Cade and Nikki. "She going to be okay with that?"

Cade looked after her, his jaw set. "We'll find

out. If she won't get in the truck with me, you can drive her."

Luke studied his brother for a minute but didn't ask what had gone wrong. He figured he knew. Nikki and Cade and been very flirty a while back.

Cade strode off in the same direction Nikki had gone without another word, and Luke figured if Nikki turned Cade down flat, he'd hear about it soon enough. So he stuck close to the barn until he saw Cade's truck, with Nikki in the passenger seat, drive by.

That was going to be a tense ride for both of them.

Then he saddled Kipper and headed out to catch up with another crew. Keeping busy had the added benefit of keeping his mind off Josie, but truthfully, she wasn't far from his mind at any given point. This was an issue. And he was worried about Nikki, too.

Cade came in late that evening. Josie had left a plate for him, just in case, ready to be warmed up. Luke hadn't known much, only that Nikki's father had a stroke and she'd needed to get home right away. Josie had waited for Cade, hoping to get more information on how Nikki's father was faring.

"I don't know if you ate already, but there's a plate in the fridge," she said when he came in. "How's Nikki doing?"

He gave a harsh laugh. "I don't know. She won't talk to me. She's very close to her family so I'd guess this is very hard on her. Being so far away."

Josie held up the plate and he nodded, helping himself to a beer from the fridge. "Thanks." He popped the top off and the metal cap danced on the counter. The bottle made a clinking sound on the granite when he set it down. The only other noise was the hum of the microwave. Josie leaned on the counter and said nothing. Cade was in his own world, and she wasn't going to try to break in. She already knew Nikki had feelings for him, even if he didn't realize it, but Josie wasn't going to say anything. They'd have to figure it out themselves. God knew she wasn't in any position to hand out romantic advice.

"She said she didn't know when or if she'd be back," Cade said. When he fell silent, she pulled the plate out of the microwave, set it in front of him and added silverware. "Said she wasn't sure if it was worth it to come back. Thanks," he added.

"You're welcome." She studied him for a minute. He looked bewildered. She stifled a sigh. Unless Nikki gave her the go-ahead, there wasn't anything she could really do here. Neither of them wanted to admit their feelings.

Maybe like someone else she knew. She got protecting yourself. She really did. But she also wondered—why couldn't they all have a shot at a happy ending? Or at least, a happy right now? Why were all of them unable to take those steps?

Since she had no answers, she let it go.

"I'm sure she's feeling awful over her father," she said. "When she has a chance to see how things are there, she'll be able to make that decision easier. Her job is here. She loves it here. You know she does." Because that was true. She knew Nikki did. The other woman had told her so.

Cade forked up a mouthful of beef she was willing to bet he didn't really taste. "Yeah. She does." Then he looked at her and actually focused on her. "You going to leave Luke?"

Josie floundered for a moment at the change in subject. "What? I'm not leaving Luke. I'm going home, like I'd planned from the start."

He shrugged. "Looks the same from here. He wants you to stay."

Those words tugged at her heart. He hadn't said that to her and she hadn't said anything about it to him. They didn't go there. "Oh, Cade. Don't say that, okay? Don't make this any harder than it already is." It was as honest as she could be.

He looked at her intensely for a minute, then mopped up gravy with a roll. "Going to suck for both of you. I wish there was another way."

*Yeah, me, too.* But Josie just said nothing. His blunt statement was true. There wasn't another way. Wanting it to be different wasn't going to change anything. All she said was, "If you hear from Nikki, will you tell me?"

"Yeah. But I won't. She'll let Luke know what's going on."

He sounded sad, mad and resigned all in one, and she just said, "Okay," and let it drop.

What a pair she and Cade were, she thought as she trekked off to bed after Cade had left the kitchen. Wanting something they couldn't have, for very different reasons. Or maybe all four of them were like that—wanting what couldn't be, and not knowing how to change it. If they should even try to change it. In the case of her and Luke, she couldn't stay, and there was no way Luke was going to leave the ranch he'd dedicated so much time to, the place he'd spent nearly his entire life. She'd never ask him to do so.

And that, right there, about summed it up.

Cade's statement had been spot-on. It was going to suck. And she wished like crazy she knew a way to change it.

Josie spent a restless night—Luke hadn't come to her room last night, and she wasn't sure why. It shouldn't matter.

Plus, her dreams had been the sort that she couldn't remember after waking up, but they left her feeling discontent and slightly out of sorts. So she was very happy to get her morning cup of coffee in her hands. She knew all too well the signs of a day that would end up being fueled by caffeine.

Maybe all those years of running in high gear had finally caught up to her. Though she hadn't realized it at the time, she'd been in a constant state of stress from one thing or another. Since coming here, that had all faded into the background. There were still things she needed to take care of back in Los Angeles. But she wasn't overcome with it anymore.

It was as if being here gave her the space to breathe. Space she hadn't even known she'd needed.

She stepped outside on the back deck and heard the noises from the barns. The workday started long before daybreak down there, though the sunrise was hitting the peaks of the mountains and turning them pink, the rest of the area was still the grayish dark of early dawn. Hank trotted around, not straying too far from her, but checking out what had come through his territory overnight. She took a deep breath of the crisp air, feeling it clear her head of the leftover muzzies from her night. Maybe she wouldn't need all that caffeine after all.

Of course, in LA she wouldn't step outside and take a nice deep lungful of smoggy air. It wasn't really the same.

So maybe she wouldn't go back to LA.

That thought kept circling in her head as she prepared and served breakfast, and accepted a quick kiss from Luke before he went out the door. He didn't say why he hadn't come last night, and she wasn't going to ask.

"You want to take a ride with me this afternoon?" he asked her quietly, after letting her know Nikki had made it back to Minnesota okay and her father was stable. "There's something I'd like to show you."

"Sure," she said, far too pleased by the prospect of time with him. "I'd like that."

"All right. I'll be back up here around eleven, so any time after that is good."

She said she'd be ready and watched him go out the door, allowing herself for just a moment to dream that this was their life. That she was a part of this, that they came down together in the mornings from his room and in the other room, their kids still slept, little versions of Luke with his gorgeous eyes. It was so much the opposite of what she'd ever wanted—or ever thought she'd wanted—that she slumped against the counter for a moment because she wanted it so badly it took her a few heartbeats to find her breath.

She'd never wanted anything like this with Russ and she'd been going to marry him. She'd thought their life would go on much as it was, just as an official team. But this—with Luke—was entirely different. And it made leaving very important, because she was sure that he didn't want the same thing. He'd never given her any reason to hope, despite the nagging feeling of belonging that had dogged her since she'd arrived. It felt as if she'd come home.

Right. Home. To a place that was about as opposite from the life she'd led as she could get.

How could that be possible?

She got ready for her ride—her new boots wouldn't be done until just before she left Silver River. That was a bittersweet thought, but they were going to be so pretty she wasn't sure she'd have worn them out on the trail anyway, even though Skye had assured her she could.

She'd bought jeans at Schaffer's last time she'd been in Powder Keg. Because the wind was a little cool today, she put on a long-sleeved T-shirt—also purchased in Powder Keg—and grabbed the hat Luke had bought for her on the trip. Looking at herself in the mirror, she almost didn't recognize herself. This woman looked happy and relaxed. Josie stared at herself for a moment longer. There were no shadows under her eyes. No tension lines around her eyes or mouth. Her skin was clear and almost glowed. She wore no makeup other than a touch of mascara, and hadn't in a month. The changes she'd undergone here were startling. She hadn't realized how pale and wan and tense she'd been for years.

She gave herself a final quick once-over and hurried downstairs, slipped on her aunt's boots and headed out. She put Zippy in the cross ties and saddled him herself, remembering that he would hold his breath when she tightened the girth. She gave him an affectionate pat, and he turned his head as far as he could in the ties.

"We're friends now, right, big guy?"

Zippy's answering chuff could have meant anything, but she chose to take it as an affirmation of his affection.

She got him all ready to go, then led him out to the yard, where Luke and a group of other cowboys were just coming into sight. He greeted her with a grin when he got close enough.

"Give me ten. I'm going to take out a different horse today. Kipper can take the afternoon off."

"Is he okay?" she asked, reaching out to stroke the horse's neck.

"Yep. Just need to work out one of Nikki's horses a little bit, and this is a good way to do it."

He took care of Kipper and saddled a new horse, this one a splashy paint named Zeke, then they set off.

"Where are we going today?" she asked as Zippy plodded along next to Zeke. She enjoyed these opportunities to see the ranch from horseback. And okay, to spend time with Luke. She was running out of chances for both.

"You'll see," he said, and slanted her a grin. "I can tell you it was one of my favorite places as a kid."

She was touched he'd share something like that with her. "All right. I can't wait."

They rode in companionable silence, with Luke occasionally pointing out this and that, and Josie just basking in the sun and his company. She was happy right now. Just—happy. On the back of a horse, in what to her was the wilderness. Funny how life worked.

## Chapter Fifteen

It was a good hour or so on horseback, but Josie's body had acclimated to riding and she wasn't sore when they dismounted and ground tied the horses. She planned to pick up riding again wherever she ended up. He pulled a blanket and some lunches out of the saddlebags and they set off a little way on foot. Josie could hear water, and she looked at Luke quizzically. "There's a river out here?"

He laughed and dropped a kiss on her cheek. "Silver River Ranch, remember? But here it's more of a creek. It widens farther downstream."

She shook her head and mimed slapping her forehead. "Of course."

They came through the trees to a clearing as the sound grew louder. "And here there's a bit of a waterfall."

Josie stepped around him and her eyes widened. It was a waterfall, all right. It fell maybe twenty feet below to where the rest of the river wended its way off the ranch. "How pretty! Look at the rainbows." The water caught the light as it fell and the resulting rainbows flashed in the sunlight.

"It is. We've come here for years. As kids, not sure about as adults." No real reason to as adults, unless maybe his brothers brought girlfriends here. He hadn't brought anyone here until Josie. It was secluded and quiet and beautiful and the one place that represented the ranch to him. "I'm sure there are other places my brothers went. We all had secret places we liked to hide or hang out in. Just the way of kids, I guess."

"I guess," Josie murmured, her gaze still on the waterfall.

"Did you?"

She looked at him, surprised. "Did I what?"

"Have a place like this. Not like this exactly," he said, gesturing at the water, "but a place you could go to get away when you were a kid?"

She stared at him for a long moment, her expression changing from thoughtful to sad. Then she shook her head. "No. No, I guess I didn't. We moved around kind of a lot when I was a kid. It seemed as if I'd just settle in and we'd have to go."

Luke spread the blanket on a soft patch of grass, and she sank down on it and played with the grass with her fingers. "Did you have a parent in the military?"

"No." Her smile was a little twisted. She looked at him, then away. "My dad was— Well, he was a con artist. Not only that, but a bad one. I didn't know that at the time, of course. Eventually he went to jail and my mom divorced him, but I was almost in my teens by then. She'd had plenty of issues of her own."

That hadn't been what he expected. Somehow he'd assumed she'd been raised in the same affluence she'd appeared to have had in Los Angeles, since she wore it so naturally. Anger flashed through him. Selfish adults. "I'm sorry to hear that."

She sighed and lifted a brow. "Which part?"

"All of it. No kid should have to go through that."

She smiled at him. "I survived. And I'd say that I did have a place I went. I cooked, even then. Someone had to, and I didn't mind it."

He tucked a piece of her hair behind her ear and smoothed her cheek with the back of a finger. Her skin was so soft and smooth. A sharp, sweet contrast to the roughness of his hands. "You've come pretty far since then."

She shrugged. "We all have. My dad's out of jail and works for a construction company. He's remarried. My mom is a manager at a bank. She got her degree. I'm actually very proud of them both. They just—they just weren't any good together. I don't think either of them had really grown up before they got married."

Still. The adults had put her through the wringer, and that wasn't fair to a kid. "I'm sure they are proud of you."

She smiled at him but didn't answer, then pressed her lips to his for a slow, sweet kiss. He wanted to lay her back on the blanket right then, but managed to hold on to ask another question. "Josie. Are they proud of you?"

She sighed and shut her eyes. "Yes. But they don't understand why I didn't marry Russ. He'd charmed the hell out of them. So it was just easier not to go into all the details."

He understood that. He'd done much the same. But still. He stroked his hand down her face and under her chin, and when she lifted up he kissed her again. Before it could go further he pulled away and had to smile at her little huff of frustration.

"I want to show you something."

He stood, and she took his outstretched hand. He tugged her a little harder than necessary and she stumbled into him. He kissed her again and she laughed into his mouth.

"What?" he asked.

"We were doing that pretty well down there," she teased, pointing to the blanket.

He stole another quick one. He had every intention of having her naked on that blanket as soon as possible. "Yep. But first come see this."

He took her hand and led her toward a well-worn but overgrown path. She had to walk behind him, and she kept her free hand on his back. He loved the feeling.

They came out next to the waterfall.

"Luke, what is this?" she asked from behind him, loudly, to be heard over the rushing water, as she peered over the edge. He squeezed her hand lightly and led her under the waterfall, into a cave of sorts. She gasped.

"Are we under the river?" she asked, looking up

and then out the curtain of swiftly falling water. "Oh, my gosh, Luke. I've never seen anything like this."

The expression on her face was one of pure wonder. It was loud in the cave, a bit of an echo from the noise of the water, so he put his mouth close to her ear. "Yes. We are. Pretty cool, huh?"

The cave was maybe ten feet wide and ten feet tall and probably twenty feet deep. At some point the river above would wear through the ceiling, but that was a long way off. The rock was pretty durable. It was also cold and damp, so he led her back out and up the trail to the blanket.

"That was so cool," she said, her eyes bright. "Did you go there as a kid?"

He grinned and lay back on the blanket, hands behind his head. "Yeah. We weren't supposed to. And we were expressly forbidden to jump. The currents at the base are strong, and it's not really that deep for the height of the jump. So we didn't do that. There are better places along the river for that."

She stared at him. "I don't think I'd jump in the river," she said solemnly, and he laughed as he tugged her down to him.

"No?" he whispered into her mouth and tugged her shirt up and over her head and reached for her bra clasp so fast it made her laugh. "Will you get naked next to one instead?"

Her response was a moan as her breasts fell free of the bra, and he had his hands and mouth on them, teasing, flicking, sucking. When they were naked and she was poised above him, the dappled sunlight slanting on her sleek body, a goddess all his own, she looked down at him and said, "I've never done this outside." There was wonderment in her tone.

He gripped her hips and let out a half laugh, half guttural groan as she slid down his length. Slowly, slowly, inch by hot, wet inch. "Josie. Now's a great time to start."

And she did.

Back at the ranch later, Josie thought this was the best time she'd had with Luke yet. Their lovemaking was phenomenal and hot, and something about it touched her on a soul level, not just the physical. She'd told him about her unconventional upbringing and he hadn't run away or flinched. The part about her dad being a con man, and ex-convict to boot, was often a bit of a relationship killer. In fact, she'd never told Russ, though he'd found out anyway, no doubt through a private investigator. In retrospect, if she'd hired one first she could have saved herself a lot of trouble.

Anyway.

They'd just been together, in an easy way she wasn't used to but enjoyed. Just Josie and Luke. No cameras, no rushing off to put out some kind of fire at a restaurant. No using the moment to make someone else look good. Just the two of them, together. It made her feel wonderful and valued in a way she wasn't used to. As thought there was more to her than her career—and even that had taken a backseat to Russ's. Somehow she'd lost sight of her own life and been enfolded in his.

That wouldn't happen again.

As soon as they got in the barn, Luke headed back to a stall in the far corner that was in the partial light. He turned with a grin and reached for her hand.

"Look." Luke tugged her to the open stall. Inside, lying on the clean straw was a pretty dog. She was snapping at her sides a little and whimpering, but she gave a little wag of her plumy tail when she saw them.

"Is she okay?" Josie asked, worried.

"Yes. She's in labor. We'll keep an eye out. This isn't her first time. Her first labors were smooth. Her name is Taffy."

Josie stood outside the stall and watched, rapt, as the puppies entered the world and Taffy licked and nudged each one, her warm tongue rolling them around in the clean hay. Luke had grabbed some clean towels. But the littlest one wasn't moving. "Luke," she started, but he was already in motion. Taffy nudged the baby and looked at Luke, who picked up the little brown puppy. It was so tiny and delicate in his big hands, and he handled it with such infinite care that Josie's eyes watered.

"Can you help him?" she whispered and Luke sent her a worried look.

"I don't know. Sometimes you can, sometimes not. We'll know in a few seconds, though." He held the puppy upside down and rubbed firmly with one of the towels.

Josie held her breath and let it out in a rush as the puppy started to struggle a little in his hands, and he carefully set it back down, where Taffy started to lick it and nuzzle it, clearly as relieved as a dog could be.

And Josie realized, watching him with the dog and

puppies, that she'd gone and fallen head over heels in love with this man. Her heart both ached and wanted to fly. She was leaving in just a week, and there was no way for her to stay. She had to be back for the court hearing, and her whole life was in California. But seeing him with the puppy, the gentle way he treated Taffy and helped her, just made her melt inside. Somehow, despite her best efforts not to, she'd managed to fall for him. Wholeheartedly.

And, she feared, foolishly.

Luke gave her a little bump with his elbow. "We did it."

She hoped her mix of emotions didn't show on her face as she looked up at him with a smile. "We? I didn't do anything. Well, except pray."

He smiled back, and the sweetness of the moment wove around them. She wanted to capture and hold these fragile moments as if they were butterflies landing on her hand. Savor them, so when she left, she had something to look back on.

Taffy made a little whiffing noise, not a bark exactly, and Luke reached over to rub her head. "You did good, girl," he said softly. "Real good."

Josie wanted to cry. She also wanted to lean into his side, to say those little words that were swelling in her heart, but she knew once they'd been said, she couldn't take them back. She didn't want to make the last of their time awkward, or worse, find out that he absolutely didn't feel the same way and therefore she'd humiliated herself. He took her arm and steered her away from Taffy and her new puppies in the quiet, warm stall, and gave her a quick kiss. As he headed out and she went back to the house, she wished again, for just a moment, that all of this could be real and lasting. That the sense of belonging she experienced here was for real. It was a foolish fantasy, not to mention a dangerous one.

For now, she was determined to stay in the moments as they came to her and Luke. She sort of tucked them away like little jewels to savor after she'd gone.

A short while later, Josie stood in front of the window and looked out at the jagged mountains and the wide expanse of green that spread at their feet. She was putting together dough for rolls for that evening's dinner. The longer she stayed at the Silver River, the more she grew to love it. It was so peaceful here.

Alice smiled at her when she came in the kitchen from the back door. "Well. You look happy."

"I had a good afternoon," Josie said cheerfully, which was true, and she couldn't of course go into all the pieces that had made her afternoon so wonderful. Her relationship with Luke wasn't something she wanted to talk about with his mother, no matter how much she liked the older woman.

"That's good to hear," Alice said, and didn't ask any further, for which Josie was grateful. "I made a pie this afternoon and thought I'd drop it off for dinner."

Josie peeked under the tin foil covering the fragrant plate Alice handed her. "Mmm. What kind? Apple?"

"Yes, apple raspberry. Jim picked a bunch for me. Usually I do it myself, but this year I can't be out on the uneven ground like that. I made pies for them, too. And I made a little tart for myself," she said with a laugh. "So no, I don't need any of this, before you ask. The boys will decimate this anyway, so make sure you get a piece before they get to it if you want some."

"Believe me, I will." The pie looked lovely, like something from a magazine, which told Josie that Alice had probably been baking them for decades. "Maybe I'd better hide it in the pantry until after dinner."

Alice laughed. "Maybe." She turned toward the door, her cane light on the floor. She was moving better, Josie noted.

"How are you doing in your house?"

Alice turned back and smiled a little. "Wonderful. I love this house, have always loved it, but that little place is mine, and I really missed my own space and my own things. I really have the best of both worlds here. My kids nearby and my own place. I'm very blessed."

Josie smiled at her. She knew so many people who just ran through life without really looking at what was passing them by. It was possible she'd been one herself. Out here, you were kind of forced to slow down and look. That was a good thing. "Yes. You are."

Alice left, and Josie made a mental note to tell Luke she was moving well and he could relax a little bit about her health. She doubted he would, but it was worth a try.

She looked outside and saw clouds gathering on the horizon. It was still sunny here, so the clouds looked especially ominous and dark in the bright light. Someone had mentioned snow on the peaks this morning. This must be the storm that was bringing it. She tied her apron on and got to work, only to be interrupted by a knock at the door. With a frown, she went to answer it. No one out here knocked. They just walked in. And more likely, they bypassed the house altogether and went down to the barns.

She left the dough for the rolls on the counter and hurried to the door. She yanked it open to see Russ standing there. He opened his mouth, and she blinked at him.

*What the heck?*

She shut the door right back in his face, pressed her hands to her mouth, and stared at the door like maybe she could vaporize him. Her pulse pounded in her ears. This couldn't be right. Russ? How could he have found her? More important, why would he care? He'd made it perfectly clear he didn't want to see her anymore, and she'd been very clear it was mutual. Plus there was the court case she had against him. He wasn't supposed to be contacting her, except through her lawyer.

There was another knock, harder this time, and she yanked it back open. "What do you want?" No point in pleasantries.

He arched a brow. "That's not a very friendly greeting for your lover."

She couldn't help it. She laughed, and saw his face flush. Good. He was getting annoyed. "That's because you're not. What do you want?"

He gestured at the door. "May I come in?"

She hesitated. It wasn't her home, and she didn't

want him, even as a guest. So she shook her head and stepped outside. Annoyance flashed across his face, but he moved aside. She shut the door firmly behind her and crossed her arms. "Make it quick, please."

He stared at her and she simply stared back. Now she wondered what she'd seen in him. He possessed none of Luke's quiet authority or sincerity. He was good-looking, but now he looked pale and weak, and far too smooth in comparison to Luke's rugged good looks. How could she have been so blind to what this man really was?

He couldn't hold a candle to Luke.

His expression was too smooth and she knew it well, bracing herself for the usual onslaught of flattery mixed with insults. "Josie. You're looking gorgeous as always. The cowgirl look works for you. Being out here in the backwater appears to agree with you."

She couldn't help it. She laughed, again. Hard. So hard, in fact, the tears came and she doubled over, her hands on her jeans-clad thighs. Miffed and clearly confused, Russ stared at her. "Josie. For God's sake, what is wrong with you?"

She leaned on the door and wiped her eyes. "You. God, Russ, you'll never change. If only I'd realized that way sooner." Like *way sooner*. Like before she'd started dating him. She was much, much wiser now. "Why are you here?"

His eyes were hard now. "I came here to offer you your job back."

## Chapter Sixteen

All laughter fled and a kind of rage filled Josie. "What?"

He tipped his head at the door. "Can we take this inside?"

Josie turned and walked in, not bothering to see if he followed. She didn't want her job back. There was no way to get her restaurant back unless he handed it over to her, and she knew that wasn't going to happen.

Russ sat at the counter and looked around the room. "Nicely set up for a home kitchen," he said. "But of course, Ryder has money to burn. Can I get a drink?"

Josie took a glass from the cupboard and willed herself not to throw it at him. Instead, she filled it with water and set it in front of him with a *thunk*. "I wouldn't know about that. But yes, my aunt knows her way around a kitchen. She designed this one years ago." What, did he think Luke had suddenly remodeled his kitchen to suit her?

He took a drink and winced. Plain old water. That was another thing. His drinking had gotten worse as they'd been together. He was good at hiding it. Too good.

"Do you have anything stronger? That drive was hell."

"No," she said coolly. "Nothing I'm going to waste on you."

He set the glass down and smiled at her, but it was hard around the edges. "When did you get so disagreeable, love? Is it all this time in the sticks?"

She shook her head, then tapped her finger on her lips. "Let me think. I think it was when I got lied to, cheated on and stolen from by my fiancé."

"Josie—"

She interrupted him. "What do you want from me, Russ?" He wanted something. That much was sure. He wouldn't have come all this way otherwise. "You already took everything I had."

He didn't even have the grace to look chagrined at her quiet accusation. "Now, Josie. That's not true. You couldn't make a go of it on your own, remember? That's why I helped you out."

Right. Helped her right out of thousands of dollars and her reputation.

When she said nothing, just stood there with her arms crossed and her gaze level, he sighed. "I want to give you a thirty-percent stake in the restaurant in exchange for you dropping the lawsuit."

Josie's jaw dropped. "Thirty percent?" she repeated. Was he kidding? After all he'd put her through, he thought a measly 30 percent stake in her own restaurant would make her drop everything and come back? He clearly thought even less of her than she'd thought.

He beamed at her. "Yes. And you drop the lawsuit."

"No."

He frowned. "Josie, it's fair. You couldn't make it work."

She advanced on him and saw him fidget on the bar stool. "No, Russ. I made it work just fine. Which you hated so much you came in and ruined it for me, because you couldn't have me be successful on my own. There is no way in any hell that I'd work for you again. Now get out of here, and rest assured I'm calling my lawyer to tell her about this visit."

He cursed and started toward her. "Be reasonable—"

Before Josie even knew what happened, Hank was there, all hackles and teeth. His low growl and sharp barks had Russ throwing his hands up. "Call that mutt off, Josie!"

Josie crossed her arms. "I don't think so. He's a good judge of character."

The back door banged opened and Luke strode in just as the front door slammed. Hank had run to the door and was still barking hard. "Josie! Are you okay? What's wrong with Hank?"

"Nothing," she said as the dog trotted back in and licked her hand. She patted his head and his tail wagged, all happy now. "Russ was here. Still is in your driveway, I think."

"Did he hurt you? Do you want him arrested?"

She shook her head. "When he raised his voice, Hank took exception. And no, I just want him to leave." Forever.

Luke made a quick call. "Jim will escort him off the property and all the way out to the main road to make sure he leaves." He reached for her, and she went willingly into his arms. He smelled like fresh hay and the sun and the scent that was just Luke. "What did he want?"

"To offer me a small stake in the restaurant I founded in exchange for me dropping the lawsuit." She pulled away. "That reminds me. I need to call my lawyer and fill her in."

"Guy's got some nerve," Luke muttered. He bent and patted Hank, too. "Good dog," he said. "You got rid of the bad guy."

Josie laughed. "Yes, he did. Russ couldn't get out of here fast enough." Then she sobered. "I'm sorry he came here. I know how much you value your privacy."

He caught her chin and kissed her softly. "It's not your fault. Anyone with a computer can look up where I live. It's not a secret." He straightened up. "I doubt he'll be back."

"Probably not," she agreed, and went into the office to make the call to her lawyer. Still. She felt bad that she'd brought him to Luke's house.

The lawyer took serious exception to Russ's visit and promised to make a heap of trouble about it. Josie hung up, satisfied. It was why she'd hired her. She needed someone to force him to pay attention. It did shame her, though, to realize that Russ thought so little of her—and so much of himself—that he could make a paltry offer like that and think she'd come running back like a puppy.

He'd had no respect for her, then or now.

Luke stalked to the barn, anger fueling every step. If only he'd been there. If he'd intercepted the guy, he wouldn't have gotten anywhere near Josie. She'd been upset, even though she'd tried to pass it off. It had shaken her.

He wasn't a violent guy, but he would have loved the chance to run the asshole off himself. Better yet, land him in a small-town jail where no one cared who he was or how much money he had. Be good for him.

Luke's phone buzzed, and he slowed as he pulled it out, recognizing the number as his agent in Nashville. Rob called him every few months to try to bring Luke back to the stage. Luke always said no. It was a dance they did each and every phone call, yet neither of them terminated the agreement. He wasn't sure why. Probably because Rob ran interference for him, dealt with things like offers so Luke didn't have to. Plus, he liked the guy.

"Luke," Rob said. "How're things in Montana?"

They spent a few minutes on the obligatory small talk. Rob did his job well and he protected Luke's privacy, even if he didn't fully understand how Luke could just walk away from his career like he had. The reason Luke kept him on? He wouldn't find another agent who would do the same.

"So what's up?" Luke asked, bringing Rob around to the reason for his call.

"Hear me out before you say no. Okay?"

"I always do," Luke pointed out, both amused and ashamed by the observation.

"Yeah. That's because you're too polite to hang up on me. But you don't really listen. So I'm telling you, listen to this. Okay?"

"Okay," Luke said and moved to stand under the maple tree that was just beginning to change color.

Rob detailed a concert series that was medium-size venues with a couple other bands. He would be a guest performer, not the main draw—though Luke wasn't sure anyone would pay to see him anymore anyway—and it would be released as a new album. The band wanted him to guest on a new single.

"This is a way for you to get back out there and boost your sales. You still sell pretty strong, and you get a lot of airplay. But this will be like the icing on the cake. And if you wanted it, maybe a way back into Nashville."

A way back into Nashville.

Luke just stood there. A few weeks ago, he'd have turned Rob down flat. But now—he thought of the songs he'd written over the past few weeks, how they just seemed to come out of nowhere, pour out of him like a part of him had been unlocked and set free. Having the guitar in his hands again was like being reunited with an old friend. "When do you need an answer by?"

There was the tiniest of pauses, but Rob was enough of a professional and knew Luke well enough to keep his response low-key. "End of the week. I'll email you the details."

"Thanks, Rob. I'll let you know." He disconnected and stared at the phone in his hand, not quite sure why he hadn't said straight-up no like he had all those times before over the years. Then he looked up and saw Josie walking toward him, her hair in the braid she'd taken to wearing and her hat on her head. She looked like a cowgirl now, not the city girl he'd feared she'd be when she arrived. Except for the tennis shoes on her feet, but even they were more practical than the three-inch-heeled boots she'd had on when he met her, if not as sexy. He did miss those damn boots.

Hell, who was he kidding? Everything about this woman was sexy. Whatever she did or didn't wear. When she was smudged with flour from the kitchen or dirt from a ride. When she talked and laughed with the ranch hands, or his family, or him. He wanted her with every breath he took.

Not just physically. He wanted her in his life, every day, from here until forever. The realization rocked him to his core.

She stopped in front of him and gave him a slightly quizzical smile. It was then he realized he'd been staring at her. So he gave her a little smile and quick kiss on the mouth to cover his suddenly roiling emotions. "Hey. Everything okay?"

"Everything's fine. I talked to my lawyer." She recounted the conversation quickly. "Russ will regret he bothered to come here."

"Good. You deserve so much better than him,

Josie." And better than himself, as well. "Are you sure you don't want me to call the cops?"

She touched his arm lightly. "I'm sure. He's made enough trouble for himself just by showing up here. I looked out the window and saw you over here on the phone. Everything okay?"

He looked down at his phone and slipped it back in his pocket. "Yeah. Just had a call from my agent." Without really knowing why, he shared the details with her and watched her eyes grow larger. He never told anyone when Rob called, though he imagined they knew he did. He never wanted to justify why he'd decided to turn down yet another gig.

She clapped her hands. "Luke! That's so exciting. Wow. Are you going to do it?"

Her excitement was contagious. But he was still cautious. "I'm not sure. I need to think about it." To talk himself into it? Or out of it? He wasn't sure.

She lifted to her toes and kissed his cheek lightly. Another first, given they were outside, where anyone could see. "I know my opinion doesn't matter, but I think it'd be a wonderful opportunity for you."

He caught her hand and looked into her eyes. "What do you mean, your opinion doesn't matter?" Because it did. A lot. More than it should, considering she was leaving soon. She'd come to matter to him. Really matter.

She gave him a little smile that was tinged with sadness and shrugged. "You know what I mean. I'm leaving. This doesn't have anything to do with me. It's your life and career we're talking about here." Her voice faltered a little bit, and then she brightened up. "What are you thinking?"

Her words and her sad expression hit him in the gut. No, she wouldn't be here to see him off. To greet him when he came home. It seemed as if she might be feeling that loss as keenly as he was. He tried to bring his thoughts around. He didn't want to go down that path right now.

"I'm not sure," he admitted. "I've always said no before, and I think it shocked the hell out of Rob I didn't do it this time, too." He had to grin. Rob's startled pause after Luke's agreement to think about it had been priceless. Years of turning the other man down had clearly taken its toll.

"So why didn't you? What's changed?"

Josie's quiet questions gave him pause. He didn't have an answer. Things had changed somehow since she'd been at the Silver River. He couldn't really put his finger on it, but it was there, hovering under the surface. As if somehow she'd woken something in him that he didn't know he needed or missed. She'd shown him how to be comfortable with himself in a way he hadn't been in years. Maybe ever.

"I'm not sure," he repeated, and rubbed a hand over his face. "It just— Maybe it's time." He could hardly believe what he was saying.

She leaned on his arm, and the soft press of her breasts against him distracted him for a moment. "I think that's great, Luke. I think people will be thrilled to see you again."

He laughed. "You think they'll remember me?" Then the memories welled up of his divorce, the awful ending, the headlines. The prying. Would the press show up here? Russ had found it easily enough. He didn't want to go through the whole thing again. "On second thought—"

She laid a hand on his arm and squeezed. "No. Don't talk yourself out of it. Talk to your brothers. Your friends here. I think you'll find they all support you."

Her words warmed him. "You think?"

She shrugged. "Why wouldn't they?"

He could think of several reasons. He'd been gone when his father had died and they'd needed him the most. He'd brought Mandy here and they'd had to deal with all the associated wreckage that decision had caused. The parade of people who had wanted a piece of him, or to use his family to get to him. But he was touched that she was so solidly in his corner.

He rubbed his hand over his face. "I don't know, Josie. It didn't go so well the last time."

She touched his arm. "That was a long time ago. Talk to them, Luke. You might be surprised."

Luke did as Josie suggested that night at dinner. He asked her and his mother to eat with them, too. He looked at them and wondered again if he was doing the right thing even considering this gig.

"I had a phone call today," he said casually into a conversational lull, and Josie started to rise, murmuring something about the kitchen. He laid a hand on her arm, as close as he'd been to her in front of his family. "Stay. Please."

She sat back down as Cade said curiously, "What kind of phone call?"

He took a deep breath and set his fork down. "From Rob. He had an offer for me." He filled them in on the details, since he'd had a chance to run into the ranch office and check his email. They all listened quietly, and Josie's eyes never left his face. He drew strength from her quiet presence. "So it'd mean I'd be gone for a lot of next summer," he finished. "And I'd have to head out to Nashville to meet with everyone and do the single before that."

"Oh, Luke," his mom said, and he winced. Of course she wouldn't want him to do this, after how badly it had gone the first time around.

He shook his head. "It's okay, Mom, I won't do it. I'm not even sure why I was considering it."

She slapped her hand on the table and he actually jumped. "Oh, for God's sake, Luke, I wasn't going to tell you not to go! I was going to say it's about damn time!" When Luke's mouth fell open at both the sentiment and the mild profanity, she leaned over and laid a hand on his arm. "Honey. You've been hidden away here for a long time. You have a great talent and shouldn't hide it. There are people out there who would love to see you, have you share your music with them. I hope you decide to do it. It's not our decision. It's yours."

Cade and Jake nodded, and Josie gave him a little grin. Not quite an "I told you so" but close enough.

He cleared his throat. "What about the press? The stories? Everything that happened the first time coming back out?"

Cade shrugged. "We'll deal. It's too remote out here for anyone to really be bothered to stick around for long. As far as the rest goes, well, that's your call. It's your past. Nothing happened in there that looks bad on you."

He thought back through those years. He hadn't been a bad husband, sure. An overwhelmed one, maybe, with his crazy wife and unexpected success.

"You were young and out of your depth," his mother said quietly, echoing his thoughts. "No one's going to hold that against you. What do you think, Josie?"

Her head came up, surprise in her eyes. "Oh, this isn't about me."

"Of course it is. Luke values your opinion, don't you, Luke?"

He nodded, and realized again it was her opinion that mattered the most, and she wasn't even going to be here. She was clearly uncomfortable pitching in but she said quietly, "I think it's a great idea."

To Josie, this felt a lot like a family meeting—which it was—and she was out of place here. She wasn't family, as much as she liked them, all of them, and as much as she loved it here, it wasn't her home. Wouldn't be her home. She rose and grabbed a few plates, shaking her head when they tried to rise to help her.

She took them in the kitchen and loaded the dishwasher, trying to clear her mind. She was in far too deep here. It was much too easy to pretend she was a part of this, that she had a say in Luke's life because he valued her, because they were a couple—when in reality, they were just a temporary item, bound to end when one of them left in a week.

A week. Almost at the point it could be counted in hours.

## *Chapter Seventeen*

She swallowed hard and started when Luke's strong arms came around her from behind. He held her close, his chin on her head, and she could see their reflection in the window as she lifted her dry hand to press on his hands. They made a good couple, but it was every bit as transient as the reflection in the glass. Tears burned her eyes, and she willed them away. Moments like this were gold. She didn't want to lose them. Enveloped in his arms, in his scent, she was safe and warm and as close to loved as she'd ever been.

"Thank you," he whispered in her ear, and she turned in his arms to look up at him. He loosened the circle of his arms but didn't let go of her.

"For what?"

He kissed her nose. "For making me talk to them."

Now she laughed. "I didn't make you do anything, Luke. You know that."

He was completely serious. "No. But you didn't let me talk myself out of it."

She thought if he'd been against the idea, no one would have been able to talk him into it. But she didn't point that out. "Are you going to call Rob tonight?"

He shook his head. "I want to sleep on it. Or not," he added, his voice low and sexy.

She laughed even as his tone set off heat inside her. "You're insatiable."

"It's you, Josie. Something about you that just makes me crave you all the time." He said it with a note of wonderment in his voice. She felt the same way but didn't think it would be a good idea to tell him so. She needed to start pulling away, to protect herself as best she could. Still, she couldn't bring herself to withdraw when he leaned in and kissed her.

In the end, he helped her in the kitchen, then went to her room with her. When they came together in the dark, her heart ached just a little. The words she so badly wanted to say were trapped in her throat. It would change everything in a way that wasn't fair to either of them. So she said them in her head and carried them in her heart. *I love you, Luke.* She turned her head to press a kiss to his bare shoulder, grateful for the dark that masked the tears threatening to fall.

It wasn't until later, when the bed dipped as he rose and her door opened and closed ever so quietly behind him, that she let the tears come.

When she talked to Allie the next morning, her friend picked up at once that something was amiss. "Spill," she demanded, and Josie stifled a sigh. She didn't want to share her feelings. To put them into words would make it too real, might make the pain later too much to bear. She wouldn't want Allie watching her too closely when she went home, monitoring her for signs of heartbreak.

"There's nothing to spill," she assured her friend, keeping her tone light. "Unless you count Russ showing up here."

"What?" Allie asked, incredulous, and Josie filled her in on the details of Russ's unannounced little visit. When she finished, Allie breathed, "Wow. The nerve. He's something else."

"Yeah. You know, the thing is, a few weeks ago I'd have negotiated something to get my restaurant back, even if it was only part ownership. But now—" She stopped.

"But now…" Allie prompted softly.

"Now I wouldn't settle. He'll never sell it, and I won't get it in the court case." It still made her sad, but somewhere along the line she'd decided she deserved better than the scraps Russ decided to toss her way. If only she'd realized it far sooner. "I've let it go. I'm ready to move forward." It was liberating to say the words.

"I'm so happy to hear that, Josie. I was really worried about you. So. How's that handsome cowboy you're working for?"

Josie tucked the phone on her shoulder and reached for a dish towel. She chose to keep her answer evasive. "They're all fine. They work hard. They're nice men, Allie."

"I'm sure they are, but I was asking only about

Luke," she said bluntly. "When you talk about him your voice changes. You mention the others, but not in the same way. Are you falling for him, Josie?"

"No, of course not," Josie said with a laugh that was a teeny bit forced. Darn it, Allie knew her too well for Josie to keep this kind of thing from her. Hoping her friend didn't catch it, she hurried on. "It'd be the dumbest thing I could do. You know that. I'm leaving here soon. It's not as if anything could ever work." She winced and slapped her hand on her forehead. And that was too much of a protest right there. She'd flung open the door. Allie was far too astute to not barge straight through it.

"Who are you trying to convince? Me? Or yourself, Josie?" Allie's voice softened with worry. "Maybe it's too soon after Russ? I mean, it ended so badly."

Josie gave a little laugh. "You know what it was like," she said. "I know now it wasn't really a relationship. I didn't love him. I thought I did, but I didn't." And she knew this thanks to Luke. The depth of her feelings for him were far beyond anything she'd ever felt for Russ. She wasn't going to say that, though. "I never think about him. I don't miss him. I don't miss what could have been. He never would have changed, Allie. He proved that when he showed up here. I'm better off without him." That was all true, right there. She wished it had all ended differently, where she hadn't ended up losing so much and being played for a fool, but she was very grateful Russ was out of her life before she'd made the horrible mistake of marrying him. Of believing love was something far less than it was, and settling for it. She'd make sure she didn't make that kind of mistake again. Ever.

Luke, though—Luke had shown her what it could be. And, oh. The sense of loss spilled over her. Luke, she'd miss with all her heart. She pressed the towel to her eyes. She didn't want to break down on the phone and give herself away.

Allie's sigh carried clearly through the connection. "Well, that's good. I just don't want to see you go through that kind of thing again. It was awful."

"It was," she agreed. It had been humiliating and horrible, but it was only her pride that had suffered, not her heart. But still. "I'm not going there again." She was smarter now.

They chatted a little bit longer about far more neutral topics, and when Allie got another call, they hung up. Josie tried not to promise she'd tell Allie if things went anywhere with Luke. They already had.

Josie put the phone back on its base and looked out the office window. The day was sunny, but there were streaks of clouds. Something Allie said nagged at her. That Josie sounded different when she talked about Luke. She didn't want to sound different. She wanted to sound exactly the same no matter who she was talking about. Because it might be too late not to be in love with him, but she needed to keep it to herself.

Luke took a break midmorning to call Rob back. Since he'd made up his mind, it seemed pointless to wait to get things rolling. Rob was thoroughly shocked but thrilled. They talked awhile longer, and Rob promised to get back to him in the next day or two on all the dates once he'd informed the band. He told Luke it might be a quick exit on his end, so to be prepared to leave on short notice. They'd send a plane for him.

That alone made him shake his head as he disconnected the call. Send a plane. He rested his foot on the bottom rung of the corral and watched Jim work the horses. Never would he have thought he'd be the kind of guy who rated a plane, even when he had been. Now it was starting all over. The whole thing felt surreal. It had changed so fast. This time, though, his eyes were wide-open. He was in full control of his career.

But—Josie.

He shut his eyes just for a moment. He hoped he could be here for the rest of her stay. There was an odd ache in his chest when he thought of her leaving. He'd been trying to ignore it but it was stronger now, that the end was in view and coming up fast. Too fast.

He realized Jim had said something to him. "What was that?"

Jim inclined his head toward the horse. "I said, what do you think?"

To be truthful, Luke had barely noticed the horse even as he'd been tracking its movement around the ring. His thoughts were far away. "He looks good, Jim. Really good." He knew it was true because he'd seen this particular horse worked before.

Jim came over with a small frown. "You okay, boss?"

*I'm about to lose Josie for good. Hell no, I'm not okay.* But he couldn't say that. "Just fine." The lie stuck in his throat. If Jim had noticed and commented, he must really be in bad shape. Since he was leaving—even though it wouldn't be for all that long—he threw himself into the chores with renewed vigor. This place wouldn't miss him. It ran like a machine, with everything in its place and by people who knew exactly what they were doing. He and his brothers were damn lucky.

But there was something missing, something he hadn't wanted to acknowledge he was missing until Josie came into his life. All too soon, it'd be missing again. This time, though, he wasn't sure how he'd go back to life being the same as before. Because it wouldn't be, without Josie.

He shut his eyes on the revelation. Hell. He'd fallen in love with her, let her into his life and his heart and she couldn't—wouldn't—stay. It wasn't her fault. It was his. But when she went home, he'd be left behind once more.

He'd vowed never to let that happen again.

A clean break would be easier for both of them. A phone call to Rob, and that plane would be on its way within the hour. He could clear out and save both of them the trouble of a prolonged goodbye. It seemed like the best idea. Plus, the sooner he got away from her, the sooner he could get over her.

Swallowing the suddenly sour taste in his mouth, he pulled out his phone.

Josie knew the moment Luke walked in the door something wasn't right. She could see it in his posture and his closed expression. So instead of going to him, she moved casually to the coffeemaker to pour a cup she didn't really want, hoping to cover up the sinking feeling in her stomach.

"Is everything okay?" Her tone was normal but her hand was shaking a bit, so the coffee splashed out of the mug. When he didn't answer, she gave up the pretense of coffee and turned. "Luke?"

He had his hat in his hands, and she knew from the look on his face that whatever he had to say, it was bad. "Are there more problems with the cattle?"

He shook his head. "No. I'm leaving, Josie. In an hour and a half, I'm heading to Kalispell to catch a plane to Nashville."

Josie's mouth fell open. Now? He was leaving now? She gave her head a little shake. "I don't understand. I thought that was still a week or so away."

His face was impassive now. "I decided it was best if I went today. No point in waiting, you know?"

She stood very still and looked at him. He met her gaze, and she saw none of the tenderness and heat she usually did. Had the whole thing been a mirage? Had she just imagined that maybe he felt for her what she felt for him?

But then, she caught just a hint of remorse and realized what was going on. A little bit of hope popped up. "You're running away." Running away meant he had feelings for her, even if he was handling them badly.

He shook his head. "No. What would I be running from?"

She moved closer and heard him take a sharp breath when she stopped right in front of him. "Me. Us."

He looked at her, and his eyes were the cool icy blue they'd been when she'd met him for the first time.

"There is no us, Josie. It was great while it lasted, but it's over now. You're a city girl. You don't belong here."

*You don't belong here.* The words hit her harder than a slap. She'd felt as if she belonged, for the first time, when she'd come to the Silver River Ranch. And now this man—whom she loved—had just told her she was mistaken. That none of it mattered.

She took a shaky breath as first pain and then anger washed over her, sharp and hot, and she welcomed the sting of it. "I see. Well, how lucky for you I won't be here when you get back. Good luck, Luke. You'll need it."

She turned and walked out of the room, her back straight and her steps measured, not willing to let him see the tears that had already begun to fall.

By the next morning, she was dry-eyed. She'd cried half the night and was in some sort of a lovely welcome fog that insulated her from her pain. At some point it'd wear off. She knew this. In the meantime, she'd work damn hard to not feel.

She'd heard Luke leave yesterday. Heard him pause at the base of the stairs, but he hadn't come to her door. Not that she would have answered it. At least, she was pretty sure she wouldn't have.

She'd also packed her bags. She had decided to leave today. There was no point in her staying and prolonging the agony any longer. There were plenty of meals in the freezer, and her aunt would be back in less than a week.

She changed her flight and asked Cade, when he came in, for a ride to Powder Keg. She could call a cab from Kalispell to pick her up. Pricey, yes, but worth it.

He shoved his hat back. "Of course I'll take you. I'll take you all the way to Kalispell, there's no need for you to take a cab. My idiot brother— I'm sorry." He shook his head. "We all thought you guys would get married."

Cade's words nearly knocked Josie to the floor. They made an unfortunate hole in her fog, and some of the pain seeped in. She swallowed hard. "Well, you thought wrong." While an extreme understatement, it was all she could think of to say.

Alice came in the door and came straight to Josie and wrapped her arms around her. Josie squeezed her eyes shut tight, trying to hold against the torrent of emotion she could barely contain. Too many holes had been punched in her fog. "Please don't apologize," she rasped. She wouldn't be able to bear it. "Please."

Alice squeezed her, then stepped back. "Then, I won't. But I will say he's running, Josie. From what he feels and what he's afraid of. I hope the two of you can work it out."

The ache in Josie's chest sharpened. "There's no chance of that. We're too different and live in completely different worlds. Now, about the meals—" She changed the subject, and after exchanging a look with Cade, Alice went with it, for which Josie was grateful.

She'd miss them like crazy. All of them. When it came time to leave that afternoon, she didn't let herself look back, just focused hard on her hands in her lap, as if maybe somehow they held the answers she needed. But all the same, it seemed as though she'd left a significant portion of her heart behind in a place she would never belong.

*Chapter Eighteen*

Josie stood on her balcony and overlooked her view. She'd bought this condo because she could see the ocean in the distance on a clear day, and those were rare. She could see the 405 freeway, congested as usual, and the sea of roofs and parking lots lined with palm trees and stretches of green here and there, dotted with the sparkle of pools. The heat shimmered over the pavement.

She couldn't help but compare it to another view she'd grown to love, one that involved cowboys and cattle and horses and green pastures and huge mountains. It was all tied up with the one man she couldn't get out of her head.

She shut her eyes for a moment. It had only been ten days. Ten days since she'd left Montana. Eleven since she'd seen Luke. She'd used the time to begin a job search in earnest. She was moving on with her life, as hollow as she felt without Luke in it.

It would pass.

She turned and went back inside, leaving the slider open. It was October in Los Angeles, but it was far warmer than it had been in Montana. She wore capris and a tank top. Casual outfit, after the suit she'd worn earlier to court.

Russ had agreed to pay her for damages in exchange for her to drop all charges. After his little visit to her at the Silver River, he'd pretty much tied his own hands. The money would be welcome, but she couldn't muster up much more than a deep-seated relief it was over. He was out of her life for good. She'd wanted to call Luke, but of course, she couldn't. Forcing down her disappointment, she'd called Allie instead.

"Meet me at The Cantina at three," Allie said. "I'll buy you a drink. You need to celebrate this!"

Josie had agreed, but her heart wasn't in it. Still, she had to keep moving forward, so she changed clothes again and headed out to the little café.

Allie showed up in a whirl and gave her a huge hug and a squeal, then pulled away and looked hard at Josie. She frowned. "Josie. You look like hell. What is going on?"

Josie burst into tears right there in the café.

The waiter, drawn over by Allie's bright bubbliness, paused uncertainly. Allie gave him a smile. "I think we need some more napkins."

"Sure. Be right back." He hurried off and Josie shook her head, sniffling.

"I'm sorry. God. I'm a mess."

"Yes," Allie agreed. "You are. Now spill. Is this about Russ?"

Horrified, Josie looked up and actually managed a laugh. "God, no."

Allie patted her hand. "Good."

The waiter placed two glasses of water and a stack of napkins on the table, then withdrew. Josie made a note to tip him handsomely even if they didn't order anything. She grabbed one of the napkins and patted it on her face.

"Josie?"

She sighed. "It's all good with Russ. I accepted a settlement in exchange for dropping the charges. It was fair. He's made a lot of trouble for himself and I just want to be done with him. Now I can move on free and clear." But to what? That was the problem. Everything she wanted was in Montana. But how was she going to make a living there? Not to mention Luke hadn't asked her to stay. In fact, he'd left so fast, as if he couldn't wait to get away from her.

"But," Allie prompted gently.

Josie took a deep breath. "But there's Luke. I just— I fell in love with him. And he didn't feel the same way."

"Oh, honey." Allie covered Josie's hand with hers. She couldn't help but notice her friend's sparkly gold manicure on top of her own nonexistent one. "Are you sure?"

She thought back to the moment he'd told her she didn't belong. "Yes. I am sure."

Allie narrowed her eyes. "So he's an ass."

Josie choked on a laugh. "No. He's not. That's the thing. If he were, this would be so much easier." Because she wouldn't have fallen for him in the first place.

Allie squeezed her hands and sat back. "I'm sorry, honey. What can I do to help?"

Alcohol and ice cream weren't the answers, and she'd already tried both. Plus, she wasn't sleeping well again. She hadn't taken any of her sleep meds the night she'd had too much wine, but she had the night she'd had too much ice cream. She took a deep breath and let it out slowly. "Nothing. I'll be okay. I've been looking for other opportunities. I'm thinking personal chef. My mentor from culinary school offered to set me up with an interview. I'm going to take her up on it."

Moving forward was her only choice. Sometime, the pain would lessen. It hadn't even been two weeks yet.

"If you need anything, you call me. Promise."

"I promise." She hugged Allie. "It'll take some time, but I'll be okay." She had to believe it. If she could convince herself, then maybe she could make it happen.

Josie got in her car and drove the three miles home in about an hour. Lots of traffic, lots of lights, lots of congestion. And the time of day didn't help, either. She hadn't missed this at all. She could have most likely walked it faster, even in her heeled boots.

She hadn't taken the ones Luke had ordered for her out of the box other than to try them on. They'd arrived three days ago. They were gorgeous and fit beautifully. She'd written Skye a heartfelt thank-you note, but they made her unbearably sad. She'd put them away in her closet. If only it were that easy to deal with the rest of the memories—pack them away in a neat box in the closet. Done.

She parked in her carport and made her way inside the glass-walled lobby of her building. A cowboy hat across the vast room immediately caught her attention, but she willed herself to ignore the silly leap of hope. Those hats were all over, even in this area. She'd never really paid attention before, but now she saw them everywhere she looked. It was foolish to get all quivery and then let down every time one caught her eye. So she turned toward the elevator, her mind skipping ahead to her evening. Takeout again? Allie was right—she should celebrate her victory over Russ. It wasn't too late to call her mentor, who was in New York. She'd get that interview set up.

"Excuse me, ma'am," came an all-too-familiar and low voice behind her. Josie froze, her hand outstretched to push the button on the elevator, then pivoted slowly to see that the cowboy hat did, indeed, belong to Luke. Her mind went completely blank even as that crazy little flare of hope spiked.

She took a deep shuddery breath as the elevator opened behind her. He motioned toward the door and she got on. He followed her. The door slid closed, and she wished like crazy she wasn't stuck in the small space with him, enveloped in his scent. Her hand shook as she pressed the button for her floor. All she wanted was to throw herself at him and hang on. Instead, she focused on the floor numbers that seemed to be going by very slowly. "What are you doing here?"

Dang it, her voice wobbled. She swallowed hard.

He cleared his throat. "It was brought to my attention that I was an idiot."

"Oh?" That little flare of hope leaped higher in her chest, but she didn't dare take her eyes off the numbers slowly ticking off as the elevator rose. Because she didn't want to look at him and see something that would break her heart.

He shifted beside her. "Yeah, *oh*. I owe you an apology, Josie."

The elevator stopped at her floor and the doors slid open. She stepped out, not looking to see if he followed. Her hands were shaking so badly that she could barely get her keys out, much less the right one in the lock when she stopped at her door.

She felt him come up behind her before his big hand closed over hers. The warmth and roughness of his palm on hers made her shiver. "This one?"

She nodded, unable to speak.

Inside, he pushed the door closed and set the keys on the table near the door. She heard the clank. She walked to the other side of the room, which was as far as she could go and still be in the same room, and finally faced him. "What kind of apology, Luke?" Because she really couldn't take it if he came all this way to say he was sorry for not loving her. No, that would crush her.

He stood there, looking big and sad and out of place in her modern condo. She missed him. Missed everything about him. "For not telling you how I really feel."

She shut her eyes. Oh, God. "It was pretty clear, Luke. You didn't have to come all this way to make sure I understood. I got it." She turned, intending to lock herself in her bedroom. Or the bathroom. Anywhere she could fall apart. This wasn't going to help her move forward, darn it. But he crossed the room with that impossibly long stride and laid his hands on her shoulders.

Then he kissed her. A sweet, gentle kiss that quickly turned hot. He pressed his lips to her forehead. "Josie. I didn't get to tell you I love you."

She went stiff. Surely she hadn't heard that right. "I'm sorry, what?"

He ran his hand down her cheek. She loved the roughness of his palms, the workingman's hands. "I love you," he repeated. "I was too afraid I'd screw it all up if I admitted it to myself, much less you."

Hope bloomed into something much sweeter as she searched his eyes and saw nothing but sincerity. And anxiety. "So—you ran away?"

He took her hands. She looked down at them, her smaller ones engulfed in his larger ones. "Yeah. It seemed easier. As if I'd spare you some kind of pain by running away."

She arched a brow. "Spare me?"

"And myself," he admitted with a wince. "I guess I thought if I loved you and I left first, it would somehow make me feel better." His hands tightened on hers. "I was wrong. And my family made sure I knew what an idiot I am."

She couldn't help but smile at his chagrined tone. "Really?"

"Really. I'm sorry. I didn't want to screw up."

Unable to stand that close to him and not touch him, she burrowed into his chest and felt his arms close tightly around her. Oh, yes. This was home, right here, wherever her cowboy was. "Luke. I love you. How could you screw up saying 'I love you'?"

He laughed and pressed his cheek to her hair. "I did, clearly." Then he squeezed her a little tighter. "Josie. I love you. So much. I was too afraid to take the chance that you wouldn't stay."

She understood. She did. "You never asked me to stay, Luke."

"I didn't think it was fair," he explained. "It's the middle of nowhere. I didn't want you to be miserable. That wasn't fair."

She'd been miserable without him. She stepped back, but not out of the circle of his arms. She tipped her head up to look at him. "That was a choice for us to make together, though. Not you to make for me." It was important that he understood that—Russ never had. She couldn't take the chance of being run over again.

"I know. I guess I thought I was trying to protect you, but really I was worried about putting myself out there." He took a deep, shuddering breath and rested his forehead on hers. "Holy hell. These have been the longest days of my life."

She rose on her toes and pressed her mouth to his lightly. "Mine, too."

His hands already starting to roam, she took his

hand and led him to her bedroom, where she proceeded to show him just how sweet forever would be.

*Nine months later*

Luke came offstage after his first appearance performing in public in too many years. He'd just done an encore. Amid all the people backstage who congratulated him and pumped his hand stood Josie. She wore a T-shirt with his name in sparkles across the chest—he'd been a bit stunned by it—and the boots Skye had made for her with jeans. She threw herself into his arms as soon as he cleared the crush of people. He was sweaty and hot and pumped. It had felt good—so good to be out there, to feel the crowd's energy and excitement.

"You did it," she said into his ear—it was hard to hear, what with the roar of the crowd in the background—and he kissed her quick and hard.

"I did." He threw back his head and laughed. "Thanks to you." Thanks to Josie and her quiet dedication, he'd settled right back into the life he'd thought he'd left behind. This time was different, though. She was along for the ride as both his fiancée and his personal chef. It made for a calmer experience for him.

She smiled up at him as she looped her arm around him. He accepted a bottle of water and took a long drink. "Feel good?"

"I do." He dropped a kiss on her head. They were due to say those words at the end of the month. He couldn't wait. When the tour was over, they'd return to the ranch, where Josie would take over the diner in Powder Keg. Donna was ready to retire and had been more than happy to hand the reins over to another cook she trusted as much as herself.

The noise of the concert muffled as they went behind the venue. "It was amazing to hear you perform," she said. "They love you."

He shook his head, still amazed. "It's been a hell of a ride. I never thought— But I'm grateful beyond words."

She laced her hand in his as they walked through the humid night air toward his bus. He could clearly see their lives rolled out before him, all the way up to rocking chairs on the porch and grandkids at their feet. There was no one he'd rather spend forever with than Josie.

\* \* \* \* \*

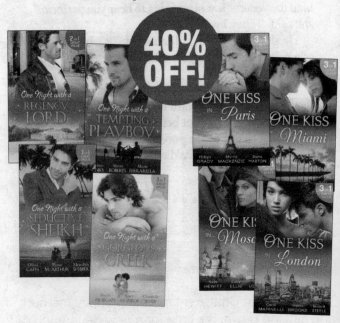

# MILLS & BOON®

## Seven Sexy Sins!

*CATHY WILLIAMS*
To Sin with the Tycoon

*DANI COLLINS*
The Sheikh's Sinful Seduction

### *The true taste of temptation!*

From greed to gluttony, lust to envy, these fabulous
stories explore what seven sexy sins mean in
the twenty-first century!

Whether pride goes before a fall, or wrath leads to a
passion that consumes entirely, one thing is certain:
the road to true love has never been more enticing.

### Collect all seven at
### www.millsandboon.co.uk/SexySins

# MILLS & BOON®

## *Cherish*™

**EXPERIENCE THE ULTIMATE RUSH OF FALLING IN LOVE**

---

## A sneak peek at next month's titles...

### In stores from 20th March 2015:

- **The Millionaire and the Maid** – Michelle Douglas
  *and* **The CEO's Baby Surprise** – Helen Lacey

- **Expecting the Earl's Baby** – Jessica Gilmore
  *and* **The Taming of Delaney Fortune** – Michelle Majo

### In stores from 3rd April 2015:

- **Best Man for the Bridesmaid** – Jennifer Faye
  *and* **The Cowboy's Homecoming** – Donna Alward

- **It Started at a Wedding...** – Kate Hardy
  *and* **A Decent Proposal** – Teresa Southwick

---

Available at WHSmith, Tesco, Asda, Eason, Amazon and Apple

*Just can't wait?*
Buy our books online a month before they hit the shops!
**visit www.millsandboon.co.uk**

**These books are also available in eBook format!**